Dear Reader:

I'm delighted to present to you the first books in the HarperMonogram imprint. This is a new imprint dedicated to publishing quality women's fiction and we believe it has all the makings of a surefire hit. From contemporary fiction to historical tales, to page-turning suspense thrillers, our goal at HarperMonogram is to publish romantic stories that will have you coming back for more.

Each month HarperMonogram will feature some of your favorite bestselling authors and introduce you to the most talented new writers around. We hope you enjoy this Monogram and all the HarperMonograms to come.

We'd love to know what you think. If you have any comments or suggestions please write to me at the address below:

HarperMonogram
10 East 53rd Street
New York, NY 10022

Karen Solem
Editor-in-chief

TO LOVE A LADY

"Your clothes and manner are a disgrace. As you transformed Moorsedge for the holidays, I shall henceforth transform you for Society," the Earl proclaimed.

"I shall be so stiff you shall have to bend me to seat me at table," Merrie said in a wicked whisper, giggling as he leaned closer to hear. "How's that!" she ended in her normal voice, and he jumped up.

"You are incorrigible! I shall rue it," he said.

But Merrie was quick to assure him she would behave. But first, for this one last day, they must all be free and filled with the joy of the season. "And that includes you, my lord. You are ordered for Christmas, at least, to allow the man in you to overcome the lord."

Smiling suddenly, the Earl took a step toward her. There was something in his eyes that had her thoughts veering from the glee of Christmas into a shockingly indelicate bypath. Reaching over, his lordship casually touched her bottom lip with his extended finger. "Your lip is trembling. From fear? Anticipation? Desire?"

THE SEASON OF LOVING

Helen Archery

HarperPaperbacks
A Division of HarperCollinsPublishers

HarperPaperbacks *A Division of* HarperCollins*Publishers*
10 East 53rd Street, New York, N.Y. 10022

Copyright © 1992 by Helen Argyris
All rights reserved. No part of this book may be used or reproduced in any manner whatsoever without written permission of the publisher, except in the case of brief quotations embodied in critical articles and reviews. For information address HarperCollins*Publishers*,
10 East 53rd Street, New York, N.Y. 10022.

Cover illustration by Elaine Gignilliat

First printing: December 1992

Printed in the United States of America

HarperPaperbacks, HarperMonogram, and colophon are trademarks of HarperCollins*Publishers*

10 9 8 7 6 5 4 3 2 1

To the original Merrie: Astera,
my sister—it was so much fun
growing up with you.

And to our loving mother:
Calliope-Carol . . . and
father, Thomas.

And, once again and always, to N. N.

And to all people who believe in the holiday spirit.

1

A merry lady must by her very nature be due for a fall. That axiom was ground into Miss Merrie Laurence while joyously, and yes, merrily, traveling along in a farmer's gig, when, of a sudden, she felt herself flying through the air.

That gig had the audacity to be blocking the path of the earl of Warwick. His lordship was dashing along at a perfectly respectable speed for a sportsman in his own well-sprung curricle, when he was thus obstructed. There was some slight collision, and the gig had the worst of it. The farmer jumped off in time, but the gig's passenger, the young lady, was thrown for a loop-the-loop. She and the wheel separated themselves from the gig at precisely the same time.

The wheel revolved, and she resolved to give the careless driver of the curricle some home truths about not only his driving but his gross inconsideration for other people. Not to mention their property.

The bonnet she had placed on her head with such pride at the beginning of her journey was now covered with mud. So much for the impressive appear-

ance she had hoped to make at the manor. Her pelisse, as well, had streaks of mud. As for her body, the
last thing she checked, it was not overly bruised, for
Miss Laurence had landed lightly on her bottom. She
was too much of a lady to rub where she felt the most
sensitive, but she did brush herself off in the vicinity
thereof. As for her bonnet, that was given a thorough
shaking ere she placed the squashed thing back over
her bright red curls.

"Oh, fiddle!" she exclaimed. Often did Merrie find
it an infamous discrimination that gentlemen had
such a lovely selection of accommodating words
when the need arose to express one's agitation. Ladies, however, were basically limited to pallid oh-
dears. Hence she'd come up with her own expletive
that had a bit more force while remaining essentially
ladylike.

Now she needed several oh-fiddles. She applied it
to the bonnet, to her bottom, and definitely to the
happenstance. At no time while looking forward to
the moment of her arrival had she seen herself covered with mud. And yet up to this moment, she had
managed her first journey from home with unexceptionable efficiency, if she said so herself, from stage
stop to stage stop. Upon arriving in Yorkshire and
finding no means of transportation waiting for her,
she had not been thrown into despair. Actually, Merrie's style was never to despair about anything.
Rather she always overcame—as in this case when
spotting the farmer and his gig. A conversation of a
few seconds, a dimpled smile, and tuppence had
solved her problem forthwith.

And then came this oversetting, proving that one
could not prevent all mischances by a sanguine tem-
perament. But one could bear all with tolerable cheer.
And she quickly put herself to the task of being helpful, that being her forte, and soon the farmer, if not

pleased at the loss of his wheel, was viewing it as less of a disaster.

Meanwhile, the gig continued to form a monstrous obstruction in the earl's path. Observing that both passengers were up and talking, not to say chatting at some length, the earl felt there was no need for concern beyond that which he felt for himself at being detained. But he did condescend to instruct his groom.

"You are to remove the gig from Moorsedge's road and as well discover the reason for its initially being here," he began in his languid tones. "And you'll perceive that I am waiting and my horses are also waiting. And all of us are fretting."

The groom was off in a trice, knowing how little the earl could bear being inconvenienced. His voice was never raised, and even now the volume was low, but that did not allow anyone who knew his lordship to suppose that he would suffer to be kept standing for more than a tolerable time.

Yet when Selfers saw the condition of the gig and the plight of the young erstwhile passenger, he felt it behooved him to return to his master and relay the difficulties of the travelers.

"I do not recollect asking you for the history of that equipage's incumbents," the earl said, still in his low and languid tone. "Has that obstacle been removed from my path?"

"No, my lord, I'm having summat of a difficulty there as the wheel be gone."

"Your difficulties undoubtedly would be of interest to your cronies in the stable. They do not concern me. Have the farmer and yourself and that other person put your shoulders to the gig and shove it to the side, to clear the road. And then you may all three convene and commiserate as long as you have inclination."

Selfers knew enough not to contradict. Rather he

went hurriedly back and with the aid of the farmer, and at the helpful direction of the young lady, the gig was moved sufficiently aside for the neighing horses of the curricle, truly prime ones, to pass by. The earl was known throughout London as a first-class whip, not to mention being a proud member of the Four-Horse Club. He was proceeding to prove his mettle and merit by passing the gig without pause, when another obstruction appeared in his path.

It was the person with the squashed hat. A female. His lordship's pampered pair, finding themselves again approaching a collision, this time felt themselves obliged to rear. The earl easily controlled them and turned to face the new obstruction. "Are you perfectly sensible that you nearly overset my horses?"

"Are you perfectly sensible, sir, that you have totally overset me and the farmer's gig?"

The voice was not that of a Yorkshire lass—she would have known better.

"You are addressing me?" he asked with enough incredulity to put her in her place for presuming to do so.

"There is no one else on this road. There is no one else who has had the audacity to run down a poor farmer's gig and then compound that effrontery by being concerned merely with the removal of that gig from his path. Are you not concerned at all as to the welfare of its passengers? I do not see you jumping down to be of assistance and to express your regrets."

That had the earl almost ready to pop his eyes out of his aristocratic skull as he stared in astonishment at the young person advancing toward him. She was a contradiction in terms. She sounded like a lady and looked like a peasant. For the first time in his privileged life, the earl found himself almost at a loss for words. But not appreciably so. As always, he found one point that could not be dismissed. He was in the right!

"This is a *private* road to Moorsedge. And thus, it is not only a gross effrontery for that farmer and his gig to be on it, but as well, to be on it in the dusk without the use of a lantern to make his presence known, which exceeds his original trespass. And further, you compound the offense by committing a trespass of your own by loitering."

After putting himself to the bother of explaining another's faults, his lordship expected the usual response of bowing or an expression of obligation for his condescension. But this person had the infamous nerve to giggle, and counter, "Oh, I perceive. You are jesting. You are, aren't you? One could not seriously believe you are accusing me of loitering after *you* smashed my means of conveyance and tossed me on this road where I am now loitering. No, indubitably you are possessed with the subtlest sense of humor, too subdued to be readily discernible. But to the point, sir. As you'll perceive," she continued, moving almost directly to the side of the curricle, "it is rather cold. And my portmanteau has landed somewhere in the bushes. If your groom would please place it in the back of your vehicle, I expect we could proceed with tolerable speed."

"The fall has clearly disordered your senses."

"Why?"

"You expect me to take you up?"

"Certainly. You would not wish to leave me stranded in the road? While you have not shown yourself to be a gentleman, I expect you make claims of being one from your equipage and servants. It is best always to assume there is some decency in one's fellow man. And if one gives another the opportunity to behave so, he invariably does not disappoint. As I expect you shall not."

Of a sudden the earl found himself smiling. He was not certain what amused him so—her audacity, her philosophy, or the combination of the two. But, egad, one could not but smile, if not gasp, at his being lectured on the social conventions by a lady whose disgracefully plebeian attire made her rather a figure of fun and whose hat, now that he had the misfortune to observe it closely, one could only charitably say, resembled an inadequately plucked chicken on a bed of wilted lettuce. A rare jest indeed, for her to be chiding him on not being a gentleman, when she had so forgotten herself and the basic rules of decorum by addressing a stranger without being introduced. And he said as much.

That did not properly chasten her. Instead, she airily replied, "I expect chance has made its own introductions. In moments of such exigencies I do not feel it is necessary to stand on such points." And then she further astonished the earl by going into peals of laughter. "Forgive me," she explained when she could speak. "It is just that you almost sounded like the kind of person who would stand by while another was drowning, and when asked why assistance was not offered, claim justification since you were not acquainted with the victim, and thus felt it would be regarded as an imposition to intrude in his watery demise."

The earl did not give her the compliment of a reply. He had wasted sufficient time. Selfers had returned and was explaining that the farmer was walking home and would come tomorrow for his gig.

"What possible interest do you imagine I have in the appointments and schedules of that mushroom?" the Earl responded, by now sorely tried at the entire experience.

"Me apologies, your lordship."

"Ah, *that* explains it!" Merrie exclaimed.

His lordship was condescending enough to turn his head in her direction. She took that as sufficient indication of interest to elucidate. "You are a *nobleman*— naturally you feel no need to be a gentleman as well, I daresay. Yet a title does not entitle you to incivility. Rather the reverse. One would hope that a lord more than ever would likely show us all the way."

The earl, although having expressed himself as having no interest in the whereabouts of the farmer, now realized it materially concerned him. For if the farmer had left, this hybrid lady-peasant was clearly in his charge. He frowned, and said with as much nobility as he could muster, having had that timely reminder, "I expect you are visiting somewhere in the neighborhood and wish to be escorted there?"

"How quick you are, your lordship. That is exactly so."

"Hmm. As I have explained, this road leads only to Moorsedge. Your farmer must have taken a wrong turn. I shall have Selfers stay here with you and on my reaching Moorsedge send back a conveyance to escort you where you wish to go. Is that sufficient for your exaggerated claims of assistance?"

"Not a jot. I should scarcely wish to be standing here all that time. Not with this cold wind coming off the moor, and myself, as you can see, with such a light pelisse. Nor is it sensible for me to wait here half the night just to be escorted directly where you are going yourself."

That last statement had the earl sitting up from his lounging position, alert and at attention. "You are on your way to *Moorsedge?*"

"Again you come swiftly to the obvious. Precisely. That is obviously the reason I was on this road."

"You are applying for a position there?" he countered, his voice if possible even more starched in tone.

"Ah, not so quick this time. I am not. I am visiting."

"You are visiting Moorsedge!"

"Yes. Is not that convenient? Moorsedge is not only my destination, but probably my destiny," Merrie cried out, clapping her hands together. "What a gratifying coincidence of direction brought us here. Now we may arrive there together."

"Somehow I shall endeavor to restrain my delight at that prospect. It certainly falls somewhat short of yours. Nevertheless, if I am not fatiguing you overmuch with these questions, I should wish to know—"

"Could you possibly contain your curiosity for a few moments, your lordship? I am more than willing to answer any and all inquiries, but I would request first to be taken up so we can begin our journey. Also, as I mentioned, there is the most improper wind that is invading my attire to the very skin. Grossly indecent, your Yorkshire winds and ways."

At that his lordship was at last shamed enough to signal his groom, and even assisted in placing her beside him before springing his horses. They were off. The groom surprised his master by placing a fur coverlet on the lady. It was not done at his instructions, nor indeed at his desire. Not that his lordship objected to this freedom with his coverlet, but Selfers had broken one of the cardinal rules of servant and master by disproving the social assumption that servants never heard conversations occurring directly under their noses. And his lordship found it presumptuous for anyone to dare trifle with any of his cherished assumptions. He was with every aspect of the evening seriously displeased.

Meanwhile the person cuddled appreciatively into the fur's warmth and appeared to be almost dozing. That was not what the earl wished. Rather he felt this was the appropriate time to discover her reason for being on the road to Moorsedge. And he proceeded to rouse her.

Accommodatingly, she shook herself awake and was soon talking freely. She'd been traveling for several days by stagecoach, and it had been a trifle fatiguing. Not that the company was distasteful; she'd made friends with quite a few passengers who had started out rather dour, but before the trip was over, they'd all come together and had a jolly time of it. One of them, a youngster, actually, had gone alongside the coachman and taken the reins and they came close to being overturned, but he proved to be a capital whip. Not, she owned, as top oars as his lordship. And here she must parenthetically interpose how much she admired the way he'd given the gig the go-by, to the veriest inch.

That was more in the toadying style his lordship was accustomed to and he'd just relaxed, when she continued: Of course he *had* overset the gig, for which he must be faulted, but observing the way he was presently driving, he was by no means cow handed. So the crash must be considered an exception, and he had no need to blush for his sportsmanship. This to a top Corinthian who had established a new mode of catching the thong of his whip that was still being copied.

His lordship was left to digest her review while she carried on with what she assumed were kindly remarks. If she'd known his lordship would be so gracious as to order his groom to give her this excessively comfortable covering, she would not have spoken to him as she had on the road. But didn't it show how correct she'd been—that there was good in every man, no matter how starch faced and toplofty he seemed.

His lordship bowed at that, and she laughed,

claiming she had not meant he was perennially a starch-face, just upon sudden meetings!

By now they'd reached the gates of Moorsedge, and Merrie must remark on the stone carvings on the supports and peer to read the inscription, which he refused to aid her in deciphering. The only thing that silenced her was the sight of Moorsedge itself. It towered before them like a giant coming out of the mist, and she could do naught but gape. And then Merrie, never cowed for long, commented in some transport, "Why, it's positively Gothic! Like something out of Mrs. Radcliffe's novels, I daresay."

His lordship assured her the towers did not contain secret rooms where young ladies were hidden, although he could not answer for what they might contain in the future.

"Ah, there!" Merrie exclaimed, highly pleased. "Did I not say you were possessed of subtle wit? How amusing we shall find this Christmastime ahead!"

That had him muttering that the prospect was too alluring to contemplate, but she had no occasion to respond, for they'd come to the doorway and she was already being handed down by the waiting footman.

The abundance of lanterns had the lady remembering herself and she abruptly removed her disgraceful bonnet. Out tumbled the most shockingly glorious red hair he had ever observed. And without the distraction of that brim, he noted a pair of sparkling green eyes that could easily have several of his dandy set writing poems to their depth and size and expression. But it was the dimples that decided the earl that her company had not been so onerous, after all. Indeed, he concluded with some condescension, she rated a full appraisal through his quizzing glass.

"Heavens! Do gentlemen really do that to ladies, without a by-your-leave?" Merrie protested, which immediately gave the earl the clue he needed that her upbringing was not of the best, for genuine ladies were inured to being thus appraised. But she was laughingly objecting, "Do please lower your glass, your enlarged eye is giving you a decidedly Cyclopean appearance."

"You are a *bluestocking!*" he accused.

"I am the daughter of a well-known scholar and admit to having read more than is generally acknowledged as fitting for gentlewomen or certainly ladies of the nobility. On the other hand, I expect, like them, not all of it has lasted in my idea-pot. One tends to have so many thoughts. Especially around this season, don't you think?"

As they were ascending the granite steps, of such monstrous proportions that she must hop a bit, the earl could not help but insert, "Are you expected?"

She turned her twinkling green eyes on him and laughed again. "You are under the assumption that I am forcing my presence on these poor unsuspecting people? Nothing of the kind. Yes, I am expected. In fact, your lordship, I daresay we are both here for the same reason."

"I scarcely think so."

"But of course, I have come to spend Christmas with the family. Have not you as well?"

"I have," he said grimly, and his thoughts were running on the possibility that this young lady might be one of his younger brother George's ideas of a holiday jest. "Are you acquainted with my brother George?"

"No. Is he as delightful a companion as you?"

"I asked merely to determine who has invited you to spend Christmas here. To be blunt, you are not my acquaintance. Nor, apparently, my brother's."

"That leaves . . ." she teased, egging him on to the obvious.

"I see. My mother."

"Again, you hit the nail on the head. How precise are your strokes! The countess of Warwick was so good as to write and invite me to spend above a fortnight here for the holidays."

While he was digesting this, Merrie made a return perusal of his elegant, perfectly featured face with its bored expression. She had suspected upon his being first addressed as his lordship that he was the young earl. Nevertheless, she kept hoping he was merely a holiday visitor, a somewhat nobler version of herself. But when he mentioned his brother, she could no longer deny the obvious. This was to be her host, after all. Oh, fiddle!

The earl of Warwick. And she had casually ordered him to take her up. Small wonder she'd put his back up. With so much consequence, how would he take her further announcement? And so with unholy joy she began her revelation. "Prepare yourself, my lord, for another shock, pleasant or unpleasant whether it be, but . . ." Here she was unable to stop herself from pausing dramatically, and when she had his total attention, concluded, "I am your relation. We are *cousins*, no less. But you need not fear. I expect our relationship is a distant one. So you may continue to keep your distance from me. Although, since we are going to experience such a joyous time together, I expect we shall find ourselves, with some necessary reservations, becoming fast friends."

His lordship's noble features betrayed him; he winced.

2

After having so silenced and nonplussed his lordship, Merrie matter-of-factly went about the serious business of making herself look kempt. For a decent presentation to the countess, she must be fit to be seen. And so she forced her wild curls back under the wounded and wilted bonnet, smothering underneath the fire of her hair. Then she straightened out her pelisse, which was too small, being her mother's, and tended to ride up in the most awkward way. And at last Merrie deemed herself as ready as she could be, under the circumstances, and under the earl's still astonished eye.

Before her, the door to Moorsedge was of such proportions, two footmen were required to pull it open. The butler, supervising, was precisely suitable for this place—old, set in his ways, yet imposing. Another person to disapprove of her, she perceived. Oh, fiddle! She simply refused to be intimidated—either by the manor or man, or manner of either—and promptly she sallied forth.

The butler was observing the lady with a great deal

of reservation. One could not but be struck by the mud-green velvet hat and its remnant of a white plume brokenly waving above it. The muddied color was in large part the contribution of his lordship, though admittedly, even before, the velvet had seen better days. But to be fair, so had the butler, who finally allowed his eyes to travel from the hat to the lady's face and there received another shock—she was smiling at him. That familiarity could not be endured!

Another stroke against her, his lordship felt, satisfied. Ladies did not smile at servants. Actually, they were usually unaware of their existence. Although the earl, knowing Walters since a child, did unbend sufficiently to inquire after his health and was informed with some pride that it was, as usual, indifferent.

Here Merrie was quick to offer her concern. Walters, seeing she'd come with his lordship, forgave the hat and allowed her one of his very rare spasms that passed for a smile.

Which was something of a victory for the intrepid Miss Laurence. And she continued smiling while she walked forward on her own into the massive armor-lined hall lit by candlesticks on pedestals, and having at least half a dozen sculptured, sizable oak doors.

Behind one of them, the countess of Warwick was taking forty winks. The commotion in the hall shook her, if not alert, at least awake. She straightened her ruffled cap and sat up. Of late, her ladyship was unaccustomed to noises in Moorsedge. Since her husband's demise, she had gradually retreated into reclusive, reclining ways.

A fire roared at her side. One thing the countess insisted on was a warm room. She needed it for her health. And so every floor, indeed, every suite she was liable even to pass through, was ordered to be kept fully heated despite the cost. She had been a widow for almost a decade. From his London home, the earl, her son, whom she could no longer remember as a child, or even convince herself that he'd ever been one, let alone hers, ran Moorsedge completely. That was deftly accomplished through the steward, who gave orders to the housekeeper and butler and reported back to him. His lordship ruled all. Which left naught for the countess to do. And so that was what she did to perfection.

Actually, there had been a time, early in her widowhood, when Lady Warwick had considered coming to London and establishing herself at the Warwick town house for a season, but the earl had quickly discouraged that, picturing the inconveniences to herself, not to mention to *himself,* and she, not one to push, had sunk back into his past, with the result that, henceforth, her ladyship's occupation and preoccupation was her health. Quacking and nostrums became her only interest, and her pains her only distinction.

Having grown comfortable with neglect and her self-absorption, the countess was jolted this year to be noticed. She found it too late and too tiring. Yet her son, accustomed to giving orders rather than consulting another's wishes, simply announced that he would be giving her the pleasure of a holiday visit. As well, he would be accompanied by several of his most elegant friends, all expecting varied entertainments, which she undoubtedly would easily plan and oversee.

His visit was meant as a kindness, the way selfish people perform them—willing to give attention when it is in their interest at last to do so. For assuredly the earl thought himself quite a decent chap. And this party was proof of his beneficence. That he wished most eagerly to claim this season's newest diamond, Lady Jane, for his own, and had devised this invitation as a means of taking her away from her other flirts, he did not allude to when patting himself on the back. As well as Lady Jane, others accepting were her parents, the marquis and marchioness of Dansville. For himself, he was including Lord Pavraam, his closest friend, and Sir Oswald, a rattle but a jolly good sport of a fellow. And as a further example of his generosity, he'd invited two rather dull matrons of his mother's age. The list was completed when his lordship was suddenly struck that with Sir Oswald and Lord Pavaarm, the competitive edge would be against him for Lady Jane. So he added a rival of that lady's, young Miss Florence Prichard. And thus neither lady would be able to feel herself the favorite.

The principal reason for his returning to Moorsedge, after nigh unto five years' neglect, was that he wished to see the lady of his choice in the setting she would eventually be placed in, if he condescended to propose. For after many years of pleasure, the earl had sensed that it was time to do his duty to his lineage by setting up his nursery. Which necessitated a wife. Both Lady Jane and Miss Prichard had been attempting all last season to persuade him that each would best suit that prime role. Unfortunately, so many young ladies had seemed fitting during the social ease and dalliance of a ballroom acquaintance, but always another young lady had come along of equal qualifications. One simply could not choose.

It was his hope that by limiting the ladies present to two, he could force his discriminating palate somehow to swallow one. Lady Jane was precisely his ideal —theoretically. She was a perfect lady, not only in title, although that materially weighed, but in her manner, her speaking (or lack thereof), dress, and mostly, in her awe of him. She had one flaw, which obviously went with a diamond of the first water; she was cold. Stone cold. He would find that quality unexceptionable for the wife of a friend, but for himself he had hoped for something more. He hit upon the idea that she would unbend somewhat in a more intimate setting, and under a holiday atmosphere. It could very well be supposed that with the Christmas warmth, Lady Jane would seem warmer herself, or at least convivial enough to spark some answering joy in his own heart. So far she'd only inspired approval, yet that was more than Miss Prichard aroused, with her blank stare. And so the odds were clearly on Lady Jane's side. Admittedly his invitation to these two ladies gave them a mark of distinguishing notice, but he could not actually spend time in the hinterland of Yorkshire without some diversion, perhaps even a challenge. Speaking of which, it was a dashed pity ladies did not fight duels over gentlemen. He should not have disliked being the prize. And it would have eased him of the fatigue of choice. Possibly ladies did combat, if not with swords, with tongues; and so he might find himself vied for after all.

And another reason for a visit to Moorsedge was that it was long past due. Thus, he could accomplish several ends with one mission. Principally, he told himself, he was bringing the party to Yorkshire to delight his mother. And he told her the same. And told both her and himself that he owed her this treat.

Lastly, his purpose for his gathering was the season. One did this sort of thing at this time, he supposed. And so one was being properly conventional.

The pleasure Lady Warwick derived from such distinguishing notice could only be described as overwhelming. For she was knocked flat on her bed for a full day afterward. Judicious use of her vinaigrette and a foot cataplasm as well, enabled her to pass the first throes.

The next morning however the letter was still there —with its dire threat of people converging on Moorsedge. A cup of tisane kept at the ready, she forced herself to read it anew.

After squeezing her memory, her ladyship vaguely placed Lady Dansville, and regretted the effort, for her recollection brought forth only a cold fish of a lady who continually quoted from *Burke's Peerage*.

Several attempts at writing her regrets to her son had her ladyship in such a watering pot of a condition that she could not send a single effort, for the blots. And so she simply did what she always did in such an unbearable situation, she took to her bed and forgot it.

As the time drew near, she sometimes recollected something looming over her, but dismissed it. The housekeeper Mrs. Prissom, a sennight later, had the indecency to request orders for the guests. *Guests*— the word threw the countess into a tizzy, and she gestured the word away. Apparently the earl had sent a note to his steward Mr. Smithers, who in turn inquired of Mrs. Prissom on the progress of the preparations. At a loss, the dear lady brought the coil to her mistress. Forced to it, the countess gave orders: Mrs. Prissom was to do what she thought best. But the trouble was, Mrs. Prissom was not best at thinking on her own. And so the two ladies stared at each other in dismay with not a single constructive idea between them. The butler ended the awkwardness by bringing in the mail.

A small note from a distant relation, Miss Merrie Laurence, sufficed to change the frightening direction of both ladies' thoughts; and with some relief, the countess dismissed Mrs. Prissom with nothing further said on the matter.

Saved from considering the frightening future, the countess fell to cogitating on the pleasant past, which included the history of her relationship with the Laurences. Actually, it was the mother with which her ladyship was acquainted. She had been a Miss Letty Aldrich who had caused some commotion by refusing to marry a lord of some standing, rather choosing a penniless scholar. Everyone had felt that sufficient reason to cut her completely, but not Lady Warwick, she of the kind and romantic heart. Having herself been imposed upon to accept an imposing earl instead of her own heart's desire, she could not but admire another who had stuck to her original choice, buckle and thong. Indeed, not only had her ladyship sent wedding congratulations to the couple but a wedding present as well. And subsequently she had even refused to excise Mrs. Laurence from her Christmas list. And thus Lady Warwick became the yearly reminder to the Laurences that society had not totally turned its face. Every Christmas, ahead of the season, in fact, came the countess's copperplate message for the holiday and always a monetary offering for the children.

With that annual guinea, it was not likely the Laurence children would do less than pronounce her ladyship as the very symbol of their season. And this year, when Merrie was taking on more and more of her mother's responsibilities, she took it upon herself to go beyond her mother's one line of gratitude, and replied in full. And her reply brought a reply.

To own it, the countess felt there was a confident yet soothing tone to Miss Laurence's letter which she was in sore need of at that moment. With what threatened from London, it would not be amiss to have someone on her side, and by her side. So on an impulse, the invitation was written. Upon receiving a jubilant affirmative, the countess called the housekeeper and triumphantly announced that she had some instructions, after all. Mrs. Prissom was to prepare a bedchamber for *her* holiday guest!

As if all the fates were conspiring to keep Lady Warwick away from the comfort of her couch, the

very next day, her youngest son, George Dickens, after enough Christmases having been spent at friends'
estates to make his mother accustomed to it, arrived
home. Her ladyship could not help but feel hardly
used to have him come down from Oxford ere she
expected him. Being one who always made his mother
most anxious, George continued in his predictable
pattern. At Moorsedge for not above a day, he took a
toss from his horse and appeared in her ladyship's
sitting room, blood freely running from the gash on
his forehead. Which naturally caused the lady to fall
directly into a swoon. The doctor arrived to find
George off on another ride, having wiped the blood
off himself and applied a court plaster, but her ladyship was still suffering spasms. She had just come to
her senses and was coming down for tea, when
George arrived with his hounds at his heels, which
canines overset the tea tray and fully partook of the
spread.

Today George had been considerate enough to stay
away, understanding that his mother could not en-
dure more than a judicious dosage of his lively personality. He should be visiting friends for at least a
couple of days, and so her ladyship had dared seek
her ease in her own saloon when the sounds in the
hall had her concluding that George had played her
false and was returning early.

But she maligned her second son. It was her first
son, the earl himself. A much worse calamity—say
even, a catastrophe. For he was to bring more than
dogs at his heels, she recollected in a transport of
alarm.

"Brett," she was just able to whisper. And then in
some peevishness, "You were not expected so early?
Were you?"

So much for civilities, the earl thought, but he nevertheless kept strictly to them, giving his mother a

passing peck and wishing her the best of holidays ahead. She did not respond to that.

Indeed, she seemed noticeably less chatty than he recollected. It had been more time than he thought since they'd last met, and she either had aged or there was some truth to her many complaining letters. Nevertheless, he did not make the mistake of inquiring as to her health, for he knew that would end all hope for any other discussion. And his principal reason for returning must be immediately addressed. He spoke in a louder tone than was usual for his lordship, as he did not seem to have her undivided attention. His earlier arrival, he explained, was due to his eagerness to observe the preparations for the holiday visit of his friends.

Pointedly his mother did not reply, which roused the worst forebodings. And he said softly, but with some grimness, "I have not as yet inspected the main rooms, but still I perceive no signs of holly or wreaths, nor fresh polished floors . . . no signs at all of a bustle."

Her ladyship knew it was time to take the medicine of confession. She was quite an expert at swallowing disagreeable doses and hoped her son was as stalwart. Almost holding her nose, she disclosed, "I have written you several notes to cancel the festivities, but through some mischance or another, they were never sent. It is fortuitous, therefore, that you have arrived early and can communicate with your guests to that effect. Dr. Erdom assures me there is no possibility I should be up to the exigencies such an undertaking would require. And further, George is home and bleeding all over the carpets. My only hope is in this new procedure Dr. Erdom is suggesting—it is warm ale and cold compresses, done precisely at the same time—"

"Forgive me, Mama. You know I am no believer in

quackery. Can it have escaped your memory that Moorsedge is mine? I have beneficently allowed you to remain here rather than removing to the dower house. But under no circumstances are you to say what shall or shall not occur in this estate. My orders are to be carried out—to the letter."

"I am not up to it. I am not even up to this discussion. I am beginning to feel the palpitations again. My vinaigrette!"

Her son found the vinaigrette under the pillows and handed it to her silently. A few whiffs and she was able to face him. But she had nothing else to say. She had performed all.

"Very well, Mama," the earl said coldly. "I shall not expect anything from you. But I intend to have my friends here for the holidays. They are expected and will be arriving."

He sat down suddenly, shaking his head, mainly at himself for having trusted in his mother's ability, when he had long despaired of her being fit for anything. He had some hopes yet of the housekeeper and suggested as much to his mother.

"Ah, poor Prissy, she is as overcome as I. As for her idea of entertainment, I expect you are forgetting, not having honored us with your presence for so long, but she is past the age for anything of that sort. She raised your father, you'll recollect, and, of course, yourself. She was very good at lottery tickets. And pick-the-straw!"

"Mother! I am not inviting children! Ye gods, what am I to do?"

The countess did not have the slightest suggestion, or wish to offer one. The earl was totally flummoxed at his situation. In London one could simply call Gunther's and at least the food would be delivered, with the very choicest ices and confections. And in the city, as well, he had an entire staff he could rely on for household preparations. But here, there was no recourse. And in the midst of all this despondency and confusion came a clear, calm voice saying joyously, "But I can manage everything without the slightest effort."

Mother and son turned. It was Miss Merrie Laurence at the threshold. So overcome had they both been in their dispute, her entrance had been unobserved.

"Did I not tell you, your lordship, our meeting was providential? I had no realization how prophetic I was." And then turning toward the perplexed countess, she curtsied and quickly kissed the lady, "I am Merrie," she said.

"She is indeed," the earl said with a groan.

3

Instantly Merrie turned her full attentions toward soothing the startled countess. Her voice took
on the consoling quality of one entering an invalid's
room in which the last rites were clearly the next and
only recourse. That was a treatment her ladyship
could not help but favor, and soon she was allowing
the young lady to fix her pillows and arrange a stool
for her feet. Tea was called for. And Merrie took that
moment to remove her hat. She placed it carefully and
proudly on the marble table near the fireplace and
then returned, her fiery hair loosed, seeming to bring
with it the warmth of a fireplace to the waiting lady.

His lordship had discounted Merrie's entrance remarks as he did the lady, but his mother, never questioning that another would be found to take on her
responsibilities, was now quite sanguine about the future, and in this new ease she turned toward her son,
claiming had not his dear old mother, after all, come
to the rescue, as she had when he used to hide in the
armor and find himself lost in there.

With strained patience, the earl requested his

mother keep to their current dilemma, but she was
still preening over having had the foresight to invite
this young lady. Did not her son owe her some gratitude? she hinted. And in civility, he was forced to
offer it her, regardless of his true feelings. Only then
did the countess continue on with a topic of more
immediate interest—the exact degree of relationship
between themselves and Merrie.

It was during this excursion into "second cousin,
and my aunt on my father's side" that the earl finally
recollected the Laurences for himself. There was constant dispute between his parents when he was a mere
nipperkin about a cousin of theirs who had given a
marquis a slap on the shoulder and disgraced them
all. That had been unpardonable, in his father's opinion, and his wife should have ended her recognition of
the couple. Subsequently when at Oxford, Brett had
met Godfrey Laurence the scholar, and even read one
of his historical treatises, which he recollected finding
rather more tolerable than the usual dry stuff. Some
occasional flashes of wit had permeated it, and he
expected that explained this redoubtable girl's own
light manner.

He did not himself find ladies of her sort tolerable.
They always allowed their little reading to go to their
heads and spill out continuously in unwise displays.
Society ladies knew enough to be monosyllabic—in
his presence, at least. And if they did volunteer an
observation, it was sufficiently commonplace to allow
him the comfort of his superiority. But more offensive
than Miss Laurence's conversation was her appalling
appearance. She was so shabbily, so demonstrably,
poor! Yet inexplicably she displayed not a whit of
embarrassment about her clothes being an insult to all
observers and particularly to his fastidious eye. Even
without that outrageous hat, her dress had obviously
seen many years' wear. And her kid half-boots were

not only scuffed, but, he observed with disapproval, had been refurbished with spots of ink on those scuffs. Shamefully plebeian.

How he was going to introduce her to his set—to Lady Jane and her parents, no less—left him at point non plus. His only hope was that she would remain silently on the sidelines, perhaps as a companion to his mother, although from his first hours of their acquaintance he was not completely sanguine that would occur. Her entrance words disabused him of his last possible ease.

As he had been evaluating her, she had been listening to the countess's full medical history. That began circa her husband's death and included each and every one of her intervening illnesses up to the present. Not spent, her ladyship continued with other unkind strokes of fate, such as her eldest son having gone off to London and forgotten her existence, and then her youngest son being away at school and forgetting her existence. Until they both chose this year to remember her and descend upon her simultaneously. Which was too much for her nerves! And with the thought of all the guests descending on her as well, was it any wonder she was palpitating again?

Merrie quickly, soothingly assured her that she had nothing to fear. "But as I have already stated, I shall take over. Surely it is providential that you have sent for me, your ladyship. What forethought! You need not lift a finger. At Christmas, naught is more splendid than that we all adjourn here to enjoy it together. And your sons can only add to your comfort at this season of happiness. And guests will make it even more enchanting. I daresay we shall have the jolliest Christmas ever. For of all the holidays, this is my favorite. In fact, Christmas is *my* holiday. I was born during the Christmas season and have ever made it my first concern. In short, I know precisely how to entertain everyone who will arrive. Leave it all to me, your ladyship. It will be our happiest time ever."

"Good God," the earl exclaimed in trepidation. The young girl's green eyes were dancing at the thoughts of Christmas joy ahead. He had a definite impression that he would not be able to contain her, that something had been unleashed in his home that would not only make the holidays memorable but might have a significant effect on the comfort and placidity of his life ahead.

"I knew I was correct, if not divinely inspired to invite you," the countess said with relief. "I shall leave everything in your hands then, dear Merrie." And with a sigh, she roused herself to retire from her couch to her chambers and the waiting bed there.

Merrie turned to face the wary earl. He resented mostly being put into a position where he had to do what he did not wish to do. Miss Merrie Laurence had continually been putting him in this kind of dashed circumstance from the moment that she had all but ordered him to take her up and transport her to his home. And now it appeared that he was going to have to turn the entire control of his gathering over to this unknown and suspiciously volatile quantity.

Yet what else was he to do at this late date? His mother had left him no other recourse. Walters could scarcely be counted on to handle anything of such magnitude, and his dour aspect would not be conducive to seasonal cheer. Which left naught but his lordship himself. Naturally he would add his input, but the overall management would necessitate attention to plebeian details and the demeaning, not to say unmanning, task of consulting with housemaids. Neither was his forte. Actually, he concluded hopefully, it was just the occupation for a lady. And since this lady seemed so willing to undertake all, what was he to do but accept her offices? Not only that, but he should dashed well have to show himself grateful. Ye gods!

Miss Laurence was awaiting the word to come from the earl's set lips, as he so obviously was attempting to find some other solution. When he turned to her and nodded, she would not allow that as sufficient. Rather, unfeelingly, she brought it out in the open.

"You wish me to handle all this, do you not, my lord?"

"I should be most obliged," he answered gruffly. "However, they are gentlemen and ladies, and as such, expect some degree of . . . gentility."

"Which you fear I lack?"

"Precisely."

"Well then, I expect I shall have to tone down some of the more bawdy Druid influences in the festivities and keep it a wholesome holiday gathering. That is, always with the understanding that your aristocratic friends are wholesome themselves."

He was not certain whether she was hoaxing him about the Druid touches, and then realized she was.

"I did not mean to imply you would not remain within the bounds of decency," he allowed.

"Thank you. I always endeavor to keep my decency." And then she grinned with a great deal of enchanting friendliness that he could not but respond to—at least marginally.

"You need not be alarmed, my lord. I promise you a Christmas you will never forget."

"That is exactly what I fear," he said. And with a slight bow, he hurriedly took his leave before he had to look this holiday gift horse in the mouth and be forced to acknowledge that he was being hoaxed.

Alone, Merrie looked around at the drawing room of such a size that the saloon in the Laurence lodgings back at Oxford would have filled a mere corner. And how delightful was the fire going at such a roar, how it warmed her to the heart. Upon her word, she could not imagine that the Warwicks could have so much, and yet the mother be so sad, and the son such a cold and indifferent character. She thought of her two young brothers and how they would make this place seem so much more merry and livable in a wink. And her dear sister Esther, who would have room for all her books. And dear father, who would probably be able to have an entire room in this place for the peace and quiet he needed to do his research. And her wonderful, hard-pressed mother, who had been a lady and given it all up for love, and found herself well loved, and yet never without a worry since. Clearly the Warwicks would be of inestimable help to her family —she just needed to be of help to them first. And after that, logically and happily it followed, they would be sufficiently grateful to spread the goodwill. It being the season of goodwill, after all.

Quite astounding. She had not been at Moorsedge above two hours, and not only was she welcomed but put in charge. Merrie was looking about in complete bliss when the housekeeper arrived to show her to her rooms. Her portmanteau had been brought up and unpacked. Merrie nodded and was about to follow, when she noticed that her bonnet was missing. It was not on the table where she'd laid it. Not under the settee where she'd sat. Not by the fireplace where she'd warmed herself. Nowhere.

And then Merrie remembered the earl eyeing it with distaste. She had a vague suspicion his lordship had disposed of it, but instantly dismissed that supposition. Not until actually before the fireplace did she observe something smoking. One look proved that it was her plumed bonnet. There was no possibility it could have fallen behind the screen on its own. His lordship had done it. He was the only one who *could* have. Or *would* have.

For a moment she bemoaned the loss of her only bonnet of distinction. True, it had been muddied, again by the earl's thoughtlessness, but she'd hoped a good cleaning would have resurrected it to a tolerable degree of presentability. But now, as it slowly turned to ashes before her eyes, she felt herself bereft—very near beheaded! That was one act that ought never to be forgiven. It bespoke a degree of presumption that boded ill for their relationship, since the earl could be so free with her belongings.

Unless . . . And here the perpetual optimist in Merrie surfaced. Unless he intended to gift her with a new bonnet as a Christmas surprise. Appeased by that conclusion, Merry was all felicity again as she left the drawing room.

As an afterthought, and this being a time for giving as well as receiving, Merrie wondered if there was not a particular item of apparel his lordship prized, that she might not cause to fall victim to an unfortunate accident. She must give that some thought, she decided with a small anticipatory grin.

Obviously there were many surprises ahead for her, and she would be returning them in good measure, in the spirit of the season ahead.

4

Apparently the earl had had sufficient of country company for one day and ordered that the evening meal be sent to everyone's rooms. The countess approved, as she was greatly fatigued and set to retire. But Merrie had enough energy to need just a few moments of reclining on the comfortable settee next to her roaring fireplace to be up and ready to explore the entire mansion. Certainly she was prepared to carry on with her examination of his lordship's character.

That, of course, she divined, must be the reason he wished to dine alone. To keep away from her. Rather than being put out of countenance, Merrie was tolerant of his lordship's reluctance. He would soon find, as did most people, that he could not do without her. Which reminded her of the people she could not do without—her family.

From the moment she had left their lodgings in Oxford, she'd seen herself as an explorer, or rather as the member of the group sent out to find aid for the party left in dire situation. Without a qualm Merrie had taken on the task of rescuing her family from the poverty and despair that threatened to overtake them.

She had to giggle at that point. For in truth, no member of her family ever succumbed to despair. While it had been practical for her to come to establish connection with their noble relations, and her mother had agreed that she should do it, neither her father nor sister had felt it necessary. They were quite happy in their meager circumstances. Mr. Laurence, a renowned scholar, found his joy in the publication of his historical works that eventually provided his family with the necessities of life, if not the comforts and certainly not the amenities. Esther found her joy in being her father's assistant in research, for which her remarkable mind showed quite a bent. Her brothers at seven and eleven found joy in everything, particularly in shouting and wrestling each other and racing around the rooms and disturbing the books left everywhere, so that their father was always finding that the very tome he needed for authentication had become the bottom block of a particularly impressive tower built by his sons. Without the slightest annoyance, he removed the pivotal block and walked away, already reading, and unaware of the crash and groans behind him. They brought their complaints to Merrie, who helped stack the books again, assuring them that this time, as the tower was shorter, they could jump over it; and immediately they perceived the advantage in this new diversion and cheerily went forth to hop along.

Her mother would companionably jump the books along with Merrie and the boys as she walked by on the way to the kitchen. Nothing of material nature would cause Mrs. Laurence to swerve from her set path in life of caring for her husband and children. And having sufficient of those, she noticed no lack of anything else. Indeed, having chosen this path of warmth and love over position and honor, she was not one to have second thoughts, especially since she found herself protected from regrets by the cozy barrier of family, unity, and caring.

But Mrs. Laurence, having been brought up as a member of the upper class, had never learned the method of humbling herself to ask for assistance. She was still left with the false notion, no matter how often disabused, that everyone would eventually be accommodating. To prevent her mother from the constant collision with reality, Merrie, even as a young girl, had begun taking over the dealings with the outside world. She it was who persuaded the poulterer and the greengrocer into extending credit. She, further, who willingly sat with the lonely elderly lady, Mrs. Pinch, the owner of the lodging house. During one of these companionable chats, Merrie explained "printings" and that her father's earnings depended on readers, showing the ilk of those by revealing an actual letter from the prince regent himself. That is, it was written by Rev. J. S. Clarke, his librarian, but signed in His Highness's own hand. Mrs. Pinch instantly stood up and curtsied to the paper, feeling blessed to hold it in her hand; so much so, her head kept bobbing in obeisance over each word of praise, as if to a royal proclamation. Afterward Mrs. Pinch jumped to the conclusion that Mr. Laurence was the prince's very own writer. Not only was she honored to have the Laurences living in her establishment, but more than willing to await His Highness's convenience for payment. "They be of the prince's household," she told the neighbors proudly and with a knowing wink. When the moneys came in and payments went around, all felt themselves honored to have, even secondhand, received a touch of their regal prince regent.

This year however, the Laurences were a great deal

in arrears, there being some misunderstanding with Mr. Laurence's publisher about previous advances. In due course they should receive some settlement, Mr. Laurence airily assured, already intent on research for his next project. But in the meantime Christmas was also due; and once more they would have to make do.

Gifts could always be managed for the two young boys—mittens could be knit, small toys bought or made. But Merrie and Esther must continue to mend their old gowns, not having had new ones in over four years. Merrie, always ready to alter things for the best, had in the interim found a trunkful of Mrs. Laurence's old dresses from her extravagant social youth, and two were selected as sufficiently serviceable to be remade into, if not fashionable creations, at least tolerable coverings.

She was needle-witted enough, if not needle-adept, to take up a beribboned bonnet and denude it to add them to Esther's gown. That young lady's blond hair had blended beautifully with the golden ribboned touches and the ribbons also covered Merrie's large stitches. She would never be able to make her living as a seamstress, but she had a spirit of the holiday within that somehow spurred her on to meet any challenge at the time. The result was that Esther looked, they both agreed, quite fair and festive. As for herself, she chose a cream twilled silk and added a matching shawl to disguise the waistline, which was not the currently fashionable high-waisted style. The prize of the trunk, however, was a hat, the ostrich feather standing up at some height and looking quite plumy, both girls agreed. They refreshed it as much as possible and planned to give it to their mother on Christmas morning, hoping the change of ribbon would mask its familiarity. The gift for Esther was an advance copy of Mr. Laurence's latest publication, suitably inscribed in gratitude for her assistance in his research. Another such would go to Merrie for her making a final neat copy for him that would be easily read by the printer, and for adding her occasional humorous touches.

The holiday gifts thus provided for, the main concern was the meal. A goose this year would be beyond their means, not that last year's skinny little bird had provided sufficient. A goose was wanted as a symbol of their lack of want and their ability to join the rest of England in having something special to table at holiday. But potatoes in their jackets must suffice. At least Mrs. Laurence had long been saving the ingredients for her famed plum pudding, which was always the high point of the meal. Beforehand their mother was slightly nervous that it would not be properly done, or that it would break in the turning out. And so when the pudding came out of the copper easily, letting out a stream of satisfied steam, the two girls and the watching sons and Mrs. Laurence herself let out an equally satisfied puff. And when Mrs. Laurence gazed proudly down at the firm pudding and drenched it with half a quartern of brandy and set it afire and tossed on a sprig of holly atop, it was wildly applauded even by Mr. Laurence, who felt the occasion sufficient to put down his notebook, remove his glasses, and laud his wife's effort.

And Mrs. Laurence always smiled in great modesty, but in complete expectation of receiving naught less but full praise from her loving family.

Thinking of that moment now in Moorsedge, Merrie could not half hold back the tears. She would not be there this year to see the lighting of their pudding. The countess of Warwick's card of Christmas greeting had changed the family's usual routine.

Every year Mrs. Laurence looked forward to the coming of the countess's card, for it was the one last link with her previous life. Proudly the card was set on the mantel for all to note. When things were the most desperate, it was the habit of the Laurences to remark one to the other, "We can always apply to the countess." But soon all was overcome by their undaunted spirits, and the countess was left undisturbed, unaware of how close she'd come to being applied to and how often her name had been invoked during the twenty-five years' gulf since the two ladies had last met.

This year again the countess's card, as always, arrived ahead of time. Merrie took it in before setting off for the shops with only a sixpence extra to spend for Christmas, and where to put it first?

The foods certainly called out to her: cheeses, bacon, sweetmeats, tins of teas and coffee. But certain other necessities laid claim as well: soap, matches, a broom—for theirs was worn to a stump—bags of salt, and extra candles for her father's dimming eyesight. And then the impossibles: all the displayed birds at the poulterers, extra firewood for the unbelievable luxury of a continuous fire, and lastly, a boy's kite. Without questions, she came home with the kite, for it was such a splendid one that promised a full spring and summer of running on the Oxford grounds.

Her mother would have preferred the cheese; Esther, the candles for her father's eyes, and yet Merrie had bought the kite. It was typical of her hopeful nature and her belief that the greatest necessity of all is joy.

And yet the need of all the items she had just seen at the store, and the bravery of her family in doing without, had Merrie staring at the countess's Christmas card with an inspired conclusion. The countess would no longer be the family jest, but the family's savior. Actually, if she were ever to be made use of, this would have to be the year. At four and twenty, Merrie had given up all hope that there was any future for herself, but Esther was now approaching eighteen; another year, and she too would be firmly on the path to spinsterhood. And this year was chosen because Christmas itself was going to be rather shabbier even than usual. One could accept anything but a stinting at Christmas.

Before second thoughts could intervene, Merrie took pen in hand and wrote to her ladyship, in her most engaging yet determined style, all about herself and her family. She hoped it would elicit a more sizable holiday gift than the usual guinea, even possibly some recognition for the future.

Instead what had arrived was an invitation—indeed, an immediate summons for her to come to Moorsedge for the holidays. That was more than Merrie had expected or even wanted. For of all times to be away from her family, Christmas was the last she'd choose. Not to see her mother's plum pudding being brought to table, not to see the boys' faces when she presented the kite—nay, she could not go from home at Christmas.

And yet, she could not possibly *not* go from home. For her mind was filled with hopes of what could possibly be done for her family. Further, there would be the joy of traveling, something she had always wished to do. And across so much of their country, clear up north to Yorkshire, well, she could not but admit that would be monstrously fine.

"But it's your birthday as well a few days after," Esther objected. "Surely you can stay for the holidays and visit her ladyship subsequently."

"I would if I could, you know that, Esther dear, but she seems to need me at the present. Whatever comes to pass it would be at least a foothold for us."

Eventually all were brought to see the wisdom in that, and Merrie was sent off with much hope and love—and with her mother's contribution of the ostrich-feather bonnet on Merrie's head.

Before leaving, Merrie had helped decorate the lodgings with greenery, not wishing to miss the communal joy of that, and lastly, she took a sprig of holly from each member of her family to place in her room in Yorkshire, so that when she looked at the bouquet on her dresser, she would be celebrating Christmas with them symbolically. A hearty kiss went with each sprig and many a tear, and thus launched, Merrie was off.

The first thing Merrie unpacked from her portmanteau was the five holly branches, and she touched each sprig in the name of the giver and put the holly next to her bed. Mrs. Prissom and a maid had brought her supper on a tray and Merrie gasped. She had not joined the other travelers at the various stops at the inns for meals, rather relied on the bread and cheese and other comestibles brought along and eked out for the four days' journey. The travelers always returned to the coach with tales of rounds of beef and other hearty viands that had Merrie's mouth watering. After one such stop, a generous countrywoman, sensing the young girl's need, had brought back a piece of kidney pie and Merrie had scarcely been able to mumble her gratitude for the taste of it.

Yet all the last day she'd had naught to eat and was fair gutfoundered. Being overturned on the road had added a chill in the pit of her empty stomach, so a cup of tea would have been most welcome. But the spread put before her by the smiling Mrs. Prissom included an entire pot of tea. And as well, a thick wedge of ham that at home would have fed the whole family. Upon seeing the buns and cakes, Merrie's eyes misted for not being able to share them with her brothers. But despite that wish, when left alone, Merrie could do no less than fall to with relish.

"My stars!" Merrie exclaimed when she was finished and was fuller than she'd ever recollected. If this be a snack, heavens, what could Christmas dinner be like?

And at last, lacking a wrapper, dressed in her worn nightdress, which despite the fire in her room still allowed the chill from the casements to reach to her skin, Merrie ran about to warm up. That gave her the occasion to observe her chamber. The large four-poster canopied bed would allow room for stretching and even rolling about. Next, she was in wonder at all the candlesticks filled with tallow. Feeling so plush, she could not resist lighting a full branch. The added light revealed portraits hanging in the darker corners of her room. There was one lady in a rose gown and holding a rose who was smirking down at Merrie, and Merrie could not resist grinning back and curtseying. But the tapestry on one wall was nothing to smile about and ought be replaced, for it was quite a realistic hunting scene with dogs snapping at a cringing fox. Merrie had a premonition of her being the fox and his lordship at her tail, for if ever a gentleman looked as if he would relish that unspeakable sport, it was the earl.

Her thoughts of the earl were not conducive to a pleasant night's rest, nor was the memory he evoked of the loss of her feathered bonnet. But she deliberately shook out of her head all such memories, and sank into the featherbed. In not above an hour she was up at the sound of singing in the hallway and rushed to her door.

A young gentleman was weaving his way down the hall singing a Christmas carol at full volume. Giggling at the joy in his voice, Merrie was closing her door when he began veering toward the staircase, a few feet from plunging down. Heedless of not being properly attired, the young lady came to his rescue, stopping the young gentleman from pitching forth.

George Dickens, the earl's younger brother, stared

at the incredibly beautiful lady before him. His senses were disordered, he admitted, which explained this vision. But the vision continued talking to him, and smiling, wishing to be directed to his rooms!

"Egad! Why am I so fortunate as to be given you?" he exclaimed, and grabbed the adorable lady by the hem of her large white nightgown. Her blazing red hair was loosed and fell to her waist. Deep green eyes were twinkling at him as she kept attempting to lift him from the floor, and then held him in her arms for support. That had George so atremble in delight that she must needs hold him closer . . . and all George could pray was that he would not awaken and discover she was merely a bedpost, or worse, Mrs. Prissom.

"Who are you?" he finally dared whisper, entranced.

"I am Merrie," she said, and urged him to direct them to his room.

He was nothing loath, pointing to it and asking with wonder, "Are you for me? For Christmas?"

"She is not—you jug-bitten scamp!" came a cold voice.

Both Merrie and George turned to observe the earl himself, resplendent in a blue satin dressing gown with golden trim. He was, as always, immaculate and in control and disapproving.

"You have met my brother, I gather."

"We have not as yet been introduced, but I discovered he was about to pitch himself down the stairs, and was directing him to the safety of his rooms."

"You are not suitably dressed for your Samaritan efforts. I expect you are giving him other thoughts."

"What thoughts?" she asked, bewildered. This was promptly answered by George, who sensed her retreating, and, fearing that his brother was going to take her away from him, as Brett always got the best in the world, moved quickly and planted a full, intoxicated kiss on her astonished cherry mouth.

She broke away and let the young gentleman fall unaided at her feet.

"You forget yourself, sir," she said, somewhat annoyed, but kindly. "I am your cousin."

"Kiss me, cousin," George whispered, crawling toward her again. "Don't let Brett get you. Don't deserve you, by George! That's me, I'm George! Belong to me, don't you? I saw you first!"

He was beginning to sob at his loss and Merrie was commiserating, at which point the earl stepped in and signaled that the young lady was no longer needed on this occasion. But when Merrie did not immediately move at his direction, rather stood staring at George coming toward her, the earl said harshly, "Are you desirous of a repeat of his performance? If so, we have not all night to await his reaching you. If nought else will suffice you ere you return to your chamber . . ." he began, and his black eyes mocked as he approached, and then, in a sudden move, kissed her himself.

Not the slobbery, misdirected kiss of the brother, but a deep, harsh, overpowering kiss that astonished her, both that it had occurred and that it had felt so shattering.

"Satisfied? Now will you retire?" he asked when he'd stepped back. And his voice was amused at her open-mouthed shock. "Close your mouth, or I shall do it for you," he continued, almost laughing now.

That, at last, had her able to speak indignantly. "Holiday cheer is fine in its place, but I expect both of you have overindulged in it!"

And she ran to her room and slammed the door on both the Warwick gentlemen.

"You're not going to take her away from me, are you, Brett?" George whined. "She's everything a gentleman ever dreamed of . . . and she was going with me. Into my room!"

"Was she, old boy?" Brett asked, and kept his eyes on Merrie's closed door. "I wonder if I stepped in too soon. Perhaps I should have seen whether she was going to escort you there or not? There might be less to this young lady than the goodly appearance she has presented."

"A dashed goodly appearance," George eagerly agreed as his brother dumped him on his bed. "Round atop and green eyes like holly leaves and lips like berries. No, dash it, like the sugarplums I used to get on Christmas morning. Aw, give her me, Brett, and I'll never ask for anything else. I want her, for Christmas."

Brett gave the usual answer one gives to children and besotted younger brothers. "We'll see." And then he slammed the door and walked quickly back to his apartment. Egad, he thought, he wouldn't mind getting her in his Christmas stocking himself, and his black, black eyes slowly lowered their lids as he recollected her *en déshabille*. She certainly looked a great deal better unclothed than clothed. And he thought of the hat he had thrown on the fireplace. And smiled. And he thought of seeing her in his brother's arms. And frowned. And then he thought of her in his arms, and he lay down on his featherbed. And dreamed.

5

The next morning Merrie was up at the unheard of hour of six o'clock, and already walking about Moorsedge to grasp the extent of her task ahead. Most ladies, and certainly Lady Warwick, would have lain abed until at least ten before descending to break their fast. Merrie was satisfied to take a cup of tea and a biscuit in the housekeeper's room while discussing with dear old Mrs. Prissom the holiday decorating.

"Her ladyship cannot abide our putting out the greens. We munnot set out even a sprig o' holly! Nay, not since the late earl cocked up his toes. It fair bursts my heart, how Christmas be forgot."

Merrie smiled widely at that, sensing a fellow respecter of Christmas, but Mrs. Prissom still seemed reluctant to do more than stare at the young lady, and Merrie, hoping she guessed the cause of the reserve, added, "I certainly do not expect you to follow my orders without hearing directly from Lady Warwick. I was just being beforehand. You shall be told that I am to direct the holiday preparations, to save the dear countess the slightest exhaustion."

Mrs. Prissom's white cap bobbed up and down, but that was not the reason for her silence. At last, at Merrie's continued questioning she said what she felt. "This be Yorkshire. We mun respect Yorkshire ways."

"But of course," Merrie exclaimed, relieved to find the impediment so minor. "I would certainly not wish to do anything that would not be in keeping with the traditions of the family and the locale."

"The old ways be best," the old lady said, nodding.

"Yes, indeed! You must tell me everything, and I'll see what can be done at this late date. In the meantime, it would not be amiss for a general cleaning, and I am certain the earl would wish you to hire several stout and hearty maids from the village to aid the staff in all the extra work."

Mrs. Prissom was nodding her head, agreeing to all that as well, and when she subsequently stopped in for a talk with her ladyship and was told frankly that "dear Merrie" was a cousin, and Miss Laurence was to be in full charge and she was not to be the slightest bit disturbed, Mrs. Prissom stopped dragging her feet and began to hop to, as much as a lady of her advanced years could hop. Thus, the cleaning commenced. Chandeliers that had not had more than a feather duster shaken at their tips, were lowered and shined, luster by luster. Banisters were polished and carpets taken up and shaken out.

It was noon by the time the earl left his chambers, now dressed in country clothes of breeches and a relaxed cravat, and he was well satisfied at the evidences of preparation already in progress.

He informed Walters that speed was of the essence and several helpers from the village should be hired. Told that had already been seen to by Miss Laurence, he felt a combination of peevishness and pleasure.

Certainly he wished her to be ahead of him in the task he had assigned her, but somehow he resented her being so prompt. He would have liked to be able to give her some reprimand.

"At least twenty maidens and ten young strong lads," he altered, to have some authority, and Walters bowed and went about the ordering. Soon they'd have so much help here there'd be naught for his own staff to do, he worried. He began to make work. Plate and silver was to be polished. The ancient portraits in the family gallery were to be thoroughly dusted, including the frightening portraits of the first earl—both the head-and-shoulders view and the life-size figure in Crusader armor. Those were usually avoided by the village staff, for superstition would have it that the first earl walked if disturbed, which explained why even his suit of armor was left for years to gather coatings of dust and rust.

The present earl, who prided himself on never letting dust settle on him, was finished with his morning repast and off to discover whether the Christmas sprite, Merrie herself, was actually cleaning or had retired back to her rooms. He was anxious to see her again. Each time he did, she was doing something surprising, from ordering him to take her up, to last night's carousing with his brother. Of course, that last act could be interpreted as one of kindness, but he was too jaded a man to believe in so much innocence. The more innocent a lady prided herself on appearing, he often found, the more devious was her aim. Usually she was after money or position, depending on her standing . . . probably both.

In truth, there was something about Miss Laurence's dimpled smile that had him convinced she was laughing at him and maneuvering him into some awkward position. In short, she did not know her place. Not that he knew her place either. For while she was born a lady, her circumstance must assure a lack. Further, she'd come here in the capacity of a relation, but had willingly taken on a servile duty. And then her actions last night had certainly stamped her as beneath his touch—even while touching her. A true lady would not have appeared in the hall sans a wrapper to cover her ample charms.

And this Miss Laurence certainly had proportions that would equal the most sought-after Cyprian. For a moment he allowed himself to indulge in imagining her in satins and silks rather than her worn nightgown, the top of which was of such a size it had half slipped off her shoulder as she was wrestling to lift George to his feet. That was when he'd had a near viewing of her firm attributes. Impossible to dismiss that image. . . .

Distracted by his thoughts, the earl had ambled toward the stable in something of a daze out of which he was rudely shaken by another merry surprise.

Riding into the stable yard were George and Miss Laurence, racing. At the last moment, the minx had the audacity to jump the wooden fence, and was into the yard before his strapping brother and his wild steed Blazes had made the turn.

"I won!" she exclaimed, and was off the animal and handing it to the groom.

George was dismounting with a laugh. "No fair jumping! If I had known we could do that, I'd have won."

"Nonsense. One wins by taking chances. There was no rule we could not jump fences. You did not challenge me to race to the stables with the stipulation that one must keep to the road. In fact, you already had the advantage since you knew the road, and I did not. And so I created my own road."

And grinning at her, George had to admit his having an additional advantage in Blazes. Merrie had bested him fairly.

"It is never fair when one is allowed to create one's own rules," the earl said, approaching the laughing pair.

Merrie turned to face his lordship. She was dressed in her old pelisse; no elegant riding habit, and not a riding cap on her curls. They were either allowed or had fallen into wild abandon about the flushed, triumphant face. Egad, she was beautiful when aroused, he thought. As an expert on doing so to scores of ladies, he had some comparisons. For a moment he wondered what her face would look like in that other form of exercise in which he so enjoyed instructing ladies, and he lost track of her response. She had said something to him, because George was laughing. He fell back on his cold, eyebrow-lifting evaluation and his all-purpose "Indeed."

"In thought and in deed," she responded. "One must fly with the wind when it takes one up. But I expect your lordship is too correct ever to allow himself so to give in to the spirit of any occasion."

The stable hands were peeking out, amazed at the beautiful lady who had come flying in like a huntress. Her wild red hair had them all gasping, and her laughing with Master George and then even daring to bandy words with his lordship had them further amazed. His lordship saw their attention to the lady as she walked away, and was displeased. His frown had them all rushing back to their jobs and by the time he'd turned his head back, the cause for the disturbance had already returned to the house. George was taking Blazes to his stall and his lordship followed him.

"She invited you for a ride this morning?" he questioned carefully, that point being quite important to discover her true objectives here.

"You mean our cousin? No, she was out riding when I overtook her and egad, I thought she'd been a dream last night, and there she was in the morning. And I said, are you real or an image of my hopes, and she said she hoped she was as real as possible, and laughed that tinkling laugh of hers and gave me to know we were related, and that Mother had invited her to spend Christmas, and by Jove, that was first rate, I said. And I apologized for not being myself last night, and she was dashed decent about it, said she had young brothers herself whom she had to take care of. Not that I liked being put in that category."

"I understand her brothers are children, and not likely to have imbibed," the earl interjected. "She seems to have a tendency to alter the facts when she wishes . . . to her convenience."

"Come, come, Brett. Miss Laurence hardly implied her brothers were tosspots. Rather that she'd protected them from their mother catching them out in a hobble. And that, I wager, is why she came to my aid. I don't think she remembers that I kissed her, for I apologized for it, and she assured she never regarded gentlemen's amorous inclinations when they'd overindulged, adding that overindulging appeared to be a family failing. So I gather you'd been imbibing last night as well. Felt a jolly good deal better, not having made a cake of myself alone. And so, bro, I dashed well don't expect you to ring a peal over my head just because the squire's son and I dipped rather deeply at the village inn."

"You are adult enough to control your actions and not have to account to me for them," his brother said coldly and realized he was deucedly offended at the young lady's putting both of them in the same category of being so foxed they needs must make fools of themselves with the ladies. He had not had more than his usual brandy, and he would have liked to inform

her of that. Except she probably would have said that
excused him less for his taking a liberty. And he
would have replied that the excuse was not in his
drinking but in her dress.

He was deep in breaking straws with Miss Laurence when his brother called him back to what was
actually happening.

"I dashed well wouldn't have believed being home
would be so jolly. This place has been like a tomb
ever since Father died. And now you're here and
you're bringing a bunch of nobs and . . . there's
Merrie! This will be a Christmas that will be something like!"

"Did she give you leave to address her by her given
name?"

"No," George admitted with a rueful grin, "I just
think of her that way. She's so Merrie . . . and yet,
not like a chum, you know . . . more like the companion you'd dreamed of all your life, who would
laugh with you and race with you and yet be so adorable through it all."

"George!"

"What?"

"I hope you are not forming a *tendre* for this . . .
lady. Remember she is a poor relation. And to be
totally forthright, she is several years your senior."

"What do years matter in matters of the heart?"
his brother said earnestly, his blue eyes starry with
first love.

"Ye gods," the earl exclaimed, "she has not been
here a day and already she has created a problem of
major magnitude," and he raced back into the house
to see what else and who else she was turning on their
heads at this moment.

Merrie was in conversation with Walters and Mrs.
Prissom, for which his lordship could not fault her, as
that was her assignment. In the next moment Brett

was astonished by Walters's gesture: he bowed respectfully to the lady. All his life he had believed implicitly that butlers could be counted on to sniff out those not worthy of recognition. From the time young Brett had become earl, he'd been put on the right path by Simpson, his butler at the London Warwick House. And although at this point he no longer needed a hint, his confidence in Simpson's opinion was demonstrated by still bringing a doubtful friend for a drink just to receive Simpson's imprimatur.

Thus Walters's and to some extent Mrs. Prissom's respectful attitude toward Miss Laurence had him refraining from addressing her as if she were a servant, although she had at times reacted as if he were hers. Indeed, now she walked into the library without waiting for his permission: and once there, indicated that he could sit, clearly establishing herself as a lady giving him audience. And at his demands as to the state of the preparations, she showed no fear that he would be evaluating her.

"All things are progressing splendidly. I am particularly pleased by your forethought in suggesting the extra lads from the village," she said with an approving nod his way. There was the barest twinkle in her green eyes which indicated she knew precisely how her composure was discomfiting him. Nevertheless, she kept to his question. "Certainly if we are to have an authentic Yorkshire Christmas, we shall need as much assistance as possible and everyone putting their shoulders to the wheel."

"What do you mean, an *authentic Yorkshire* Christmas?" the earl exclaimed, somewhat alarmed. "I told you these were *ladies* and *gentlemen* attending. We must keep everything elegant. Nothing of the wild nature of this area."

"Your father, I am told, was a believer in keeping Christmas as it was done in this area. A genuine old-fashioned Christmas, with Yule log and Master of Misrule and greenery everywhere." Her eyes were alight at the prospect.

"Holla there! I did not say—"

"Nonsense. If your friends wished to have a London Christmas they would have stayed there. They are coming to see how it is done in the country, and to do it in halfhearted imitation of a London event will have it falling short of that, and being one giant naught. We shall honor your father and your heritage and tell all your friends you are proud of both by carrying on the traditions of the place and the season." And without waiting for him to bring further objections, she continued with a topic he hoped she had forgotten. "One of the first Druid traditions is to go into the forest and bring in the mistletoe. We shall have to have some of that hung, but I feel that the Warwick men do not need any inducement in that area, and so I request you to restrain yourselves. Kisses should never be forced, you know," she added, as if having to inform him of the social niceties.

Turning a bright red for the first time since his youth, the earl objected, "I did not force you! You invited those attentions by your apparel, by Jove!"

"I am quite astonished that a gentleman of your standing could have such little control that the mere sight of one shoulder should so overcome him. I have lived in Oxford, with young scholars all around, and never found myself so subjected to advances as I have in a mere day here. It must be country ways, but I expect while we are having a country Christmas, a gentleman should observe it more as my father would do—as an interesting investigation of the past. And not an opportunity to misbehave!"

And once again, she left him flummoxed. He'd been reprimanded like a commoner. He, the earl of Warwick. And somehow all he could think of was the kiss. All this discussion of it and the promise of more with the mistletoe was certainly directing his thoughts in that direction. Was that her objective? Was she a master seducer . . . or the most innocent maid? He spent the rest of the morning wondering about that, and somehow forgetting the two ladies coming whose very purpose was to win his interest. With determination, the earl forced himself to think of Lady Jane, recollecting her serene blond appearance, and that cooled him down a few degrees. Almost immediately he felt himself reestablished as the lordly lord he was. And he sent a mental sigh of gratitude to that lady. Thank heavens she was coming. Lady Jane would put them all on the correct footing. If she did not, his lordship had full confidence that her father and mother, Lord and Lady Dansville, once acquainted with his poor relation's upbringing, would put Miss Merrie Laurence in her proper place.

Not that he wanted someone else to squelch the sprite. The earl had a great and growing desire to do that himself, which promise roused the earl to be present when the mistletoe was hung in the hall to show Miss Laurence an authentic Warwick Christmas embrace. To be historically correct, he should, by Jove, emulate his ancestor, the first earl, who was known to have brought back several women from the Crusades and placed them in the tower. Lord Warwick grinned and wondered if she knew that story. If Miss Laurence wished things authentic, he would give her authentic. She'd never get her breath from how authentic he could be!

At the same moment, authenticity was also Merrie's topic of concern, while conferring with the oldtimers at Moorsedge, such as the harper who played for those revels, and the younger balladeer who assisted him. It took a full morning, but Merrie was pleased to have come away with many a song and

dance that could be added to the entertainment. As
the days advanced Merrie was kept more than tolera-
bly occupied. Yet she always took time to ride every
morning with George, as well as spending several
hours each day with the countess. By dint of her
knowledge of nostrums and her own sympathetic
heart, day by day Merrie was fast winning her way
into the countess's favor. Actually, her ladyship was
soon wondering how she had ever done without the
bright young lady making everything smooth for her.
To Merrie her ladyship's nerves took precedence over
all, as she established a strict regimen: mornings of
rest and afternoons of amusement. The library was a
prodigious source of entertainment. Promptly Merrie
began daily readings to the countess, done with such
pleasure, as if Merrie had not previously perused the
same works. Even her ladyship was aware that she
had. For Merrie was good enough to skip the boring
parts, where the author had the poor taste to make
judgments (as if one did not have enough of that in
life), and go right to the action of the plot. So the
countess was skimmed through Fielding in a wink
and raced through Mrs. Radcliffe in a shudder.

And soon the countess discovered she was not exclusively interested in her physical complaints any
longer, although she would not immediately desert
those old friends and boon companions of her desola-
tion. It was just that she was too preoccupied to give
them the full attention they had once enjoyed. Eventually, Lady Warwick owned herself extremely surprised at her sense of well-being, attributing it all to
Merrie's miraculous cure of talking one into a rapid
recovery. The countess had heard of healing hands,
but Merrie obviously had a healing tongue—or even
more, a healing laugh.

6

On the very day when the party of lords and ladies was to arrive, Merrie assigned George to go to the woods to supervise the gathering of more boughs of holly and ivy, the first batch not being sufficient. The branches of mistletoe which had yet to be hung at the drawing room entrance would, she promised, await his return.

Meanwhile, Merrie was occupied checking on the bedchambers with Mrs. Prissom and found all to her liking. Every bed had been aired, and herbs passed over the linen to give a refreshing scent. Some of the brocade hangings were fading, and should have long been refurbished, but there was no time for this. All that spit and polish could accomplish was done.

Fires were lit throughout the house and Lady Warwick prepared for her ordeal with assurances that she need only make token appearances. Her ladyship walked about the estate and found it all delightful. Indeed, the place reminded her of the days when her late lord was alive, and they'd had jolly Christmases together.

"Actually," Lady Warwick said, "I would not use the word jolly in regard to my husband. He was a gentleman more concerned with proper observance, and he was satisfied if things were done according to custom, but not for the joy of it."

"And your sons . . . surely they found Christmas jolly?" Merrie interposed.

"George, of course, found everything jolly. But Brett, I expect, as he does now, just barely tolerated the events."

"Pity."

"Yes," her ladyship admitted with a sigh. "It has been so long since I recollect our sharing any closeness. Actually, I feel he would resent even my interest in his affairs. Although I have some. Indeed, I have been hoping one of these ladies coming will have sufficient attraction to rouse him somewhat out of his particularity. Lady Jane and the other lady are, I daresay, being auditioned for the role of his consort . . . or countess." And she allowed a small smile at her admission.

Merrie could not help but gasp. "Are they not affronted to be put into such a demeaning position?"

The countess's eyes widened. "Affronted? Demeaning? What could you possibly mean? Both ladies, I expect, are eager to engage in the contest for my position here. That, after all, is the very purpose of their upbringing—to marry well. And, if it is not too immodest in a mother to say, Brett is and has always been vastly in demand by all ladies. First, because he is an earl. But more, he is statuesque and excessively fine featured with most impressive and penetrating dark eyes. Unfortunately, I have recently felt them too penetrating. They bore right into one, actually, while George has the gentle blue eyes from my side of the family. A lady could scarce go wrong in preferring George, for Brett has a streak of formality that reminds one uneasily of his father."

That revealed a great deal about the countess's marriage, but Merrie was too much of lady to delve. Her sympathy aroused, she brought several additional pillows for the lady's present comfort to atone for her past discomfort.

Perhaps the ladies of the ton coming here did not mind a touch of coldness, Merrie thought, and her mind wandered into attempting to decide whether the earl's dark eyes were cold or hot, but unquestionably they had the ability to transmit shivers to the on-looker by their implacability.

All the while her ladyship was talking of past Christmases here in Moorsedge, and caught Merrie's attention by describing servants being dressed not in livery, but in mummers' outfits. "It was quite a romp. So much more entertaining. Costumes give everyone a general release. The servants were a bit wild, but his lordship could always control them with a mere frown."

"Do you think the mummers' costumes are still in the attic?" Merrie asked with a surge of hope.

Her ladyship assured her that everything was in the attic. Naught was ever thrown away. "That is the result of a tradition-bound household, I expect. Clutter."

The two ladies exchanged grins at that summation. They had really begun to understand each other and enjoy each others' company. Merrie took the opportunity to bring up a topic she felt her ladyship should be informed about. "Your son seems to have formed a rather excessive attachment to me. He follows me everywhere I go and, actually, is underfoot."

"Brett!"

Merrie laughed loudly at that image and said quickly, "Hardly. I meant Mr. Dickens. I was hoping his *tendre* would wear out or that it was just high spirits, but I feel I need your advice on how to handle him. I have tried speaking gently to him."

"With George? Nothing less than hitting him on the head with a hammer will have an effect on that ruffian."

Merrie was delighted that her ladyship was not concerned over her son's infatuation. She assured her ladyship she had not encouraged him and that she saw him in the light of a younger brother.

"I have no doubt, my dear Merrie, that you have behaved properly. And that George has behaved improperly. He always gives one a turn. If he were not running after you, he would be out with his hounds or shooting at something and bringing in the bloody carcass. It is a much safer sport for him to be chasing after you, my dear. It is never wrong to love, even if the feeling is not returned. Is it?"

Agreeing to that generally, she could not specifically as regard to George or herself. "Actually, I am beyond the age when I can hope for that kind of love."

"Nonsense!" the countess exclaimed. "I have not been a recluse all my life. I had a gay season. And I remember all the diamonds of the first water, and frankly, I do not believe one could hold a candle to you. Your beauty is not just outer but inner as well. I would not be the slightest bit dismayed if you returned George's feelings. I should think the scamp fortunate."

Mentioning him seemed to bring him forth, for immediately came the sounds of riotous laughter and shouting, and quickly Lady Warwick picked up her pillow and retired to her own sitting room.

"Try to get Georgie to speak slightly lower than a shout, would you, Merrie dear?" she whispered as she retreated.

Relieved that her ladyship would not be faulting her for her son's infatuation, Merrie went out into the hall to discover the cause of George's latest commotion. With him was Bruiser, a rather excessively large dog that was a combination hound and mastiff. The eager Bruiser was almost a duplicate in personality to George. They both jumped about, albeit one yelled while one barked, and there wasn't an ounce of meanness in either. Merrie approached both with outstretched arms, a touch on the arm to George to warn him to keep his voice lower as his mother was resting, and a pat on the head to Bruiser who jumped up and nearly flattened her while licking her face thoroughly.

"Oh ho, there, Bruiser boy, you've got the correct idea. Wouldn't I just love to kiss the lady myself."

"I am all aquiver to think," a lazy, elegant gentleman's voice intervened, "that Bruiser is setting the standard of gentlemanly behavior at Moorsedge."

All three reprimanded turned to face the elegantly attired earl, now presenting himself in more formal attire in preparation for greeting his guests. His cravat had several additional inches of height, and he had changed to pantaloons and Hessians. A fob and quizzing glass completed his toilette. Through that very quizzing glass, he was observing Merrie and Bruiser and George. Each one received a full disapproving moment. George was cowed, Merrie affronted, but Bruiser was fascinated by the gleaming light the quizzing glass reflected into his own, and came forward to investigate. His manner of observation was not subtle, rather he jumped up on his lordship's freshly brushed and uncreased pantaloons and made a grab for the shiny object.

"That's torn it," George whispered to Merrie, and no sooner had the words come out of his mouth than they became prophetic. Bruiser tore the quizzing glass off his lordship's waistcoat and went running with the thing in his mouth. George followed him; a merry chase ensued. His lordship was annoyed, but had the intelligence not to vent it on the hapless animal. Certainly not when a laughing young lady was handy.

"We are expecting the most elegant members of the ton. Do you think they would find it suitable to have a hound racing about the place? I should think you would have spoken to George about Bruiser."

Astonished, Merrie faced his lordship. "I have the responsibility of arranging the entertainments and accommodations. I expect controlling your brother and his pets would be more in your line of duty. Besides, I expect if they are people as well as lords, they must see George and Bruiser as naught but overgrown children. High-spirited and perfectly lovable."

His lordship's dark eyes gave her that hard, frozen stare that usually reduced people to quivers. And when he spoke, his voice was equally lacerating. "You find my brother . . . lovable? I have seen his actions toward you of late, Miss Laurence, and hoped you would have had the decency to warn him off by now. Unless . . ." He paused. His face revealed his astonishment at the thought invading his brain.

"Unless?" Merrie challenged, undismayed.

"Unless, it is part of your stratagem to improve your position in life by snaring a halfling before he has had a chance to meet ladies of his own set."

"And if that were my conniving purpose, I certainly should not be admitting it to you so openly, until I had achieved it. Actually, I suspect your brother has developed something of a *tendre* for me. So in essence, I have achieved it. Fortunately for you, I am aware that he is too young to be taken seriously. His mother and I have discussed it and . . ." Merrie stopped herself.

"And?" the earl insisted, sensing something she was reluctant to disclose.

"Well, frankly," she paused and, unable to resist taunting him, finally admitted, "your mother has given me her blessing. She feels that I would have a beneficial calming influence on Mr. Dickens."

"You say what? Egad, are you announcing your engagement to my brother?"

"No," Merrie soothed with a grin, "you may rest assured *that* is not my purpose in coming here."

"And what is, by George? I mean, by Jove," he faltered.

"George is safe from me. A lady could not have designs on such an artless, gentle soul. One would have to be beastly indeed."

"And what is your purpose then? In less than a fortnight you have won over my mother and my brother, and the entire staff jumps to your command. I order something and find you have already thought of it."

"Are you objecting to my efficiency, or my lovableness?"

Staring at the dancing green eyes, the earl wondered indeed which of those attributes he found the most objectionable. He met her glance directly and said matter-of-factly, "I fear you, Miss Merrie Laurence. You are too charming, too lovable, too eager to please us all. One is only so accommodating when hoping to achieve something substantive from another before one becomes sufficiently aware to protect it. Yes, I fancy you are playing a deep game indeed."

Merrie did not quake at that blatant summation. Rather she asked amiably, "But, my lord, if you are so suspicious of me, you must fear losing something? I wonder," she mused, "what could you possibly have that a mere poor relation should seek?"

"I'll not scruple to be forthright in my response. Obviously my wealth . . . my position!"

"Disappointing. For you have so much of both,

even if I were scheming to take a little, what would you lose? No, you are not afraid of that, for it is in your hands to deny me wealth, as you continue to clutch onto yours. Yes, I gather you are a perfect nipcheese. Witness the shocking state of your hangings in all these rooms. Heaven knows when Moorsedge has been refurbished. And as for my seeking wealth for myself from you—rather I have been diligently working for your interest without the slightest request for recompense. Although, *entre nous,* I expect you owe me a new bonnet!"

The earl's brooding eyes narrowed. She waited for him to confess his culpability as regards the demise of her bonnet. But his only reaction was a slight smile and the raising of one eyebrow. Yet that was enough for Merrie to conclude that he had indeed done that dastardly deed. She was further incensed by his quickly ignoring that side issue and reverting to his original charge. "I do not hesitate to inform you, young lady, that I am fly to the time of day. So you need not think you can easily gammon me. Not only are you here to improve your own position, but that of your entire family," he concluded with a gleam in his eyes as if he had caught her out.

Merrie, however, was not discomfitted, and admitted frankly, "Certainly my entire family. Do you really think I have no feelings for my relations that I could abandon my mother for years to convince herself that she is an invalid, and refuse my own brother's request to join me in London with the remark that it is not 'presently convenient'? Heavens, I am not such a cold fish! Anything I achieve would naturally be spread to those I most love."

The thought that this young lady was so much in the confidence of his family that they complained to her about him was not to be endured. Brett's dark eyes bore into her as he demanded, "Admit it, you have come here to gull my mother into wasting the ready on you and yours. Well, egad, I must disappoint you. Her funds are entirely in *my* care."

"I am well aware of the mere pin money in her charge. And that you look over her household accounts as if she had not brought you up and even possibly, at one time or another, diapered you."

"That is scarcely the point of . . . of our discussion," the earl exclaimed, his hackles up. "My diapering is not only irrelevant, but *indecent* to mention."

"Faith, you ought not to be so shy," Merrie observed with a choke of laughter. "Even as a mere mewling babe I assume all the conventions were strictly observed."

Sputtering, Brett accused her of unwarranted levity in the midst of a serious discussion.

"Levity is never unwarranted—it leavens our lives and makes them bearable, I've found."

The two were bandying words back and forth, and the earl was determined to annihilate this ebullient lady and quash that bubbling spirit out of her, when Bruiser and George returned. George had raced through the entire first floor, both wings, chasing Bruiser and his prize.

"I wrestled it away from him," George admitted proudly and handed his brother the tattered, slobbered-over quizzing glass.

The earl viewed it with finicky disdain, crying out pettishly, "Thunder and turf! 'Twas my favorite piece!"

"Oh, I say." George laughed. "No need to get into a lather. It could be cleaned and fixed up, I daresay."

"Give it me," he said coldly, "my valet will refurbish it. Egad, my most prized possession—blast you, it was Father's."

At that, Merrie reached over and took the quizzing glass. "Ah, pity. It is sadly twisted. Perhaps I can fix it. . . ." And she walked toward the fireplace to have a better view, and somehow the thing slipped out of her hands and over the firescreen and into the flames.

"Oh, dash," she said, looking helplessly at the earl. "The thing seems to have fallen into the fire. Who could believe something like that could happen?"

The two eyed each other. An understanding was clearly transmitted that tit for tat had occurred. His lordship was uncertain whether he admired her for it, or wished to reprimand her.

"It is certainly difficult to believe such an accident could occur unwittingly," the earl said in a voice stiff with sarcasm.

"What do you mean, Brett?" George demanded hotly. "Certainly it was an accident. Why, the thing was slippery from Bruiser's spit!"

The earl winced at that. Bruiser, hearing his name, came close and now went after the earl's fob and with one jump had disarranged his meticulous cravat.

George let out a shout and leaped for Bruiser, with the result that all three fell to the floor in a tussle. There was a medley of barks and shouts and affronted oaths as the three rolled about in a tight pile. Merrie was quick to rush over to disengage the rolling three and promptly fell on top of the group.

More oaths and exclamations.

"Miss Laurence, you are disarranging my coiffure," the earl announced in a long-suffering tone, as he was attempting to disengage his head from under Merrie's arm while she was helpfully attempting to release his cravat from Bruiser's hold. Into that coil came George's shoe, pushing the toe of it into Bruiser's mouth. They were in a tumbling embrace indeed, with the earl's face now totally covered over by Merrie's bright red hair.

He smelled the scent of it—like herbs and flowers. The earl almost reflexively slowed his struggling, beginning to enjoy the situation. Putting his arms around the helpful relation and feeling the full, solid warmth of her, he moved his head a bit and could almost nuzzle her neck as her soft white skin brushed against his mouth, and he felt his entire body flooded with the warmth of being near her. Abruptly she turned her head and looked directly into his eyes, and the two of them stopped moving as they stared at each other.

Merrie blushed almost equal to the color of her hair as the earl's dark eyes began to sparkle. He pulled her closer to him, and his lips went from her flushed neck to just above her trembling lips, and he was about to capture them when Bruiser bit him on the chin. The earl was thus instantly shaken out of his sensual enjoyment of the situation and vigorously struggling again. So all four were once more rapidly rolling when Walters opened the door.

"Lord and Lady Dansville and Lady Jane Dansville," he announced.

The noble party gasped as their hosts came rolling toward them on the polished floor, right to their feet. George, in a convulsion of laughter, was finally able to rise and pull Bruiser to the side. Merrie was left in his lordship's arms, but he was already shoving her away and George was giving her a hand up. Disheveled, with one sleeve off her shoulder, Merrie was still half laughing, half aghast as she glanced at the absolutely impeccable young lady in the forefront. Her golden hair was neatly arranged in two small curls that just showed under her blue velvet bonnet. Her pelisse was blue velvet as well, and she had a matching reticule. But what stifled all of Merrie's welcome was the expression on her ladyship's face—not surprise, not confusion, but rather disdain.

Turning to the elder couple behind, Merrie viewed similar faces with similar expressions. Except Lord and Lady Dansville had had years to perfect their disdain, the lips curled to perfection, the eyebrows raised just so.

"We seem not to be expected?" Lady Jane whispered in a voice that would soon become anathema to Merrie. It was the softest and coldest voice she'd ever heard. It slithered up one's spine like a soft, cold touch. Yet even in a half whisper, she was able to make her point.

The earl, rather than apologizing, said coolly, "You have arrived in time to witness a . . . family exercise period."

That nearly set Merrie off again. It had George guffawing and Bruiser barking.

"Yes," Merrie said quickly, "it is a regular morning activity. So encouraging to the dogs. And decidedly conducive to a healthy familial outlook the rest of the day."

The earl caught her eye, and a slight smile in his had her surprised. Turning to his still unappeased guests, he said smoothly, "You need not fret. It is not obligatory for the rest of you. Nor indeed does the countess indulge in it, finding it too strenuous."

"I expect she would," Lady Dansville said faintly.

The earl made one of his perfect and envied bows and welcomed the nobles to his home, and the butler and Mrs. Prissom were soon there to take the guests to their rooms. Stopping Lady Jane just as she was ready to follow, Lord Warwick said smoothly, "I am most grateful for your lovely presence. In the spirit of the season, shall I suggest the greatest gift for us all will be to hear you play the harp. . . ."

Pleased and reassured that the earl was once again the elegant gentleman she remembered from London, Lady Jane merely smiled and whispered something that was obviously a compliance, for the earl nodded and smiled.

Not till the party departed did Merrie realize with some affront that she had not been introduced to the nobles—as if she were a housemaid. So much for the welcome planned. The earl was to have been waiting at the doorstep, and she just behind, part of the welcoming group, in lieu of her ladyship. Thus from the first moment she was to have established some credibility. Rather, she'd been seen with her dress up and her face flushed, like a common tavern girl. Her eyes were flashing at the outcome.

The earl returned from escorting Lady Jane to the bottom of the stairs, ready to reprimand George, Bruiser, or preferably Merrie for the scene. He was intending to say something about her "entertaining" the guests earlier than expected, when his words were forgotten as he viewed the flushing, flashing Miss Laurence. Gad, she was so alive! Expecting her to look insignificant in comparison to Lady Jane, an acknowledged diamond, he was shattered and silenced to see Merrie glowing and alight, like a dashed Christmas candle. He was soaking in the view of her, as one would a sunrise, and any attempt to call up Lady Jane's face to put hers out was ineffectual.

He had not remembered Lady Jane's eyes as being so pale, nor her stature so insignificant. But it was Lady Jane's voice that astonished him. He'd oft not heard all her words at a ball and always attributed that to the music. Actually, he'd not really found a small voice in a lady a fault, never assuming before meeting Merrie that a lady's remarks were worth listening to.

He frowned at his disappointment, and Merrie half correctly assumed she was being blamed for the outrageous contretemps, and quickly struck back by reminding of her previous retaliation. "Pity you did not have your quizzing glass to give the lady a glimpse of your eye."

"She is familiar with it. Ladies are accustomed to gentlemen's magnified eyes staring at them," he replied, somewhat pleased that she'd been shaken out of her usual cheery good nature by Lady Jane. Apparently with one glance, that lady had succeeded in making Miss Laurence aware of the great gulf between herself and his friends. "One does not need a quizzing glass," he pressed his point, "to remark her pure perfection, from bonnet to her elegant slippers. And further, she plays the harp so delightfully, one has the sensation that a Christmas angel has come to life."

"Unfortunately there isn't a harp for her to play," Merrie said with secret relief.

"No fear. I have ordered one precisely for the lady's amusement. It should shortly be arriving."

"I look forward to the pleasure of hearing it. Unless you wish me not to be in attendance?"

"What do you mean?" the earl asked with a frown.

"Since you did not introduce me . . ."

"Ah, that's what gnaws, does it? You don't like being overlooked? Well, with all the lords and ladies, I expect you'll have to become accustomed to it. Only special ladies can shine in this exalted company."

And restored to his own sense of position, the earl nonchalantly bowed and retired to his apartments to remove the Bruiser touch and restore himself to an elegance suitable to his new arrivals.

7

In a few days' time Merrie's assessment of those who descended on Moorsedge for Christmas was that they were quite a motley group. The marquis and marchioness of Dansville were a petrified couple who walked about the place with a permanent look of disapproval. Naught seemed to please them—neither the saloons nor the meals, neither the games of whist nor backgammon played afterward. Lord Dansville only came alive when he brought up his favorite subject of snuff. On that he could talk for hours, detailing the various kinds and mixtures and how to ensure that one's stock did not dry out or catch cold. Merrie, giving herself the impossible task of thawing him out, as she did to all, discovered that weak spot and went jumping into it. She wished to know what type of snuff was suitable for ladies, which had him finally slightly smiling at the image of a lady using a snuffbox. She had him demonstrating the variety of ways a gentlemen could take snuff. At last, after all this attention, his lordship unbent enough to honor her with his opinion on the rest of the group; they were all clearly beneath him, and as she did not disagree but just glanced at him with amusement, he took it as compliance and concluded that she was a singularly intelligent lady, and would not subsequently join in his wife's and daughter's snickers at her country clothes.

Lady Dansville rarely came to life, except to complain that nothing was up to her standards, not the food, not the service, and definitely not the company. Lady Jane echoed her mother, but in such a soft voice one continually had to assume the disparagements. Except when the censure was personal, then Lady Jane made more of an effort, and unfortunately could be heard.

"It really is not the thing for a lady to go riding without a habit," she said one morning. "An ordinary pelisse has the tendency to ride up while one is riding and a gentleman might then be subject to seeing more of a lady's limb than is permissible."

Merrie, in just such a pelisse, did not answer that she did not have a riding habit and that she was dashed well not going to allow that to prevent her from going on her morning constitutional with George. Instead she fell back on her usual response to her ladyship, claiming not to have heard Lady Jane's words, and as her partner was waiting, could not remain for their repetition.

Galloping across the moors jollied Merrie out of her temporary annoyance. Nothing improved one's spirits as much as feeling the wind in one's hair and riding along with a companionable escort. She said as much, as they neared the rock formation called Warwick's Cliff and reined in to gaze about. George readily agreed that the company could not possibly be improved, though regrettably the same could not be said for those gathered in the mansion.

"Whatever possessed Brett to invite Lady Pauley?"

he complained, having been chosen to bring that doddering lady in to supper, when she had clawed his hand, leaning on it.

"She is come as chaperone for Miss Prichard. We are, I understand, indebted to one or two precipitous snowflakes for being spared her elder sister, as well. But you need not fear her company; for one night in ours, and Moorsedge's drafty rooms, and she has caught quite a violent chill. And we are indebted to the duke of York for Lord Pavraam's desertion. So our party is just the Dansvilles, Miss Prichard and her companion Lady Pauley, and perhaps Sir Oswald, who has not yet arrived."

In the distance one could see the stone walls that divided the flat moors, and the few random wind-tossed trees holding on to the ground by their straining roots. The chill off the moors prohibited loitering long. A few moor sheep went by without looking their way; naught disturbed the silence till of a sudden a bird flew by making soft sounds. Ah, there was peace there, and a power.

"If I knew no one would be watching, I would ride *ventre à terre* up to Warwick Cliff and then dismount and race to its top ledge to see half the world."

"Let's do it!" George challenged, his eyes sparkling.

"I should be back at Moorsedge. There are several more things to be arranged for the Christmas celebration ahead."

But George was off, and Merrie could not resist following. They rode to Warwick Cliff, and then both dismounted and ran to the edge to look down. The world was there spread like an open palm ready to give its all to them, and George, watching the wild wind seizing Merrie's hair and making a billowing sunset cloud around her head, saw her as a goddess one should bow before and worship. In a twinkle he was doing so, telling her how much he loved her, and how beautiful and yet spirited, and what jolly good fun she was, and that he could not bear to think she would be leaving after Christmas, and would she remain always with him as his wife.

Merrie, who had been startled at feeling George's embrace around her knees, was even more astonished by his proposal. But no sooner had her flailing hands dislodged him than he was on his feet and taking her fully into his arms.

"Mr. Dickens, you are to desist. I have explained to you that I see myself as your sister, as you are my brother. That is the limit of our relationship. Please do not make it difficult for us to be together."

His eyes took on a whipped-dog look and the anguish came out in his voice as well. "But you must love me. I could not feel so strongly about someone . . . and they not feel it back. Just let me kiss your sweet mouth once, so I can say my life had some meaning."

Merrie decisively demonstrated *her* meaning by shaking her head and turning away, keeping her back to him. Abashed, George, after a few moments of hopeless waiting, finally left. With relief Merrie heard him departing, and then, surprisingly, returning. Turning around with some irritation, she found herself face to face with Lord Warwick.

Suspicious of Miss Laurence, the earl had kept up his surveillance, especially when she went off with his brother. And what he had seen was complete justification. Folding his arms across his chest, he glowered at Merrie's flushed face, which had him abruptly understanding George's losing his head over her. Merrie's lips were swollen from George's clumsiness, and all that the earl had prepared to say to her vanished from his mind as he stared at the full berry red lips that he felt were pulsing, and he could almost feel pulsing under his. She stared at him confused, waiting for a rake down. The moment of staring grew to a noticeable length. And then both were astounded by the earl's next action. He simply stepped closer to her and placed his lips on hers, softly at first, and then slowly increased the pressure. All the while, he moved his hands up and down her back, pushing her closer into his embrace, until she began to feel herself unwinding into a soft, sweet center. Still his kiss went on, deeper, breathing with her, and she felt herself suddenly going weak in the knees, slipping from his arms and dropping down on the ground into a swoon.

He took that as an invitation and fell down on the ground with her. There was a slight sheen of snow, and it jolted her alert, causing her to sit up in alarm.

"What are you doing? What is occurring?" she asked in terror.

Brett smiled lazily. "What? Have you never felt the pleasure of love, my dear cousin?"

"No," she said softly. And then shaking herself out of the sensuous entrapment of his soft voice and strong touch, she bolted up. "I am not part of the Christmas festivities. I give no more kisses. And if there is even an ounce of gentleman in you, no more shall be taken against my will."

"Certainly never against your will. I need never attempt that, when most young ladies are anxious to share their favors with me. There are two come here for that very purpose."

Reaching her horse, Merrie turned and viewed him skeptically. "You brought those two young ladies here to examine them for their fitness to be your wife. Both have in essence confided as much to me, Miss Prichard with anxious hope and Lady Jane with a soft warning. At least, I think that is what Lady Jane said, for she whispered it. Therefore, if you have two such candidates, why do you waste your time in forcing your advances on one to whom they are most distasteful? If you are under the assumption that I can be trifled with because I am without my parents here, let me inform you, you have double reason to behave with utmost propriety to me, for I am under your *mother's* protection, and thus, relatively, yours. To treat me lightly is to demean your mother and yourself as well. I have volunteered to help you, but there is a limit to how much use you can make of my services."

"I always make unlimited use of any lady's services," he said calmly, but somewhat sobered by her reasoning. "You should not let yourself become so discomfited over a mere kiss. You are past the age when one should be so missish over a mere friendly exchange."

He was cowed enough by her remarks not to say any of the things he had planned about her morning rides leading George astray, and he even quietly helped her mount and yet allowed his hand to linger on her leg which was exposed as her tight pelisse had ridden up, just as Lady Jane had warned her.

Miss Laurence lightly used her whip to flick away his touch and rode off like the wind. Enraged by the sting of the whip, he mounted and rode after her. It soon became a race for more than the declaration of victory. Both sensed that if he caught her, he would make her pay for that slight lashing, and Merrie had her job lot of a horse riding its old heart out, while Lord Warwick on his mighty steed Caliban was soon alongside. He pulled her off the horse and placed her before him, and they rode on.

For a moment while hanging suspended between horses, Merrie had felt she would be dashed under their hooves, and hung on, but upon feeling herself secure, she sensed the greater danger of his arms.

"Do you enjoy rough play? I'm not adverse to it, if

it pleases you," he whispered in her ear, and then kissed her on her neck and let his mouth roam through her flaming hair. His body behind her back was warm and all-engulfing, and they rode up and down and up and down, treading the miles, flying over the land, and his arms around her waist held her so firmly, so inexorably, she felt herself melting into him. Riding as one, they reached an abandoned wooden shack, broken down by wind and vandals. Brett reined in and Caliban neighed in anger at the termination of his run. Merrie herself protested his lordship's handling of her, half turning her around and fastening onto her lips, allowing not a second's pause between the string of kisses that went deeper and deeper into her senses. And Brett's strong hands kept her head from moving away from that fusing of their lips. Although she groaned a bit, he kept her silent and floating. A wild rush of sensation was spreading throughout her body that despite the chill wind warmed her all over. Caliban, now pawing the ground, distracted Brett sufficiently to lean down to soothe the beast below them.

"We'd best get into the shack," he whispered, smoothly dismounting. Looking at her stunned expression, a small satisfied grin flashed on his lordship's face; and that was sufficient to wake Merrie out of her humiliating obedience. The moment he touched the ground and reached up for her, Merrie gave the restless Caliban the signal, and they sprang off.

The obliging wind not only cleared Merrie's head but scattered Brett's protesting calls as she rode away, leaving him stranded in his little derelict shed.

Probably he had taken many a maid there during his youth, Merrie thought grimly, and then grinned at not only escaping him, but leaving him miles from Moorsedge.

In her one glance backward, Brett had been standing and shaking his fist at her retreating figure, deserted and seriously displeased.

For how long, she wondered, should she let him stew there before sending a stable hand with another horse to the rescue?

Her nobility fought with revenge. At last she remembered that despite his cavalier treatment, she was not a lady who enjoyed putting others to discomfort, even Lord Warwick. So a stable hand and extra horse were dispatched on their Samaritan way.

In a short time Sir Oswald arrived, and she was quick to greet him in his lordship's name. He was out riding, that was all the information Merrie would divulge.

"Dashed uncivil of the old boy. I turned down the duke of York to show me face here. Want some appreciation, demme," exclaimed Sir Oswald in a tiff. He was a small gentleman with an excess of gestures, as now when he was waving his arms, one almost expected him to take flight.

"In his stead, I shall give you all the appreciation you could possibly wish," Merrie was quick to insert in appeasement. "Walters has a morning repast on the sideboard."

"Egad, couldn't sit down in all me dirt. Must change, what? Could stand a jolt of something warming, though. Coming on to snow, I should dashed well think."

"It shall be sent to your room."

Too young to be the housekeeper. Too ladylike. Relative? Sir Oswald wondered. This lady was too beautiful not to be fully investigated. He took out his quizzing glass. By now Merrie had become inured to these examinations. She even grinned at him. He grinned back.

"Dashed beauty, ain't you?"

"So I've been told by all the gentlemen here. But

my father always believed that beauty is a mere surface attribute and should not be traded on or commented on."

"Father ain't in society, then. We do naught but
comment and trade on surface things."

Merrie laughed fully at that, and the two exchanged glances of mutual approval. She quickly told
him who she was and in what relationship she stood
to the family, and how she was acting as hostess for
the countess, who was not up to fulfilling that pleasurable function.

"No dowry, then?" he asked with his amazing
openness.

"Not a jot."

"Pity. Would have asked for you on the spot.
Might still do so and live a life of poverty just to be
near such a beauty."

"You wouldn't find life with her a particular pleasure," came the voice of the lord of the manor, just
arriving and assessing the situation.

Merrie's eyes twinkled as she observed that he was
still in a well-stoked rage. "You must forgive his lordship. He is in something of a pelter. He was unhorsed
today, and we had to send a stable hand to his rescue."

"Egad, Brett! Never saw a horse that could bolt
under your leg." Sir Oswald gasped, giving his friend
a warm handshake.

The earl smiled at his friend's assessment, and
regained some of his spirit. "Apparently Miss Laurence here has a way of making animals lose their
heads." He paused and, giving Miss Laurence a formal bow, added somewhat penitently, "As well as
gentlemen."

She accepted that as sufficient apology, and with a
smile to both gentlemen rushed to consult with Mrs.
Prissom.

Alone with his friend, Sir Oswald was even balder. "Now, that's something worth one's spending Christmas in the country! I was dashed well just going to look in and ride on. Not that you ain't enough of an attraction, old boy. But I heard you've got the Dansvilles. Season's cold enough without them."

"Bite your tongue. You know I am seriously considering Lady Jane."

"Well, you ain't the fun-loving Brett I went to school with. That chap would have unhorsed you himself for having become too aware of your dignities. Need a little shaking up, I daresay."

He was being shaken up by Miss Laurence, the earl admitted later. Something of a sparring match between the two. He had burned her hat, she burned his quizzing glass. She struck him with a whip, he whipped her into a frenzy. Last point had been hers—stranding him on the moors.

Tonight at dinner he would show Miss Laurence how it felt to be stranded. He had scarcely said a word to Lady Jane and nothing beyond a civil greeting to Miss Prichard. He would jolly well concentrate on the two young ladies he had invited to Moorsedge for the specific purpose of attracting him. If only his poor relation would stop distracting him from his set purpose, that is.

No doubt after dinner he would have the pleasure of being entertained by the two ladies in the approved fashion. For the harp had arrived and Lady Jane would play particularly for him, as she had at the London assemblies, and which he'd found rather pleasant and soothing. And Miss Prichard had promised to sing. Therefore Miss Laurence, who had no talents but a ready tongue and an impish smile, would be quite cast down. Just as he'd thus concluded, the earl noticed the mistletoe put up at the doorway of the drawing room. And he groaned. Miss Laurence had one unbeatable talent—kissing. And he should dashed well not wish any of the gentlemen here, certainly not Sir Oswald, and not his brother, to use the excuse of that Druid bough to feel her berry lips. Frowning at the full-berried branch, the earl signaled a footman to remove it. The man did not question or in any way betray his astonishment at the order, and yet Brett was unable not to mumble as he walked away; "Some ladies apparently don't need any more encouragement in *that* direction!"

8

Expectations, like balloons, have a way of rising and then falling flat when filled with too much hot air. So did the conversation that evening. Lady Warwick, who had been persuaded by Merrie to attend the first full conclave of the guests, was beginning to regret her appearance.

"Your presence will give the dinner dignity. Actually, having the countess and hostess there will be rather like an official imprimatur," Merrie urged.

"Nonsense," Lady Warwick replied, although pleased that the girl thought she would add so much. "More than likely none will even be aware of my presence. Certainly not Brett. And I shall be forced to talk to Lady Pauley and Lady Dansville, and both are insufferable."

Lady Warwick's prediction was correct; her son was not the slightest bit appreciative of the great sacrifice she'd made to her health and humor by appearing. She was attired in a rather faded gown, not having patronized a dressmaker for several years, and looked like a relic from past Christmases. And after dinner, Lady Pauley took her aside and began to confide all her many symptoms. Not accustomed to anyone having more symptoms than she, Lady Warwick was in a tiff. Rather than finding themselves fellow sufferers, it became a contest of which one had more doctors despairing over the complexity of her case and which one had tried warm ale first for insomnia and doses of straight camphor for coughs, not to mention burning pastilles for excess sensibility.

Lady Pauley had the floor for above twenty minutes describing in detail the procedure of cataplasm applied to the soles of her feet for general debility and the castor oil packs on her abdomen for gastric distress, when Lady Warwick interrupted to complain of a present pain in her head, which won her final points. Meanwhile Merrie was attempting to draw out Florence Prichard, who, nothing loath, was revealing the many beaux who had writ her letters of adoration, as well as poems to her dimpled elbows. Lady Jane whispered that a lady ought not reveal private correspondence, and the two ladies had a discussion as to whether that was done or not done in polite circles. Merrie, never having had even a note to her pinky, stepped aside, allowing the society ladies to come to cuffs.

Their testiness could be explained as jitters before a performance, for directly the gentlemen finished their brandies, all were to adjourn to the music room. The harp was quivering, awaiting Lady Jane's gentle strokes. The pianoforte, less tremulously, awaited Miss Prichard.

In the meantime Lady Warwick requested Merrie's company in the library and no sooner closed the door than she exploded, "That Lady Pauley is insufferable with her sufferings. One would think she is the sole support of all the nation's surgeons. No one else has had as interesting complaints, she assumes. If only she were aware of how she is boring everyone, she would shut her mouth and suffer in silence."

"Perhaps it is the only thing she finds of interest. One always talks of one's main concerns. Lord Dansville's foreign travel tales during dinner were not the height of interest. Especially since the acme of each story was how various foreigners—Swiss, Portuguese, French, and Italian—not aware of who he was had been put in their places by the announcement of his title. And Sir Oswald is a dear, but his *on-dits* were not amusing to us, for we do not know the people involved. And Lady Dansville's discussion of her heritage perhaps would concern her descendents. The secret of good conversation is to share an interest, I expect. I had thought that Lady Pauley and you might find some coincidence of connection with the various cures you have both tried. Nostrums and such."

Lady Warwick closed her eyes in despair. "I hope sincerely you are not accusing me of being as boring in tales of my illnesses as she is! If I thought that—"

"Oh, no. No, indeed. Why, I find every one of your complaints riveting, because, frankly, I find you interesting. Wishing you well so much, I am constantly in concern. But you are much better of late. You have so much more to discuss beyond cures. All the books we have read. When Lady Dansville ruled that there was no need for libraries, nor for any books beyond the Bible and *Burke's Peerage*—which apparently is her Bible—your answer was prime."

Somewhat mollified and pleased, the countess turned the discussion to Lady Dansville, and they had the pleasure of finding themselves in complete agreement on not only her but her daughter Lady Jane. "I scarce understand a word that girl says. I feared my hearing was going until Lady Pauley ordered her to take a deep breath and project her words ere she sent us all to our ear trumpets."

Merrie grinned at that. "I daresay it would be best if we all let her words fade away into the ether, unattended."

Lady Warwick laughed loudly at that. "Heavens, I hope she is not going to be my daughter-in-law. I shall have to borrow Lady Pauley's trumpet without doubt."

That introduced the topic both had been avoiding —which of the two ladies the earl had singled out for his marked interest. It could not be determined by his behavior at dinner, for he had flirted outrageously with each one equally, until both had turned quite pleasurably pink. At those times his lordship had turned to see if Merrie was appreciating his dalliances and found her observing him with an amused expression, as one would watch a performance not taken seriously. This goaded the earl to further gallantry, until he addressed a compliment of such excess that Merrie could not help but mime applause, and he bowed in her direction, forgetting the ladies he had been complimenting, till they loudly protested that he was turning their heads, and he had to turn back to them.

Throughout the meal, George had been silent, viewing Merrie with despair. After all that had happened to her today, Merrie realized she'd forgotten that George too had attempted to take liberties with her this morning. So she finally gave him a generous smile, and he perked up, either feeling himself forgiven, or that his advances were not too distasteful to her. George was too far away to converse with, but he spent the rest of the meal gazing at the lady with the blazing curls as if she were a sparkling star. Occasionally Brett harshly interrupted one of those gazes of adoration, and he remembered to swallow.

At last they had all gathered in the music room. Lady Jane's harp was carried to the forefront. Lady

Dansville arranged her daughter's silk gown till the folds fell just so. Next, Lady Jane carefully removed her lace gloves and a small ring. There was some coughing, and the lady patiently waited until that had totally subsided. Then just as she had struck her first note, Sir Oswald disconcerted her by coughing, and she looked up at him reproachfully, causing Merrie to bite her lip to quash her giggle. Thankfully, she did so. Not another sound came from any of the audience, and at last Lady Jane thought it proper to begin again. This time her father coughed on the first note. Once more, she looked reproachfully at her audience and put her hands down. Another wait. Then again, hesitantly, suspiciously glancing about, Lady Jane poised her hands above her harp. She waited an extra second, and then plunged into a chord. There was a universal coughing from Oswald, Lady Pauley, Lady Warwick, her father, and George. But although red in the face at that point, Lady Jane was trooper enough to carry on until the coughing finally subsided.

It then became clear that her playing was better when people coughed. For when not feeling in competition with those hacking sounds, she played in her usual genteel style, and it was so faint that the many sounds of chairs being moved—attempting to come closer to hear every other note—drowned her out totally.

When Lady Jane was finished, everybody was uncertain whether to applaud or simply mime it, fearing she might find any loud noise offensive. But her mother led the loud applause and everyone was relieved enough to know she had finished and that at last they were permitted to applaud and cough and speak out in wild liberation.

It was Miss Florence Prichard's turn next. She approached the pianoforte and banged away so loudly no one could hear whether anyone was coughing or not. She had a vigorous style that was accompanied by the bobbing of her head, which had the various brown tendrils flying. When she finished, she rose and everyone vigorously applauded. Merrie turned her glance on the earl and gave him such a look of compassion that he flushed red and was even more offended than if she had said a hundred cutting things about the ladies of his choice. The annoying part was that he was bored by both these ladies as well, and had found their performances, at the most, amusing.

"We have another young lady in our midst," he said, eyeing her with droll revenge. "Miss Laurence, surely you can entertain us as well?"

"Of course," Merrie said promptly, not at all overcome by his daring her. "With Christmas so nigh, I expect we all are in the Christmas mood, and so I shall play us a carol and hope to have you all join in." Behind the pianoforte, her rather common drab cream made-over gown no longer dominated as it had when she had walked into dinner, and the earl had been able to compare her so unfavorably with the two fashionably dressed ladies and even Lady Dansville. Picking Sir Oswald, George, and Lady Warwick to be her chorus, she began, "God Rest Ye Merry Gentlemen." Although her voice was drowned out by George's base and Oswald's tenor, here and there the bright tone of it and the joy of her face induced the earl to come closer. Soon he was singing along with them, and Lady Warwick was remembering the days in this very room when her two sons had sung this very song for her and gotten a sixpence from their father, and she requested that they repeat the performance. While George was nothing loath, and began, the earl was ready to demur when Merrie said forcibly, "I dare you! I sang at your request. Show your nerve!"

And so goaded, he let out his baritone. When the

two sons finished the rousing carol, their mother had tears in her eyes and Merrie was applauding them as if it had been the greatest glee she'd ever heard, and Sir Oswald was saying "Top ho!" and the earl found that it was rather jolly to be singing after so many years of ennui.

And soon Miss Prichard had come to stand beside him and give her soprano and that had Lady Jane joining, and before everyone knew it, they were having quite a delightful Christmas glee.

George, who had a rather pleasant voice, sang one of the newest songs being sung in his crowd; it came from a current poet named Leigh Hunt and had been set to music. It was entitled "Jenny Kissed Me," and though the name was Jenny, he sang it to Merrie as if it were to her. " 'Jenny kissed me when we met,' " he began, and expectantly came close to that lady's chair for the finish.

> Say I'm weary, say I'm sad,
> Say that health and wealth have miss'd me,
> Say I'm growing old, but add,
> Jenny kiss'd me.

He was much applauded, and after his bow, Merrie threw him a kiss, which gesture was also applauded by all.

That led to requests for everyone's favorite love song, and Sir Oswald rendered his to Miss Prichard, and soon she joined him in his chorus; they found they had matching voices, both obstreperously loud and high, and so they formed a delightful duo. It looked clearly as if Lord Warwick was losing one of his ladies. Lady Jane remained faithful, and whispered a song to the earl, which Brett applauded vigorously, despite his not having grasped a single phrase, claiming himself much moved. And then he shot a defiant

glance at Merrie, who was also applauding her ladyship, and agreeing there was much there to move one
to tears.

He came close to her and whispered with a laugh,
"You minx! If you find her ladyship deficient, why
don't you show us how a lady would sing to the gentleman she loved?"

But Merrie, as director, claimed her prerogative of
announcing the end of the singing and the beginning
of the drinking. Indeed, Walters with his impeccable
timing was already bringing in the tea and spread for
those who still had appetite. And after a cup, Lady
Pauley and Lord and Lady Dansville retired. Lady
Warwick was surprised to find herself filled with energy, and she whispered to Merrie that she certainly
was no longer to be included in the invalid class in
which *certain* ladies belonged. Rather she stayed up
for the youngsters' discussion around the fire. The
talk was principally of past Christmases, and of specters that walked on Christmas Eve. George and Brett
were entertaining with tales of their ancestor, the first
earl, the one who had returned from the Crusades
with three ladies in his train.

"A deuced rum touch the fellow was, I own," Brett
confessed, "A genuine blot on our escutcheon, for he
visited the tower room and summoned a different
lady on a different night to, eh, have a discussion, and
thus determine which one he wished to choose as his
life's mate. And upon making his choice, the other
two ladies were so distraught, they joined hands and
jumped from the tower to their deaths. Rather dead
than without the love of this fellow, apparently. And
since then on certain windy nights, one can hear the
laments of the maidens and their shrieks as they fall
to their demise."

"But that is not the full tale," the countess interposed. "A few years and children later, his wife, or

the lady chosen, similarly jumped from that tower room, and so the earl was left alone. And they do say that he often haunts Moorsedge when a lovely lady is here, seeking to find his lost love and perhaps this time keep her."

Lady Jane said something. By her expression one assumed it was that she was slightly alarmed.

"Yes," George added enthusiastically, "we oft hear his armor rattling around the halls searching for a beauty to stay with him, or seeking to send her to join her sisters in a plunge to her death. He announces the lady of his choice by knocking at her door, and no one is ever found in the hall, but eventually the lady takes a plunge, either into love or, in the name of love, off the tower."

Merrie's clear laughter eased the tension that had been growing, as Lady Jane and Miss Prichard were listening for the sounds of the armor rattling, and vowing to barricade their doors this very night. "Obviously the earl had a difficult time keeping his women."

"You are not a romantic?" Brett challenged her. "Don't you believe in a lady jumping to her death rather than living without the gentleman she loves? Do you not believe feelings can be that all-enveloping?"

"A gentleman who had three ladies deliberately brought to Moorsedge to make his selection"—and she paused here while everybody realized the present earl had similarly at least two young ladies in Moorsedge for his selection—"sounds rather like a man with no heart whatsoever. And for such a passionless man, one should not give one's life, not even one's affection. It is my opinion the ladies should have gotten together and pushed the gentleman himself off the tower."

The earl laughed at that conclusion and that challenge, and admitted he must henceforth keep a watch against any cabal of ladies with designs on his person. And he looked deliberately at the three women there and laughed at their discomfort.

A few more tales of the first earl and his walking suit of armor and his banging on ladies' doors, and the ladies were insisting on being escorted to their rooms by the gentlemen, for fear of running into the earl.

Merrie walked to her room, unafraid and unescorted. Not above a half hour later, she heard a knocking and opened it with a grin, expecting to see George playing tricks, but no one was there. With some wary alarm, Merrie looked out into the hall and still did not observe anyone lurking even in the distance. Her candle flickered eerily as she quickly returned to her room. And then, admittedly, she felt momentary concern. But she would not dwell on it, concentrating instead on Christmas preparations. But that night she dreamed of the first earl knocking and then coming through the door, and joining her in bed. And she awoke in a blush.

9

It was Christmas Eve day. Merrie had been waiting for it and the next one—the great day of Christmas—ever since she'd first come to Moorsedge.

From her father's tales of Christmases in other countries, with which he always entertained them on Christmas Eve, Merrie was long enamored of one Swedish custom featuring the eldest daughter representing Saint Lucia. Dressed in a white gown with a brilliant red sash and a crown of pine boughs with seven lit candles haloing her head, Saint Lucia appeared at each person's door bearing breakfast treats. Ever since Merrie had been eleven years old, she'd been representing Saint Lucia for her family and decided to continue that tradition at Moorsedge, declaring herself daughter of the house. Accompanied by Walters and two maids holding the goodies and morning chocolate or tea, Merrie knocked on door after door with her holiday preamble.

This welcome was received by each person at Moorsedge according to his or her joy in Christmas. Lord and Lady Dansville accepted their morning repast as if Saint Lucia were merely another servant to be dismissed with a joint nod of their heads. Considering Saint Lucia's head was ablaze with candles and her eyes sparkling with the joy of the occasion, that was rather a prodigious act of noble indifference. Their reaction being particularly daunting, Merrie could not help but regret having chosen their chamber to begin with, and a somewhat wilted Saint Lucia carried on toward Lady Pauley's chamber. There the saint was greeted by a scream. And further, frightened by the fiery candles on her head, Lady Pauley tossed a water pitcher in Saint Lucia's direction. After successfully ducking that dousing, Merrie attempted to explain the historical tradition of the occasion, but Lady Pauley merely accused Saint Lucia of bringing on her palpitations, which would undoubtedly lead to her having to spend the entire day in bed.

Back in the hall, Walters gave her a look which said, "I told you so," without his committing the solecism of saying it. Nevertheless, Merrie could not allow the tradition to be so quickly dismissed.

Her next room, fortunately, was Lady Warwick's. And yet Merrie-Saint Lucia hesitantly peeped in.

"Oh, you darling child!"

That exclamation, and Lady Warwick's fondly smiling and rising from her bed to greet the spirit of Christmas, did much to restore the seasonal delight to the bludgeoned saint. Bowing, Merrie offered her goodies and her wishes for a delightful Christmas for the great lady, who was great enough to ignore the candles and hug her vigorously and then with pleasure accept both the chocolate and several treats, all the while smiling at the blazing girl. Perching on her bed, Merrie confided her failure so far. At the mention of Lady Pauley's throwing water, Lady Warwick was incensed, and thought one might as well attempt to douse the Yule log, and did people have no Christmas spirit at all!

This from a lady who had ignored Christmas for the last five years, and had thought herself too ill to partake in the festivities. But a remarkable change—say rather a renewal—had taken place in the countess since Merrie had arrived. Admittedly the companionship of reading, talking, and sharing confidences had lifted her out of her decline. But the final step toward renewed health had been precipitated by the antics of Lady Pauley. Never had Lady Warwick wished to appear less like that shocking example of self-indulgence. And so she vowed no longer to spend any substantial part of her days in her room, but rather to be an active participant in all the Christmas plans.

Somewhat heartened by the love and smiles of the countess, Merrie entered the chamber of Florence Prichard, and found the girl entranced by the custom. She was up and anxious to try on the crown herself and quite willing to laugh with Saint Lucia and accept her good wishes and the delicacies from the servants. And when Merrie departed her room, she felt the earl could do a great deal worse than choosing that lady for his lady. Which brought her to Lady Jane's chamber.

Merrie entered determined to give her ladyship every opportunity to show her better nature, and joyously went through her wishes and offerings. Whereupon Lady Jane demonstrated that she had no nature whatsoever by not reacting. At last, her continued silence dried the words on Merrie's lips, and the two just stared at each other. Merrie was awed by her ladyship's abundantly lace-trimmed nightdress that included a matching nightcap all in an explosion of lace on her beautiful blond head. But her face was so expressionless that for a moment Merrie had the sensation she was addressing a petrified doll put on the bed merely for decorative purposes. At last, the doll inclined her head and accepted the tea. She whispered something, which Merrie could not quite hear, but sensed was a dismissal, and she left. Outside, Merrie shuddered, for that lady left her with the feeling that a pitcher of cold water had indeed been thrown over her blazing candles, although Lady Jane had merely stared ahead.

Heavens, if the earl chose her, he might as well bed down with an effigy!

Her last three rooms were those of the gentlemen: Sir Oswald, George, and lastly, the earl. Once more Merrie considered whether it would be indecorous of her to enter their rooms. That was not specified in her father's description of Saint Lucia's sojourns. To maintain some decorum, Merrie decided to send in Walters, and request their coming to the door to be greeted by Saint Lucia. At that message, Walters inclined his head with approval; he'd been fearing the lady would forget herself and actually enter the gentlemen's chambers, and he'd been wondering how to give the hint to this irrepressible lady that such acts would be shockingly indecorous. She was grinning at his look of relief and whispered, "I am not that unaware of the proprieties, Walters."

"No, miss," he said woodenly, but added, "and I expect you would not enter, even if requested to do so by the gentlemen?"

Merrie shook her flaming head, and the candles flickered her agreement.

It was Sir Oswald's turn to be greeted, and his valet stepped aside for Walters to enter. Merrie moved a respectable distance away from the doorway as Sir Oswald, in a shocking dressing gown of exuberant print, came cheerily to the door and received her blessing. True to Walters's fears, he attempted to coax the Christmas angel to enter.

"I shall give you such a Christmas cheer in here, my dear, you shan't forget it for the rest of the year."

"Remember yourself, Sir Oswald. I am Saint Lucia, and as such should be *reverently* greeted, or you shall receive ill fortune the rest of the year."

Slightly superstitious, the buck stopped his joshing, and bowed low to the saint and accepted her good wishes with pleasure and even kissed her hand, as she offered him the treat.

She walked away smiling, and with an approving nod from Walters for having handled that gentleman as a lady, or in this case, a saint, should.

There was no hope of George's pleasing Walters's finer sense of propriety. He was out in a dash and swinging her around, until he extinguished a good half of her crown. Merrie was forced to enter his rooms after all, with Walters, to relight her crown from his fireplace. Incorrigibly George insisted that she stay awhile and bless his entire room, as he'd never had the pleasure of an actual saint visiting him, and he should dashed well not allow her to make it a mere courtesy call.

"That's what it is," Saint Lucia warned, but smiled. "Besides, Mr. Dickens, you have many things this morning to attend to, such as a visit to the attics for the clothes we discussed and the other objects you are to collect."

Recalled to his exalted role, for he had been chosen by Merrie as the Lord of Misrule for tomorrow's celebrations, he agreed he would keep up to scratch, but still would not let her immediately depart, saying this and that. At which moment Bruiser began expressing himself as vastly intrigued by her candle crown and jumped up to dislodge it. George lunged at the dog and held him off while the lady made her timely departure, throwing back a few appeasing breakfast buns to whichever one of her pursuers reached them first.

It was the earl's apartment next which was situated in the other wing and quite extensive. One could enter one of his sitting rooms and still be a respectable distance from his sleeping area, and so Saint Lucia dared to cross his threshold and wait before his fireplace.

He entered dressed in a rather conservative brown dressing gown, although his dark hair did not have the usual carefully brushed-back look he favored. Tousled, he looked younger. And his dark eyes usually filled with ennui were lively at the anticipation of greeting that saint. The sight of her had his eyes further lit, as if reflecting her many candles. "Egad, what a beauty! You look as if you were an actual candelabrum. Your hair is not really blazing, is it?"

"Please do not be familiar in your addresses, my lord. Recollect I am a saint," Merrie said primly. "Actually, I am Saint Lucia, here to wish you the joy of the season and to promise if I am well received you shall have a year of good luck and joy . . . and of course, love."

Spellbound by her crown of lights and her promise of love for the year ahead, the earl was one step away from lifting Merrie in his arms and taking her into his inner chamber. He imagined her without that white robe, and yet with candles all about her as he laid her on his bed, and somehow from the fiery blaze in his eyes, Saint Lucia sensed some of his thoughts, and she stepped back a step or two. "I have come to give you a treat," she said softly.

"I hope to heaven you have," he said, his voice coaxing as he took another step toward her.

When he reached her, she had stepped back almost to his outer door, and he followed, leaning close, blinded by the lights on her head.

She was gasping at his nearness, and, remembering

the occasions when he had taken the opportunity to kiss her, looked around and saw that Walters was there, and felt reassured.

"Here's your treat," she said, still in her breathless voice, and as he leaned closer yet, she took a bun and stuck it in his half-open mouth, and shoved it in.

He stepped back to choke on it.

"Walters will give you the chocolate that goes with it. And I the blessings for the season." And having done so, she bobbed a mock curtsey and rushed out of the room while the earl was drinking down the chocolate to wash away the crumbs in his throat.

When he had his breath, he opened his door and watched the Christmas sprite of a girl laughing through the halls. Never had he seen, in all his years of diamonds of the first water, a lady of such sparkle and joy who could tempt any gentleman, even one as experienced as himself.

Walters was serving him some tea and he took that as well, and another bun left behind by the Christmas sprite.

"Did she enter any of the other gentlemen's rooms?" the earl asked suddenly, eyeing Walters imperiously.

"She did not," Walters lied, conveniently forgetting her having gone into George's room to relight her crown. "Both of us waited in the hall. She was not subject to the slightest discourtesy, except by Bruiser, who took exception to her candles and attempted to dislodge them."

Satisfied, the earl nodded.

"The young lady is planning many a holiday surprise, your lordship. The entire staff is to participate, and we are all rather grateful to you for the announcement of holiday remembrances."

His lordship frowned at that and dismissed the man. Brett dared not comment on those holiday remembrances since he had forgotten about them, but evidently Merrie had stepped in. A moment before he had felt the greatest amiability toward her, but this acting without consulting him as she ought had him miffed. Nevertheless, she'd saved his groats, and he did not have the right to call her to account. Then too, that timely reminder of gifts had the earl hurrying off to the village to make whatever purchases possible in such a rustic area. Naturally, presents for his noble guests had been purchased at the best London shops, including several fans, objets d'art, and snuff boxes. The loveliest fan was one of hand-carved ivory sticks delicately covered over with a spun web of pink lace. Originally this exquisite object had been meant for Lady Jane, but her ladyship had not shown herself worthy of it. Oft in London, the earl had been uncertain about that lady as his choice, for he was somewhat put off by her stiffness; although then he'd attributed it to an excess of social decorum. But here in the country, where manners were somewhat relaxed, Lady Jane seemed, if possible, even more lifeless. Or was that in contrast to that minx Merrie, who made everyone about her seem lacking in spark and fire? The use of the word fire recollected his first image of her this morning with the crown of candles and her lips parted in expectation at his reception of her. And he had been hard-pressed not to run to her and lift her up in his arms, and say, "You darling, welcome . . . welcome to my heart."

Stopping himself short of the realization that their poor relation had lit something of a fire into his heart, the earl frowned. Good heavens, what was he thinking? Her position made her suitable only for a tumble, or at most, an affair. He could not disgrace his title and standing by allowing himself to become entrapped by one beneath him.

Yet the thought of tumbling her had his face blazing as he set off for the village. No, he reprimanded his inclination, he would not give Miss Laurence that choice fan. It belonged to a lady of Lady Jane's ilk. He would find something in the village that would be more suitable for Miss Laurence. Some little inexpensive gewgaw that the child in her would probably more enjoy.

Upon his return, the earl entered to find Sir Oswald kissing Miss Prichard, and being applauded for it by the rest of his guests. Instantly he surmised the cause and was confirmed by the sight of a branch above the two heads. Mistletoe! By Jove, hadn't he rid the halls of that weed to prevent this very thing? And yet he must behave as if he thought this mistletoe prank were the greatest boon. Immediately he fell into the clichéd behavior every gentleman assumed in the vicinity of that Druid vegetation, pretending both surprise and joy, and looking about like a positive bumpkin to see which lady would inadvertently pass beneath. Miss Prichard was delighted to do so inadvertently once more for the earl's benefit. And in all civility, he could do no less than Sir Oswald. Her lips were soft and willing, and he found her quite a warm armful. Perhaps there was more of a bumpkin in him than he'd realized. Beginning to enjoy the simple pleasures of this game, the earl and Sir Oswald fell to a shoving match as to which one could stand closer to the weed.

When the earl spotted his mother passing near enough the mistletoe, he pretended she had passed directly beneath and gave her the first resounding buss of his adulthood. The countess was delighted and hugged her son in return, and laughed and laughed as George jumped in and made it a family embrace. And all the while Merrie was applauding the endearing picture of the Warwicks *en famille*.

But so many kisses had been given and taken that

half the berries in the mistletoe had been claimed. For each kiss necessitated the plucking of a berry, and when all the berries were gone, that privilege of free kisses would similarly be lost to the young swains. Before that occurred, both Sir Oswald and George were attempting to catch Merrie in the vicinity, but she was quite careful not to come close enough to be judged within its perimeters. And then Lady Dansville, resenting that she and hers had to stand there as witnesses to all that jollity, ordered her husband to follow her. He did. And she positioned herself squarely under the mistletoe. He leaned over and gave her a dutiful peck.

It was the example for her hesitant daughter, and Lady Jane approached reluctantly. Under that seductive plant she planted herself with a long-suffering expression that clearly said, Have I come to this?

She had. And the earl had as well, as courtierlike he made quick to kiss her beautiful lips. Surprisingly they were not as cold as expected, and as she did not quickly duck away, he gave her several more hearty smacks.

Lady Jane was all smiles on eventually running away, and Lady Dansville was nodding in satisfaction at a distasteful task well handled. At that moment, Lady Jane turned to eye Merrie, and found the young lady clapping her hands at the good fun all were having, and for a moment, the discussion she and her mother had had the night before that she must look out for the encroaching "poor relation" seemed less essential. Perhaps the lady was just simple, and was really enjoying all this frivolity. Simple and common. The commoners, her mother had explained, fully enjoyed this season since they had no position to uphold and no dignity to preserve, and thus could fall unrestrainedly into all the frolicking.

Sir Oswald and Miss Prichard were at it again, and finally had denuded the mistletoe down to its twigs.

"Ah, dash it!" George exclaimed, "the berries are finished, and I did not get a single kiss!"

His mother objected that she had kissed him, and with everyone heartily laughing at the young man's peevishness, the party retired into the drawing room. There were books from the library set out for those who cared so to entertain themselves, with writing paper and sealing wafers and standishes for those who wished to carry on their correspondence. Fires were lit and confections in glass bowls invited. All about it was clearly Christmas. The scent of pine boughs filled vases and had one thinking of treks through a forest glen. Indeed, the outdoors had been welcomed in, as the greenery of holly and ivy decorated every pier glass and every portrait. As well, the mantles of every fireplace were crowded with greenery and all ablaze in candles. One particular table was loaded with packages in brown wrapping, each exuberantly trimmed with fir and holly accents. Hourly it became more laden. The earl was just adding his purchases when he turned and saw Merrie hurrying off, closely followed by George. Grimly, he gave them a second to feel themselves alone, and then light-footedly crept behind.

Merrie had gone directly to the portrait of the first earl in his full armor, and with George's assistance she was balancing herself on the chair below to add twigs of mistletoe discreetly between the greenery already there.

When she turned triumphantly to face George, she announced, "That's for his attempting to visit me last night."

"Did he, egad?" George cried, helping her down.

"He banged at my door quite excessively, and I concluded he is not only offended by all this talk of his spooking but also rather neglected. And so I am giving him a welcome and announcing that I have not the smallest belief that he ever conducted himself as less than a gentleman. Obviously he simply wanted a lady's love and did not quite know how to win it. And so he lost one after another of his loves. Pity he never learned the way to win a lady is to give love—wholeheartedly—without playing flummery games of selection."

"That's what I've been trying to do to you, dash it!" George exclaimed, and then pointed out the mistletoe. But Merrie claimed she was decorating and that put her out of the weed's power, and further that he had work to do; and refusing to play any more games, severely ordered him to his task. Left alone, she gazed up at the first earl. Taking up half a wall, the portrait was of him in his armor, charging with his lance held out.

"Is my lady inviting me into her bedroom?" came a soft voice.

Merrie jumped, but then turned and observed the present earl, which caused her to fall into relieved laughter, acknowledging, "You fooled me for a brief second."

"You didn't answer? Are you attempting to seduce the earl?"

"If reports are true, one could hardly seduce anyone so primed. Actually, I dreamed he came into my room last night, unbidden, and took me up into the tower room and there the two of us . . ."

"The two of you . . ." the earl encouraged, his voice rasping.

"Jumped out of the window!" she concluded. "And so I felt he was too melancholy a gentleman, and should partake of the joy of this season, which is not death and forcing and hurting, but giving and laughing and sharing . . . and true love."

And with that Merrie started up the stairs. He followed her until she'd reached the landing, where the portrait gallery was. She went in and looked at the face of the first earl, this being a full-head version, without armor. He looked amazingly like the present earl—dark eyes and a ruthless look about them. His usual set expression now, as she neared, seemed less severe, almost in a smile.

"Ah," Merrie exclaimed, "there, you see, he's less unhappy. Moorsedge is cheerier all around, haven't you found? Your mother has never been fitter. I was so delighted that you gave her a demonstration of your true feelings today. No one enjoys being alone and unloved on Christmas."

There was a sadness to her words, a sigh that disconcerted his lordship. "Are you telling me *you* feel alone and unloved? You!" he exclaimed.

"That is scarcely surprising. For I am without those I love best—my mother and father and brothers, and most of all my sister, who is my dearest friend. You have all been excessively kind here, but one cannot help but remember other seasons. At this moment I would be cutting chestnuts with my mother for a stuffing, and wondering if the bird will be enough to make sufficient servings. It is difficult to have Christmas without the resources to celebrate fully. We were not to have a goose at all this year, and yet your kitchens have a gaggle of them. Bruiser will have more of a feast than we ever had at *any* Christmas. Or than your cottagers have, I expect. And yet, there was open love at Oxford. And here, one has to keep pushing to stop the evil feelings from overcoming. Lord and Lady Dansville are always making remarks about poor Miss Prichard. You have created a competition that should not be present at Christmas. I believe you should make your feelings known to one lady, so that the other can enjoy her Christmas. It is the only decent thing."

"I say, are you under the assumption that since I told you you could arrange the Christmas celebration here, you could as well arrange my life?"

"I was merely suggesting," she said, ready to walk back down the stairs when the earl stopped her.

"Very well, if we are to invade each other's privacy, I suggest that you stop tempting my brother. I shall in no way allow you to wed him. He is not to be your goose no matter how deprived you feel. Spare me your sad tales, and let us be honest. Without any bark on it—are you setting your cap for Georgie or not?"

"Not," Merrie said directly, but could not hold back a touch of a taunt for his uncaring reaction to her previous circumstance. "But . . . Mr. Dickens has asked for my hand."

"And?"

"And . . ." Merrie paused, toying with him a bit further, and finally concluding with a small smile, "and, I feel I need an older man. To control me."

Her eyes were dancing as she said that, putting rather pleasant ideas in his head of controlling her in several ways, when the realization of what she'd said hit him and had him stiffening in outrage.

"Are you offering yourself to *me?*"

"Certainly not! You could not control me. I need a gentleman of more . . . understanding. We ladies like to be treated with a gentle hand. Stern looks put us off our feed. You notice I am keeping this in equine terminology, for the only time I have seen you showing any concern is for your horse Caliban."

Amused at that, at last the earl grinned. How was it that this young minx could so easily throw him off balance, he wondered, concluding that he would like to master her indeed. Then suspecting she had deliberately brought him to thinking those thoughts, immediately Brett pokered up, concluding coldly that if it was a mate she was looking for, she had best set her sights lower to spot a gentleman on a par with her limited qualifications. For himself, keeping it in her own metaphor, he preferred to gallop alone. "And if I should ever consider harnessing myself to another, only the most prime-bred animal shall team with *me*."

Unfazed, Merrie said airily that even a horse from the wealthiest stable might lack good lines, and when put through its paces show up as a slug at heart.

At first the earl smiled, assuming she meant Lady Jane, which showed a proper jealousy for that exalted lady. But upon meeting Miss Laurence's direct gaze, he suffered a monstrous shock at the sudden realization that she was alluding to him! But he recovered enough to claim that he was a remarkably good judge of horseflesh, so she need not concern herself. He would easily find a suitable mate for himself, as, indeed, he could for her.

At that Merrie clapped her hands in delight. "Are you offering to be my matchmaker? What a delightful idea! A perfectly *cousinly* approach. But if you're suggesting Sir Oswald, both of us are somewhat behindhand there—Miss Prichard has caught his eye. Obviously you've lost one of your choices. Best find me another gentleman. And I suggest for yourself you quickly snap up this somnambulant Lady Jane before she wakes up and falls for Walters, who is the only one as stiff-faced as she and her family, which will leave you in the equally degrading position of being left with either Mrs. Prissom . . . or me, after all!"

And laughing at that, Merrie rushed away, leaving the earl wondering how he had been brought to this pass. For it was true that Miss Prichard and Sir Oswald seemed to have become jolly close. Yet rather than feeling himself put out of countenance by that, he felt a strong relief, as if one of his burdens had been taken off his shoulders, and he only wished for Lord Pavraam to make a late appearance and do as much with Lady Jane.

Face to face with the first earl, the present earl would have welcomed a confabulation. The old boy had the right of it, tossing his ladies off the tower turret. Women were a dashed nuisance. Although, as he stared at the old earl, he wondered, with a shiver, if the chap were planning to take Merrie away from him. He remembered with some peevishness that she'd said he'd come banging on her door. It could have been George playing a game, but he had been properly astonished when she told him. And Sir Oswald would never rouse himself from his bed; it was too much effort.

A steady glare at the dark, sardonic eyes that so mirrored his own, and the earl whispered, "You've had your share of ladies. This one is mine." And then as he said it, he felt the old boy approving, and putting wild thoughts in his head of taking the lady to the tower room and showing her an actual flight of passion. By Jove, he could give her and himself the sensation of plunging through the dark, and he wondered if he could rid himself of his guests soon enough to have her alone.

Although he attempted to shake off such thoughts, the earl found himself later in the day going up to the tower room and observing it. He ordered the maids to rid it of some of the dust and to place fresh sheets on the canopied bed. He did not allow himself to face why he had done it, but he felt his blood running wildly through his veins at the thought that he had.

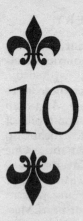

10

On Christmas morning, after breakfast, all were to assemble to view the gifts. Merrie in her sojourn in the attics had uncovered a wealth of items that could be made into unexceptionable gifts. Spotting a red flag, she nearly pounced on it as a gift for Brett to be accompanied by a note of explanation that he must wave it before others to signal when he wished to come to cuffs with them. But Christmas was hardly the time for an unfeeling jest. Rather she would give him her father's current book on ancient Greece, having brought a copy originally as a gift for the countess, but felt her ladyship would quail at the size of it. As for the earl, he would likely skim through it as he did through life. An amateur painting of two hounds—one looking remarkably like Bruiser—was snatched as a gift for George, whose devotion to that splendid animal showed what a dear and loyal heart he had. Often she wished herself a few years younger. He was just the correct age for Esther, however. Indeed, Merrie had written her sister about him, with the hopes that she would leave her studies long enough to lark about with Mr. Dickens, if in the future Lady Warwick were to fulfill her promise of inviting both sisters for another visit.

More dusty paintings were found, but these were of hunting scenes, and she dismissed them. And then in a drawer of a buhl cabinet she came upon a pile of miniature portraits—faces that had once meant so much, at least to the subject, now mere debris. One miniature had as its subject another middynasty earl, who bore a close resemblance, through the same smoldering black eyes, to both the first and present lords. Unable to think of a fit recipient for that, Merrie still pocketed it. A few moments later she spotted a great find, a discarded riding outfit, only to discover disappointedly that it was several sizes too small. The hat, at least, might have fit, but it was missing. A hat was certainly owed her by the earl, and Merrie had hopes of one from him for Christmas. Naturally, it could not be anything like the one he'd ruined, with its genuine ostrich feather. Nor, she sighed, could it equal the bonnet Lady Jane was wearing upon arrival that had awed Merrie to her bones. It had *two* ostrich feathers on the imposing brim, and was a light blue velvet, which made her ladyship's watery blue eyes a deeper hue. Merrie had not been able to stop gazing at it, until she'd caught the earl's amused glance at her marveling. Whether he was remembering the contrast between her own bonnet upon arrival or whether he was just triumphant that the lady he had chosen was so much an object of envy, she did not trouble herself to divine.

Most of the gowns in the attic were the heavy brocades and velvets of yesteryear, nothing like the present slim, high-waisted diaphanous gowns. With her meager wardrobe and the countess's permission to take whatever she wished from the attic, Merrie did not deem it greedy to snatch up a green velvet cape.

Sprucer than her worn pelisse, and so warm, it could even double as a dressing robe when she was up of a morning. Another find: two fans with torn panels, which could easily be repaired and given as her gifts to the two ladies. She was not a prime seamstress, but she could sew a rip, and the material was fine, if slightly yellowed.

Coming jubilantly down the stairs with her Christmas booty, Merrie rushed to repair and wrap them for the Christmas table. She trimmed them all with greenery of such abundance that the wrapping was prettier than the gift inside. For the countess, Merrie had long been planning a special gift, ever since she'd discovered the cat in the stables had given birth to a litter. She had carefully chosen the prettiest of the group, one that was all white, except for a V-shaped black spot on its head. He or she—Merrie wasn't certain which at this young age—was decorated with greenery and taken into her ladyship's room first thing on Christmas morning.

But the countess, reverting to her old fear of contagion, was alarmed at the wiggling little animal. Calmly, holding the cat in her arms, Merrie sat next to her new friend and began to chat about the reason for this gift.

"It is generally said that petting a kitten relaxes one's nerves. As you no longer need a composer, this should suffice. I have christened it Vinny, for the V on its head, for your victory from invalidism, and also, for vinaigrette. It will take the place of your reliance on that. And further, you are such a loving person that upon my returning to my family, and the departure of the guests and your sons, you will have no one on whom to demonstrate that generous, loving nature. And so I felt I would leave you Vinny to keep you company and to comfort you . . . and to love you as all things and people must, upon knowing you."

Her ladyship stared at the earnest, concerned look in the young lady's green eyes and was profoundly moved. She had not acknowledged that dear Merrie would soon be leaving her, and indeed, that thought brought on her first palpitation in a while. Merrie, quick to discern her discomfort, not only put her own arms around the lady but placed Vinny in her lap. Absorbed with protecting the kitten from falling, her ladyship had no time to grasp her heart and collapse. Shortly, the kitten was licking her fingers, which Merrie pronounced a sign of its instant affection for the countess, but the lady, having been a mother, assured her that was just a nursing gesture. And she ordered a bowl of milk to be brought, and what with feeding it and playing with it, a full hour passed before Merrie said proudly, "You see, Vinny stopped you from having palpitations faster and with more lasting effect than your vinaigrette!"

And the countess, still stroking the now contented kitten in her lap, had to laugh and admit Vinny was quite as effective as her vinaigrette. But upon the young lady's leaving, pleased with the success of her Christmas gift, the countess immediately stopped smiling. For really it had been Merrie who had saved her, as in the beginning she had pulled her out of her state of illness and loneliness. It was *Merrie* she must keep. And with that conclusion, which she deemed a life-and-death situation, the countess, nodding decisively, paid a morning visit to her son.

His lordship's valet was surprised to find the countess, still in her morning robe, knocking for admittance. He roused the earl and whispered the unpleasant tidings.

Unlike his London self, the earl did not castigate his valet Biffens for not dismissing all morning visitors. Rather, he instantly pulled on his dressing gown and attended his mother in his sitting room.

In a few moments, her ladyship made her wishes known.

The request was startling enough, but that the countess was holding a common cat in her arms, and cooing to it between her words, was equally astounding. But naturally, the earl was quickly able to put all together.

"That animal is a gift from Miss Laurence, I collect?"

The countess was pleased to nod and introduce him. "Vinny—an abbreviation for vinaigrette, since she felt I would no longer need the offices of a reviver. And it is true I am much improved, but I shall be devastated again if I am left alone. That is why I need Merrie to remain with me, and I know she will not wish to do so if her family is in need. She has been reading and rereading a letter from her mother, and I know their circumstances are not prime. She spoke of wishing she could collect the leftovers from our Christmas table to send to Oxford."

"Oh, did she attempt that pathetic ploy on you as well?" And while his mother looked at him in confusion, the earl thought out this situation while walking around his room. The idea of Merrie living here with his mother was not what he would wish, he realized. Several material objections to that came to mind. First, that George would inevitably elect to remain at Moorsedge as well. And thus, without his own presence to bring everyone into an awareness of the absurdity of the connection, before many months, Miss Laurence would become his sister-in-law! And shortly she would bring her entire family to squat at Moorsedge. And then they should never be rid of the Laurences. It was his lordship's belief that once one engaged in a charitable act, there always popped up a dozen more cases in even more need of charity, until one was awash with the unwashed. No, thinking of others inevitably led to forgetting oneself, not to mention one's position.

"I feel we should . . . that is, it is incumbent on us to grant her family an annuity," Lady Warwick said with a deep breath, rushing to have it all said before her son could say nay. "Recollect, they are our relations, or at least connections, and one would give money even to a stranger at this time of year. And we'd be giving the dear child the relief of never having to worry about her family's welfare, so she could be free to be completely happy. She ought not have any burdens—that is like tying stones around the neck of a lark, and not permitting it to soar."

"I have no objections to an annuity," the earl began, and his mother was ready to exclaim in relief, when he turned his dark penetrating eyes on her and made an addition to that. "However, an annuity for her family is only part of the solution. For is it really best for the young lady to remain here with you? What future do you see for her? That of being your lifelong companion? Or did you have some idea of her marrying?"

Her ladyship flushed.

"If you have Georgie in mind, I request that you not throw away his life on a family so clearly beneath us. And it is hardly fair to him. He has not had a chance to see other ladies of his own age. A chance to grow and expand. Perhaps he might not wish to be burdened down so immediately."

"Merrie could never be a burden to anyone. She would only add joy to whomever was fortunate enough to win her hand."

"Perhaps. *We* might see her as charming—now under the influence of Christmas and her Christmas spirit. But once out of this specialized background, we might very well find her sadly common. Actually, I have promised her I shall find her a husband who is suitable, and I believe that course is best all around."

The effect of his remark on the countess astounded the earl. Instantly she cried out and raced to embrace him. Having forgotten the kitten was in her arms, it too fell upon him and was running across his shoulders as his mother plastered his face with kisses.

Really, this was becoming an outrageous habit! One had relented in regard to the mistletoe, but so much embracing for a gentleman of his decorum was not to be endured.

And then, as she moved away and began speaking, he realized with a shock that the kissing had been the least offensive reaction.

"I am so overcome!" the countess was gushing. "But of course I knew you were not the uncaring gentleman you've been affecting. Your solution is exactly what I've been secretly wishing. For myself as well. And for dear Merrie, she has made it clear she did not feel Georgie would be the correct husband for her. And I do want her to be happily married. Yet whom could I find here in Yorkshire? And then, you—dear, dear boy—have instantly shown us the only way. Unquestionably the solution for her and for me and George is to come to London with you. And there under both our auspices, Merrie can have a season. Ah, gracious me, it has been so many years since I've been there. To be actually going there again! But what else could I expect of my firstborn, whom I so labored to bring into this world? And now, now, you are making every pain worthwhile!"

To such a statement, the earl could hardly inform her that his idea had been to find some suitable gentleman and bring him to Miss Laurence's home at Oxford. He opened his mouth, but naught came out. In contrast the words were still running freely from the countess as she was now recollecting, with much flutterings and deep sighs, her own first season.

"Such attentions as not to be believed! Such gentlemen of style and consideration! Your father was just one of my beaux. Unfortunately he was the one chosen by my father. But now I shall go to London again and relive all those delights through Merrie. Clearly you have some of *my* family in you, after all, and are not completely the cold, uncaring man your father was . . . eh, I mean, the formal man. And to think I'd despaired of finding a warm heart within you. But Christmas has shown me my mistake, and I shall ever love it for giving me back my son . . . my child."

Still his lordship was speechless. Hence, obligingly, Lady Warwick summed up their conversation. "And so we are agreed, then. We all go to London, where you shall find Merrie the perfect mate. Are you to divulge the joyous news to her? Or shall I?"

"My dear mother, I am not certain that I . . ."

"Indeed, you are not certain how to tell her. I shall do it for you. Ah, I understand now, this offer is your Christmas gift to her and to me. None could be more loving. . . ."

Thus, it was decided. Hardly could the earl alter any of those plans at this juncture, not without disabusing her of the belief that he possessed the generous nature she was ascribing to him. After all, she was his mother, and he wished her to think highly of him, he realized with surprise. And then too, it was not so dashed unpleasant a solution. For actually it was his idea, so it had to be correct. He'd wished Miss Laurence married to someone other than George; and as head of the family, he should probably have had to support the couple, as he was going to have to support her family. Therefore, would it not be best to find her someone financially flush enough to take over some of that responsibility from him? And he could not but admit that taking Miss Laurence back to London with him would have some interest. Certainly it would help diminish his growing preoccupation with the lady. For here in a Christmas haze, Miss Laurence seemed to predominate. But in a social setting, her inferiority would clearly be demonstrated. And further, he was not averse to Miss Laurence viewing him in his milieu where everybody was all admiration. For nothing else could so effectively demonstrate how much he'd condescended by toying with her this fortnight.

Having arranged all to his satisfaction, his lordship actually sat down and wrote out a draft for the first year's annuity for the Laurence family, promising his mother that his solicitors would arrange all the details. So excited was the countess at the amount of the draft in hand, that she scarcely knew the way out to her own chamber. Indeed, so flummoxed was she that Vinny was forgotten behind.

Spotting the white fluff at his feet, the earl emitted an oath. Immediately he scooped up the animal and rushed to the door, calling after her ladyship. She was gone. During that abrupt elevation, the kitten had promptly relieved itself all over his lordship's first-stare dressing gown.

"It needed only that!" the earl exclaimed. Dropping the culprit, the outraged lord called for his valet, who immediately brought a fresh wrapper.

"What is to be done with the animal, your lordship?" Biffens asked a few minutes later. "He is scratching at your dressing room door."

With a long-suffering air, the earl opened the door. Joyously the kitten ran up his boots, dulling them, after all of Biffens's efforts to perfect their shine. "You are overstepping yourself," the earl whispered to the mewing thing. "Are you under the impression that I have become your mother?"

Biffens choked back a laugh that was silenced by a scowl from the earl. And then with some satisfaction, the earl ordered, "Biffens, you are to have the happy opportunity of returning the animal to my mother, with my compliments. Everyone is grossly mistaking my nature of a sudden. There is a limit to the amount of common things I intend to take under my wing . . . eh, protection."

And as Biffens rushed off with the mewing animal, the earl walked a pace. "Confound Christmas for having gotten me into this bumble broth!" he exclaimed. "And thank heavens it only occurs once a year!"

Unaware of all the plans for her future, Merrie was rushing about completing her own plans for Christmas Day. She checked first in the dining room and had the relief of noting that the Yule log was still blazing. Last night it had been brought in with much ceremony by Walters and staff and placed in the grate and lit, as required, with a brand of last year's log. There was many a superstition about the Yule log. The one prohibition, never to be challenged, was having a squinting person present while the log was being lit. Naught could be more ill-omened. Merrie had whispered the injunction to George, who naturally squinted through the ceremony, having her shaking her head at him and his mother concerned that he was developing a sty.

But despite that, the log was still glowing this morning, which boded well for a joyous holiday. That was immediately proven when her ladyship, in high gig, took Merrie aside to relay her breathless news. Merrie could not have been more astounded. The annuity for her family left her in wonder. All credit was of course given to her ladyship. So profuse was her gratitude that her ladyship had to share some glory with her son, for he had decided the lavish amount, and further, his was the proposal for the season in London with Lady Warwick as her companion.

"But surely his lordship would not want me there," Merrie cried out. And while the countess was assuring her the earl was most eager, Merrie recollected him saying something about finding her a husband, and although wondering at it, she at last believed. "Probably he wishes to separate me from his brother," Merrie concluded, but here too her ladyship assured her that George would be accompanying them—that he, in effect, was to have a season as well.

"Ah, that begins to make sense. He wishes George to meet a better class of lady, so that my charms will not seem so special to him, I expect."

Her ladyship was honest enough to admit that she felt that was part of the reasoning, but was not that Merrie's wish herself? Did she not say that George should meet younger ladies?

"Yes, indeed," Merrie said, but stopped to cogitate a moment. She had her own plans for George and began posthaste to put them in operation. "Speaking of younger ladies, do you think the earl would mind if I invited Esther to come along? For while I should certainly need no companionship better than yours, some accompaniment would be desirable for the afternoon outings when you needs must rest. Despite your new strength, you are basically delicate and should conserve your energies."

Her ladyship eagerly acknowledged herself the height of delicacy, and that a younger miss would not be amiss to spell her in their outings. "We shall just bring her along," the countess decided. "And once she is there, Brett will adjust to her, I expect."

Delightedly Merrie agreed to that inspired tactic and rushed to write a joyous letter home that would include the overwhelming evidence of their newfound financial security. Her heart was pounding at the thought of all her dear ones' faces upon viewing the amount. How she wished she could be there! Certainly Esther and her mother would see the relief of it. Mr. Laurence would probably be too preoccupied to grasp the benefit. Yet he would soon feel it, for he could engage a scrivener, shortly to be needed upon losing both his secretary–daughters. And more immediately, for all the Laurences, the sum would provide a New Year's goose in compensation for their lack of one on Christmas Day. Ah, was she not correct always to believe Christmas was the most miraculous time? How else to explain the wonder of the earl's total transformation into a good angel?

The seraphic earl himself was at that moment approaching. Catching sight of the cause of her great joy, Merrie threw herself into the astonished earl's arms and gave him the soundest Christmas hug.

When she stepped back, still abubble with her gratitude, she said, "You have given my parents such a happy Christmas . . . you are really the spirit of goodness to me and mine!"

Embarrassed that she had taken it as such and yet moved, his lordship frowned. "My dear Miss Laurence, recollect! 'Tis not a gift. Rather an *agreement*. All is granted you on the understanding that you are to discourage George and to allow him the freedom to find another lady. Further, once we are in London, you are to allow me to make certain changes in your appearance before I introduce you around."

Merrie's face of joy fell. "What changes?" she asked suspiciously.

"Your clothes and manners are a disgrace! As you transformed Moorsedge for the holidays, I shall henceforth transform you for society . . . into a *lady*. And that means you are not to throw yourself into a gentleman's arms. Regardless of the incentive."

Merrie thought a bit. "Very well. I shan't throw myself into your arms. I shall keep you at a distance."

"That is not what I meant exactly," he interposed. "I mean you are to behave like a lady in London. Toward all gentlemen. That includes George. Lady Jane might very well be your model," he concluded.

Merrie stared at him aghast.

Frowning at that, he continued. "She is the epitome of a lady. While one can be freer here, in London there are definitely more restrictions."

"I shall be so stiff you will have to bend me to seat me at table," she said, but it was the way she said it that made the earl despair. She whispered the entire sentence, and then giggled as he had to lean close to hear. "How's that?" she ended in her normal voice, and he jumped back.

"You are incorrigible! I shall rue it," he said.

But Merrie was quick to assure him that she would be unexceptionable. But before their London stultification, here for one last day, they must all be free and filled with the joy of the season. "And that includes you, my lord. You are ordered for Christmas, at least, to allow the man in you to overcome the lord."

Smiling at that proviso, the earl allowed that he was looking forward to doing so, and she had best be on the lookout for it!

At which point he took a step toward her. There was something in his eyes that had even Merrie's thoughts veering from the glee of Christmas into a shockingly indelicate bypath. Reaching over, his lordship casually touched her bottom lip with his extended finger. "Your lip is trembling. From fear? Worry? Anticipation? Desire?"

Merrie felt the pressure of his finger sealing her lips, and as he named those emotions, she felt every one of them. And then he smiled and released her lip, putting that finger under her chin and lifting it close to him as he bent down, closer . . . closer. . . .

"I say, where's the mistletoe?" Sir Oswald interrupted, eager to have a kiss himself.

"There is none. The lady and I were just about to seal a bargain," he said smoothly. And as the rest of the company entered, he abruptly remembered himself and quickly reported to Lady Jane's side, escorting her to a chair.

George positioned himself faithfully at Merrie's side, anxious to be close when she opened his gift, for it was time for the presents to be shown. The table was filled to toppling with them. And everyone was chattering and laughing, allowing the child inside to take charge, as wrappings were torn open and exclamations and thanks were given around. George was well pleased at her image of Bruiser and would have left to bring him to view his reflection, or a close relation thereof, if he had not first wished to see Miss Laurence's reaction to his gift. Assuming a jest, she received jewelry. It was the most ornate and most expensive and most tasteless golden and diamond brooch she'd ever seen. In despair at hurting his feelings and worrying that she should not accept it, she turned to the countess with imploring eyes.

"It is a family gift, and as such may be accepted," her ladyship pronounced, and Merrie smiled her thanks to George, while attempting not to observe the earl's reaction. But she could not resist a peep at him, which revealed not only a frown but a glower.

She shrugged as if to say, she could not do less than accept it, while he turned away, as if in disinterest. But actually his lordship felt the gifting of a family heirloom proved how correct he'd been in the need to separate George and Merrie. And feeling Miss Laurence had received more than her share, he decided against giving her his special fan, after all. Up to that moment he'd been uncertain which of the ladies to honor with it. Miss Prichard's turn came and he easily chose one of the lesser fans, with which she was nevertheless most delighted. Lady Jane and Miss Prichard had both received Merrie's old fans from the attic. Miss Prichard had been kind enough to say, "Lovely . . . antique?" But Lady Jane had merely put it back in the wrapping as if it were indeed part of the debris, and gone on with her next gift. Humiliated, Merrie had blushed and attempted not to mind.

But Lady Jane demonstrated quite a different reaction to quite a different fan when she opened her gift from the earl. Not only did it single her out for special attention, but the fan itself was an object of monstrous specialty. The pale pink lace on it was of such delicacy it seemed made of blushing cobwebs. Her satisfaction was obvious as she ran to show it to her mother, who approved with an august nod.

"It is Titania's fan," Merrie exclaimed, agog.

"Certainly not," Lady Jane whispered. "Not everybody gives leavings."

"I meant . . ." Merrie began, and then was stilled.

The earl felt a stab of regret that he had chosen Lady Jane for the gift, after all. For he himself had thought it looked like something the queen of fairies would have worn, and strangely, it was too magical, too pulsing to be happy in Lady Jane's hands. She waved it and waved it, and with each gesture it lost some magic. And then he watched Merrie quietly going through the abandoned wrappings and finding the old fan that Lady Jane had discarded and taking it as her own.

Touching the faded lace and gently fluttering it, the discarded fan took on a fairy's sweep as the green eyes of the lady above glowed and glowed.

Catching Brett's eyes on her, Merrie quickly closed the fan, but was reminded that she had not given him her gift and graciously handed the earl her father's tome. His reaction surprised her, for rather than just an indifferent nod, he looked the volume over with some interest and made her blink with the comment that he had read her father's other books and would read this one with pleasure as well.

"You read?" she said, that comment escaping from her ere she had time to censor it.

"You think I am an illiterate?" he taunted.

"No, that is, I meant, I thought most lords did not concern themselves with more than their social life. And yet you have a rather excellent library. Your father's?"

"Again you undervalue me. Compiling it was my very first act upon coming into my authority."

Merrie's estimation of him jumped several notches. "The collection is first oars," she said. "Not just the works of Scott and Byron now being generally read, but the Greek classics, including an edition of *Medea* my father has long despaired of finding. And all of Shakespeare, no less!"

"Monstrous deep, ain't I?" his lordship mocked, putting on the exaggerated airs of a society fop. "Stab me, even been to that fella's plays, and stayed awake, oddsblood—to the gory ends."

Merrie was laughing and begging pardon for so belittling him, when she stopped midword and gasped. "Oh my stars! Does that mean *we* shall see a Shakespeare play in London? *Hamlet? Macbeth? The Tempest?*"

He assured her these wonders indeed were in store, and further, if Kean were playing, he should take her to Drury Lane not only to see him perform, but to introduce her to the actor. She looked at him as if he were Merlin and could perform the greatest feats of magic, her eyes almost tearing at these promised pleasures. Brett could not resist smiling and beginning to anticipate the London season himself.

When it came time for Merrie to open his lordship's gift, although demurring that she'd already received the most spectacular present possible—the promise of seeing Kean in Shakespeare—still she tore open the wrappings with great zest.

It was a peasant's straw hat. One look and she cried out in pure pleasure—not the chagrin the earl had expected from his jest. He'd bought it to taunt her for her predilection for hats and to remind her of her peasant standing. But she saw it as just a hat, and a new one at that, and was grateful.

In fact, Merrie immediately placed it on her head, and rather than making her look like a country miss, the wide straw brim above her glowing face and around the golden red of her hair took on a fashion plate's dash.

So much for its derogatory intent. She'd defanged his gift as she'd depeasantized the hat—just by her joy in both. And the earl rather preferred that she had not seen the affront; for, upon reflection, he wished her to be completely happy on this day.

Even more did he regret the country hat when Miss Laurence wore it subsequently during the ladies' constitutional in the garden. Lady Jane and her mother exchanged barely concealed glances of amusement, and even asked loudly if the cows were soon to be milked.

Yet Merrie did not react to that—either not understanding the linking with her hat or refusing to give either the ladies or himself the satisfaction of her understanding. But the earl felt the humiliation of the gibe and was himself insulted, and thought less of them and more of Merrie, as she paraded around the stone-walled garden, waving her mended fan and proudly modeling her brand-new Christmas hat.

11

The pinnacle of the celebration was Christmas dinner. The guests were ushered in by footmen whose livery was made festive with greenery. Merrie had even found a red carpet in the attic that served for the company's parading into the dining room, where the table was resplendent with polished silver plate. But most spectacular was the display on the sideboard of every bit of Warwick silver unearthed from chests and brought to a prime polish. There were flagons, cups, beakers, goblets, ewers, and even more impressive, the full shining helmet of the great Crusader himself, the first earl of Warwick. Two Yule candles, decorated with holly, balanced the spread. And in the corner, seated on a small stool, was a grinning old man holding a small harp and stroking out Christmas tunes for the guests' entrance.

Everyone sat down with pleasant smiles on their faces that holidays call out, looking about approvingly at each other. The ladies, except Merrie, were in prime finery. Lady Jane wore white crepe and a single strand of perfect pearls. Her blond hair in its usual severe topknot was softened by several ringlets, and she looked rather like a Christmas angel. Miss Prichard had a pink gown with a ruffle, and she was perky and pretty and prepared to enjoy both feast and festivities. Lady Warwick was dressed in her best blue satin and Lady Dansville was impressive in a cinnamon silk gown with several rows of pearls. Only Merrie was dressed, as every evening, in her outmoded cream twill, but that was made somewhat festive by threading ivy around the bodice, secured tonight by the diamond brooch given her by George, who noticed it with approval. Never having worn jewelry before, Merrie felt herself rather grand, but the main reason for her smile was the anticipation of the after-dinner entertainment she'd planned down to each carol.

The earl and the other gentlemen had honored the occasion by changing into formal fashion. The earl had even deigned to display his most imitated cravat, *coeur d'amour*. It flowed from his strong neck in an exuberant but precise eruption and had a ruby stickpin in the center to depict a heart.

At the countess's tinkling of the bell, the butler entered in the lead, followed by a retinue of servants carrying dishes on silver trays. Roast beef rare for one end of table, roast beef well done at the other. And in between a chorus of pies. The favorite, mince pie, showed in a goodly number, as well as veal and ham pie, but the most applauded was peacock pie, authentically decorated with its own feathers. A leg of mutton appeared for those of simpler tastes. And in encore: frumenty, or wheat boiled in sweetened milk and richly spiced, served the night before for Christmas Eve and specifically requested by Sir Oswald and George. On every spare space on the table were golden oranges and brown nuts and jellies and even little cakes. Finally the high point of the holiday feast for many: enter the plum pudding. When Walters set the pudding afire, Merrie could not resist, as at home, clapping her hands. George and Lady Warwick laughed fondly, but the rest of the guests sent her disapproving looks, as if she had overturned her glass, and she was squelched into silence.

Rather than good tales of happy Christmases past, as was the pattern at home, or her father telling the history of every tradition, the conversation here remained as usual. Lord Dansville took the lead with personal reminiscences. Sir Oswald, socially adept, between munches added compliments on the spread. That called to his own mind the most delicious dish he'd ever eaten—would they believe he'd discovered it during a hike through the Lake District upon his stopping at a cottage. It was tripe—and never was a humble meal offered him with more pride.

"Indeed," Lady Dansville inserted, and looked so vindicated she could hardly swallow. It soon became clear that she'd often said that peasants were in a great deal better state than they pretended. Especially in London, where the underclass always went about with hands held out. Especially at this season. "One has to hear them sing and give them sixpence or not be allowed to pass. As if one would wish to have Christmas degraded by their voices."

Merrie blanched, mentally canceling her plan for the staff's joining the caroling.

"There is much in what you say, my dear," her husband agreed. "One must put it down, all this cant in vogue about hovels and children in need. Put it down and keep the peasantry down. Somehow they survive, don't they? One always sees more and more of them about."

Suddenly, in a pure clear voice, Merrie sang the last chorus of *Good King Wenceslas*. " 'Therefore, Christian men, be sure, Wealth or rank possessing, Ye who now will bless the poor, Shall yourselves find blessing.' "

There was a moment of shock while Merrie matter-of-factly continued eating as if she had never sung. The rest continued dining as well, regally pretending that Merrie had just been inspired by the season to carol, and had no other reference. But the harper took that as a cue and played the carol throughout, finishing with a flourish of chords, fingers moving like lightning, showing Lady Jane's sluggish strokes on her grand harp to be totally amateur.

Lady Warwick took the occasion to relate her husband's always having this very same harper for all occasions. The harper responded by playing the late earl's favorite carol, at which the countess nodded, remembering that she knew there was a reason she disliked that particular one.

Naught else was said till the forks were put down and Walters removed the cloth. He was quickly followed by a footman carrying a huge silver bowl of exquisite workmanship. That elicited cries of approval. The wassail bowl was placed directly before the earl. Walters bowed and waited. The guests waited. This was the moment when the head of the household would rise and make a speech. The wassail was mixed of wines sweetened and spiced, and within, roasted apples bobbed merrily.

Scooping up a silver cupful for his official taste, the earl brought it to lip. The brew was excessively hearty and reviving. Lord Warwick signaled his approval and wished all to partake and to partake of the joyousness of the season. In reply everyone cried out: "wassail, wassail, wassail!"

And then the harper began the wassail song, accompanied in voice by the two balladeers at his side. After one chorus, Merrie signaled that they were all to join in the salute, and she and George stood up and

sang along, joined by Sir Oswald, Miss Prichard, and
Lady Warwick. The earl made it official when he nodded and sang as well, so the rest of the company stood
and added their voices. The chorus was simple
enough for all to follow:

> The brown bowle,
> The merry brown bowle,
> As it goes round about-a,
> Fill
> Still,
> Let the world say what it will,
> And drink your fill all out-a.

Silver cups were passed around. Each person, Merrie announced, must make his toast. It had previously
been the custom for everyone to drink of the same
cup, but now only those who wished to share need do
so. But each must give the table a toast and drink
their wassail down.

And so it went. Good health was proposed. And
Sir Oswald spoke of a good dame for all worthy gentlemen, and that was well applauded and drunk to.
And Lady Warwick made a gracious welcome to all
her guests that was much approved and also much
drunk to. Lady Jane, after two cups, was heard to
speak: "Honor to the Warwicks!" And the earl bowed
to her. Merrie wished all their most secret hope's ful-
fillment. To which George chanted, "Hear, Hear!"

The arrival of the wassail bowl had brought much
hilarity, although the conversation was not noticeably
wittier, just that the listeners were less critical. Everyone seemed to catch the contagion of happiness, and
when the ladies retired, the gentlemen had some
rather racy jokes to tell that would have not only
shocked the departed females but themselves as well
on soberer days. College pranks were recalled and

George claimed that his brother was renowned at Oxford for his having climbed a bell tower and rung it on Christmas Eve. And Brett remembered it with glee and was laughing. His usual haughty eyes were soft, and he was floating in the enjoyment of the moment.

When the gentlemen joined the ladies, they were all well primed for fun and frolic. And that was what Merrie and George had planned. Immediately George was declared Lord of Misrule, whose every whim had to be obeyed. Donning an Elizabethan ruff and cape, he was officially crowned by Merrie with a wreath. In return, he appointed her Lady Misrule and Merrie departed to dress her part.

George's first order was to Miss Prichard: she was to dance with Sir Oswald. And both were nothing loath. Following, there was an edict for Lady Warwick to sing her favorite carol, and she laughingly obliged. By then Merrie had returned, accompanied by a footman carrying piles of clothes. From that collection of ancient costumes found in the attics, Merrie had chosen her own green velvet gown. It had a wide skirt which showed her small waist and a plunging bodice, which showed her full breasts. But most spectacular was her headdress, a fan-spread of peacock feathers that framed her blazing hair and accented her white face and red lips to the point that the gentlemen could not refrain from rapt attention.

Immediately George used his power as lord to order that she must embody her costume by joining him in a slow dance called Pavon. At the soft strumming string sounds, the two costumed dancers appeared like specters from another time, slowly stepping to the music before the blazing Yule log. Except that George kept missing the steps. Irritated at his brother's ruining the performance, Brett pushed George aside and led Lady Misrule through the paces. His eyes could not stop feasting on her. For she seemed, indeed, to be a queen of this night, moving with the grace and beauty of a peacock, as with her every swaying move, her peacock-feathered crown bowed a blessing of bliss on all observers. And the two dancers, in the formality of the ancient pattern, touching only by fingertips, yet coming closer with each measured step— tantalizing themselves and the onlookers in their continual parting and coming together, parting and coming together. And then not quite together, after all, by their stepping around each other, weaving a spell of motion linked by everyone's riveted eyes, but mostly increasingly, unblinkingly by the jointure of their own.

When the dance was concluded, the couple from the past came back to the present, bestirring themselves to recollect where they were, and allowed their hands and eyes to part.

Annoyed, Lady Dansville claimed their version of the dance was not fitting. Certainly she did not recollect such a sensuous performance in society. George explained the movements were not meant to be seductive but rather reminiscent of the stately strut of a peacock. Looking significantly at Merrie, he added that all beautiful things reminded one of peacocks. This was not the direction Lady Dansville wished the conversation to go. She was about to further protest, when George, as Lord of Misrule ended the discussion by ordering that the costumes be brought forth.

Miss Prichard was chosen first and draped in a brown cloak, handed a chunk of pie, and announced as Miss Mince Pie. That set her off into an uproarious laugh, and obeying the instructions, with not the smallest hesitation, she fed all the gentlemen directly into their open mouths. When the pie was gone, Sir Oswald was feeding on her fingers, and still she was laughing, feeling herself quite a mincing miss of mincemeat. Meanwhile George had found a sword and was dubbing everyone with their misnomers. Lord Dansville was pronounced Lord Wit. Lady Tart was given to Lady Pauley who had come down for a few moments of Christmas cheer and to complain of the noise. She was given a drink of wassail and that quieted her. And more wassail was passed around as the dancing continued. Faster and faster reels were performed. And then the games began. For Blindman's buff Sir Oswald was blindfolded and tickled by long straws as he searched for a lady to embrace and found Miss Prichard by peeking above the narrow blindfold. George was looking about to select the next blindman, as Miss Prichard and Sir Oswald were too occupied to continue, when surprisingly, Brett put down his wassail cup with a bang and announced that he was "it." He would bluff them all, egad!

The colors seemed to reach out from the room and warm themselves around the earl as he approached. The red of the fire and the holly berries and the greenery everywhere—'twas like a second spring in the house, plants and growth and people laughing. He recollected spring at Moorsedge, as the blindfold closed all from sight, and he was, in mind, back on the moors, a lord chasing a maid from one of the farms through the heather and catching her.

Love, love, love was flowing through the room and over him, as three lovely maidens were waiting for him to choose one. Miss Prichard obligingly stood directly in his lordship's path; but she'd already been caught by Sir Oswald and he, as lord of the manor, did not want second helpings. He was to be served up the first taste, egad! Droit du seigneur! And there stood the serene and stunning Lady Jane, the epitome of everything he had been valuing all his life: calm, controlled, and terribly civilized. But that was the rub, he did not feel dashed civilized tonight.

Rather he felt a wild man with all the wassail roaring in his veins and egging him on as he stumbled through his cheering guests. A voice was telling him which way to go—this way, that way, but his prey was hiding from him.

He stopped to get his bearings. There was a smell of the burning log and scented candles and the sound of a jig as the harper kept at it. But the voice drew him out of his drawing room and caused him to tear off his blindfold and his high cravat, and position himself directly beneath the first earl's portrait in full armor. Ah, if he had that armor he could really charge about. He could, by gad, take all three women up to the tower room and have his choice of them.

But he did not really want all three. He wanted one. And she was ducking behind his mother and behind George, not wishing to be caught. He would have to knock them down to reach the blasted minx! And the first earl was laughing at him for allowing such minor obstacles to dissuade him.

He was a descendant of that wild earl, was he not? He would find the woman he wanted, if he had to throw out of the tower window everyone else who stood in his way!

The first earl was laughing and taunting. And Brett, needing to join with his ancestor in truth, went to the sideboard displaying the first earl's helmet and sword. He placed the helmet on his head, visor down, seeing sufficient through the slits, and took up the sword and marched back to the waiting festive gathering.

A stunned silence. Then, full applause greeted his transformation. Sir Oswald by-Joving all over the place. And his mother smiling in a motherly way. And Miss Prichard jumping up and down. And Lady Jane nodding at him silently.

The earl went toward Merrie, and raised the earl's

massive sword and swore allegiance on it to her as his lady. Then letting it clatter to the ground, his lordship took the beautiful lady into his arms, and they danced the rest of the reel. Eyeing her through his visor for several rounds, he was suddenly made more vulnerable by Miss Laurence calmly leaning over and raising it. And then, Merrie stood back. For as if she'd removed a shade from a light, the full blaze of his black eyes fell unshielded directly on her, and she had to call up all her strength not to blink his burning gaze away.

And the dancing continued: jigs and reels, that had them all whirling around. But the earl and his lady would not be parted, going from dance to dance in their own daze. And still the harper played, as the log crackled and the roomful of candles flickered, and the lords and ladies danced. And the harper was chuckling, quickening the pace yet, controlling them by his rapid fingers . . . faster yet, and faster still, until several of the ladies were feeling breathless and dizzy and even the gentlemen were gasping.

Lady Dansville walked up to the harper and silenced him with a stare. And the dancing stopped. There was a limit for decent English lords and ladies, and it had been reached. It was time to retire. A winded Lady Jane curtsied to Sir Oswald and followed her mother. Miss Prichard gave her partner George a reluctant smile as she left. The countess, having succumbed to Lord Dansville's request for a whirl, had revolved herself into a pleasant evening and was throwing wishes for a good night's sleep to all as she and the stragglers went up the stairs. Only the earl and Merrie and George remained. And finally Lord Warwick quietly removed his helmet. Merrie went into the kitchen to bid the staff good wishes and graciously give permission for their own festivities to carry on, while George gave coins for the New Year to the harper and balladeers.

And dash it, the earl was left mightily unsatisfied. He took another drink from the wassail bowl, and then, on the quiet, took a footman aside and bade him bring the wassail bowl and one cup to the tower room. Meanwhile George, reluctantly removing his ruff and cloak, said what a jolly Christmas this had been, and he spoke fondly to his brother about his appointment of Miss Laurence, who had turned it all into a magic time. And he spoke of his gratitude for Brett's inviting them to London, concluding, "So there's that for us all to look forward to. And, Brett, would you sponsor me for the Four-Horse Club? I'm not the top sawyer you are, but a dashed good driver."

Scarcely in the mood for such a topic, Lord Warwick felt like roaring through his hall, and yet he had to stand there discussing qualifications. Soon George was assured that his brother would do all he could for him, and he smiled like a satisfied child and called to Bruiser, who was gnawing on a Christmas bone, as dog and owner retired to a well-earned sleep.

Alone, Brett walked in and out of several rooms, looking for something . . . or someone.

She was just leaving the servants' hall, carrying a candle to make her way up the stairs. Merrie had not removed the peacock crown. The candle adding a glowing outline about her gave the illusion that a lady from the past was approaching, in search of her lover. And that lover was he. The knowledge seared through him: he was the first earl and she his chosen lady, and almost in a rush, he approached the lady. Her green eyes were emerald as she stared quizzically at him. And he drank in every detail of her. The peacock crown made Miss Laurence into more than a mere lady, but rather a queen, the queen of his castle. And he put out a hand to her, not wanting to speak and break the spell.

She gave him her hand, and curtsied her good-night, turning up the stairs. In a few steps, he caught her around her small waist.

Merrie pulled away and calmly instructed the earl that the festivities were over. "No more masquing and mummery. It is all concluded. Tomorrow we return to the reality of our lives, and the guests' departures."

The earl did not answer.

She continued up the stairs, and he simply followed behind like a silent shadow. Merrie increased her pace. When the staid lord had appeared with the helmet, she had assumed he was slightly over-wassailed, but by now she hoped he'd begun to come to himself. Yet the closeness of his steps to hers made her leery. At the landing, she was turning toward her room when he finally spoke.

"There is one more ceremony that has to be performed before the night is over," he said softly but with an intensity that made her heart jump.

"We have finished the festivities," she said, stepping away.

"There is *one* more," he insisted.

"And what is that?" Perhaps there was a final observance she should not omit, a procedure handed down from his ancestors. And then the thought of his ancestor the first earl, and his wearing the helmet, caused Merrie to catch her breath. But in the next moment, he told her.

"We must go to the tower room."

"No. No, indeed. If you wish someone to accompany you there, wake up Lady Jane. I am heading for my chamber."

"You are the organizer of all these festivities. You cannot leave it incomplete."

"It is complete. Christmas is over."

"We must drink its demise over a wassail cup together. From the *same* wassail cup, as you said—otherwise this Christmas will be . . . ill omened."

He was pulling her toward the tower stairs, and she was pulling away.

"We completed the ceremony of the wassail bowl, and it is safely in the kitchens."

"Ah, but it is not. It awaits us in the tower room. And one lone silver cup to drink the last toast."

For a moment, as the warmth of the singing and celebrating was still coursing through her body, Merrie wished to run up the stairs with him and drink another toast. But the burning coal of his eyes, as if one could light another Yule log from it, made her aware that he was too much afire. And she feared catching it, and she feared that if she were with him a second more, they would both blaze together. And she stepped back from him, the searing source. But he took her hand, and the warmth leaped into her again, up through their hands and into her own heart, and though she recoiled, she could not resist basking in it awhile, as he led her up the tower stairs. She felt herself rising without effort of her own, almost floating over each step, reaching the threshold of a narrow stone-walled room, and being pulled over and into it. The casement through which the ladies had jumped or been thrown caught her attention, for it was partially open, and she could not help but walk directly toward it.

A metallic sound made her turn, only to see the earl at the door, viewing her with extreme satisfaction. And shaking her head in bewilderment, she could not understand how she'd come up there.

"I willed you here," the earl answered with a soft laugh. "But *you*, as well, willed to come, for we both know we must always be together." And then nodding, he announced, "And now, on to our ceremony!" And he went eagerly toward the wassail bowl, filled the cup, and handed it to her. Obediently she drank it. And he took the cup and drank from the same spot, finishing it off. And filled another.

"I drink to you, Peacock Lady. Are you an Elizabethan ghost of joyous pleasures past?" he asked, becoming more and more exhilarated. But as she did not respond, he answered for her. "Yes, you are. I know you are, and I am no longer the present earl of Warwick, but the first earl, and I have brought you here to my tower room so we may drink to *us*—drink to combining our past and present in one . . . as we become one."

He tossed the cup down at that and laughed, and the lady stepped back slightly. Blinking, he peered closer, for she seemed to be floating away, disappearing into the shadows. Doggedly, he neared to keep the Peacock Lady before him. No longer was she Merrie, with her usual pixie smile that willfully led him about. Nay, before him stood the queen of his heart with a message for him from the past, and he bent toward her trembling lips to hear it, whereupon he sensed those lips needed comfort to stop trembling, needed to be gently covered over by his own.

And softly he did so. And then continued kissing at either edge of her lips, attempting to make the sides lift into a smile, for he wanted her happy and laughing in his arms, for she was, he swore, the lady of his heart, come to him on Christmas Day as his own, and he said the words easily to her then.

"My lady, I bow to you." But he did more, he actually got down on his knees. "I make confession of my abiding love for you. I have watched ere you first came to my castle and known you were mine, and my heart cried that I could not claim you. Lifetimes come and go, and there is only one love for two souls like ours, and we must claim it while we have the chance. For neither generations of men to come, nor those past, nor present, could love you through all their lives as much as I do in a single moment. This moment that is ours."

Joy filled Merrie to the brim of her soul at that declaration. And smile she did, and put out her hands toward him to raise him up. But as he rose the two candles in the tower room went out in a breeze from the casement, and heavy shadows separated them. A sensation struck Merrie that a third person was there. The lantern Brett had brought up with them was still lit, and she went to it and lifted it higher.

Around the room, she saw naught but the long-ago whitewashed stone walls, one worn tapestry, a bed . . . and Brett. He took the lantern from her hand and placed it carelessly on the floor, next to them, leaving them lit, but the rest of the room in darkened shadows. Merrie was aware of the rest of the room, but his lordship was not, he was concentrating only on her. Now his hands were slowly going up and down her green-velvet-clad arms, as if in comfort, but really to pull her toward him. And he was whispering, "Look at me, my love."

She met his eyes then and forgot the room, and felt herself flowing toward him again, and he brought her into the comfort and warmth of his arms, lifting her, and putting her down on the bed. Their kiss was an acknowledgment of a month of passion—passion denied, passion refused, but yet passion that would not finally be shoved aside. And there he kissed from her mouth across her face, up to even the eyelids of the eyes that bewitched him—her witch's eyes, he said, wishing he could step behind those eyes, so their joining would be total. He locked his mouth on hers, the two sharing one breath, as if they had grown together and henceforth had to breathe and live and love as one. And he claimed her with kiss after kiss.

Then as from a distance, between each kiss, she heard a chanting, "Merrie, Merrie, Merrie." That murmuring entered into the lady's consciousness slowly, seeping, bringing back other times her name had been called. Her mother saying, "Merrie, my dear child," and her father saying, "Merrie, my love," and she abruptly came to her senses.

Forcing down the tumult within her, she turned away from the heat of him and pulled herself, as if from the bottom of a fiery pit, up, up off the bed, and standing up, she gasped and groped her way toward the door.

It was bolted. He had done so on their entrance. That was the sound she'd heard. Thoroughly shaken out of all emotion but surprise, Merrie faced him coming after—faced him with a look of a child just slapped.

That expression of betrayal reached through the fog of his senses, and he wanted to apologize and let her out, but dear God, he knew himself enough to know he could never let her go again. Not now. Not for the life of him. And sadly, but with deep gulps of breath, he shook his head.

She attempted once more to lift the bolt and could not. And she rested against the door, head down, as if in submission or helplessness, letting him reach her, touch her, but then, at that moment, her head went up and she cried out—a wrenching cry from the bottom of her heart.

But the cry was not directed at him; rather her entire attention was focused past his lordship's shoulder, past the lantern area of light, to the darkness beyond. And lifting up her hand to point, she was just able to do so before being overcome by sobs and shudders of total terror.

12

Brett, his brain befuddled by drink and by his own emotions, which had never before so strongly possessed him, could not grasp what was happening to her. Following the direction of her finger, he saw naught but the half-open casement rattling from the high winds around the turret. Returning his glance to her, Merrie's stare was still riveted to the spot across the room with an unwavering focus that could not help but alarm. Once more he looked behind himself, and once more saw nothing but what he had seen before. And then she groaned and clutched herself in panic, continuing to shudder and stare. Then forcing more breath out of her stiffened lips, she cried softly, "Angels and ministers of grace defend us!"

At that he grabbed the shaking girl and demanded to be told what she saw, but she was not hearing him or feeling his restraint as she said softly, "It calls me," and then began walking by him into the dark, intent on a thing beyond. Cajoling now, the tone of her words clearly showed her desperation. "Be you a spirit of health or goblin damned . . . speak, I'll go no further."

Yet she took another small step forward and gasped, "It waves me forth again." And here Merrie quaked noticeably and half sobbing took another unwilling step closer to what she had fixed her eyes upon. "Still am I called! I'll follow it. . . ."

"What's this?" Brett exclaimed, sobering a bit, eyeing the enchanted lady walking toward the window—the very window from which the ladies of the first earl had fallen to their deaths. That thought came to him, and almost shook him back to his senses. One more moment of observing her gliding steps moving her toward destruction and Brett was completely roused and made a jump, landing in her path, a barrier to her next motion. "Stop," he demanded, attempting to get her attention, for she still looked fixedly over his head.

And then sobbing, she struggled intensely to release herself from his holding her back as her next words came, wrenched out of her. "My fate cries out and I must follow."

"No, blast it, *no!*" Brett said thickly, holding her back.

"Unhand me, gentleman!" she pleaded, and when he would not, cried out, "I'll make a ghost of him that lets me! I say, away! I *must* follow!"

And still gazing beyond, Merrie attempted one last time actually to throw herself toward the window, but Brett would not slacken his grasp, and now rather began shaking her out of the trance until her peacock feathers went flying, releasing her hair to flaunt about her.

"Merrie, darling, wake up. There's no one here but you and me."

Yet she continued to make gestures toward the window, but fainter and fainter; and next she whis-

pered, but this time, he noted with relief, to him.
"Take me out of this chamber, lest I succumb. I must
be out of here, or I am done for!" And she held on to
Brett's arm with all her might.

"By Jove, yes!" the befuddled earl exclaimed, and
led her toward the bolted door, and there quickly un-
handed her to pull back the bolt and throw open the
door with such vehemence that he fell down at her
feet.

Not pausing, Merrie skipped over him and scurried
out into the safety of the hall, where she stopped just
long enough to throw back a warning, "Do not remain long in there!" And then she was gone.

It took the groggy earl a moment more to rise and
go toward the open door, but Merrie was no longer
visible. He wondered whether she'd even been there,
as he dragged himself back across the tower room and
sat down heavily on the bed. The bowl of wassail was
still there. He took another swig and glanced around.
"Wassail," he said softly to the empty room. The window rattled a bit, as if in reply, and Brett said, "Blast
you," and fell across the bed into a deep sleep.

The earl awoke the following morning to find himself in the tower room. His eyes could see where he
was, but his brain could scarcely recollect coming
there. While moving about, he stumbled over the gob-
let still holding dregs of wassail, and he took a sip to
clear his mouth. The smell began to remind him of
events that had occurred on Christmas night. They
came at him like spigots of cold water, turning on and
off with dousing revelations. Had he really worn the
earl's helmet before all his guests and made a blasted
spectacle of himself!

Groaning, he tried to shake off more oncoming images. But they were inexorable. Visions of Miss Laurence—the two dancing, walking up the tower stairs

to this room, kissing, and then he alone at her feet, saying . . . what? He could not recall his words, but he was cringing enough at his actions.

Looking at the floor where he'd knelt, he saw several peacock feathers from her crown, scattered. Unable not to, he bent down to pick them up. Holding them, strong emanations came, but no picture. Rather they tickled his mind, feathers that they were, while he blankly, fixedly stared. Then wrung out from him was a thought, a logical conclusion: faith! If they were scattered about, someone had pulled them off her!

Dear God, he hoped he had not offered her an intolerable insult. If he had, he must make immediate reparations by offering himself in marriage. That last word stumbled in his mind, it being such a stranger there all these years. Yet if he had in any way offended her . . .

Taking another sip of wassail, Brett had a recollection of their sharing a further wassail toast up here. And that relieved him. That was anodyne to his worst fears. A convivial evening, after all, he assumed. And he went toward the door with a lighter step, when the door itself gave him pause—in his step and assumptions. It showed him Merrie struggling with the bolt. And he cursed. Cursed the door, and then himself. Confound it, he'd bolted the blasted door to keep her in. He remembered that distinctly. And there was worse remembering to come—the sound of her desperate voice imploring, "I must be out of here or I am done for!" The earl could just wince at that and hide his head in his hands. Had he dared that? And worse?

Before the worst image could assault him, Brett had pulled aside the accursed door and gone rushing down the tower stairs. In his haste, he missed a step and reached for balance to the banister, and saw that his hand still clutched the peacock feathers. That stopped him midstep to concentrate on them again.

And this time a clear memory clicked into place, of himself actually shaking the lady until the feathers had gone flying off her head. He sat on the step and shook his head, denying that possibility. Not he! A courtier would never have forced a lady into surrendering. It just wasn't done.

And yet the picture was there, unshakable. In dismay, he dropped the feathers on the last stair to the tower and went on the run toward the west wing where her room was situated. His lordship was about to knock and throw himself at her feet in apology, when he regained control of himself and stepped back, forcing himself with some semblance of his old hauteur to walk back to the east wing and his apartment.

He must completely recollect what had occurred before he came face to face with her, to know in what attitude he must present himself.

The only excuse for his behavior was that he was not himself. More than being jug bitten, or more accurately, wassail bitten. In truth, he had not been himself since first meeting Miss Laurence. She'd shaken him up and rearranged him indeed. For he never recollected, even as a lad, being beside himself with passion. Not with all his Cyprians and lightskirts, not with the many married ladies of his set had he so lost control—unless last night he'd blended with the ghost of the first earl who had loved women with such gusto that he needed three to appease his lust and desire. Yet in truth neither spirit nor excess of spirits could excuse him, he admitted at last.

Biffens came toward him to ask if he wished to be shaved and prepared for the day. He longed to refuse to do so, to allow his face to remain haggard and unshaven to reflect more accurately the turmoil within him, but he remembered that he had guests to escort to their coaches; he had servants and a younger brother to continue to set an example for. And so resolved, he allowed his toilette to begin.

After his morning ablutions and dressing for the day, the earl, to some small extent, felt the elegant lord of society again, prepared to face the day's challenge with some aplomb, including making reparations to the offended lady by offering her the ultimate sacrifice of marriage. She deserved no less; she would be expecting no less. Possibly had arranged for no less . . . egad!

That last thought skidded his heart-sinking to a stop.

Was she not the one who oversaw the mixing of such a powerful concoction in the wassail bowl? And was she not the one controlling it all—the dancing and the games? And had she not earlier been the one urging him on this one day to forget his title and act as a man? Indeed, further, was it not she who had originally come to Moorsedge to win a future of luxury and title? And she too it was who after capturing his brother relinquished him only upon spotting a more likely target—himself! It all fit. Her campaign was masterly. Every maneuver was calculated to subtly show him that the other two ladies invited were less appealing than she, by setting an unladylike agenda and games at which a true lady would be bound to fail, and she to shine. And by God, how she'd shone all last night!

Yet he must not be sidetracked by her blatant appeal. His only salvation was remembering how she'd led him to this point. Shortly, triumphantly, his lordship had recollected a welter of her deliberate acts of seduction since her arrival at Moorsedge. From coming to his rooms with a blazing crown of candles to racing with him on the moors and teasing him by pretending to be willing to come to the shepherd's hut

while intending to ride off, leaving him walking back
—smoking!

Actually, each time she looked at him she aroused
his senses, and then left him strung up, twisting in the
breeze. And then last night dressing in that Elizabethan gown to prove she was the most beautiful of all
the ladies, her beauty crowned by peacock feathers.
Blast her, what was a gentleman to do but seek her
out?

It was not enough he'd promised to find her a husband in society. She wanted the most important gentleman of society. Himself! He who'd eluded the most
exalted ladies of the ton, even a royal connection.
Lady Jersey had affectionately raked him down for
being so selective. "All the ladies fall for your charms,
my dear Brett, surely there must be one worthy of
you. Don't you think it's time to choose one and put
the rest of us out of our misery?"

He'd laughed with her, but felt that was pretty
much the case. Whatever young lady was chosen as
the season's most desirable, he was certain to win,
and then drop her and go on to the next lady. Ladies
once captured scarcely held any lasting charm. What
justice then that the prime catch of the ton must take
a young miss from the edge of poverty as his countess
—all because of a drunken night's spree? A lady without the smallest amount of social polish who would
undoubtedly disgrace him again and again.

And what would his companions say when despite
all the high expectations, he'd been caught by a commoner? There would be a prodigious amount of polite laughter behind his back, he had no doubt. Miss
Merrie Laurence was unquestionably beneath his
touch, yet the thought of touching her aroused him,
and could not be summarily dismissed, which brought
forth his greatest qualm—having to wed when he did
not even recall the act that led to this parson's trap.

But he was in her hands—and he must ask for her hand in marriage. He had no right to do less and still call himself a gentleman.

His mother had not yet arisen, nor had the other ladies, he was told by Walters as he entered the morning room.

"Am I the only one awake?" he asked, pretending casual unconcern.

"None of your guests are up, my lord. They have not rung."

"Nor, eh, my family. My mother? Or brother?"

"No, my lord."

The earl waited. Under what category would the butler place Miss Laurence, or was she in a class by herself?

He was forced to put it into words. "And Miss Laurence?"

"Ah, she has long been up and out."

"Dash it, man, must I drag every word out of you. Where the blazes is she?"

"Miss Laurence?"

"She!" his lordship said grimly, losing his patience completely, and rising from the table without having taken more than a bite. "Where the devil is she?"

"Riding, my lord."

And grumbling, his lordship went out and had Caliban saddled and went riding himself. The stable hands did not know in which direction she had ridden, and so Brett just rode about on the moors, immediately spotting her.

She was riding in a green velvet cape over her old pelisse. No other lady he'd ever seen could sit a horse as well. But then she walked with grace and danced with it, and last night . . .

Thoughts of that nature not being allowed until he'd come to terms with the lady, he reined them in and rode on.

At the sound of Caliban's hoofs, Merrie turned her horse in the other direction, making the earl even more determined to catch her, setting Caliban to a gallop.

Then at the last moment, Miss Laurence abruptly changed tactics and made a quick turn toward him. He was jolted by that, and by his realization as she rode directly to his side, that he had never seen a lady look so magnificent. Her hair was loose and flying up behind like a cape of fire, and the green cape was flying out as well, so that she seemed to be winged, not an earthly creature at all. Their horses were snorting as they came face to face.

Yet Miss Laurence's eyes were averted, causing the earl to surmise that she was already punishing him for unforgettable actions. Deuce take it! He didn't even remember what he had done.

"I came immediately to express my apologies for last night," he said stiffly, all along eyeing her anxiously, hoping for some clarification.

That caused Merrie to meet his glance after all. He looked haggard, but more—shamefaced! Could he have forgotten all of last night—part of it—or just enough to reduce him to this abject state?

She decided not to put him at ease immediately, for his bolting the door alone deserved some moments of continuing on tenterhooks. "One cannot but feel relieved that some aspects of Christmas have concluded," she said coldly.

"Indeed," the earl said miserably. "Er, to what particular aspects are you referring?"

Not willing to have him continue so woebegone, Merrie asked frankly, "You are having some difficulty recollecting our moments in the tower room?"

"I am," he admitted with humiliation. "I recollect that I took you there . . . and . . . then?"

"Bolted the door," Merrie supplied severely.

"Ah, I was afraid of that, and humbly apologize. I was not myself."

"No, indeed, you were the first earl. You swash-buckled about like him from the moment you put on his helmet. The entire gathering was much amused."

"The devil you say," he ejaculated, and shook his heavy head. "And then . . ."

"Ah, there are significant lapses in your recollection?"

"Somewhat," he said brusquely. "But if I offered you an intolerable insult I do not expect you even to be speaking to me this morning. Rather you should have been placing all before my mother."

"I am, you'll recollect, good-hearted. I could forgive you myself for your presumptions without having recourse to distressing the countess."

"Blast it—did I force myself on you? In which case you should be so overcome as to need a . . ."

"Vinaigrette?" she inserted helpfully, and he flinched. Her attitude gave him pause, and he said, "Are you *not* overcome because that was exactly your aim—to put us both in such a position where I could do no less than make you an offer? Egad, tell me! Am I to ask for your hand or not?"

"You are not."

"Then I did not? . . ."

Affronted by that insinuation, showing how little he thought of her honor, she said coldly, "You did insult me last night, by locking me into the tower room, and then placing me on the bed."

"Dash it." He groaned. "Then I owe you a pro-posal, it seems. You have achieved your aim of be-coming mistress of Moorsedge."

"That has never been my aim."

"Did you not tell me at our very first meeting that Moorsedge was your destiny? And have you not been attempting to attract me since coming here, so that I could see you as the preferred choice over the other ladies? And did you not order the mixing of the wassail punch and tell me it was a custom for us all to drink of the same cup?"

She stared at him, aghast at his turning the facts of their acquaintance so upside down. Her eyelids, which always intrigued him for the width between that space and her arched, delicate brows, now were half closed as if she could not bear the pain of his remarks. He was spellbound, watching them slowly opening to reveal a look of blooming disdain. He was cowed and ready to acquiesce in whatever condition this lady would demand; everything seemed different with her before him. As the two linked glances, his lordship began to feel that marriage was not the most distasteful of alternatives. Worse would be never being able to look into those expressive, glowing eyes.

But she committed that very deed, turning and riding away. A lock of her hair whipped across his face, and Brett felt himself branded by it. He sat frozen on his horse, watching her increasing the distance between them, before he shook himself alert and rode after. He rode across her path.

"I am giving you an offer of marriage," he had to shout over their horses' hooves.

"I refuse it. Nor do I think it necessary, for while you forgot yourself as a gentleman by forcing me into the tower room, you absolved yourself by opening the door and letting me leave. I expect you came to your senses. At just the opportune moment."

"I did?" And his disappointment in himself had Merrie almost laughing, despite her hackles being up at his presumption. Nevertheless, she kept her face composed.

"You are free to propose to Lady Jane, and I free to find, as you promised, a gentleman in London who would perhaps have . . . less of a problem!"

"What the devil do you mean by that?"

"I mean with your inability to hold your liquor. To that I mostly attribute your actions. Did you have any other reason for your declarations to me last night?"

"I can always hold my liquor," he claimed proudly. "However, I must admit your charms were so excessive that I was swept up by them, my beautiful peacock lady. You bewitched me, but I remembered who I was and who you were—in time."

"Yes," Merrie said, not helping him out by any more details.

She began to ride back to Moorsedge, and he let her go. And then once more he could not let her quite leave him so unsatisfied. He caught up to her again. "Since I did not remember, why did you not take the opportunity to become my countess? I was ready to offer you that."

Merrie deemed it more of a retaliation to tell him the truth. And she did so with a matter-of-fact tone that made the words seem all the more unquestionable. "I expect because as enticing as being mistress of Moorsedge would be, and being related to the countess, it would not be worth it, if one were forced to have to take *you* along with the package. I shall settle for your continuing to keep your original promise of taking the countess and me to London, and there finding me a husband who would love me freely, without needing to attribute his enchantment to my witching powers. My aim has always been to contribute to other people's happiness. Why then would I put myself in a position of being constantly spurned or regretted? I believe in love. Naturally, I desire a gentleman who could love with all his heart, and not be ashamed to own it. Those are my qualifications, and I hope you are able to find me a suitable mate to fulfill them."

Turning on her horse she gave him a sweet smile at that, and then rode like the blazes back to the stable.

And this to the most sought-after bachelor of the crème de la crème. This to the Corinthian! This to him! And why the deuce, once he had her alone in his tower room, had he let her go? There was something more to this. Something that minx of a girl had done. He was dashed certain she was laughing as she rode away.

"Blast her!" he yelled to Caliban, who merely neighed in response. He'd find her a husband, by Jove, and a wife for himself, so that he could forget her witchery. But he kept feeling the place where her long hair had whipped across his face. "She's marked me," he said with a groan.

Merrie was no sooner in the morning room and had taken a sip of her morning tea, than the earl marched in and sat beside her.

"On my way here, my eye caught the tower room casement, and I had a certain flash of memory."

She bit delicately into a roll. He watched her tongue go over her lips for a flick and lost track of what he'd come here to face her with. But when she looked up at him again, and he could see the devilry in her eyes, it all came back in a rush.

"You were pursued last night by two gentlemen, if I recollect completely. One who kept beckoning you toward the window."

Merrie laughed then, unable to hold it back. "Ah yes, you rescued me from the first earl, your lordship. And I am much beholden to you. You stood between me and him and even were good enough to tear open the barred door and help me escape from you, er, from him."

"And did you actually see the earl, or was that just one of your manipulating ways to escape me?" He took his hands off the table and plunged them under the cloth so she could not see the fists he'd turned them into as his body raged, waiting for her answer.

She answered by not answering. "What do you suppose?"

"I suppose the entire thing was a jest on your part. And I expect you have been laughing at me all morning, especially when I came and humbly proposed to you," he concluded, and his face was blazing with hurt pride.

For a moment she considered keeping to her original story, but was actually too honest to continue it. "I briefly thought I saw him. I have sensed him following me around the manor at other times. And then, when I needed rescuing from you, I felt him strongly there, and used his presence to help you come to your senses. But that I was alert enough to find a way out of the humiliation you intended to inflict on me in no way excuses your actions. You are still beholden to both me and the late earl, for not having to marry me this morning."

She took a last sip of her tea and stood up to leave. He reached out to touch her to understand his own confusion, and because frankly he did not wish her to leave. Feeling his touch she could not resist saying, " 'Unhand me, gentleman, my fate cries out.' "

The purport of her quote struck him as if he were a gong. He felt his head reeling as he recollected she'd said something similar last night. Then more of her remarks came back, and he cursed softly as he understood at last how she'd gammoned him. "Egad, Shakespeare!" he exclaimed, still holding on to her hand and now concluding, "You played *Hamlet* last night. The ghost scene. And I, like a proper moonling, fell into your every direction."

Merrie's eyes could only be said to be gleaming with unholy amusement as she responded unabashed, "Actually you were rather befuddled and did not know your lines, but I improvised around your, er, staggering. And then you were good enough to follow directions to the extent of opening the barred door. For which I was prodigiously grateful. However, I did warn you not to stay in the room with the earl. He has a way of wanting to rid himself of his rivals—or become them."

The earl flushed like a youth, remembering it all now, his sense of union with the earl goading him on, the completion of having her in his arms, and then worse, her ridicule in the face of his humbling declarations. Double blast her! Not only had she brought him down a peg, but to his very knees.

"If it is a husband you want, I shall find you one," the earl said with all of his old hauteur, "but it might be a trifle difficult to find one who would enjoy your humor and your making him the butt of it. In the meantime, Miss Laurence, I suggest you prepare yourself for as speedy as possible removal to London. Wit like yours should be appreciated by the best wags. And you need have no fear, we shall unquestionably find someone suitable to your class and style and acting talents. Actually if you were able *almost* to win me, I expect any other gentleman will be mere child's play."

"A modest reply, I must say," Merrie responded coldly, angry enough to break loose from his grasp finally and leave.

The earl was left to talk to his teacup. The leaves formed a pattern very like a whale. She'd made a whale of a fool out of him, he moaned. But in a way he had to admire her. What an opponent—up to every rig and row, not only that she thought to play the *Hamlet* scene with him, but that a lady would know it well enough to use it. She really had a way of keeping him on his toes. He felt a slight smile of admiration on his lips and called them shortly to account. But traitorously they continued to smile.

My fate cries out, indeed! Was she his fate? he wondered, but cried out against that. For his wounds were raw.

13

London in February was not quite the height of the social season. But enough people had congregated for Merrie and her younger sister Esther to be astonished at all the activities.

"But this is nothing," the countess assured her delighted companions and their escort throughout London, Mr. George Dickens, eager for some seasoning himself.

Remarkably the earl countenanced their invasion with a minimum of alarm. Even the introduction of Esther into their group did not cause him to raise more than an eyebrow. Certainly not his voice, nor his temper. Merrie had allowed the countess to explain the addition while she stood mute. Actually, Merrie had had very little to say to the earl since their final discussion at Moorsedge, and as for his lordship, he was behaving as if she were the slightest of acquaintances.

Simpson, his majordomo, was in full control of the house on the edge of Regent's Park, and made it clear that he would resent any interference in the smooth

arrangements between himself and the earl, even by
the countess, and most certainly by either of the two
young ladies. Perhaps the old Merrie would have
delved enough to discover if the staff was happy, as
she had at Moorsedge, where she had arranged for
medical care for the cook's son and lessons to be
given in the village for the children of their cottagers
and staff. All was done under the countess's name,
and her ladyship was the one thanked by the Moorsedge people, but most knew who had started it all.
And Merrie had wished to know their happy news as
well—who was attempting to improve himself, and
which child had a lovely voice and had hopes for joining the village glee club that went from town to town
to entertain.

For Merrie was one who could share other people's joys as well as sorrows. A good many nobles of
the Lady Bountiful variety saw it as their duty to help
the unfortunate, especially on their own estates. But
Merrie had been a Lady Cheerful, wanting joy to
spread from family to family, and being just as concerned with a birth as with an illness. People can sym-
pathize when another is troubled, but truly joining in
another's joy is rarely wholehearted. Envy is the barrier, and self-concern. But Merrie had had no envy,
except of Lady Jane's bonnet with the plumes, and
she had mastered that, and admitted that it probably
looked better on the pale lady than it would have on
herself, and so she was able to enjoy it as just a beautiful sight. That being her nature explained why she
was at her best during Christmastime—the season of
sharing with other people's joy, the season of love for
the family, for others, and for the world.

Thus it was so astonishing that love itself had altered Merrie. Not that she admitted in the smallest
degree to being one of Brett's conquests. But he'd affected her openness by causing her to close down, as

she focused her thoughts exclusively on him. She was, in effect, preoccupied by his lordship. And that gradually had her forgetting to concern herself with the others about her. Therefore it was a prodigious relief to find in the beginning of their residence in London that his lordship was rarely at the Regent Street house.

At Moorsedge they had all been housebound, sharing every aspect of Christmas together, but here, society and London itself called with constant diversions. And as for his lordship, he slipped immediately into his old pattern of spending most of his days at Manton's Shooting Gallery, or Gentleman Jackson's Boxing Establishment, and most of the evenings at various of his clubs, White's, Boodle's, or Brook's, gambling and exchanging scandal. And lately he'd almost taken to establishing a residence at his club, even dining there rather than at home *en famille*.

To compensate for his lordship's dereliction, Merrie had the joy of being with her sister. Equally comforting was the constant kindness of the countess. And always George's happy, spirited, loving self. The most exciting distraction, however, was London. She had once come to the city with her father several years ago, but they'd limited their explorations to libraries and museums, while this time with George and the countess the outings were less cerebral. Socially, they were limited to afternoon teas or soirees with old friends of the countess. They were returning from just such an affair when they were stopped by the earl in the hall. He gave them all a critical observation through his quizzing glass. His examination was returned in good measure, for his outfit was a marvel to behold.

"Bang up to the nines," George said at the earl's creaseless dark jacket, a yellow brocade silk waistcoat, and the most shockingly form-fitting knit pantaloons in a delicate fawn color. But it was the white cravat that most astounded all three ladies and his brother. It rose with the accordion folds into a huge bow just below his tilted chin.

"I have just created it today, in response to urgings that we do something to celebrate the wedding of our Princess Charlotte to the prince of Saxe-Coburg shortly to be performed for all our edification. I call it tie-the-knot." He pointed to the knot. "Indissoluable, don't you see? Gives a gentleman pause, lest he become equally . . . entangled."

While his mother and George were in rapture, Merrie could not resist adding, "There is always Alexander's solution to any knotty problem, which appears to be your solution to any connection, as well."

Amused, the earl smiled for a moment. It had been too long since he'd been in Miss Laurence's challenging presence, and he could not resist parrying, "I own I endorse cutting. Especially a judicious pruning of one's family tree, lest common vines choke off one's reach for air."

Merrie grinned. "Ah, your need for air explains the elevated cravat. Or is its purpose, like blinders on a horse, to assure not seeing anything beneath you, while appearing every inch a lord?"

"I regret not being able to return the compliment," he said with as much starch in his tone as in his cravat. "Not only do you not look every inch a lady, but there has been no appreciable improvement in your appearance, which, as you'll recollect, was one of our conditions for your season. We are no longer in the hinterlands of Yorkshire. One must strive to live up to London standards. I have urged my mother to take you shopping, but as usual it seems to be too much for her, and so to do it correctly I shall have to do the thing myself."

Not following the gist of their verbal sparring, that last reference to herself had the countess speaking up,

"But my dear Brett, what are you saying? I have already taken both of these delightful ladies for a buying spree. We had the most enjoyable time, did we not, girls?"

They quickly nodded. The countess had taken them around, and they were now wearing the perfectly acceptable white muslins of a lady in her first season, and Merrie as well had lifted her wild red hair up into a topknot in blatant imitation of Lady Jane's style. Esther with her blond hair freshly styled *à la Grecque* looked so adorable that Merrie felt a double pride. Merrie's sisterly pride was only assuaged by George's praises for Esther. Considering all their primping and pleasure in their new apparel, to have his lordship find no appreciable difference in their appearance was beyond tolerating.

Ignoring his mother's attempts to point out the suitability of her choice, and the unexceptionable results on dear Merrie, the earl said with a long-suffering sigh, "Prepare yourself, Miss Laurence, I shall take you to Madame Bliss's tomorrow after nuncheon. You may not be beyond salvation."

Merrie was reflexively set to refuse, but he did not wait for her comment, putting on his beaver hat and strolling out without a backward glance.

There was silence as the door closed. Then George and Esther spoke up almost together, using superlatives for her appearance. Only Esther said "lovely" and George "top ho," but the sentiments were the same. The two looked at each other and walked into the library for a discussion. There was not the smallest justification for the earl's assessment, not to mention his rudeness. It was amazing how often the two found a coincidence of opinion. Especially on Merrie, for George still loyally worshipped her as he had at Moorsedge. Although to his disappointment she was no longer his partner in frolicking. No longer did she challenge a fellow to races, laughing through the ride to her triumphant finish. Indeed, she was acting as if she'd never engaged in such wild starts. London or society or something else was inhibiting her. Dash it, she even seemed somehow older. Perhaps that was because Esther was with them, and she was always attempting to set a proper example for her sister. And then too, somehow he and Esther were always left on their own.

No quicker entrance into Esther's heart was there than praising her sister. And she had many tales to tell him about Merrie, and about their happy family, which made George envious, for he'd generally grown up ignored, his father dead, his brother in London and uninterested in him, and his mother too ill to be disturbed. He held back nothing in his confiding to Esther about his life and of course about his hopes of marrying Merrie. Although encouraging him, Esther warned that Merrie had a habit of refusing gentlemen. Half the Oxford students who came to study with their father had already made her proposals, and she had not relented. "We always thought she never meant to wed, but just be our good fairy watching over us and all who came within her ken, just as she came to your home and you told me made a difference to all, from maids to her ladyship. But now, how strange is her determination to wed to someone of society. That was not anything that ever appealed to her. Nor does she sparkle as before. A complete puzzlement."

George was equally puzzled by his own feelings; for Merrie's lack of regard no longer smarted, especially since Esther was always there to soothe him, as when she concluded shyly that in her opinion there was no more perfect a gentleman for her sister than he. That could not help but appease, and indeed, please.

Eventually he found he preferred talking to Esther than to anyone else in the world. She was so serious, and yet so anxious to hear his opinions, as if he too had similar weighty observations to make, that shortly he found himself coming out with more and more worthwhile remarks.

At her suggestion, George read guidebooks, so that on the family's expeditions, he it was who was the authority on all observed. And it was dashed exciting being the one turned to for the facts and having them at his fingertips and actually hearing his mother say, "But we must ask Georgie. He is better than a guide-book." In fact he was a walking, parroting guide-book, egad; he laughed at himself, but could not resist parading his knowledge. At the Tower of London, George could point out King Henry the Eighth's ar-mor, and he could quote Anne Boleyn's last words before being beheaded, and even how many carats in the various crown jewels. Yet the high point of that Tower visit for everyone was the lions. The countess saw a direct relationship to her Vinny. Esther was so overcome by sympathy for their imprisonment, she actually put her hand out to stroke a mangy mane. Observing it, George felt his heart sink, and he jumped quickly to insert his own hand to deflect the beast from Esther's. Thankfully the lion had just eaten and did not find either hand worth disturbing his snooze. But when both George and Esther were safely away from the beast, he could not remember decorum but rather openly hugged her in relief. At that moment, it was clear to both that their feelings for each other were more than intellectual.

Merrie, joyous at Esther's rescue, came quickly to hug both, and the countess, after merely suffering a spasm in alarm, rushed to join in this family together-ness.

"I scarcely know what came over me," Esther was

explaining, "except I saw the beast as the one rescued by Androcles, so sad and in need of one removing a thorn."

And Merrie understood, but momentarily questioned their father who had trained them to live in myths. Yet George became a mythlike figure by his act and Merrie said as much, which had the gentleman preening, especially when Esther softly and hesitantly added, "He is an exceptional gentleman in every respect."

That evening Esther and George read the fable of Androcles and the lion, and Esther henceforth called George Androcles, albeit in private. Daily this couple had many things they privately exchanged, mainly George's sudden interest in archaeology, as Esther spoke of her father's works. Their visits to museums became more frequent and led to Lady Warwick's drawing the line in her attendance, using those times to rest at home with Vinny in her arms, or have tea with some friends from her youth.

Along as a chaperon, Merrie often developed a pain in her leg and needed to rest before certain works of art, while Esther and George carried on with the tour, leaving Merrie smiling at them from a distance with prodigious satisfaction.

The social season had certainly begun, but the earl's houseguests had not yet been presented, for his lordship had sent word that he would let them know when it was the propitious time.

It was George's view and Lady Warwick's, having had years of Brett's not wishing them in his milieu, that he would never feel they were sufficiently prepared for that honor, or that he was delaying that honor as long as he could.

Therefore, his wishing to dress Merrie was the first indication that that moment was at last approaching, and George was not overly dismayed by it. He took

the occasion to comment to Esther that neither she
nor her sister had anything to blush for, and, indeed,
that she, Esther, was prettier than any of the society
ladies. "With your lovely blond hair and those dark,
speaking eyes, everything about you is prime. Your
appearance, your kindness, your mind, and your understanding, loving heart."

As George was saying this to her, he felt himself
overcome by his emotions and leaned across the
drawing room settee, where they had both convened
to talk over Brett's orders to Merrie, and kissed her in
a brotherly fashion on the cheek. She blushed so pret-
tily that he wished to see another blush, and he kissed
her again. And then she was fully flushed, and he
laughingly continued her high color by continuing his
kisses, and then he slid from her full red cheek to her
soft open mouth, and the kisses he gave her there
were setting him flaming as well.

He pulled away and stared at Esther. "Ye gods,
how is it possible for me to love both sisters?"

And thus, he made his declaration. And Esther admitted she had been in love with him from the moment she met him. He was so special a person that he
ought to be married to a special lady like Merrie. "I
never thought anyone would be worthy of her until I
met you."

No greater compliment could she offer, and he felt
it, and kissed her for it, and the two kissed some
more, agreeing it was terrible to love someone and
not have one's feelings returned. Except now his feelings were being returned.

"I say, Esther, I think I love you better than Merrie. I mean that she was like a dream. I enjoyed
watching her ride away from me, and we laughed together, but she never took me seriously as a man. She
saw me merely as a . . . brother, and that can daunt
a fellow. But with you, I feel we are twin souls that

shall go exploring together, hand in hand through life."

And thus he had made a declaration, and which of the two was more astounded could not be said.

"But how can I accept you," Esther lamented, "when you belong to my sister? I could not so intrude on her choice."

"But I am not her choice. She has said over and over that I am free to love. And while she opened my heart to love, you are the one my heart has closed over and taken into it. We are a couple. You must say yes, for it would be too beastly for both sisters to turn me down, and in the space of a few months."

Esther giggled at that, and admitted that would be too much for any gentleman to bear, and so in order to spare him a second refusal, she would accept, but on one condition.

He was ready to accept anything, except bringing Androcles into their home, which made her laugh, remembering again how he had risked his life to rescue her, and they kissed over that act of bravery and love, and she had to be reminded to state her condition.

"We must not tell Merrie, or your mother, until Merrie has found her true love. And definitely we must not confide in your brother."

It was obvious that Esther had developed an aversion to the earl, for he had been particularly cold of late and had barely nodded a welcome to the young sister. And from Merrie's tension whenever he came into the room, Esther subtly understood that he was a figure to dread. George attempted to assure her, but without much conviction himself, that Brett was a "decent chap," but he quickly agreed that they ought not yet divulge their engagement to him. And he further understood the need for delicacy in regards to confessing to the lady, to whom he'd sworn eternal devotion, that in the space of less than two months he had sworn that devotion to another.

Therefore, the newly engaged Esther had special incentive that Merrie should find a beau upon her entry into society. There had to be someone out there whom her older sister would love as much as she herself did George. And so when Merrie was fuming at the earl's evaluation of her dress, Esther said appeasingly, "While you look lovely as you are now, Merrie darling, if the earl wishes to dress you more properly to show your uniqueness, why not allow him to do so?"

Merrie, after years of secondhand gowns, felt that these chosen by Lady Warwick were quite presentable. Looking at herself in a new muslin gown, she could not see anything amiss, especially when she contrasted them with her past apparel that never quite fit, being made for a shorter Mrs. Laurence and needing scarves to hide the worn marks and unseemly let-out seams. In any case Merrie felt that a gentleman should want her for herself and not her fashionable attire. Nevertheless, understanding Esther's insistence, Merrie promised herself she'd do her best to win at least one gentleman admirer so that Esther would be free to acknowledge hers. Naught pleased Merrie as much as the attachment between Esther and George. During a conversation with Lady Warwick, both agreed not to disclose their awareness of the young couple's affections until they were officially informed. But both could silently and subtly help the connection along.

"It is so joyous to see youngsters finding the correct mate so quickly," Lady Warwick said. "Georgie will never be forced to lose his love and regret it all his life, as was the case in my life."

Having often been told of her ladyship's having to give up her own choice of a mere baronet for her father's choice of an earl, Merrie, in generous spirit, once more sat down to hear the tale relived. Taking Vinny in her arms, Merrie thoroughly groomed him down to his tail while her ladyship relived her tale of thwarted love.

When she arrived at the point of her forced separation and was awash in tears, Merrie put her arms around the lady and gave her back Vinny for comfort; and somehow, with those two snuggling close to her, the sadness abated more quickly than usual, and the countess was smiling. "You are still a lovely lady," Merrie coaxed, "I see no reason for your ladyship this season to be confined merely to chaperon duty. Perhaps love can come for you a second time."

The countess was quick to deny that possibility, claiming one always loved one's first love and nothing could equal that, which edict left Merrie retiring to her room flummoxed, for she'd not wished to admit to herself that somehow her heart had been reached by Brett at Moorsedge, especially during the end of the Christmas celebration. However, she did acknowledge reveling in his mistletoe kisses, his choosing her above all the other ladies as her dance partner, and seeking her out in the game of blindman's buff. Ah, it had all been like a dream unfolding, with bright candlelight and holly berries decorating her moment of joy. Of course, he had ruined the purity of their togetherness by his carrying his attentions past the point of acceptability in the tower room, and then subsequently accusing her of planning her own seduction.

She really ought to have accepted his stiff marriage proposal—naught else would have served him tit for tat for his effrontery. Except that Merrie had too much faith in love to make a mockery of it. Obviously he was not the correct gentleman for her—she had yet to find him. But his lordship had awakened in her the desire to find a husband—actually, he'd awakened in her the need for love. And although both were staying apart, he was often, she regretted to admit, able to rouse some past emotion with just one of his careless, mocking bows or intense, all-absorbing stares in her direction. *En passant,* so to say.

A note one morning was delivered to her room, not by the footman but by Simpson himself, clearly indicating that the sender was his lordship, and her heart leaped up. Then crashed down upon reading. It was an order that she be prepared to accompany him to the dressmakers that afternoon after nuncheon.

If it had ended there, Merrie might have only been tweaked by its commanding quality. But he went on to claim that he'd been waiting in hopes she would achieve some town polish on her own, but rather she seemed to be sinking into total mediocrity. Which forced him to the fatigue of stepping in to attempt to make her at least presentable.

Putting down the note Merrie knew she had been hurt more than at any time in her life. She felt the pain spreading through her, and yet could not understand why this recent devaluation by the proud lord should affect her any more deeply than the many similar remarks he'd made to her at Moorsedge, which flicked right off, landing harmlessly at her feet.

Except she was more vulnerable since having acknowledged herself as having a *tendre* for him, even after having turned those feelings aside.

But more, being here in London and listening to the awed manner in which the countess's friends spoke about him when they came for tea was somewhat intimidating. And lastly, at Moorsedge she had been protected by Christmas, protected by still being who she was and being confident enough in that to deflect his slights.

But here in London, she'd already attempted to alter herself to suit his lordship's society qualifications. And after that concession, and his still finding her wanting, she could not in her heart but agree that she was not a society lady—it was all pretense. As he had seen through it, so would the others. Pulling down her Lady Jane topknot in disgust at her pretense, Merrie allowed her abundant hair its freedom; indeed it seemed to sigh in relief as it swirled around her tear-stained face.

But when she went down the stairs to her appointment with the earl, she'd once more put her hair in the Lady Jane style, having no time to devise another, and covered it with a new small, conservative bonnet. Never had she felt less confident. Obviously something was lacking in her appearance, and as the earl was known throughout society as being a gentleman of the most exquisite taste and manners, she would use him. Let him dress her to the teeth, and then at last she would be free of his daily disregard.

Disregard was not quite the word for his lordship's reaction to Merrie's appearance. Distaste would actually be the most precise word, as he sighed. "We are off to Madame Bliss's just in the nick of time. You are quickly losing all your sparkle and becoming . . . common. That bonnet! That bonnet!" He moaned, touching his gloved hand to his elegantly arranged dark curls as if her hat was actually paining his own temporal region.

Unable to stay sunken in blue dismals when directly attacked, Merrie spoke up, especially since the two had a history of combating over bonnets. "What is wrong with it?" she snapped. "Your mother chose it!"

"Exactly."

"Your mother has very fine taste."

"My mother has *ordinary* taste. And if you are to be under my presentation, I hope you do not imagine

I shall allow you to look like the *poor relation* you are. We shall scarcely find any takers for your hand. And that is our objective, is it not? We are preparing you to capture a mate?"

"That is my objective," Merrie said grimly. "And I shall allow you to dress me and spend all the money you think necessary into making me the desirable bait, for the sooner I am chosen, the sooner I shall be able to leave your presence. And isn't that the primary wish of both of us?"

That remark lay smoking between them. He evaded its implications, merely handing her into his carriage. Blast the girl, why had she become so coolly indifferent to him since their arrival in London? he thought, forgetting that he himself had set the mode to show her how little need he had of her in his social milieu. And having achieved what he wished, he paradoxically resented the loss of her openness. As now, as they drove along, she kept her face averted. No gratitude for his escorting her to Madame Bliss's. No obligation for all his kindness in her behalf, and he said as much, having worked himself into the deuce of a sulk. "Why do I waste my valuable time, when it is so little appreciated? Rather than showing the smallest gratitude, you behave as if it is my obligation to please you."

"But naturally it is all our obligation to please one another. Why else have we been put on this earth?" Merrie replied, astonished that he could question so basic a tenet, and then goaded further by the disbelief on his face, she said soothingly, "I daresay the less my gratitude, the more credit to you for acting so selflessly. Although"—and here Merrie paused, much struck by a revelatory thought—"I too am acting selflessly and deserve *your* gratitude for allowing you to become my creator. You insisted, nay, made it a condition of your largesse, that you alter me. Well, now I agree and give you carte blanche to make me a true credit to your reputation. Ah yes, cannot you perceive, henceforth, anything I am—from my every frock to my every action—will be laid at your door."

"That is precisely my fear," he said with a shudder, uncertain whether she was mocking or prophesying. But, dash it, she was definitely smiling. Somehow she'd managed once more to turn the tables on him and rather than her being under obligation to him, he was now obligated to her. Still every glance at that pot of a hat had him wincing and concluding that whatever the reason, it was imperative that he rescue her from his mother's stifling taste. It was criminal to cover her with such conventionality. Might as well place fig leaves on the Venus de Milo. That last thought brought images of the young lady in fig leaves, which kept his lordship well occupied for the rest of the ride.

At Madame Bliss's, the proprietress herself was there to greet them. It took her a moment to grasp the relationship between the couple, whether from picking up on the earl's fig-leaf thoughts or just the smoldering stares they were exchanging, but quickly all her doubts were resolved.

"You are here, my lord, for some pretties?" she said with a knowing wink. "A few lace unmentionables?"

Merrie blushed to her toes.

14

The palpable sense that she had committed a faux pas caused the elderly French lady to frown. It was there in the amused glance of the earl and the young lady's clear discomfort. Madame Bliss had achieved her following by her very intuitive understanding of what was wanted regardless of what was asked for. But she had misread this relationship.

The earl was good enough to put things in proper perspective. "This young lady is my, er, cousin, who is to be presented to society, and I wish her to appear as unique. Not a copy of every young miss, but rather as every young miss would wish to appear."

Dropping her Gallic twinkle, Madame Bliss quickly put on her most severe British expression, assuring him that she knew how to dress a *lady*.

"She is not quite that either," the earl said incorrigibly, continuing to elaborate. "I see her as a lady, yes, but one raised on a pedestal with just a flicker of an ankle showing to rouse the men to want to seize her off it. She must be Eve who torments, and an angel who holds gentlemen away. In *one*."

Madame Bliss, through all her years of experience, had never quite had such a charge.

Merrie, sensing the lady's stupefaction, attempted a sensible abridgement. "Dress me as a lady but with a bit more dash."

"Is *that* what I said? How deflating you are," he countered, eyeing Merrie with a taunting grin.

Feeling this was the moment for her to take charge, Madame Bliss ignored all his lordship's speech and made her usual presentation, after which the earl gave her one of his severest glances that usually sufficed to put fools in their places. "How could you suggest that insipid miniscule print on a drab silk background? Lord above! Have you no eyes? The lady is a dashed beauty and ought to be dressed brightly in reds, greens, even golds. Fire, greenery, and the sun and the blue of the sky—that is she."

Madame Bliss could not accept this wholesale affront to her style sense. And although cloaking it with the utmost servile deference, she suggested that the lady had so much color herself and so much stature and perfection of form, therefore, in contrast, she should be simply dressed, else she might appear as a demimondaine. And with so sufficient a hint, she paused for it to sink in.

The only thing that sank was the earl's opinion of Madame Bliss. But she, not familiar with him, assumed his silence meant compliance and continued, "*Eh bien,* we omit the reds and golds, *n'est-ce pas?* Green perhaps, but not vibrant emerald, a paler shading, suitable to a young miss."

"That is not this lady," he said, finally cutting her off.

"*Mais oui,* it is," Madame Bliss insisted, her French temper and pride in her knowledge of what was *au fait,* making it essential that she speak out.

While the two experts continued their contretemps,

it soon became clear that Miss Laurence's attire had many ramifications. It called into question both Madame Bliss reputation, and Lord Warwick's knowledge of fashion. Further, deeper, it would tell the world not only who this Miss Laurence was, but in what manner the earl viewed her. Clearly this was becoming a contest of power and authority in which Merrie could not wholly remain uninvolved. Forcing herself into the middle of the fray, she said, "I shall choose, and that way it must reflect me." And she went decisively to the table with the materials and the fashion plates and proceeded to skim through all.

It would have been a supreme moment to prove herself to the earl and to the French lady—casually to open *La Belle Assemblée* and say calmly, "That and that and that," and awe them both by the brilliance and appropriateness of her choice. But the fashions confused her. She shut the book with a snap and turned to the materials. There was such a wealth of them—small wonder Merrie was overwhelmed. Madame Bliss had assumed her name to suggest to the clientele that a lady would be in bliss at all the beauteous designs and fabrics, and naturally the results thereof. Boding ill for Merrie's entree into the fashion world, once again she showed the new insecurity that had been touching her of late.

"I like pink," Merrie said at last.

"Pink, for my lady with such bright hair—it is not done," Madame Bliss pronounced, delighted to be able to put one of them in their place.

But the gentleman, becoming bored with the colloquy and indifferent to either lady's feelings or wishes, took charge. "I do not know why I imagined anyone else could be of assistance. Obviously neither of you knows what is correct. Nor does your collection have what I'm looking for. As usual I shall have to put myself to the fatigue of creating an entirely new fashion." And he called up the creator in himself by staring fixedly at his raw material—Merrie—and then nodding, he pronounced, "Color—greens, to cool down the fire, if that is possible for such a lively lady. Fabrics—naturally simple muslin for daytime, but for evening, we banish all heavy silks and crepes and keep to the nets, gauzes, or laces over satin to emphasize her natural grace. And style?" He turned to the pattern books, and with the tip of his quizzing glass languidly indicated at least three dozen selections, adding his own touches, so that Madame needed two assistants to take notes. Often he ordered the final design in white as well as green, for choice. "And make that a bright emerald green. Although in some cases I shall accept a paler green if the gown is decorated with an emerald hue to match her eyes."

The extent of the order had Madame Bliss forgetting her designer's integrity, replying with all deference, "*Mais oui,* you have found exactly the correct picture for the *charmante* lady. I comprehend *exactement* what your lordship wishes and shall do all in my power to please you."

"I expect that," he answered matter-of-factly, while Merrie, gaping at all the gowns ordered, could not stop herself from indicating that enough was enough; his lordship need no further fatigue himself.

"I never find it fatiguing dressing ladies . . . or undressing . . ." Both ladies gasped, but he concluded, "their pretensions." And they regained their composure, while he laughed at Merrie's pink glow.

Her temper up, Merrie said, "Madame, would you do me the courtesy of coming with me into the fitting room? I wish to discuss a personal matter about my figure."

"That would not be uninteresting to me," the earl said with a grin, but he allowed the ladies to step aside. On their return Merrie was smiling and decisive. "I have chosen the *few* dresses needed, we can leave now."

"Going behind my back, eh, to tip me a doubler! Well, I am not averse to your having several of your own selections, but my order stands. Ergo, you shall have the essentials at hand, if despite that, you are goose enough to choose to appear *lacking*—that shall be as you wish."

And without the slightest pause, his lordship continued making more selections, now concentrating on a special gown for her first appearance. "It, I expect, must be white, yet we shall surprise by the use of nuptial white lace. This lace here." He indicated a silk bobbin lace called blonde, which was so fine it was only worn for trimming. To prevent future misunderstandings, Madame explained the usual use of that particular lace, but his lordship merely dismissed what was generally done, insisting on a full gown of it.

And so Madame quickly added it to the list. That gown alone would pay for several trips back to France, the couturiere thought in delight. And yet, *mon Dieu,* he was still purchasing. She took the opportunity of his open pocket to bring his attention to her most advanced designs, dresses with heavily embroidered flounces and hems. But to those his lordship took an instant aversion and waved them away. "And if Miss Laurence ordered any of those, they are to be cancelled. I'd as lief she did not appear like a country maiden gawking at her betters."

Merrie flushed, for there went half of her few private choices.

"And nothing with wadded hems that stand out. Those are for ladies who wish to detract from the imperfections of their figures. And no ruffles, for the same reason. Actually, flounces and ruffles are passé."

Merrie rounded on him. "You have just obliterated all my selections."

"I thought so," he said with satisfaction.

"I wish to have some say, blast you!"

"Tut, tut, Madame Bliss will wonder where you picked up such an expression."

"She need not wonder long. You use it all the time."

"As touching as it is that you wish to emulate me so faithfully, Miss Laurence, I expect you should choose other aspects to ape, such as my unerring sense of style. You wished to be unique and yet lady-like—I am arranging for just that. Nothing gaudy or flouncy, and yet we shall not fall into boredom by our choice of colors—the brightest greens to complement your eyes, although when enraged your eyes take on a rather magnetic violet hue, I have noticed." He languidly came close to the enraged lady's eyes, and stared deeply in, then turned away as if justified. "Yes, undoubtedly a hint of violet. As always, I am correct. We must have a touch of that," he continued, turning back to Madame Bliss, but warned, "Naturally we must keep her basically in white, as is de rigueur, but with enough surprises to keep her original. And as for design, as I've tried to demonstrate by altering the individual style plates, she is not to appear in any of these shockingly low-cut gowns the most modest ladies are flaunting of late. This lady has no need to reveal what gentleman can quite well imagine for themselves. We shall keep her a mystery. Ergo, lacy inserts to the neck on everything. Or for daytime, gauze. So shyly covered shall she be, we shall have everyone longing to uncover her. Even inserts down her lovely arms, I say . . . not in every case, of course. But to give the aura of modesty with a dare, what say? Ah yes, she must 'assume a virtue if she has it not.' "

Merrie flinched at the quote for the licentious behavior of Queen Gertrude.

"Obviously you believe you are being 'cruel only to be kind,' but it is not succeeding."

Brett laughed at her foiling him with a riposte out of the same scene in *Hamlet*. It was daring of him to quote from that play at all. But it demonstrated that he no longer felt cowed by that memory. And as now the earl felt he had the complete upper hand with Merrie, he was quite jovial. He was even good enough to recollect that Miss Laurence had oft indicated a desire to see a Shakespearean performance, and while he would not quite allow *Hamlet*, he would seek one of the other dramas. Which reminded him to order something for that planned outing. "She will need a theater cape, as we shall be attending the full season at Drury Lane, and let us not forget, an evening cape, with an ermine-trimmed hood to hide her blazing hair and cause a commotion when she puts it down for all to see the flame of her tresses."

Turning to Merrie at that point, he was practically crowing with his new assurance of having her in full control, "That is another thing, you are wearing your hair wrong in that topknot. Not being Lady Jane, I suggest you not attempt to emulate her style. We shall call a coiffeur tomorrow."

Not waiting for her reply, his lordship turned to Madame Bliss, who was in true bliss as she was mentally totaling the bill and curtsying at his every word, and he put her in heaven with an additional sentence.

"Fill out with whatever you think a lady would need, from underclothes of the finest silk, to nightclothes, in similar luxury. Matching reticules, and of course satin slippers to suit each dress. Gloves . . . what else?"

"And fans?" Merrie could not help but put in, betraying her weakness.

He eyed her tolerantly, "No fans," he ordered, and her face fell. "I shall purchase those separately. Along with your jewelry."

"I don't believe a lady in her first season needs jewelry," Merrie said, determined to draw the line somewhere.

Madame Bliss was astonished. "Impossible! A lady must have jewelry. This is the year for tiaras, for bracelets up the arms, for cameos."

"I do not care for jewelry," Merrie said decidedly, making a last-ditch effort to have some say in her transformation. "And that lace dress you ordered, if I must be all in lace, I at least want it in a shade I like. I want it in pink."

Madame Bliss gasped. "In pink it would look . . . *très intime, n'est-ce pas?* For the boudoir."

Merrie was silenced by that, but Brett's eyes danced with devilry. "But if the lady wishes it, make one up in pink as well—no, not deep pink, more the shade a lady blushes when she has gone beyond the line."

And laughing at that, he escorted the blushing lady out.

The first ball the earl thought sufficiently significant to be honored by his bringing his protégée was Lady Jersey's Almack's affair. Only the most select were given vouchers by Lady Jersey and the other lady patronesses of Almack's, a club known for exclusivity. In addition, this was to be *the* dance to start off the season. Anything ruled by Lady Jersey had to be prime, for her ladyship had once been the mistress of the prince regent, and for many years after, the leader of all social events. This time Lady Jersey had ordered a tightening of the list, just to make the remaining guests feel themselves doubly honored, and the others left out, precisely, as she intended, like discarded weeds. With usually only the crème de la crème invited, and now even those in restriction, the countess had no hope whatsoever that Merrie would be given entree; indeed, she was losing hopes in regard to herself. And so the Laurence girls and the countess were making plans to attend a smaller rout of rejects gathering on the same evening.

Not so *au fait* with the politics of social invitations, neither Laurence lady was thrown into the blue dismals at the thought of their exclusion. They had been reared on the philosophy of making do and had made do with a great deal less than they had now, and not felt themselves martyred. And now they were rather awash in abundance, living just to indulge themselves. Each day was a pleasant round of sightseeing, calling or receiving calls, eating all they wished, and being served by an efficient staff that resented any attempt at assistance from either lady. And as a delirious culmination, a trickle of Merrie's gowns began arriving. These in addition to the gowns already given them by the countess! They could scarcely ask for anything more. And though the countess spoke about the loss of the Almack's ball several times a day, she was always assured by the Laurences that they had not the smallest desire to attend.

And then the bulk of the Madame Bliss creations arrived at once, with special emphasis on the ball gowns. During Merrie's unpacking one after another, Lady Warwick was in high gig, only bemoaning the one place each gown would have been most apt, Almack's. But what silenced all the ladies were the underclothes. Holding up those items of the softest silks and so daringly cut, the Laurence girls inquired of her ladyship whether it were not a sin to wear them, and she, although faintly blushing herself, remembered she had been a married lady, and assured the young ladies that such was not worn in Yorkshire, but would be perfectly unexceptionable here in London, she assumed. After that, the gowns with their modest lace inserts even down the arms, seemed the height of propriety. That is, until Merrie tried one on and understood the earl's fantasy, for somehow the gauze and lace inserts were so positioned as to bring more attention to those particular areas than they might have had unclothed.

There were so many gowns, Merrie grew tired of modeling, and just had them spread out on the bed and sofa and asked Esther to pick several for her own. But that young lady preferred the gowns selected by the countess. Actually, she was in the right, those were more suited to her, and so she took all of Merrie's from Lady Warwick's choosing, and one or two of Merrie's new cache that were pressed on her.

Another delivery appalled Merrie, for Madame had sent six of the gowns with the ruffles and wadded hems and embroidery, which the earl had specifically ordered her not to include. That left Merrie in a moral dilemma. Should she reveal the mistake or simply assume Madame wished to please her since they had been her request. Obviously his lordship would not wish her to make an issue; he'd made several remarks about her middle-class, nipcheese economizing. Originally viewing the sad condition of Moorsedge, Merrie had assumed the earl a clutchfist, but on seeing Warwick House and his spending in London, it became obvious that his was a worse fault—indifference to people and houses not directly under his eye.

With that assessment of his lordship's character, Merrie concluded it best simply to accept the gowns. Therefore, she felt free to try one on. The new design had its hem so wadded, the entire gown lost its drape and stood out widely, causing Merrie to grimace; obviously the earl had been right. This style did not suit her in the slightest. Esther as well refused them. But the countess was enchanted by the advanced design and dash of the appliqué; at which both girls, nodding with joy, deposited all six smack into her ladyship's lap. Demurring that she was too old for them, she found rather the boldness of the look gave her an individuality that wiped out years. And she was prodigiously pleased to accept all but two, which she found not up to the rest. Those Merrie bundled up along with a goodly amount of daytime dresses and sent to Oxford for Mrs. Laurence. Although there would probably be no occasion for her mother to wear the gowns, still she relished knowing that her mother had something now of the very latest fashion, after years of the very passé.

To keep up to the ladies' splendor, George visited his brother's tailor and returned in what he assumed was a perfect copy of the earl. Actually, he had turned himself rather into a caricature of him. For while the earl wore his shirt points high and his cravat elevated, his lordship *was* able to turn his head and even look down and see his boots. Not so with George, who was totally swathed around his neck to the point of rigidity.

"No need to tell you henceforth to keep your chin up," Merrie cried at first viewing, and upon George's finding it difficult even to smile at that without crushing his cravat, Merrie whispered in alarm to Esther, "Is that the first sign of rigor mortis? Surely it bodes ill that a gentleman cannot even grin without quashing his neckcloth."

But Esther felt that George was a marvel to behold and said as much, at which George risked destroying the perfection of his cravat by bowing to the lady. The cravat lost its folds like a fallen soufflé, and George was in despair, and Esther soothed his feelings while Merrie laughed. Further cause for Merrie's amusement was hearing that he had needed the assis-

tance of two footmen to get into his snug coat of
fashion. He was strutting before the ladies when his
brother walked in.

"You tulip!" he pronounced with a shudder.
"Egad, all you need now is a lisp, and we can call you
a Bond Street Beau in earnest."

Offended, George claimed he did not intend to
take on the social lisping, nor was he sporting all the
fobs and quizzing glasses dandies usually affected.
Since the earl had his quizzing glass and one fob dangling from his trim waist, the point was well made.

"It is your cravat that really offends," Brett said.
"You look injured! A cravat is folded round the neck
and tied in the front after one's own style."

Calling his valet, the earl removed his brother's
abomination, and gave him one of his own muslin
cravats and even deftly tied it for him in a version he
named *fledgling*, in George's honor. George ran
quickly to show it off to Esther and won her enthusi-
astic approval, while his lordship went from George's
neck to Merrie's head, informing her that her hair
was to be dressed in the next hour by the most
sought-after coiffeur, Mr. Swinton himself. Merrie,
having heard of him from the countess's friends, was
sensible of the honor being done her by that gentleman's attention, still she could just force a smile,
for actually she was dashed bored with fashion and
fashioning herself. Realizing that, the earl was astounded, not certain whether her indifference proved
how above the other ladies she was, or how out of the
social swim, by not sharing their preoccupations.

In grave consultation with the earl, Swinton agreed
that the usual topknot, even with dangling tendrils,
was too sedate a style for a lady of such exuberance of
personality and coloring. Further, she was too statuesque to have such a small head. That was passable
for Lady Jane, who was small in every way. Other

styles of current fashion were attempted but Merrie's hair fought every one.

"We must then create something unique for the unique lady," the earl said, challenged.

As usual Merrie could not help but wonder at his dedication to perfecting her. The degree of attention to detail and the interest in his face when observing hers, went beyond a creator's concern and Merrie began to suspect a resurrecting *tendre* for her. That had first been indicated during their shopping expedition for hats. No longer were his black eyes mocking but intensely concentrated and even softening while he watched her trying on bonnet after bonnet.

"You are quite a beauty, you know," he had said gruffly and then smiled, adding, "But I imagine you know."

And Merrie had looked back at him, and given him one of her very special grins, which either acknowledged that fact or not, but they had enjoyed exchanging a friendlier moment. It was short-lived. Every hat she tried on, he had waved away. Merrie was patiently modeling, until she spotted one that stopped her heart. It was an exact duplicate of the original bonnet she'd worn to Moorsedge, only grander, of course. It was a French bonnet with a tall crown and a brim of wider circumference than usual, made of green silk and topped by a large, rather exuberantly waving ostrich feather. Every feminine instinct cried out within her that this was the hat for her. Upon placing it on her head with trembling hands, Merrie took a moment before she dared take a peek, and then gave her reflection a radiant, unconditional smile of approval. She looked, she concluded unabashedly, smashing. Just as she'd always dreamed. A grand lady indeed.

With her heart in her eyes, Merrie glanced at the earl. She wanted to demand, You owe me this one for the one you burned. She wanted to say, Please do not say a word against it, for it makes me feel special. But she said nothing. Just faced him and looked it all.

He nodded.

She exhaled in relief and her dimples were deep and long in view. Even when the shop assistant came to remove the hat, she held it on.

"It is perfectly proper to give him the hat, Miss Laurence," Brett said with an amused tone. "The hat is yours. As you are probably thinking, I do owe you that one, because, you are correct, I did burn the disgraceful one you were sporting upon arrival. And yes, this one is even more of a gem than the one Lady Jane wore that so went to your heart."

And Merrie allowed herself to laugh fully at that, admiring his knowledge of her exact thoughts.

"I always know what you are thinking," he assured her, which was remarkably intuitive, but Merrie was too happy at the moment to resent his teasing. For she had her ideal bonnet at last. She was just rising when the earl stopped her.

"It demonstrates a deep streak of fidelity in you that once having found the one you wish for, you feel no need to go on to others. However, that is not, I rush to add, society's way. Nor yours, actually. Are you not going on to seek other gentlemen after having found a perfectly unexceptionable one close at hand? Not that I mean to imply that I have gone to your head. . . ."

And before Merrie could grasp how sincere he was in that offering of himself, he slid back to his seignorial style of directing her actions, indicating which hats he wished to be placed on her head with a languid pointing of his finger. And soon Merrie was developing a decided pain in her temporal region as one after another was tried and either chosen or found wanting, and she exploded, "Fiddle! If I had as many

JOIN THE
TIMELESS ROMANCE READER SERVICE AND GET FOUR OF TODAY'S MOST EXCITING HISTORICAL ROMANCES FREE, WITHOUT OBLIGATION!

Imagine getting today's very best historical romances sent directly to your home — at a total savings of at least $2.00 a month. Now you can be among the first to be swept away by the latest from Candace Camp, Constance O'Banyon, Patricia Hagan, Parris Afton Bonds or Susan Wiggs. You get all that — and that's just the beginning.

PREVIEW AT HOME WITHOUT OBLIGATION AND SAVE.

Each month, you'll receive four new romances to preview without obligation for 10 days. You'll pay the low subscriber price of just $4.00 per title — a total savings of at least $2.00 a month!

Postage and handling is absolutely free and there is no minimum number of books you must buy. You may cancel your subscription at any time with no obligation.

GET YOUR FOUR FREE BOOKS TODAY ($20.49 VALUE)

FILL IN THE ORDER FORM BELOW NOW!

YES! *I want to join the Timeless Romance Reader Service. Please send me my 4 FREE HarperMonogram historical romances. Then each month send me 4 new historical romances to preview without obligation for 10 days. I'll pay the low subscription price of $4.00 for every book I choose to keep — a total savings of at least $2.00 each month — and home delivery is free! I understand that I may return any title within 10 days without obligation and I may cancel this subscription at any time without obligation. There is no minimum number of books to purchase.*

NAME_____

ADDRESS _____

CITY_____STATE_____ZIP_____

TELEPHONE_____

SIGNATURE _____

(If under 18 parent or guardian must sign. Program, price, terms, and conditions subject to cancellation and change. Orders subject to acceptance by HarperMonogram.)

GET 4 FREE BOOKS
(A $20.49 VALUE)

TIMELESS ROMANCE
READER SERVICE

120 Brighton Road
P.O. Box 5069
Clifton, NJ 07015-5069

heads as Cerberus and Hydra together, I should perhaps need all these hats," and she waved the rest away, and started to rise.

"Sit," he said caustically. "A lady would not dream of being seen in the same hat twice running. And the warm time is coming on. You shall need straw bonnets—leghorn or fine Dunstable straw, I expect. And, for this Merrie lady, a ribboned bonnet, for her face oft gives one the sensation of being a gift one would open on Christmas morn. And yet there is a mystery there, and so we must surround her in lace. Yes, she looks particularly intriguing in lace."

As he spun around the room, sighting and choosing, another pile was brought before the exhausted lady, until Merrie at last flatly stated that it was indecent to buy so much finery; one bonnet could have bought food for her family for a fortnight.

The manager of the shop was aghast at her remark and had to defend his occupation. "But a hat is as much of a necessity for a lady as food," he assured her. And Merrie was set to argue that point when the earl reprimanded her for both engaging in a colloquy with a menial and for revealing her middle-class mentality.

"Why do I labor to turn you out like a lady when you belie it every time you open your mouth?" he snapped. And the enjoyment of the expedition was seriously impaired for both. Merrie rose in offense, claiming there was no need for his lordship to waste any more of his valuable time and money on such a lowly specimen as herself.

But the shop owner had already placed another bonnet on her head, and she, unwilling to hurt the gentleman's feelings, especially after she saw him wincing at his lordship's description of him as a menial, allowed the hat to perch on her head. This one was of the smallest crown and brimmed equally economically, yet with a point over one eye that was rather rakish. And then as the gentleman lifted the veiling and placed it reverently over her entire face and tied it behind, Merrie was intrigued enough to look. Heavens, she looked prodigiously mysterious. Not like herself at all.

"Oh yes, this one," she said quickly, belying all her talk of the unimportance of bonnets over food.

But the earl was not impressed with that confection. "No," he ruled, "it is too old for you." And when Merrie objected, he added with a tinge of malice, "You appear rather like several incognitas I have known."

It was an effective enough remark to silence Merrie's protests when it was set aside. Smiling at the success of his ploy, his lordship was up again, this time himself placing a prodigiously wide-brimmed leghorn straw on her head. She looked, he thought, like a haloed angel, but concluded, "It lacks . . . distinction. Perhaps a trim?"

The shopkeeper was quick to bring for his lordship's perusal an entire basket brimming with flowers, ribbons, and red berries. The latter reminded the earl of the holly berries Merrie had worn in her hair during the Christmas season. Predictably, Merrie's hand gravitated to the berries, but his lordship was quick to put his hand over hers to stop its motion. "Nothing so childish," he whispered. And then, when he should have removed his hand, he kept it on hers while he leisurely examined the trims, and Merrie felt the warmth and strength and control of his hand and sensed herself uncontrollably blushing. And still his hand covered hers, and she did not move hers away. She lost all interest in the trims and just felt his hand's warmth covering hers. Had he forgotten it there? Should she shake him off?

Merrie's eyes were so greenly glowing, Brett could

not resist selecting a green ribbon for the leghorn. The choice made, he slowly removed his hand, as if unaware they'd been holding onto each other. And yet Merrie felt the pressure of it all the way back to the town house, to which he casually allowed her to return without his escort, substituting his groom, while he was let down in front of his club. He bowed his departure as if he had not held on to her hand all that time, and Merrie's cheery nature was fast being seriously tested. She could not help but recollect what the countess's friend had whispered to her about the earl: that he was known as a most accomplished flirt.

So while the earl was standing next to her and the coiffeur, Merrie was alert for any of the earl's tactics, having vowed not to be the slightest bit affected by them. If he held her hand, she planned simply to pull hers away. Also this time she would not allow him total control of her person and choice. For one could change a hat or a dress in a wink, but a hairstyle would be with one constantly.

Meanwhile back to his old dogmatic style, the earl after dismissing all the suggestions of the hairstylist as commonplace, pushed the noted designer aside and took up the brush himself. With a scowl of concentration, he began vigorously brushing the lively, fiery locks that reached down to the lady's beautiful straight back. Of a sudden, he stopped the vigor of his strokes, and did it gently, dwelling on the feel of the hair in his hands. And while his lordship brushed in softer, longer motions, Merrie could not help but close her eyes for the pleasure each motion sent through her entire body.

And still Brett continued brushing, now putting his free hand directly into her soft, lively tresses, quelling the urge simultaneously to plunge his face down into the glowing locks, and totally sense the fire of her, as he smoothly, steadily stroked and stroked, bemused.

"I have an abigail who brushes my hair with more efficiency," Merrie broke in. "Are you auditioning for her role?"

Shaken out of his daze, the earl quickly lifted her hair up from her neck and let it fall forward in curls around her face. "Do you see what I mean?" he asked the stylist, who obediently agreed that this was the correct look. But how were they to attain it?

"That is up to you to devise," the earl said brusquely. "I have an appointment. When I return I expect to see the transformation as I have designed it."

Without a look in her direction or even a civil bow, he abruptly took his leave.

Provoking man, Merrie was thinking as he departed, and yet she was pleased that he'd allowed her to take charge of herself at last. Which was just what she'd planned originally. One victory for her. And she was grinning as she and the stylist devised something to her satisfaction. But her grin faded as Merrie realized that the final result was close to the earl's original suggestion. Oh, fiddle! How had that come about? She'd simply been looking for her most becoming arrangement, while he'd hit on it almost instantly. Did he know her so well? Or was his taste impeccable, after all? Yet with some anticipation, she wished him to see the results and wondered at his delay. But Lord Warwick did not return until the next day. And then while walking by, he merely nodded at the style as if he had only a passing interest in her hair or her, after all.

Merrie castigated herself for having run to him, like everyone else, for approval—like Bruiser anxious for a pat. And she gave herself a good talking to. With all this effort to transform her into a lady, why couldn't she act and feel as coolly indifferent as a lady would?

Because she was Merrie, and her feelings were more likely to soar or crash, and his lordship of late had given her sufficient of these highs and lows.

15

Lady Jersey's ball at Almack's would be the high point of the season, everyone said, particularly Lady Jersey herself. It was like seeing a copy of their social Bible *Burke's Peerage* made flesh.

As the time neared, Lady Warwick declared herself sick of hearing of it. She forbade anyone to discuss the ball with her, and then broke her own dictum by approaching her titled son with a request for vouchers, only to take back her own words immediately with the remark that such a feat was impossible, and she was "just talking."

"You know, Mama, that as a dutiful son, I find your talk is always of prime interest, no matter how unjust." And he bowed away, leaving her as usual uncertain whether he'd complimented or insulted her.

Yet next evening the earl surprised them by spending it at home with the family. He acted very much as if it were the most logical thing in the world for him to be talking to Esther about their jaunts through London, and then laughing at George about his various attempts to bribe the secret of the shine of his brother's boots from his valet. "Not champagne, dear boy," Brett had said fondly, "one always has better uses for that beverage."

And Esther had inquired as to the taste of champagne, and George laughingly assured her it would tickle her little nose, and the earl smiled and said, "I expect champagne is to wines what your sister is to women—she sparkles and gives us all a pleasant, happy . . . buzz."

And he'd kept his eyes on Merrie while saying that, wondering if she'd remember the wassail incident and blush or frown, but she did neither, she just smiled, and he found himself dropping his rapier and smiling back.

After the gentlemen had joined the ladies, and Esther was playing on the pianoforte and George was singing with her, Merrie approved the new earl. "You have been quite pleasant."

"Egad, pleasant! *Pleasant,* you could give me no greater insult. Naught I wish less than to be pleasant."

"Yet you have been, and look how happy we all are as a consequence." She waved her hand at the family scene. The countess punctuated the bliss by a slight snore, as she had fallen into a doze on the settee.

The surprising thing to the earl was that, faith! he felt pleasant. And at ease. There was something very softening in the presence of a family; he could not grasp the influence, but he felt less bored, less bitter—almost cheerful? And he realized a great deal of the joy was coming from just being next to Miss Laurence and not taunting or teasing—just the two sharing the soft feelings.

A sizable portion of the earl's pleasant sensation, he concluded, came from having news to impart to his family. He'd been brimming with it all evening. And when the countess sat up abruptly, having wakened herself by a snore, he very quickly and without a word removed the Almack's vouchers from his pocket and held them out to her.

"The vouchers! You've secured them!" His mother gasped, and kept screaming in surprise and delight and just for the miracle of it. Indeed, she refused to take them up, shaking her head and claiming, "No! I will *not* believe my eyes!"

Her son feigned disappointment, "Forgive me, Mama. I was under the assumption these were exactly what you wished to see. However, if I am mistaken, then I can easily remove . . ." And he began to re-pocket them.

"Heavens, how you tease!" the exhilarated lady cried out, reaching out and clasping the tickets to her bosom. Which reminded her to throw herself and her bosom against her son, who very civilly tolerated that and the eager questions from George and Esther.

But it was Merrie's face he sought. For her undoubtedly he had put himself to the fatiguing effort. And when the countess and the rest were insistent that he explain how the feat had been accomplished, he said, "It required the supreme sacrifice from me, but as it was my mother's fondest hope, I could do no less. Also I felt society should not be deprived of bearing witness to the perfection of the ladies here, and of course, my dandified brother."

George gave him a playful punch and demanded to know what sacrifice.

"I endured a perfectly dreadful tea with Lady Jersey reminiscing about her days of being the prince regent's mistress and how much more elegant she had been than the present Lady Hartford."

The countess gave him a warning look, and the earl remembered that he was speaking before several innocents, and amended, "She enjoys hearing herself praised and so I did so, and thus by being 'pleasant' assured our pleasure at the ball."

At that Merrie smiled, but she did not share the delight at the coming event. For she realized with a jolt what it meant—that the earl was, in essence, cutting her loose. Up to now, she had been his project; and the two, although often coming to cuffs, had been a team. But now his mission was accomplished, and he had even put himself to some discomfort to launch her well. Heavens, he must be anxious to be rid of her!

It was true that his lordship was most anxious for society to see his protégée. First, because devoting so much effort creates a wish to be applauded for that effort. But mainly he wanted her launched because daily their linkage was solidifying and would soon be unbearable. Actually, theirs was a seesaw relationship. At Moorsedge, Merrie had been in control by her leading the festivities. Here in London, he had had the satisfaction of not only ruling her but re-creating a social Miss Laurence from Merrie, the impossible, wild madcap. But even in London, his control slipped during moments of her blasted honesty and humor. There was something about the way she made no bones about making use of him, when he prided himself on never obliging anyone.

"But you must wish to make others happy," she had said, "otherwise one is always concerned with *self*, and that is quite a lonely existence."

"I have had no opportunity of being lonely ever since I met you, Miss Laurence. You are constantly putting me to use."

"That reminds me of the reason I sought you out today, thank you for not letting me forget it," she said, pleased enough to clap her hands. "I am not fully outfitted for the season."

"Pardon, but I am in charge there, and I do not

believe I have forgotten anything essential. Any additional trifle you wish, of course—"

"I need a dowry," she cut in.

The earl eyed her with a steely glance.

Quickly she explained, "It came to me suddenly, that despite all these new clothes, I shall not be able to form a suitable connection unless I have some income. I understand it is obligatory. Being so mercenary, gentlemen prefer *that* to a lady's person, let alone her character."

"And ladies as well," the earl countered, "concern themselves merely with titles and fortunes."

"You underestimate yourself," she said with a straight face.

"I was not referring to myself," he replied. But he had been, for the first time wondering how much his title and fortune had to do with his vast success with the ladies.

"I told you I did not need all that apparel and all those hats. And I've consistently refused jewelry. But I shall, I fear, need the dowry or some kind of settlement as a lure. Lady Warwick's friend, Miss Phyncot, assured me that certain ladies had let her know that I, despite your acceptance of me, must still be given only the barest acknowledgment. Which reminded me of Lord and Lady Dansville's attitude toward me at Moorsedge. And indeed that called to mind your own attitude toward me as a 'poor relation.' Are you not typical of the gentlemen I shall be meeting? Or are you unique?"

"One always hopes one is unique. Yet in my insistence that a lady have some standing, I expect I am typical. But typically I have already acted."

"Which means?"

"That I am beforehand. And you need not have embarrassed us both by this financial discussion. I have dropped a judicious word or two in the right circles and before the best-known rattles. There is no possibility that the gentlemen I shall be introducing you to will not know that while you do not have title and position, you are a lady, and are comfortably established. I have arranged for you to have an independence. It is presently in your name at my bank."

Merrie's eyes lit up in sheer delight. It was amazing how women were all alike in regard to money, he thought wearily, and she further verified his opinion by her joyous exclamation, "Are you saying I have that independence as we stand here? And that I do not have to accept any gentleman, or indeed anyone at all?"

"Quite so, Miss Laurence, at this precise moment you could return to your parents with your independence and your clothes and live free of the Warwicks. Or, you may continue to use my auspices until the most suitable gentleman has been found for you. Your heart is free to rule your selection. For you have enough income to keep a gentleman interested but not enough to make him dishonest."

"Why are you being so generous?" Merrie asked with her impossible directness. "Do you feel I am compromised somewhat by our time in the tower room?"

"Blast you, I thought we'd forgotten that!" the earl exclaimed, rising and taking a quick, fuming walk about the room. She kept her eyes directly on him until he was himself, or rather his social self again. He took snuff with a great deal of casualness and said, "You are here in London to achieve your heart's desire, are you not? That is my object as well . . . to assist in that aim." His lips curled as he continued dryly, "Isn't that what you wish—to find another gentleman to belong to?"

"Fiddle! I don't belong to anyone but myself," Merrie replied, unaffected by his constant gaze. "But I am willing to *share* myself, as I hope the gentleman I love shall share his heart, his mind, himself with me." And she hurriedly departed.

In the back of the earl's mind had been the secret dread-hope that once told of the independence Miss Laurence might jolly well cease the desire to enter society and would return to Oxford and her quiet life there, leaving him to the comfortable social pattern he'd so long established as his life. Since meeting her, he found himself questioning his every interest. His very own ton, of a sudden, had turned tedious, the ladies predictable, hiding behind fans at his every remark instead of responding honestly. Lady Jane, the personification of perfection, could no longer be met without finding her every whispery remark comic, and as much an affectation as lisping. Such mannerism! Such falsity! Was it any wonder Merrie had been such a refreshing change?

And so the earl actually had been anticipating her sparking his select social world for him as well. Unless under the ton's critical glare, she seemed lesser. About which the earl was ambivalent and ambidextrous— wanting on one hand for all to see her as special as he did, and on the other hand, hoping they would not. For she could not really be so remarkable a lady while falling short of the criteria he had set for the lady of his choice. But then, if she were to fail, that would mean *he* had failed—for, egad, she was to represent him. Again, they had become too dashed well entwined.

So as he waited in the carriage for his family to join him on their way to Almack's ball, the earl admitted that he wished not only for Miss Laurence to be acceptable tonight, but his entire entourage. George was the first to join him in the carriage, demonstrating that he'd remembered the gentleman's dress code of Almack's by being properly attired in the more formal breeches rather than pantaloons. So many rules had to be explained to them all, so as to assure that they would not embarrass him by a faux pas. As well as dress restrictions, there was time prohibition. No one arriving after twelve would be admitted, even if he were the famed war hero the duke of Wellington. Indeed, that very lord had been coolly sent away for a five-minute tardiness. And if the ladies did not stop dawdling they would find themselves having to turn the carriage around for missing the curfew.

George assured his brother that they were ready, merely talking.

Talking! his lordship cried out in a huff, and was about to get down and reenter his town house prepared to rush them, when his mother and Esther appeared. George and his lordship jumped out to hand the ladies in.

Turning to Esther his lordship inquired, "Is your sister making an entrance, or is she still not put together?"

Esther assured him that her sister was dressed and ready but that Vinny needed a bowl of milk and Merrie had stopped to assure he would receive it.

"Ye gods," his lordship exclaimed, "on her most important evening she stops to play with a cat. The mind boggles."

The countess was quick to defend the girl. "Vinny is not aware of Almack's rules, and his stomach must be appeased. You would not enjoy yourself dancing and indulging in all the comestibles while Vinny was languishing in hunger at home, would you?"

"I dashed well would. I have a very competent staff, and if all of them together are not capable of feeding one animal, I should certainly like to know it."

"Brett, are you serious? Vinny never eats from a stranger's hands."

"It is needless to debate these points," Esther put in. "She will be here before the right or wrong of it can be settled."

His lordship glared at the lady. There was something about both Laurence ladies; they were never cowed by position, perhaps because they were so lowly themselves. He eyed her with some distaste, and found to his annoyance that there was naught amiss with the miss. Rather, although smaller than her sister and a delicate blonde, his connoisseur's eye told him she was faultless as she sat composed in a rather familiar white gown with blue muslin inserts. Could it be one of the ones he'd chosen for Miss Laurence? She did not have Merrie's wild streak, being more of a bluestocking, he'd surmised, always discussing things she'd read with George. And how that young scamp accepted it all said much for the young gentleman's civility. Now they were discussing a poet named Keats, one of the current Cockney set of lower-class rhymsters. She felt his eyes on her and gave him an encouraging smile. Blast it, as if he needed that young lady to tell him to keep his patience. But the smile had revealed that there was a generous heart under all that studiousness. And on further staring, he noticed that her features were more perfect that Merrie's. The countess had often claimed Esther was the exact image of her mother, who had had several lords after her in her season, and chucked them all for love. It looked as if this girl might be able to catch some younger son. He must spread the word that he intended to give her something on her marriage, and thus he might dispose of both Laurence ladies in one night.

Just as he'd reached the point of imagining himself happily rid of all the recent inhabitants of Warwick House, animals included, and particularly one lady who had the audacity to treat him like a common beau and keep him waiting like this, Merrie arrived. But blast her, she was carrying Vinny.

"He wanted to add his good wishes for our outing," she said with a laugh, and gave him up to the pleased countess, while assuring the lady that he had filled his belly and was quite content. After several of the countess's kisses and a few from Esther and a pat from George—the earl declined a parting message to the feline—Vinny was handed to the waiting maid, and they were off.

"Are you certain there is not a mouse in the pantry that has some pithy last words he wishes to bestow on us ere we embark?" the earl asked sarcastically, just keeping his voice in control.

Merrie stared at him and pretended to think that out. "No, I believe we are now set to conquer the ton."

His lordship signaled the coachman, and they were finally off. When she said that, there flashed in his mind their first meeting when she'd been so cheery about being taken up in his vehicle, speeding onward to Moorsedge, claiming it her destiny. And she'd certainly made a mark there. Mayhap he ought to believe she would do as well at Almack's. Merrie was dressed in the ermine cloak he had bought for her with the hood to hide her hair. He wondered if he ought to have gone to her room for a last-minute inspection. But that was not done to an unmarried lady. Yet he could have insisted on her reporting to him in the saloon for a final observation. In truth, he had not wished her to know how concerned he was about her appearance, not only because it would ruin his image of detachment, but also because it might even transmit some insecurity to her. And the most essential quality for social success was confidence. It really was not necessary to check her choice, for every gown was bound to be one of his selection, and so it could hardly be off the mark. By Jove, why was he clucking over her like a mother hen? She would look unexceptionable in whatever she wore. He had done all he could by giving her the creations and style; now it was up to her to carry through. And he forced himself to sit back with all confidence in his protégée.

But he sat forward upon catching sight of the lanterns decorating Almack's doorway. The row of coaches emptying indicated that it would be quite a squeeze, which was better for a first debut; for with so many people about, whether Miss Laurence measured up or not would not be generally noticed.

Within, there was more waiting for the ladies to leave their wraps in a small anteroom ere he escorted them up the stairs to the ballroom. The familiarity of his milieu at last composed the impatient lord. Nobles of his acquaintance stopped to chat. Lord Pavraam came up, and they fell to talking about his having missed coming to Moorsedge for Christmas. It was his loss, Lord Pavraam said with a laugh, and he meant that literally, having lost a prodigious amount at Oatlands, where the duke of York had never let them leave the whist table till they were depleted. And the duchess had him walking her hundreds of dogs in the evening damp, leaving him with a deuce of a cold. He'd just recovered enough to rejoin society and was wishful of being brought up to date on the *on-dits*. The earl obliged, during which he mentioned casually, "As well, I shall be introducing a protégée of mine tonight and perhaps you can ask the lady for a waltz?"

Lord Pavraam was astonished at the degree of concern in the earl's voice. Not like Warwick. Girl must be a positive antidote to need to beg her waltzes for her. Yet he couldn't imagine the earl ever allowing himself to be put to the bother of being helpful to another.

"Want her to meet a gentleman of taste and propriety," the earl was continuing, still shockingly concerned.

"If you mean me by that, dear boy, think again. Known for my impropriety, and so are you. But no fear, I shall give the lady a whirl." Lord Pavraam was about to question the earl further when his eyes beheld a vision and he gasped and reached for his quizzing glass. "Forget my promises, Brett. Shan't be dancing with anyone but *that* vision. Who the blazes is she? Gad, what a beauty!"

The earl turned in the direction of his friend's stare, although he knew in his heart who had just come into the vestibule, and his heart was not mistaken. It was Merrie.

Nevertheless Brett gasped when he saw her. Blast the girl, she'd worn the lace gown he'd planned, but not the decent white one; rather her own choice of the lace in pink. And that, as Madame Bliss had foreseen, was rather intimate; actually subtly daring, as if the lady were in the buff and blushing for it. And yet on closer viewing it was more severe and ladylike than any of the other off-the-shoulder, low-plunge silks. For the lace demurely went up to her long, graceful throat and covered the shoulders as well as her beautiful arms down to the very wrists. He did not know whether to rake her down or bow before her. At least her hairstyle was dressed exactly as he'd indicated, in a profusion of wild, fiery curls scooped up from the back and dressed high on the crown, yet falling down each side of her face and just touching her shoulders. Her green eyes, even from this distance, he could tell were shining emerald, and she wore the green emerald earrings he had given her yesterday. Not to quibble, but dash it, she should have been wearing pearls with pink! The emeralds went best with the white lace. It offended his fashion sense, yet she was carrying it off.

Concentrating on the earrings, he was rather pleased with them. They were exquisite: small diamonds circling rather fine emeralds, from which the emerald droplets almost grazed her shoulders. The emeralds were hypnotically accenting the green glow of her eyes. His creator's sense was appeased. She was perfection.

Then Merrie reached into her reticule for a hanky, and leaning over, removed a smudge from her sister's chin. In that one gesture, she'd ruined the mystery of her appearance and become an elder sister. Then she looked across at him and grinned, curtsying to demonstrate her choice of gown, and he nodded, and she became again in a twinkle the lovable Merrie he'd first known. Complex, adorable, breathtaking lady, he thought proudly. And turning to Lord Pavraam, he said, "Care for an introduction, or would you rather just gape at the lady all evening?"

"Egad, do you know her? I should rather think I want you to introduce me! Who the devil is she?"

"Part devil, part angel. She is my protégée-cousin, Miss Merrie Laurence. And that is her sister, Miss Esther Laurence. Both charming young ladies of great breeding and—I'm sorry to say—some intelligence."

"That's torn it," Lord Pavraam said with a grin, but no noticeable diminution in his racing toward the ladies for his presentation.

Lord Pavraam as the evening progressed was not the only one who felt himself having suffered an immediate *coup de bonheur*. All the gentlemen were struck. At first the earl was vastly delighted and prodigiously relieved at her success, which he took as his own. Indeed, he received several congratulations on her beauty, and accepted them without question, for if he had not quite created her, he'd at least perfected her.

And yet as the interest increased, his lordship felt a

shaft of resentment. He'd launched her, and she'd sailed forth, never looking back. Not one anxious glance toward him for reassurance or approval. In a short time Lord Warwick had several other reasons for his pique. It was the shocking behavior of the English gentlemen of the ton. One would think they had never seen a beautiful lady before. He attributed that partly to her newness; the bucks always reacted to new ladies by hovering. But the older, more experienced and hard-to-please lords were similarly dancing attendance, forgetting their dignity. A perfect example of that latter group was the duke of Chumley, who rarely put himself to the trouble of attending a lady when all the ladies were eagerly attending His Grace. A title so superior entitled one to grand-scale toadying, both the earl and duke naturally felt. Actually, the duke was nearer the countess's age, but of such standing and wealth, he had taken his time about wedding, and thus had long established himself as society's first bachelor. Nevertheless, this evening His Grace, after a mere distant view of one particular pink-laced lady, forgot his dignity and quickly approached Warwick for an introduction.

"Ward, old boy?"

"Cousin. And protégée of my mother's, of course."

"Like a candle, ain't she? Pale pink and flaring atop. Warms a fella just to look at her. Warms you right to your bones, egad. Any fortune?"

The earl mentioned the amount, and the duke nodded in delight. "No heiress, then. Not likely the younger bucks will beat me out. She's worth a fortune in herself. She danced by me and I felt the rheumatiz in my knee heal right up."

"She is rather adept at nostrums. Was quite a help to the countess when she had a similar complaint."

"Speak to her," he said, and walked off.

The earl assumed he meant Merrie, but the duke

was rather conversing with Lady Warwick. He was touching his knee, and she hers, and finally his mother signaled Merrie away from her crowd of gentlemen and introduced her. Instantly the duke was whirling her off. Not an ill selection for Miss Laurence, the earl felt with some relief. It would add to his own consequence, and would not overly distress him, as it would if, say, Lord Rockham were to approach her.

Naturally, no sooner had he had that dread thought than his competitor with all the ladies, that rake of a gentleman Lord Rockham smoothly glided up to the duke and interrupted his dance. His Grace was enough of a gudgeon to step aside. And before Brett had finished his grimace, Rockham was dancing off with Merrie and then compounding his affront by holding her indecently close. The two whirled by and Warwick noted with a sinking of his heart that Merrie was laughing fully and not even aware that she'd come so close to her sponsor that they'd practically touched. Not a glance around, seeking him. Well launched, indeed.

In truth, Merrie did not need to seek the earl out; somehow she was always aware of where he was. Even as she glided by with Lord Rockham, she felt Brett's eyes on her back, and increased the volume of her laugh.

Lord Rockham repeated his joke and she obligingly laughed again and looked him over with approval. Although he was just slightly taller than her statuesque physique, she felt doll-like, due to his muscular build. Probably rode as much as sixteen stone, yet he danced lightly on his feet. And his face and coloring made him somewhat similar in appearance to the czar of Russia, whose fawning descriptions had filled the periodicals a few years back on his visit to London. At Oxford, Merrie had read them all and dreamed of a meeting, yet here was the perfect substitute. Blond, assured, and most importantly, appreciative of a lady's charms, Lord Rockham won her instant approval. But by the end of the dance, Merrie began to find her first reaction fading, probably as a result of the watchful look in his light blue eyes even as he laughed. Yet he seemed to be quite taken by her, which could not help but please as he continually doused her with praise.

"Don't you ever draw breath between encomiums?" she asked with a tolerant glance.

"Most ladies would rather I spoke in that vein without drawing breath, unless to gasp at their beauty. Why do you object? Can there ever be too much praise?"

"Spanish coin never rings true."

"Oddsblood, are you so modest? I am, I admit, experienced at flattering ladies, but I have never beheld an object that so merited even my most exaggerated claims. Praise for you is superfluous, since you are perfection."

"Gammon."

"I speak to you from the heart and you laugh? Are you heartless?"

"Without doubt. Now you know my fatal flaw, and beware."

And at that moment the earl and a partner danced by, and he gave Lord Rockham such an icy glance that it truly intrigued him. She was, Rockham concluded, quite a package: a beauty, with some intelligence and a great deal of spirit, but most of all, she was Warwick's, and he was playing dog in the manger, was he? Ere the lady had left his side, Lord Rockham had decided she was fair game indeed, and might turn into a tasty little pullet he should dashed well enjoy winning. Henceforth, he hovered around the lady, and as the duke had been consistently hovering, Merrie could not go anywhere without her two guards armed with alarm that the other would see an advantage and seize it . . . and seize the lady.

Finally the earl had to take Lord Rockham aside. "My dear Cyril," he said coldly, "you are making an ass of yourself. I am the lady's protector, and I have already decided that you are not to be considered in the running. In point of fact, I have practically had an offer from the duke of Chumley."

"He will never be brought to scratch. And after His Grace, I am the next best catch in the room, I daresay. Barring yourself, and since she is a relation, we need not be competing for her as of old. What say? Let's allow the lady to decide whom she wishes for her follower. For I have certainly decided there could not possibly be a more alluring lady. Haven't seen her like for many a season. But she tells me she has no heart."

"She doesn't. Best stay away."

"Oddsblood, she was interesting before. Now she is a challenge I could not possibly resist. Much obliged."

"She does not have the heart for your kind of games. She is a total innocent of the heart and concerned only with bringing joy to others. Not at all the kind of lady with the devilry you desire," he was saying earnestly. "Leave her alone, or I shall have to assure your absence."

"She becomes more and more fascinating with your every word," Lord Rockham pronounced with eyes half closed as if in anticipation of his pleasure. The earl stomped off.

In a moment Lord Rockham was once again in the crowd around Merrie as several lords and gentlemen were vying to offer her ices and lemonade, Almack's never serving spirits. Almost predictably the duke was seeking Warwick in complaint. He'd not had a moment alone with the lady. The earl promptly invited him for tea on the next day, and then both gentlemen could be somewhat easier. But Merrie riled the earl by granting another dance to Lord Rockham. Most ladies knew enough not to show such marked preference for a gentleman unless there was an understanding between them. But Miss Laurence obviously did not know the first thing about this social game between ladies and gentlemen. Deuce take her, he thought, and he realized it was his obligation to set her straight on these fine points. And, in fact, with that happy duty in mind, he felt free almost immediately to cut in on the couple.

Dancing toward an outer area where there was less fear of being overheard, the earl said with cold languor, "You are cutting a poor figure indeed. One more waltz with that notorious rake and your reputation will not be worth a farthing! Did I outfit and bring you here to become a byword? I did not. Keep your mind on your objective. You are here to win a husband. And Lord Rockham is not the marrying sort. He is, bluntly, a cad with ladies."

"Rather like you, I expect."

"Exactly like me. That is why I know enough to warn you."

"But why must I be warned? Having become well acquainted with one rake, I find I have a marked preference for them, and am intrigued to see the difference in their maneuvers. Further, I no longer need to marry. You told me I could retire on my income. Very well, I shall just amuse myself. As you have been doing with all the ladies. I shall follow you in all things, my lord."

"Go to the devil!" he interposed, having lost his noted aplomb. "If you think I have perfected you, so that everybody is remarking on your beauty and charm, just to have it thrown away on such a one as

Rockham, I'd sooner lock you up in my tower room for life."

"It's too late for that," Merrie said undaunted, her eyes alight with amusement. "I am already out . . . loose upon society, and I am going to enjoy every minute of it. You lost your opportunity. You lost me. Be content now to allow someone else to enjoy me. And I to enjoy someone else."

"The hell I will," he muttered, and his black eyes bore down into her laughing eyes. "I hope to God you are just teasing, because if you mean it, you will rue this day. And perhaps I as well. I will allow you a decent marriage to a decent chap, such as the duke of Chumley, but anything else, *anyone else,* and I no longer hold back. You are then fair game. And to hell with propriety!"

The dance was over and Merrie curtsied to him. "The battle is joined, I collect," she said with a small laugh, and extended her hand to Lord Rockham waiting close by.

The earl was questioned by his mother as to the reason for his scowl. "Why aren't you dancing, my dear boy? There is Lady Jane trying to catch your eye for half the evening. Look you, she is not dancing at the moment, it is your opportunity."

"Let her and every woman go to the devil," he muttered, and stalked off.

"Really!" his mother exclaimed, and then looking at Merrie dancing now with the duke, she smiled. George was dancing with Esther. And in another moment the countess was asked to dance by a marquis, and she was pleased to join the happy group whirling about. Only Brett was not dancing. He was standing on the sidelines, his dark eyes scowling as he followed one bright flame flickering around the ballroom.

"Egad," he whispered to himself as the realization hit him that he should never have introduced her to his set. She'd conquered here as well as at Moorsedge. Apparently nothing would extinguish her fire, or the fire she'd lit in him, which at last he had to acknowledge.

The crowd of lords about Miss Laurence was pressing her close. How dare they talk with her, smile at her, touch her, when she belonged to him? The earl had a moment when he was one brief breath away from going up to the gentlemen and growling, "Leave her, she's mine!"

But then slowly, getting control of himself, Brett smiled. Obviously the solution was to take her away from the rest. He'd never had difficulty capturing a lady he sought. He'd been keeping away from Merrie, playing guardian. Now he would go toward her . . . and instruct her on the complexities of a master seduction. His advantage over her other admirers was that he knew her every thought, felt her feelings. And then, becoming aware that he was standing there, gazing at her like a rejected lover, he gave Lord and Lady Dansville a happy evening by finally standing up to Lady Jane. She whispered something to him, and although he was not certain what it was, he felt safe to nod.

16

After the ball, the season for Merrie moved in a dreamlike state indeed. For not only were all the gentlemen surrounding her and seeking her attention, but even the titled patronesses were speaking to her. Even Lady Jane condescended to nod to the "poor relation." Gone was Merrie's fear that society would cut her or at most give her a halfhearted welcome. She had put out her hand to the earl's world and it had taken her up. No longer did she feel herself a sham; for she had been accepted as herself. If not a society lady, she was once again a merry lady.

So much revelry was there about, it began to seem like continuous Christmas. Gifts were showered down on her, which the countess claimed were acceptable, as they were only trifles. Yet they would not have seemed inconsequential to the old Merrie. The duke gave her a lovely crystal bottle, etched and gilded; for perfume, she thought, until Lady Warwick recognized it as a vinaigrette, which certainly Merrie did not use; nor did even the countess rely on that of late. Nevertheless, Merrie gave it to her, wondering at the duke's lack of awareness of the lady he was pursuing. Sir Percy wrote her a sonnet to her left eyebrow and Lord Rule to her right one, which poems Esther read aloud, stopping to correct the meter, while Merrie listened with each honored brow lifting and twitching alternately.

Lord Pavraam gave her so many flowers, her boudoir and Esther's were turned into veritable hothouses. Even the earl surprised Merrie by not ceasing to give her gifts, especially a wardrobe of exquisite fans of hand-carved ivory or shell or froth of lace, after which she need never bemoan not having Titania's fan. But two of them were special and had her doubling over at the double entendre, for they were both peacock fans, one of the actual feathers and one of delicate black lace stitched in a peacock pattern.

Yet for all his more gracious actions, the earl was not yet part of her court, but continued to be seen at the various assemblies with Lady Jane herself. It lowered him in Merrie's opinion. Surely he could see how superficial a lady she was. Apparently being a lady was all that mattered to his lordship. But as she did not lack for lords' attentions, Miss Laurence need not repine or think about him above several times a day.

Then too, ambivalent man, he favored her with several dances and was curiously unmocking, even making an occasional compliment, each one seeming to be wrung out of his soul, and coming after an entire dance of silence; and each one she cherished more than all the poems and flatteries of all the other gentlemen. After a silent dance between them, in which they had both just felt their way through every motion and breath, he had said softly, "I wish you and I were in this ballroom alone, and every one else . . . gone to blazes!"

And that one sentiment, coming from his heart and reaching hers, had more value than all the comments on her eyebrows, her eyes, her comparisons to the sun and stars and heavens.

At first assuming his attentions were roused by the competition, she continued to flaunt her popularity, and never allowed him a hint of partiality. Nor did she favor any of her other admirers. Rather she made this a jolly game indeed, entitled seek-her-favor, and she set the rules, becoming Lady Misrule for all their gambols and pranks. A gentleman could win her approval by doing a good deed to an urchin in the street, or by dancing with a lady none would so honor. Any act of kindness was known to receive one back from Merrie, on the principle of casting one's bread upon the water. She kissed Sir Malcolm for visiting his ailing aunt not seen for several years; and the story was all over the ton that this one act of kindness had resulted in Sir Malcolm's being mentioned in the poor lady's will. For she promptly died, whether of surprise at someone's finally paying her attention was not disclosed, but much assumed. In his new flush of wealth Sir Malcolm proposed to the "merry lady" who had shown him the way to "true happiness." Since his true happiness was wealth, Merrie was uncertain whether it was an apt test of her philosophy, but certainly he was never merrier than henceforth. As for herself, she gained a most persistent swain, coming close in dedication to her chief admirers, the duke and Lord Rockham.

Whoever her escort on a particular day, Merrie was assured of enjoyment by insisting on the company of Esther and George or the countess, ostensibly for propriety's sake, but actually because Merrie always found more joy when her family was about her. If the duke became too verbose in his long-winded tales with no conclusion, George was always obliging enough to put a period to these wanderings by saying something of this ilk: "In short, Your Grace, you traveled through Switzerland."

"Er, exactly."

And when Lord Rockham became too warm, the countess would remove her fan and begin to fan both herself and Merrie in a mimed reprimand, and Merrie would laugh her silvery laugh, and Lord Rockham would find himself stalled. "Oddsblood, ain't a fellow ever to have a chance to show his talents? Some of these pretties have taken me a lifetime to perfect. Never thought they'd have ladies giggling."

But he was good-natured about these rebuffs; her failing to respond instantly to his usual maneuvers only made Merrie more desirable. Her challenge only whetted his appetite, as did his having finally to struggle for originality.

"Just be sincere," Merrie would say with a twinkle in her eye. And then she would spell out the word. "Just in case you have never heard it. In which case I recommend a thesaurus."

"You wound me, Miss Laurence. That a lady known for her kindness could be so cruel to a gentleman who is offering her not only sincerity, but his entire heart in the bargain."

"How often have you given that heart, my lord?" Merrie countered with amusement, and the countess, laughing as well, interposed to suggest that perhaps he had a convenient cache of hearts to give out to several ladies of a season.

Merrie fell into whoops at that remark, and Lord Rockham, smiling thinly, felt it essential to have some moments alone with the lady. But her family was always about. While the group had been walking through the gardens of Green Park, Lord Rockham resorted to a devious turn by actually turning Merrie down a secluded lane.

"Are you trying to lead me down the garden

path?" Merrie exclaimed with mock alarm, but allowed him a few moments' private stroll. Yet he took advantage of that opportunity to seize her hand and kiss it on the palm.

"For shame, my lord. I granted you a moment of privacy, and you instantly abuse it."

"You have me in a flame, you fiery creature. I cannot think of anything but your jeweled eyes—they glow into my soul and leave me wild with the need to look deeper, closer into them. I believe in there I shall find heaven."

"You are looking in the wrong direction for that place. I suggest you elevate your glance skyward," Merrie exclaimed, stepping back from his attempt to stare directly into her eyes.

Yet he would not allow her to turn from their face-to-face encounter, exclaiming, "You have bewitched me. Oddsblood, I cannot sleep but I dream of those lips." And he pulled her close seeking not salvation but oblivion in her lips. The kiss was interrupted by George's calling out her name, and in a few moments George and Esther had discovered them. With a curse, his lordship released Merrie.

"You forget yourself," Merrie whispered. "And you forget that I am a lady—taking such liberties!" She walked huffily away from him. And the next day on her visit to Hyde Park with the countess, she refused to allow him even to take her up for a short trot in his high-perch phaeton.

Realizing he'd overstepped the boundaries of propriety, he sent her letter after letter of profuse apologies. She at last forgave him, just not to have to read through those verbose, wild missives. As well she had to be fair, and while she'd allowed Lord Warwick several kisses in the past and continued to speak to him, she could not act more severely to her new suitor. Yet her feelings were not judiciously ruled. She had been

more alarmed by Lord Rockham's one liberty than
Brett's several kisses throughout Christmas. Of course
Lord Warwick had had the excuse—he for giving, and
she for accepting—of those being mistletoe kisses
. . . and later, wassail kisses. Also in the season for
loving, one could not but expect some such demon-
strations. For look how circumspect the earl had been
subsequently; certainly he'd not attempted anything
of the sort here in London. Oh, he'd touched her
hands, and there had been that delicious feeling when
he brushed her hair, but otherwise he'd been most
respectful of her person. Mayhap it was the influence
of Christmas that had made his kisses at Moorsedge
seem more engulfing than Lord Rockham's. As a penance, Merrie had Lord Rockham take up in his phaeton Lady Beaumaris, known and much avoided for
her waspish tongue, but amusing to Merrie. After his
lordship had borne that noblewoman's company with
civility, she rewarded him by accepting his invitation
to a play, naturally with George and Esther included.

Nothing was as delightful to Merrie as going to
plays. She had not as yet had the opportunity to see a
Shakespearean performance, for all her escorts preferred the lighter comedies, and the duke was ad-
dicted to the spectacular showings at Astley's where
harlequins cavorted and horses pranced on cue. Admittedly Merrie had prodigiously enjoyed Astley's
herself, especially the lady who stood up on her horse
and jumped through a hoop of fire. That had Merrie,
Esther, and George all on their feet cheering for an
encore.

So much for Brett's promise of Shakespeare, Merrie thought as the season advanced. She dropped
hints, but the earl was above them all. Nor did he
honor her with a personal invitation to any affair.
Either he was playing a deep game or losing interest,
Merrie concluded. But the countess heartened her by

confiding that her son regularly attempted to draw out information from her on Merrie's every thought, outing, and beau. Not having been a belle in her day for naught, the countess knew when to be vague and when to be precise. And she was not above teasing her son, something she would never have done before Merrie. "It's so loving of you to be concerned about us. But, believe me, dear Brett, we have a great many protectors here in London. You need not put yourself to the bother. I recollect you never wished your family to be a burden in your social jaunts. And Merrie, Esther, George, and I are deliberately attempting to give you all the freedom you always wished."

The earl eyed her cautiously. "You have changed considerably since Miss Laurence has come into your life," he said probingly.

"Yes, haven't we all! I am so grateful to her for my transformation! Are you not pleased to see me so well and happy? And yet not heavy on your hands?"

"If I ever gave you that feeling, Mama, I regret it," he said with sudden truth. "Deeply."

The countess was moved by his declaration, and gave him a vigorous hug. "You are still my darling boy," she whispered and walked away without Brett's having learned as much about Merrie's feelings as she had learned about his. Failing with his mother, the earl took Simpson into his confidence, the butler always being one his lordship could trust implicitly not only to know what was afoot but to keep everything confidential. And Simpson lived up to his master's expectations by not scrupling to read every invitation on the hall table, and quizzing the lady's maid, and was thus able to make a full and much appreciated report to Lord Warwick. Still, Brett's best source was George. One merely had to ask him and he'd reveal everything—where they'd been, what they'd done, who had been casting lures at Merrie or taking any liberties. And so through all these various means, Brett was able to keep Merrie under his observation if not control.

Coincidentally Merrie was also keeping the earl in mind when not in sight. As well as talking to Lord Pavraam about his and Brett's youthful escapades, she relived with Sir Oswald and his fiancée Miss Prichard the joys of Christmas at Moorsedge, culminating with memories of the earl's helmeted antics. Even Lord Rockham's kiss had been used, Merrie admitted, as a frame of reference for Brett's kisses. Brett, Brett—he haunted her, present or not present, and Merrie's only recourse was to surround herself with other gentlemen, hoping his effect would begin to dissipate or that she would finally reach him.

For the latter, her best tactic was keeping Lord Rockham at her side despite her growing dislike of the gentleman, for he riled the earl enough to keep the earl in attendance. With Brett in her train and all the other gentlemen following, Merrie was enjoying herself down to her toes. What a spree, after years of quiet academic life, to be in the heart of London's social whirl. But Merrie's greatest delight came surprisingly from the duke. After all her comments, he'd finally gotten the message and arranged to take her to a Shakespearean performance of Edmund Kean's at Drury Lane, which was more than could be said for the earl. She hoped for *Hamlet* or *Richard III,* but as they were not scheduled, she settled for *The Merchant of Venice.* Kean's Shylock, she heard, had made men weep. But on their way to the theater as George was handing up Esther and Merrie into the duke's waiting carriage, His Grace, to their dismay, relayed the possibility of Mr. Kean's not being there for the performance. "Fellow recently missed one, shot in the neck, don't ya know."

"Dead?" Esther asked in alarm.

"Drunk," George said, explaining the cant.

On arrival at Drury Lane, however, they were all relieved to discover that the actor was there and ready to perform. And he gave the performance of their lives, they all agreed during the first intermission. By the second act, Merrie was finally able to enjoy the play fully as the duke fell asleep and no longer needed her to interpret every line. With George and Esther holding hands through the trial scene, Merrie could forget about them, as well, and allow herself to be Portia on the stage. There she stood, meting out justice and having everyone rejoicing at the happy ending. In an ecstasy over the poetry and message, Miss Laurence was softly repeating the lady's speech, " 'The quality of mercy is not strain'd; it droppeth as the gentle rain from heaven,' " when Brett slid into an empty chair in their box.

Bowing, he whispered, "Portia, come to judgment, give me the mercy of your company," and Merrie shushed him, although he spoke no louder than the duke's snores.

At the conclusion, when the duke awoke, he asked, "By Jove, did you come with us, Warwick? I don't recall you here."

"You wound me, Your Grace. Does my presence make so little an impression?"

"Apparently so," Merrie answered. "Either that or a false impression."

"Ah, the effect of this play has not lasted; where be all the mercy you saw yourself handing out to us lesser mortals?"

Merrie had to laugh at his awareness of her thinking pattern, and forthrightly confessed that in her mind's eye she had been on stage. He eyed her tolerantly, and they began to accept each other, lowering their swords a bit for the pleasure of being together. The duke came along like a chaperon as Lord Warwick took them all backstage to meet Mr. Kean. The great actor was surprisingly short of stature, which was not that obvious on stage; however in an intimate setting the drama of his black eyes was even more hypnotic.

"An admirer of yours, Edmund." Lord Warwick introduced Merrie to the actor, who kissed her hand with much swagger.

"That is his Hamlet's gesture to Ophelia," a female voice interrupted, and a diminutive lady with brown hair was introduced, a Miss Ophelia Brown, who was being escorted by an animal almost as large as herself; it was Mr. Kean's pet lion Caesar. Any alarm was instantly tempered by the way that lady stroked the beast. Caesar sniffed around the visitors, who were all pretending they were quite accustomed to having the various parts of their anatomies nudged by a lion's muzzle. At last Merrie cried out as Caesar went further in his familiarities and lifted her dress high up with his paw.

Miss Brown castigated the animal and moved him a few feet away, but the duke was offended. Merrie, blushing, forgave the beast.

"It's what every gentleman wishes he could do," Brett said with the laughter still shaking him, and then leaning closer to Miss Laurence, he whispered, "I am delighted to see you are wearing the lace chemise from Madame Bliss's."

Before Merrie could object to that ungentlemanly mention of her unmentionables, Mr. Kean, who never allowed any after-theater conversation to continue without himself as the central topic, brought them back to his performance, during which Esther and George stepped aside for a closer view of Caesar. They were much enthused by the lion's presence, undoubtedly a sign to them to take courage and announce their feelings to the earl. And Esther concluded that her dear Androcles would undoubtedly be able to make the earl understand and accept their marriage.

A lull had occurred in the conversation, during which some of Esther's words carried back, and then all of George's as he swore he would fight a dozen lions for Esther.

But there was no need for words as the earl turned and viewed the two holding hands. Then, of a sudden, as if a hundred candles had been lit at once, he saw the truth behind the facade of George and Esther's friendship, and he turned back to accuse Merrie, his white face demanding her confession. Merrie attempted to deflect the moment by chatting on with the group, but it was too late, the earl had understood it all. He took a step forward, grabbed her by the wrist, and said coldly, "So this is my reward for housing and bringing you out. This the quid pro quo for my annuities and dowry and turning you into a presentable creature. Is this perfidy the way you keep to our bargain?"

"I have kept our bargain," Merrie said softly, attempting to walk away. But he held her fast. The duke and Mr. Kean were eyeing the earl with disfavor.

"I say," His Grace warned, "I hope you are not being disrespectful to the lady, and in my presence."

"You go to the devil," the earl said to the blustering gentleman, and then turning to Merrie, he pronounced bitterly, "You jade."

"You'd do very nicely on the boards, my lord," Mr. Kean put in, "but if you are to curse at a lady, one must do it either sotto voce, or gentility be damned, and let it come rolling across the pit. 'You *jade!* You *strumpet!*' And then reaching over and unclasping the lady from the lord's determined grasp, he pulled her close to himself and proclaimed, " 'Out, strumpet! weep'st thou for him to my face?' "

Merrie instantly recalled the play and, appreciating the actor's attempt to cause a diversion, seized the opportunity to act with the greatest actor in her lifetime by replying, " 'O, banish me, my lord, but kill me not!' "

Approving the lady's perspicacity, Edmund Kean rolled his eyes and became before them all the menacing Othello. Merrie recollected a few more speeches but soon faltered, leaving Kean to conclude on his own, as he really preferred. Whereupon he smothered her to silence and embarked on his suicide scene, kissing the dead Desdemona with his last breath dying "upon a kiss."

Both rose up at the applause begun by Esther and George who had hurried over to see the performance. The duke was congratulating them all, including the earl, assuming he had been part of the scene as well, during which Mr. Kean leaned close to Merrie to whisper that she was too beautiful to deal with Othellolike tempers and ought rather to stay away from all these blasted lords. She nodded with gratitude at both his rescue and advice, but nevertheless allowed His Grace to escort her out of the theater.

Merrie had had a unique evening. She had acted Shakespeare with Edmund Kean himself. It would be a moment never to be forgotten, and she would write all about it to her mother and father. But still that could not completely wipe out the menace of the earl's anger at his discovery of George's and Esther's affection. She was relieved that he remembered himself in time to swallow his wrath and for the rest of the evening be on his best, most lordly behavior.

In truth, Brett had had shock after shock. First the discovery of Merrie's perfidy in matching George and Esther right under his nose. And then when he'd simply reacted naturally to Miss Laurence's scheming, he'd been silenced and shown up by a mere playactor. And the choice of Mr. Kean's scene had not been too subtle for the earl to grasp—showing up his temper, and yes, jealousy. And as if a rhymed reprimand by a playactor was not sufficient, he'd been further silenced by Merrie's unladylike acting with the leading performer, which was as close to tying one's garter in public as a lady could come, and further naturally called up the tower scene, leaving him nonplussed. Miss Laurence had a way of creating scenes on call that continually confused him. With no other recourse but to muzzle his words and stifle his feelings, his lordship took himself off to his club.

Immediately upon entering Warwick House, Merrie warned Esther and George of the earl's having overheard them and understanding that they were pledged. That comment led to an awkward and somewhat amusing moment when George, abashed, had to apologize for his lack of fidelity to her, but Merrie, smiling, shushed them both, admitting that their love was her fondest dream come true, and indeed both she and the countess had been waiting all this season for the couple finally to confess their feelings so that they could share their delight.

That brought out relieved exclamations all around, as well as many kisses between the two sisters and the new in-law. But amidst their celebration, Merrie warned that while she and the countess would stand buff, Lord Warwick was seriously displeased, and must be dealt with.

"Leave Brett to me," George said. "If I have your good wishes and Mother's, I shall jolly well bring him around."

Merrie, uncertain with what degree of jollity he could accomplish that, once again wished them well and went off to bed.

17

The following day the earl invited Merrie for a ride in his high-perch phaeton at Hyde Park at the hour of the grand strut when the crème de la crème were driven about for the gentlemen to show off their carriages and the ladies their conquests. Everyone nodded to everyone else, and exchanged *on-dits* such as which lady had caught the eye of the prince regent, the duke of Chumley, or more ecstatically, the earl of Warwick.

But the lady in the earl's carriage was more wary than ecstatic, and her suspicion grew when he allowed the groom to walk the horses while they strolled down a garden walk.

The day was brightly sunlit, so there was no exterior reason for Merrie to have a sense of foreboding. She raised her green ruffled parasol that matched her gown, which was not really necessary as she was wearing the large brimmed leghorn straw that the earl himself had chosen with the emerald ribbon that tied under her chin. She did not need her mirror to tell her how absolutely enchanting she appeared; there are certain items of clothing, such as an extravagant ball gown, a fur cloak, or in this case, a very wide-brimmed hat, that give a lady the feeling that she is in her best looks.

Yet Brett viewed the young girl's attire with a grimace. He very well remembered selecting that hat, and Miss Laurence looked even better in it now with her red hair picking up the glints of the sun than in the shop. And the green of the ribbon was precisely correct, he praised himself, as she turned her green eyes toward him.

"Yes, you look unexceptionable," the earl said grudgingly.

"I have you to thank for my fashionable appearance, and you to thank for our exhilarating ride this morning. It is true you are a capital whip, and I wish I could catch the thong as you do."

Not allowing a typical Merrie diversion, the earl came immediately to his well-sharpened point, "I have thought all night, wondering how I could have been such a caper-witted idiot. Your reason for bringing your sister to town was all along to capture George's affections, was it not?"

"Yes."

So astonished was he at her readily admitting her manipulation, for a moment his lordship had naught to say.

And so Merrie continued, "Well, partially. I did miss my sister. But in the back of my mind I thought George was such a wonderful person, filled with fun and goodness, and he loved me so. And I loved him, as a brother, and I loved my sister, and thought since I could not return his feelings, there was a possibility that two sterling people could meet and love. And so I introduced them. And they were exactly suited. For while George is, or rather was, a bit of a scamp, Esther is remarkably serious and studious for her age.

And she has had a sobering effect on George, while he has caused her to see life in the present, rather than always looking in books and in the past. That is my father's influence, and I wished her to have a few months of joy. . . ."

"If I were *her* father I should perhaps be brought to see the effect of your argument, but I am George's guardian, and he has not had the opportunity to meet anyone but Laurence ladies."

"Nonsense," Merrie said, stopping to pick a late daffodil and cupping it in her hands for a moment, adding with full emotion, "This daffodil is of itself worthy of all the gold in the world. One cannot gild it, any more than one could a lily, and similarly one cannot make Esther more lovely and loving than she is even with all the titles and dowry in the world. And George has been to many affairs since we've been here, and danced and met the most titled ladies, and always talks of what they would be like running with him on the moors, claiming, with a grin, how they would want him to hold their parasols while they joined him in a measured step or two. And the soul in George would be crushed."

"You are crushing him," his lordship inserted with a look of offense. "Reducing him to your level. One by one you win them over—my mother, my brother, even my society, and we must all stoop to please you. And somehow you make us all less, while you take all."

She turned away from him for a moment, her green eyes almost tearing in disappointment, and then calmly faced him. "Why do I keep believing in you? But no matter—Esther and George are genuinely meant for each other. Fate has rescued George, through her, from inevitably following in your footsteps and becoming the stuffed-up noble that you are, concerned only with seeking pleasure or how best to obey the contemptible cockscomb dictums of your vainglorious set."

The earl's face was dark, as she, *she* who had deceived him, was suddenly turning it all into his error. "That is enough, Miss Laurence. You have made your opinion of me quite understood. I shan't scruple to inform you that not all virtue is to be found in the poor, relations or not. Indeed, I expect some are poor of mind and soul as well as of position and finances."

"I did not say the poor were better, but they are necessarily less frivolous. And having lived your life of late, I find it is corrupting. I find where I once would rise and lay my own fire, I now expect others to do it for me. And yesterday my abigail had a toothache, and I did not know it. I let the poor girl help me to dress, until I spotted her distress and sent her to her bed. One becomes blind to others when one is living a life of pleasure, and then the pleasures fade and one's heart grows callous. And all is boring. Where before I was happy with one bedraggled bonnet, I am now unhappy with a wardrobe of them. Unless I share them, they weigh on my soul heavier than on my head. Do you understand? But I fear you never shall. And we can discuss it all day and rake each other down, and yet the truth is that *our* philosophies of life are irrelevant. The issue at hand is that George loves Esther. And she is a devoted, darling girl who will make him superbly happy, and has already made your mother happy. These things you have been loath to do. Are you not relieved that someone else is willing to do it for you so you and Lady Jane can continue your pointless, whispered existences! I cannot understand why you object to Esther. You've met her and must know her for a sincere and lovely person. Certainly you have sufficient position not to need an addition to your family's consequence. Why not add to their joy?"

"Joy is your goal for everyone, is it?" he said with a laugh. "Yet somehow the only way people are allowed happiness is if they believe as you do. And I have shown you my way of life, and you sneer at it. Very well, why not return to the pleasure of your previous existence? I expect there are a great many lords and ladies who would be quite willing to give you a position as their maid and you may lay as many fires as you wish, and revel in your poverty."

"There is no speaking to you," Merrie said coldly, and turned back to the carriage. "It is too late for me to go back, so you need not look for that. I am now a lady and shall be forced to barter myself as ladies do, and it is similarly too late for you to pluck out of the hearts of Esther and George their deep love. Try it, and you shall only lose a brother as you almost lost a mother, and now have lost a friend."

He drove her home in silence and went directly to have a talk with George, who was quite open with him as always. "I loved Miss Laurence with all my heart, but she was a dream I had during Christmas. She claimed we would not suit. Yet I did not believe it, hoping rather she'd not find a gentleman worthy of her here in London and turn to me, but then I met Esther. And I realized Miss Laurence was correct. There is naught like having a lady who really cares for one to the heart. Esther is better for me than Miss Laurence. She sobers me, has me thinking of my worth and my future, and that is not in London. How long can one exist on mere pride over one's cravat, by Jove?"

Brett was so astonished at this new George that he did not know what to say to him. Indeed, he had noticed that George, after his first plunge into fashion excess, had returned to more sensible apparel. But George was still pontificating, albeit with his familiar endearing grin, which took away some of the sting.

"What's the purpose, Brett, of society ruling that a cravat is to become wider and taller, unless it is to assure that one's head cannot bend to view those beneath one? A stiff-necked fashion that allows one only to strut and be on display. And I don't give a groat for all the gamboling and *on-dits,* and I shudder to think what I would have been if I had not met Esther. She gives me purpose, because she is a lady with a mind and soul as well as a body to dress. And yet, her beauty is richer than all the ladies I have met here. We are going to be wed and go exploring to Greece and Italy. Might stay in one of those places for a while, and when we return I shall go back to Oxford with her and take another degree. I had hoped you'd be happy for me. But my course is set whether you approve or not. I have my own independence from Uncle Thomas, and for the life we plan to live, on a modest side, we shall not need considerably more. I ask naught from you, Brett, but your handshake and good wishes, and the chance to see you at times when we are in London."

Brett saw his brother extending his hand, and could not refuse it. Actually it was too late—a certain lady had so mesmerized Georgie—nay, say rather proselytized him until he would accept another in her stead, as long as she was of the same cloth. With the result that he had lost a young brother intended for his select circle, and now could just view George as one would a lady having taken the veil: wishing he might not wake some day to his loss and regret it. And so resigned, the earl shook his brother's hand, assuring him that he would not stand in his way, with the stipulation that he not continue to lecture him. And George dropped his serious manner and gave his brother a playful punch, enthusiastically planning Brett's inclusion in his life as his best man at the wedding and eventually as a visitor to their establishment in Athens. And Brett could do no less than civilly assure him that he should be delighted to do both.

"If we can drag you away from White's for any considerable time," George teased, and Brett bowed, but resented his brother's condescending view of him as a shallow fellow. Ah, it was outside of enough to have one's younger brother more serious than oneself. The score was to be settled someday, he vowed, and he knew with whom that should be done.

That very *who* shortly gave his lordship an approving nod upon George's announcing that Brett was a regular trump who would be the best man at his marriage to Esther. Merrie's smile was so inclusive that Brett felt himself accepted back into his own family, and he resented that she could determine whether that occurred or not. But just to cut her down to size, he could not take back his promises, not with George so committed and the countess so liberally praising him. And then Esther approached hesitantly, as would have a doe, so what could he do naught but smile at her: he would have been a monster else. He even extended his hand and she took it happily and called him "my dear brother." Naturally, he responded by simply saying "sister," which was apparently the correct thing, for it was universally applauded.

And when he went to his club that evening, he did everything twice over, once for himself and once for poor Georgie, who would never know those pleasures. He gambled and lost ten thousand pounds and then doubled it before the night was over, and went on a toot with Lord Pavraam until morning. And felt better for it—more honest, more himself. It would not be so dashed simple to change him, as she had his brother, the earl thought with pride. And he stayed away for a sennight, reveling.

Returning, he found everyone aflutter at Merrie's having received a marriage proposal.

"What is so extraordinary about that?" Brett asked, waiting for Simpson to take his gloves and depart before continuing. "Did she not receive one from Sir Malcolm as well as Sir Percival?"

It was his mother who answered, for Merrie was curiously silent. "He came in yesterday and asked my leave to speak to her. Very proper. And then he took Merrie into the conservatory and actually got down on one knee to request that she become his duchess."

"The devil you say?" the earl exclaimed. "The *duke* proposed?"

"Yes, is it not delightful? Merrie will be a duchess and will rule all society. Would you have believed it?"

Brett stared at that lady, who was not smiling. She was obviously in a state of near suspension as she waited for his response, with not even a blink of her long lids. He turned about and saw the rest of them waiting for his next words as well, and resented it. Shrugging in his most lordly way, he said, "Naturally I am delighted. This is a coup indeed. There were bets being made at White's that he would not come up to snuff. I admit I backed the side that claimed he would. I expect I shall be asked to give you away, and I shall be honored to take part in that ceremony."

Merrie's face had gone from a blush at hearing that he'd bet on her future as if she were a common gentleman's sport, to a complete paleness at his last offer.

"I have not accepted him . . . *yet*," she said. And then taking a breath, she added with emphasis, "His Grace's action has made it essential that I cease dallying. We all have to make our moves eventually, rather than continuing to stand pat. And so I am at this moment considering all offers before I make my final choice."

The earl's eyes darkened at that. In there, within his lordship the earl, there was Brett. She was reaching out to him, but he remained unattainable, re-

sponding indifferently, "I hope you are not considering Sir Malcolm or that idiot Lord Rule. They would
not suit, unless I mistake and you prefer fools whom
you can best push about. Of course, not all society is
composed of nodcocks and gudgeons." And he
bowed at that.

"I have already refused them," Merrie put in
quickly. She was uncertain why he was so bitter after
the easy, generous way he had accepted George's and
Esther's engagement. And though he and she had
come to cuffs over that, his moment of calling Esther
sister had wiped out all resentments left in her, and
she had supposed in him. Rather, she'd opened her
heart to him completely, as had Esther. They had all
become one happy family, and she waited for him day
after day to come and complete the connection.

And now he had come, and she was all at sea at his
maintaining his distance. She threw him looks of encouragement, but he remained on the opposite shore.
To pique his interest she had only her usual maneuver
and was loath to fall back on that, but could think of
no other way to shake him out of his lordly, indifferent aplomb! And so taking a deep breath, she said, "I
have narrowed it down to *two*."

The earl felt a slight dread and could not quite
eliminate all interest from his words. "And the other
is? . . ."

"Lord Rockham."

"The devil," he whispered, wincing.

"Not quite that. But I suspect he needs me more
than the duke."

"I won't allow that."

"You have nothing to say about my choice," Merrie said, and walked into the conservatory. He followed her and those outside were hoping that where
one noble had proposed, another might do so as well.

"You will live a life of debasement if you marry Lord Rockham," he said seriously.

"Do you have some other suggestion?" she asked frankly.

"If you mean shall I propose to you to save you from Lord Rockham, I shall not. I do not wish to be other than I am, living my own social life. I am not a puppet for you to pull the strings as you do to Mama and George. I do not permit anyone else to control me. You thought I would propose because you put those weapons to my head. But I say, you are adult enough to choose your own destruction. I shall not rescue you."

Merrie felt her heart lurch. There was a silence then, as both hurriedly attempted to gather up their shattered emotions. But Merrie could no longer play society games. Rather she was shamed at having done so. She had held the two offers before him as if she were an object on auction. And he had left her humiliated by his blatant refusal to bid.

"You are correct," Merrie said, resorting to her basic honesty, "I did deliberately attempt to coax you into a proposal. And that is shameful. But . . ." She gestured a hopeless inability to say more. Yet the tyrant honesty insisted that she make amends for her ploy by not protecting herself even the slightest. And so forgetting modesty, forgetting that a lady never spoke first to a gentleman, forgetting all but the feelings there between them, she said, "The truth is, I sincerely, with all my heart, love you, my lord."

"Confound you!" the earl exploded as if she'd knocked him flat with her smallest finger, and the surprise of it had him gasping. But in the next instant, he'd recovered enough to say, "I am not the total gudgeon you seem to think. I've had the most expert ladies in the world confessing their love for me, assuming once they did that I could not do less than love them in return. But I never have. Nor will."

Merrie shook her head in confusion. He was not supposed to say that. A gentleman, no matter how loath to wed, if he loved at all would not speak thusly, unless she had been mistaken—about him, about their love, about love itself. Was not love so strong and truth so strong that if one used both they could demolish anything standing in their way? Yes, love and truth must out, though hell itself stood between. And she remembered the night in the tower room that he had spoken his love, and since then he'd told it her as well, through their touching and glances. How then explain his words now? Shuddering, she recollected a similar moment, the morning after their time in the tower room. He had tossed her aside then, implying that she was not worthy, and she had stupidly attempted to show that she could succeed in his milieu with this game of high-bid proposals, proving that those he valued—the dukes, the lords—all wanted her. And yet that was not enough, as he still, still, kept pushing her away.

"Don't look as if you've been slapped, curse it!" he said gruffly, and he ached to comfort her and yet could not bring himself to do so unless it was on his terms. Therefore he used that road to take her into his arms.

"I have taught you much, Miss Laurence. Here is one more lesson. When declaring your love to a gentleman, you had best not do it when you are alone and subject to some impropriety."

Before Merrie could understand his warning, he demonstrated by taking her swiftly and harshly into his arms and kissing her. She let him kiss her completely as her confusion was quickly, joyously shoved aside by the passion she felt in his lips.

"You do love me," she whispered, "you do," and

she let down all the bars before her love and kissed him back, and they were flat against the wall of the conservatory when the row of ferns greened the moment for them, one frond leaning toward Merrie's face like Christmas greenery; and his lordship shoved it aside to reach her neck and felt her arms embracing him, welcoming him, and he it was, he sensed, being overcome, being won over instead. So recoiling, he pushed her quickly away.

"You should remember that I have made you a lady," he said, his voice sharp enough to suit the steel words, "but you are behaving like a slut."

And the new comfort their physical unity had momentarily provided was blown away. Those words could not have come from the man who'd just been holding her in his arms, but from a stranger with a shuttered face. Merrie tried to open to him, to send him all her love over his closed heart—she, a lady of complete love and he, a lord of none. And then she knew, and was saddened to her heart, and said with resignation, "No wonder you are looking for a heartless lady to wed. Ah, fiddle! You are afraid of love. Have to be half-foxed with wassail to say you love me, and now though I feel your heart is mine, you fear to risk it. Well, so be it. But someday when you are living a life of faultless propriety with your proper lady wife, and you have petrified into an effigy that is suited only for caskets, remember you threw away the chance to really love and be loved in return. Then go to your tower room and listen to the first earl, who knew there was only one correct woman in life, even if he had to rid himself of all others to find her. There you'll remember that we could have had a love not easily found in several lifetimes of searching. But, fearing to risk, you turned your back on it. As I finally am turning my back on you, shamed that I loved a coward even for a while, for the greatest cowardice is not in battles, nor in adventures, but in the fear to give and receive love." And with that, shaking her magnificent red hair, Merrie turned her back on the earl indeed.

Head up, she walked toward the anxious waiting family she loved and said with a grin, "Apparently, the conservatory only influences dukes. I am to be a duchess."

Tears falling down their cheeks, the countess and Esther followed her to her room where she smiled and wiped their eyes and assured them there were worst fates than being a duchess, and had them laughing at that.

When the earl passed his brother on his way out for the evening, George did not say a word. Yet the earl shot back in defiance, "I do not wish to be told whom to marry, damn it!"

George shook his head at him. "Your heart tells you that, and you just follow along. It's like jumping a fence—if you hold back last moment, you'll head for fall. If you go with your mount you'll sail right over, and that is the secret of love."

"Bosh!" the earl said, and walked out with a snap of his heels.

18

When Lord Rockham proposed, Merrie disposed of him swiftly.

Never having so favored a lady before, Lord Rockham was aghast at her immediate refusal. Nor did she offer him the slightest face-saving excuse of claiming that her heart was otherwise engaged. Rather she delivered a flat, unequivocal rejection. And this from a lady who was not of the first level, and to whom he had humbled himself for no purpose, after all. He said bitterly, "If you are expecting Warwick to come up to scratch, one can only feel the profoundest sympathy. Never has there been a lord so conscious of his standing. Not likely he would allow his feelings to make him forget his responsibility to his name and position, as I have done. But I am wild with desire . . . and love for you. I implore you to rethink your reply."

"Rather an insulting declaration, actually," she concluded, "and yet I collect you mean to be honoring me. Still, having been refused, it is prodigiously offensive to continue your case, and beneath you to beg."

"I! *Beg?*"

"Another word for *implore.* I make no bones about my feelings. They have never been engaged by you. Shall we join the others?"

And he had stood there, like a stock, not remembering his duty as a gentleman to escort her back to where George and Esther waited. Therefore, she turned away from his stunned face and walked away on her own.

Her sympathies might have been engaged by his plight had one supposed him to feel more than a physical fancy. But obviously he did not. And her refusal would scarcely injure a gentleman known to keep a string of ladies as he kept a string of racehorses. The duke of Chumley was beginning to seem clearly above all her other escorts. Yet Merrie's heart refused to accept a lifelong commitment to a gentleman who did not have her complete affection. She devoted several hours each morning to reviewing his good points and then waited for even a spurt of love. None sprang up.

The countess was the only one who believed the duke possessed many inestimable qualities and so Merrie regularly repaired to her to hear her expound upon them. Nothing loath, Lady Warwick spoke of his consideration, his gentility, his good spirits, and even his pleasing physiognomy. "Mostly," her ladyship concluded, "he is an accommodating gentleman. All in all, one cannot look for a better or rarer quality in a husband. It would make life so . . . comfortable."

And Merrie had nodded and was prepared to accept comfort—she so needed it, after his lordship's uncaring cruelty.

Sitting at her silver standish, Merrie realized she'd been staring at a blank piece of writing paper for upward of an hour, attempting to compose an acceptance. It was best to accept His Grace out of his presence, for her heart might at the last moment cry out and stop her. Here with a piece of paper facing her, instead of the doglike brown eyes of the duke, she was able to forget certain aspects of marriage ahead.

At the same time, Lord Rockham was also writing —his list of all the moves in his stratagem to change Miss Laurence's answer. He had already set some of those plans in effect. First he had taken up Lady Jane in his carriage. It was, he had found in his dealings with her ladyship, essential that they be away from all noisy crowds. Thus he chose a quiet avenue and even had his horses at a stand. And there, he acquainted her with his desire to wed Miss Laurence. When she wondered why she was the recipient of this announcement, he overwhelmed her with praise for her knowledge of social standing and how an earl's prestige might be seriously jeopardized by a marriage to a lady beneath him, such as his protégée.

That had Lady Jane's full attention, and she could not help but agree that it would be disgraceful for Miss Laurence to become the Countess of Warwick. Especially since she had hopes of holding that title herself. Yet, Lord Rockham complained, what else could occur as the earl would not allow him access to Miss Laurence to press his case. This was partly due to their years of enmity, and partly to Warwick's dog-in-the-manger attitude in regard to that lady. If only he could have her away from all such distractions, it would enable him to woo her successfully, and she would be his lady before the earl had a chance even to blink.

Lady Jane encouraged his plan and wished she could be of assistance.

"How generous you are! Such gracious consideration from such a nonpareil lady," he continued in his flattering vein, until Lady Jane concluded that his was a honey-sweet voice she could listen to for a full hour. But rather earlier than that he came to his point. "I am in need of some support, actually. I wish to invite Miss Laurence to inspect my estate, Fernhall, quite within driving distance, at Richmond. I feel if she should see the estate and its grounds, she would be more susceptible to my pleas. And then too, she would be away from the earl's family and hers, all hoping, I daresay, for Miss Laurence to be the next countess. But how to persuade her to come, I am at a loss."

Lady Jane had several unhelpful suggestions such as giving a ball at Richmond and other long-range possibilities. He stressed the urgency; that he'd heard the earl was shortly going to make his own request, and she was wringing her hands and speaking almost audibly as she cried out, "If only I had become some-what closer to the lady. I could request that she accompany me to Richmond, and then I should depart."

His lordship praised her plan excessively, and felt he would have been lost without the power of her powerful intellect. Evidently society was correct in its view of Lady Jane as possessing superior sense as well as beauty. And thus long did he wax poetic over her, until she was so flattered she was primed to accept anything, including his actual plan, which was that she inform Miss Laurence of having seen her sister driving out to Richmond in Lord Rockham's company, without an abigail or even a groom.

"Heavens, Miss Esther Laurence would certainly be disgraced," Lady Jane responded and said in confusion, "But why would you wish to disgrace one sister to win the other?"

He realized with a grimace that he could not rely on implicit understanding; rather this lady would need everything explained. "I should not of course actually be taking Miss Esther Laurence, that would just be incentive to have Miss Laurence join you on your ride to Richmond."

"But how could I see it, if it did not occur?" she asked, totally flummoxed.

With an inward groan, Lord Rockham persuaded her that it would be in her best interest, and in the earl's best interest, and indeed, ultimately in Miss Laurence's best interest, if she could somehow persuade herself to have seen sufficient to report it to Miss Laurence and then have a carriage waiting to escort her to Richmond.

"But I could not drive to Richmond!" Lady Jane exclaimed. "It is not what a lady would do."

"But a lady could merely make the suggestion, especially if she had both an abigail and groom alongside to prevent even the appearance of the slightest stain upon her honor."

All alarms for herself satisfied, Lady Jane was rehearsing exactly how to convey her reaction to seeing Miss Esther Laurence being driven off. "But should I feel faint at the sight? Perhaps succumb to it and fall in Miss Laurence's arms?"

Lord Rockham restrained himself with effort. "But my dear lady, you are not witness to an abduction, but an assignation. You should be more indignant than overcome."

"Ah yes, but actually, my lord, if I did see such a sight, I should rather be justified and certainly I should not put myself to the trouble of calling on the sister. Rather I should wish to cut all connection."

"Indeed, indeed," my lord said with a strain. "But we were assuming, were we not, that you were a friend of Miss Laurence, and we are not forgetting the extreme kindness of your heart, which would wish to inform her sister and prevent the young lady's being disgraced."

Recalled to her role of a friend, Lady Jane agreed that on that condition she might report to the sister, but how would they be assured that Miss Esther Laurence might not be at home at that very moment?

Such details, he assured her, he would provide for; she need not concern herself. And after her remarks were rehearsed several times, Lady Jane was prepared. She was to speak to Miss Laurence on the morrow, at precisely ten o'clock. That was a difficulty since she rarely rose till noon, Lady Jane informed him; and he must spend another half hour persuading her to do so on this particular day.

At last she was gone. Lady Jane was the weakest part of his plan, for there was always the possibility that she would reveal everything, not through the goodness of her heart but the stupidity of her brain. Thank heavens the rest of the maneuvers rested on the one person whose brain and resources had never failed him—himself.

Within a few moments of setting down Lady Jane, he drove his phaeton about the park and was fortunate enough to observe the Laurence sisters strolling. He stopped to offer his compliments in his high, ingratiating voice that so often annoyed Merrie. Shortly Merrie was even more put out of countenance when rather than giving Esther his usual bow, Lord Rockham showered her with his attentions. The young lady stared at him seriously and neither blushed nor showed any evidence of delight even when he jumped down and handed Esther a bouquet, marveling at how she exactly duplicated the fragility of the lilies in her hands. Never having been the object of an experienced rake's flirtations, she did not know how to deflect or laugh them off. And then too, being principly honest and sincere herself, she almost believed the gentleman was being so as well.

She thanked him for his compliments most graciously, but froze when he approached shockingly close with one flower extended. At which point George at last came into view. "I say, Rockham, are you foxed?"

Rockham turned and bowed. "I was just placing a flower in this lady's hair."

"I do not believe she wishes it there. Do you?" George said with a fury. Both ladies were alarmed at the possibility of the event going too far.

"Good afternoon, my lord," Merrie said quickly and took Esther by the hand and, placing her other hand through George's arm, all but propelled the trio in the opposite direction. "Shall we walk?"

And the episode was concluded, although George was rather resentful that Merrie had intervened when he was near to teaching the blighter a lesson he would never have forgotten.

Watching them depart, Lord Rockham's usual smile of satisfaction noticeably broadened. Part two of his plan had been successfully completed. Now when Lady Jane came to Merrie with her observation, Miss Laurence would not find it inconsistent with today's action. Tomorrow was beginning to shape up just as he had anticipated.

Merrie was just concluding her tea the next morning, expecting a response from the duke to her note and assumed that was what Simpson was bringing, when he instead announced Lady Jane. On the verge of asking the butler to deny her, Merrie rather put on her most civil face and rose to greet the lady. Her ladyship refused tea and Simpson was dismissed. That Lady Jane should come was curious, at such an early hour still more curious, but most curious of all was her refusing to remove her bonnet, which Merrie took time to note was a particularly smashing one. Gracious, it had a face-framing circle of blue bows under the blue brim and one large one under the chin. But

all thoughts of bonnets were obliterated at her ladyship's words. She had just seen a distressing sight that
must be shared: Miss Esther Laurence was vis-à-vis
with Lord Rockham in his curricle. *Unaccompanied,*
she stressed, and as her own carriage came abreast of
that vehicle she had clearly heard his lordship discussing their destination—his own estate in Richmond.

"Nonsense!" Merrie snapped, almost ready to
laugh aloud at the lady's load of flummery. Obviously, if a true sighting, Lady Jane had mistaken the
lady in question for Esther, who was still abed. She
said as much to her ladyship, who insisted she had
seen what she had seen. "What is your object in coming here with such a Banbury story?" Merrie asked
calmly. "You who have never shown the slightest concern for my family."

Lady Jane was prepared for that doubt and met it
head-on. "Naturally, my friendship with the earl, and
the kindness of the countess to my family put me under some obligation that, as a lady, I could not ignore.
Further, since I have my groom with me and my abigail, I am more than willing even to accompany you
to Richmond, so that by my very presence there, your
sister would be protected from all gossip. I have sufficient consequence to prevent even the slightest appearance of an impropriety."

That last mention of her ladyship's praising her
own consequence was Lady Jane's own addition to
Lord Rockham's speech, and rang so true that Merrie
was given pause and ran off checking on Esther's
whereabouts.

A moment proved that Esther was not in her room
after all, which began the first stirrings of alarm, doubled at the maid's statement that Esther had departed
before breakfast in response to a note brought round.
Questioned on Esther's demeanor, the maid answered
that the lady had been smiling as she read the note

and had slipped out with every attempt not to be observed.

At this Merrie rushed to George's room. Finding him gone as well momentarily relieved her, assuming they were together. But on second thought, Esther would scarcely forget all propriety as to go on a private outing without either herself or the countess along. And as she would not do so with George, she would certainly not do so with Lord Rockham. Something was amiss! With trepidation, Merrie called for the groom. His information left Merrie shaken indeed. Mr. Dickens had set out alone, keeping an early appointment with his friend Sir James, driving the earl's phaeton and grays to demonstrate their excellence. And as for Miss Esther Laurence, she had not been observed departing. It was not known whether she had called for or had summoned a hack.

Without leaving a note or giving notice, Esther was gone!

Returning to the morning room, Merrie, by now more than concerned, was beginning to assume that Esther had indeed been somehow fooled by Lord Rockham into actually meeting him, and then found herself in a situation from which she could not rescue herself—dear God! And there was Lady Jane, looking smug as her suspicions were proving to be correct. Merrie was long wishing her at Jericho when she recollected her ladyship's offer of her carriage. They had their own, but it would take time to bring one out, and then she would have to explain to the butler and the groom and to awaken Lady Warwick with the news, all of which actions would undoubtedly make Esther's escapade soon known to the entire town. And here was Lady Jane waiting. She eyed the lady, and once more realized that in life, the strangest people were sent by heaven to come to one's aid.

"I shall not forget you, your ladyship. We have

never been the best of friends. But at this moment of terror for me, you have taken time from your own life and risked your own comfort and convenience to aid an acquaintance. It shows me that I have never seen the extreme generosity of your heart, and that the earl had more discernment than I in marking you out for his earlier attentions."

That speech would have lost Lord Rockham all, but for one word Merrie included at the end. For at the beginning, Lady Jane, seeing the prodigious alarm in Merrie's white face had had a momentary qualm. And while she would not expose herself by confessing the truth, she was near to putting a stop to some of the ramifications by simply turning on her heel. That noble urge was halted by use of that word "earlier," which clearly implied that lately, Miss Laurence had supplanted her. And *that* her ladyship could not bear. For such a one to be chosen rather than herself with her title and unimpeachable style and manners! All Lady Jane's breeding cried out that she must prevent that misalliance. And so she pursed her mouth and said simply, "I should not delay a moment, Miss Laurence, if we are to arrive before the girl has been subjected to an intolerable affront."

"Good heavens, yes," Merrie cried out, distracted. "I shall be but a moment to send a note."

"You would not wish to do that and alert the menials," Lady Jane inserted, and took Merrie by the hand to rush her out. She was allowed time however to seek her bonnet and parasol, without which no lady could appear out of doors.

But Merrie used that moment, after all, to write a hurried note and entrusted it to Simpson to deliver to the earl mentioning her destination and asking for his assistance in case she did not immediately return from rescuing her sister. He and George must come as quickly as possible to avoid certain tragedy, but she and Lady Jane were hastening to prevent the worst.

Lady Jane, waiting in the carriage, was astonished that the lady had not outfitted herself properly, after all. Indeed, Miss Laurence seemed in such fidgets, not only did she not wait for the coachman to hand her up, jumping in herself, but worse, showed a total lack of breeding by crying out, "Spring 'em!" At that Lady Jane was excessively thankful that she did not truly intend to go along on this vulgar adventure.

Within two streets, Lady Jane complained of feeling faint, and could just manage to whisper that she must be set down at Hatchards bookshop, just ahead, for she would make a purchase and then send her abigail for a chair to take her home.

"Are you saying that neither you nor your abigail are coming with me?" Merrie asked, astounded.

Lady Jane made another one of her whispered statements that Merrie this time could not decipher in the slightest. But apparently the coachman had, for he came to a halt and was assisting her ladyship to descend. "Drive on," Lady Jane said the moment her feet had touched the cobblestones, giving Merrie, alone in the carriage, the barest of waves.

While entering Hatchards, her ladyship could not help but wonder at how little Miss Laurence seemed to know about propriety. How could she ever for one moment assume that the daughter of a marquis would take part in such a wild escapade and in the company of a woman without a bonnet whose hair was already falling victim to the morning breeze, escaping its pins and flying around her distraught face? One could only hope no one of any consequence had observed her even conversing with such a demented apparition. By the time Lady Jane had returned home with her purchases, she'd forgotten that her behavior had not been the height of nobility. For so vividly had she described the scene of Esther's being in his lordship's carriage, adding such details as his lordship's arm around the girl's waist, that she'd almost persuaded herself of having seen it and having come to the rescue of a lady in distress. Upon recollection, she remembered she had not, and that Miss Laurence was flying off in Lord Rockham's carriage with Lord Rockham's coachman to Lord Rockham's estate—totally unaccompanied!—which was the first step to an immoral assignation. Lady Jane was not exactly certain what happened to a lady when she was imposed on by a gentleman. But she had been assured by her mother that one could survive it, if one remembered at all times that one was a lady. Miss Laurence did not have the benefit of that assurance, but then her ladyship had also been told by her mother that other women did not have the sensitivity of feelings that ladies did. And further, Lord Rockham was quite an attractive gentleman, and surely more than a poor relation deserved.

Yet she could not quite dismiss the last view of Miss Laurence as the carriage drove hurriedly away, with face so white and hair flying like a fiery cloud. And that image assuaged Lady Jane for everything she had done. A woman who looked so spectacular was definitely not of their class. Just as she'd looked spectacular on Christmas in her peacock crown, and the earl had had eyes for no one but her. It was clearly best that such beyond-the-pale ladies be eliminated from the social scene lest it be tainted. Lord Rockham was correct, she had done society a service by keeping it pure.

19

Face to face with Lord Rockham, Merrie was breathing as deeply as if she had run rather than been driven all this distance.

"Welcome to my home," his lordship said with a gracious bow.

"Where is my sister?" Merrie demanded, looking about for signs of Esther's presence.

"Would you care to retire to your room to compose yourself? You seem, Miss Laurence, rather beside yourself. Whereas it is I who should be beside you, henceforth."

Lord Rockham approached her with the delighted smile of a pursuer having set a trap and finding his quivering prey caught and waiting.

Merrie's instincts warned her not to allow the pale-eyed lord to sense the wild thoughts that had proliferated during the hectic drive there. Aside from the prayerful fear for Esther's safety, she'd been battered by doubts—doubts of Lady Jane's role, but worse, doubts of her own actions. Dear God, she should have done more than written a note to Lord Warwick.

Rather she should have ordered the carriage to drive to his club and demand his escort. But then the earl might not have been there. Another method might have been to send a message to Sir James's for George. Yet both these courses would have necessitated waiting calmly until one or the other gentleman could be found, and who knew what could be happening to Esther in the meantime? And further, Lady Jane had been so insistent that they immediately leave, almost giving her the suggestion they could overtake them. Doubts, doubts—as devastatingly debilitating as fears. She would not allow either to weaken her and render her useless to Esther on her arrival at Lord Rockham's. Merrie fell back on her own philosophy that if one kept hope in one's heart, the worst could always be overcome. And that was how Merrie faced Lord Rockham—with hope and the strength thereof. In short, an undaunted lady was calmly asking his lordship, "Where have you hidden Esther?"

No response.

The pale-eyed man refused to be deflected from his lovingly devised stratagem, which certainly did not include his jumping to respond to her questions. Rather he was setting the pace of their encounter by indicating that she should be seated.

She remained standing.

"Very well, we shall both stand."

Merrie asked him again about her sister.

"Ah, yes, Miss Esther Laurence. Well, I must admit to you . . ." He paused maddeningly, and then as Miss Laurence did not rise to the bait and beg, but still waited patiently, he concluded, "I actually have not the slightest knowledge, or interest, in the whereabouts of your sister. Truthfully, one Laurence sister is sufficient for me. And I have long chosen you."

"Oh, fiddle!" Merrie exploded as she understood

the trap at last. "You and your nefarious cohort Lady
Jane have been most expert in your plan. Undoubtedly you both have had experience in abduction and
all forms of dastardly deeds. But if there is even an
ounce of goodness left in you, for heaven's sake, tell
me that you have not in any way hurt my sister. How
did you contrive for her to leave the house?"

"If you wish for an answer, you must at least be
willing to continue this discussion in a more courte-
ous manner. Come into the saloon. There if you will
allow me to offer you some refreshment, I should be
delighted to tell you every detail of my ingenious maneuvers."

Merrie forced herself to swallow her sharp words.
Coming to cuffs with his lordship would scarcely be
helpful. Once again, she persuaded herself not to assume the worst. And so nodding, she followed him
into the saloon. Passing a mirror, she missed a step at
her appearance. Her face was flushed and her hair
wild. Without thinking, she smoothed her hair as she
sat, then folded her hands before her to keep composed. The tea was brought and served. He asked
with a lift of his eyebrow if she wished to pour, but
she ignored him, and so the butler did the office and
departed. Merrie was dry and weak from her wild
ride, and wished for the tea, but waited until his lordship had drunk from his own cup, and then simply
reached over and took his.

Astounded by her act, Lord Rockham began to
laugh. "Are you under the impression I intend to drug
you? For shame. I would not win you that way. Still,
it is a particular pleasure for me to see you drinking of
my cup—the cup that has touched my lips. It is a
joining, don't you feel?"

"You are obviously quite pleased with yourself,"
Merrie said, somewhat stronger after her tea. "Begin
with your explanation, please."

"Not terribly much to explain, actually. I wished to have you. Ergo, I arranged for your coming to me, since Lady Jane was kind enough to convince you that was where your sister was. Your pure heart would naturally come to her defense, I assumed—obviously correctly."

"And Esther?"

"Ah, Miss Esther Laurence, I expect, is safely at home, after having received an urgent message from Mr. George Dickens for a secret meeting at Green Park. Oddsblood, I'm a romantic at heart, what say? No need to send a message to the gentleman, but I wished to see the couple happy. And so I expect they spent a delightful time discussing the source of the mystery messages. And if they are true lovers, by Jove, they shall be nothing loath to take advantage of this opportunity. One's faith in lovers is never wrongly placed. I assumed both would take sufficient time so that Lady Jane would be able to confuse you and send you on your way."

Merrie closed her eyes. Until this moment she had not realized how terrified she'd been that he'd hurt Esther in some way, that she'd been abducted and was in the hands of some brigand, tied up in some place where she could not breathe. To know that she had merely had a delightful outing with George allowed most of the terror of this circumstance to abate.

Then came his lordship's irritatingly shrill voice, talking on. "I could have, I wish you to note, arranged for an actual abduction of her, as I could have for you. But one prefers to do these things subtly, don't you know? With something of savoir faire. Of course the abductions were reserved as a last resort."

"And all this you have done," she exclaimed, "just to have another moment alone with me? How many times must I say it for you to understand? I do not wish to marry you. I reject you. The answer is in the negative. In other words, *no*."

"You have not understood, my dear lady. You are quite fortunate that I am still requesting that you marry me. Most ladies at this point would be imploring me to marry them to save them from the disgrace."

"Of what?"

Lord Rockham rolled his eyes in disbelief. "Are you not aware of your circumstance? You are compromised. No gentleman of any standing would even bow to you, henceforth, let alone a lady. You must be married, or the scandal will be of such proportions that not even your delightful sister would ever be accepted by any decent gentleman. And even your countess would find it necessary to send you away from her, unless we return wed."

"I see," Merrie said calmly. "You paint quite a devastating scenario. However, I expect I shall somehow overcome it. One must never despair, I have always believed. Have faith in oneself and in the people one loves and somehow all will be resolved. As long as one does not continue to act as idiotically as I have. And the height of idiocy would be if I succumbed to your threats. For as miserable as you assume my life would be if I did not accept you, your actions have proven it would be ten times worse if I did."

"Confound you! Are you made of stone? Why are you not weeping and imploring me to spare you? I could at this moment ravish you. Yet I am not that heartless."

"I am delighted to hear that. So far your actions certainly would lead one to suspect a serious lack of such an organ."

"You are amazingly composed. I tell you I intend to keep you imprisoned here until you accept my offer, and only after we are wed are you ever to be allowed to see your family again."

"Pity," Merrie said. "I shall miss them. But I certainly do not intend to marry you just to see them again. They themselves would wonder at my lack of taste."

Lord Rockham walked about in despair. "Are you . . . jesting? At such a moment?"

"I find it always helpful to jest at the most distasteful moments. One restores one's sense of balance, actually. And further, I feel rather sorry for you, my lord. How comes it that a gentleman of such a title and wealth, and not totally distasteful, I expect, to most other ladies, should have to force a lady to be his? Surely there must be some degree of pride to have prevented this extreme action? Has no lady ever loved you for yourself?"

Lord Rockham's eyes were almost rolling back in his reaction to that statement. "Oddsblood! Have you no eyes? I am most prepossessing! By gad, it is no boast to say I have been loved by more ladies than I can even count. But I have never loved any of them. You are the only lady that has won my heart, and I'll be damned first before I allow any other gentleman to have you. It is either me or no one, ever again. You shall be mine, if I have to keep you here until you are no longer the beauty who obsesses me."

Merrie shook her head, but still sympathetically. "I do not believe I have ever met a gentleman so melodramatically inclined. Have you spent all your spare time reading gothic novels? If so, I can readily see why you wish to cast yourself in the villain's role, a decidedly less boring part than that of the hero. But," she continued, rising decisively as if the interview were at an end, "since you are enacting a gothic tragedy, you had much better have chosen Lady Jane as your fellow performer. She would, I am persuaded, know exactly what you wish her to do and have long since conveniently swooned into your waiting arms. However, I must just say, I find it all rather comical and unreal. As, I regret, are you."

Goaded, Lord Rockham attempted to restore his own self-worth by assuring Miss Laurence that he was not playacting, and further that he would prove the genuineness of his feelings by resisting dishonoring her until she became his wife. "The appearance of disgrace is oft of more potency than the actual act," he concluded with a bit of his old-time leer, assuming she would at last be put into a quake.

But Merrie instead giggled as he kept reminding her of the villain's parts on the stage she'd often seen in the provinces. Blithely she responded, "I cannot agree with your point about disgrace. It rather depends on the individual, I expect. Some people are as susceptible to disgrace as others are to colds. I daresay I have always been shockingly impervious to both, which I hope does not give you a disgust of me as an abductee? But for your drama-farce to succeed, you need a poor trembling maiden, my lord. And regrettably my only reaction is to wonder why you are fatiguing us both with such antiquated flummery."

At that, Lord Rockham forgot himself and sat down while she was standing. She gently reminded him of his lapse, and he quickly stood up again. But his face was dark and his eyes fluttering. Merrie began to sense that she would not be able to lighten the moment with her wit, as she often was able to do with Brett, for Lord Rockham was obviously sunk so deeply into the scenario he was enacting that naught would shake him to his senses. Indeed he was now continuing it, breathing deeply as he approached her, and feeling at liberty, took a liberty with her person. He boldly enacted what he had so often visualized himself doing, putting his hands deeply into her loosed hair and pulling the lady toward him. At that his breaths were so harsh, she caught hers in some alarm at last. And then he placed his panting mouth on hers and began to drink deeply of her breath and self, and she felt as if she were being devoured by a beast, kiss after kiss. When he allowed her at last to pull away, he said triumphantly, "You are already dishonored, just by being here in my arms, in my home . . . in my presence."

"You perhaps would know best about that," she incorrigibly replied, "but if you wish a serious answer, I must point out that I have my own honor. Nothing you can ever do to me could stain that. You have merely succeeded in dishonoring yourself. For honor is only susceptible to self-inflicted wounds. And at the present time, yours is in rather a sorry state, while mine shines brighter than ever."

Abruptly he stepped away from her. The calm certainty of her unequivocal answer and her cold eyes and lips brought a dash of sense and awareness to the moment which somewhat slacked his passion.

"I shall have Winters escort you to my chambers. Think a while about how you wish our lives together to begin, in anger or in love. You have merely to accept me, and I shall devote my life to giving you all forms of pleasure."

"I shall never accept you," Merrie said steadfastly.

"Then it shall be your decision whether I am forced to behave dishonorably after all," he said, and he bowed and summoned Winters, who was to show her to Lord Rockham's rooms. She went willingly to be away from his lordship, hoping to devise a saving scheme.

"After dinner, we shall have another discussion," he threw after her, but Merrie did not respond, except for a small smile of relief that she had at least that much time.

Watching Miss Laurence walking of her own voli-
tion toward his apartments, Rockham felt a sense of
victory. Say what she would, she was now in his
chamber, under his control, waiting for him to come
to her. Ah, so sweet it was. What happened next
would largely depend on her. He was prepared to behave honorably, he assuaged his conscience, if she
would only allow him to—the usual excuse of dishon-
orable people, blaming the unaccommodating nature
of the victim for the dastardly nature of their own act.

The hour was late and the countess's concern for
Merrie increased with the minutes, for the dear girl
was still absent. Previously she had consulted Esther
and George, and neither had been aware of her
whereabouts. The butler had prevented an immediate
alarm by reporting that Miss Laurence had gone out
and had entered a carriage that was waiting for her.
Therefore, it was at first assumed that she had gone
to a social engagement with one of her many admirers, perhaps to a picnic at Green Park. Lady Webster
was giving one around noon, but when that hour was
long past, the entire household was thrown into
growing alarm. Esther was holding onto George's
hands with open despair. He did not leave her side
except to take himself off to the clubs to determine
subtly which one of Merrie's escorts was not about
town. The prevailing hope was that she was under the
safe escort of the duke, but George was dismayed to
find His Grace at his club. Naturally George made no
mention of his errand, but engaged in a brief conversation, during the course of which he was peevishly
informed by the duke of his not receiving a reply from
Merrie on his offer of a union, and he assumed she
was still staying indoors in mighty deliberation. Sir
Malcolm was next spotted, and even Sir Percy. Which
left only Lord Rockham, and George's heart sank at

the elimination. Rockham was nowhere to be seen. The disappearance of that lord George attempted to hide from both his mother and future wife, but it was eventually questioned out of him. The countess cried out and, for the first time in a good while, had recourse to her vinaigrette. Esther's white face was awash in tears, and George was muttering, uncertain what to do next. At last, he left the ladies in each other's arms and did what he should have done immediately.

The earl of Warwick was playing billiards at his club when his brother entered. George did not greet him in his usual happy manner, and that was sufficient to alert his lordship to some disturbance. His instincts told him that it concerned Merrie, and he took a moment and asked himself whether he wished to be involved.

One further glance at the devastated face, as George cast him a look of entreaty, and Brett, in some dungeon, was forced to concede the match to Lord Gore, and with a stiff bow excused himself to approach his brother. "Do not tell me whatever you have to say until we are outside," he whispered, and stopped to greet a few other friends, making a great show of unconcern, while within, his feelings were beginning to boil into a mixture of anger and concern for the lady.

Once in his lordship's curricle, he turned and said softly, "All right, my boy, stop looking as if the world had come to an end. What the deuce has that blasted girl done now?"

George took a moment to decide whether he should defend Merrie or not, but was so desperate he reverted to his childhood dependence on his brother and said in a choking voice, "She's disappeared."

"What exactly do you mean by that? Are you informing me that she was there one moment and then her corpus disintegrated before your astonished eyes? I should not be much surprised if she could do such marvels."

George did not reply, for they'd arrived at Warwick House. The carriage and team were turned over to the groom, and the earl then removed his gloves and hat and put down his cane before taking George to the library. Offering his brother a glass of brandy, he took one himself. "Miss Laurence has run away? Returned to her parents in Oxford?"

"No. She was seen to enter a carriage this morning and has not returned."

"And who was in the carriage?"

"We have not been able to ascertain. Her maid however reported that she did not take a bonnet, nor parasol, nor even reticule."

That did surprise his lordship. As much of a hoyden as Merrie was, she took great pride in her bonnets, and would certainly not go out without one. Departing without a reticule as well was certainly unusual. "And her sister is not aware of her destination? Perhaps she is sworn to secrecy. Not even Mama?"

"Ah, you wouldn't say that if you could see their faces. They have been fearing her dead or worse these many hours. They are attempting to encourage each other not to indulge in the worst fantasies, but you would not believe the tears."

"I would. I have seen Mama at her worst. She is back to her vinaigrette, then?"

"Yes. And cataplasm to the feet. And she has sent for her doctor in Yorkshire. Esther, who is not in much better shape, is doing all she can to keep her from total collapse, but we neither of us have much hope unless Merrie returns. I made subtle inquiry around town as to which of her escorts were around, and I met most of them, including the duke, and all asked me to send their devotion to her, so she cannot be with one of them."

"Ye gods, you went all over town making inquiry about her without first coming to me?"

"You didn't want to be involved with us."

"That is not what I said. I said I didn't want her to manipulate me, and blast it, how do you know this is not an attempt on her part to raise our fears to such an extent that we will do whatever she wishes when she returns?"

George just stared at him and rose to leave the room. "I regret even bringing you into this matter. You are not concerned about her. If you knew Miss Laurence at all, you'd never say what you did. She would never allow Mama to be so brought low, nor would she allow her sister to go through the terror. Nor even myself. Even you she would not wish to be concerned. She has a gentle heart. Don't you know that yet?"

The earl was by then seriously concerned. "Yes," he said shortly. "Nor do I like the thought that she left here without being suitably dressed. It suggests a state of alarm. It suggests that she received some note that alarmed her."

George then mentioned his fear about Lord Rockham, and that he had determined that his lordship was not at his club.

"Blast you, did you make the lady's name a byword? Inquiring about all her suitors? It will not take anyone with even a modicum of sense to put together the story of an elopement."

"What the blazes do I care what a bunch of nobs have to say, when she might be being hurt at this very moment?" George exclaimed. "She pretends to know her way, but she doesn't, because she continually believes there is good in everyone's heart. When I know there isn't. Not in Lord Rockham's. And not in *others* to whom she has been foolish enough to give the honor of her regard."

"If you mean me, I do not think this is the moment to discuss my relationship with the lady. You have done all the wrong things in discovering her plight and not the simplest and most obvious. Have you questioned the jarveys at the corner, who might have seen whose carriage was awaiting? Have you questioned my own groom?"

"We did not wish to spread the rumor, as you said. Once it is known to the staff, it will be universally known. Mama did not want the staff questioned."

"And yet you went to the very clubs the greatest rattles frequent before questioning those close at hand?"

"Naturally we talked to her maid and Simpson, and it was from him we learned that she left this morning and went into a carriage, but he did not recognize the carriage. It did not have a coat of arms."

Frowning at that, the earl ordered both his groom and his valet to report to him. Each one was individually questioned. His groom had not seen the carriage, nor had his valet Biffens, but that gentleman, his lordship believed, was always in the know and he risked hinting of his concern regarding Miss Laurence. Biffens, with a most impassive face, replied that he hoped nothing had happened to the good lady, for that would cause concern to them all. It surprised the earl to discover Biffens showing any emotion, and it said much for the lady if she had gotten through his indifference. Indeed, on his own, Biffens assured the earl that he would make subtle inquiry of the staff and other staffs. And so he was dismissed. They had not made a noticeable advance in finding her, and George was beginning to pace and despair again, when the earl summoned Simpson for further consultation. That gentleman repeated his story of having seen Miss Laurence leave the house and enter a carriage and of her being driven off by a coachman. He did not recognize the carriage. She had left no note or message for anyone in the family.

"Was a note brought to her that alarmed her and sent her on her way?" the earl asked insistently.

"There was not."

"So you know of no reason why the lady suddenly left her home without parasol or bonnet?"

"She seemed anxious to rush into the carriage, my lord. But I should say her countenance was as always —in a happy state rather than one of concern."

"There you are," the earl said coldly when he'd dismissed the butler, "we do not deal here with a case of a lady being lured away into some desperate state, as you've all been assuming. Rather with a wild, headstrong lady who was anxious enough to meet with a gentleman to forget the very essentials of a lady's wardrobe. Not an abduction, but an assignation, curse her!"

"Flummery!" a lady's voice cut through, and at first it sounded so similar to Merrie's that both gentlemen turned with hope, only to be crushed at the sight of Esther.

Brought up to date with all the facts and conjectures, Esther was insistent that her sister would not rush out without her reticule unless in some alarm, nor would she fail to leave a note for her sister or the countess.

The earl's dark eyes were now filled more with anger than the concern they had shown before. "I expect she had her mind on other things. I suspect she has eloped or allowed herself to be cajoled into an assignation with Lord Rockham."

Even as the name came from the earl's mouth, he

could not hide the rage associated with that conclusion.

"She detests Lord Rockham. She refused even to allow him to take her up for a drive at Hyde Park," Esther countered.

"Yet he was one of the gentlemen from whom she claimed she was contemplating a proposal of marriage."

That was unanswerable without revealing Merrie's tactic of using Lord Rockham as a goad for the earl, even though she'd refused him. So against her nature Esther remained silent, and the earl could think what he would. And he did.

Meanwhile Esther was thinking of Lord Rockham and his pale blue eyes, as if once having an object in sight, he was primed to strike, and she said quickly, "Where does Lord Rockham live? Perhaps we should all pay him a call, just to see if he is keeping her there."

"That is not a very sensible approach. We should just be denied admittance. I have already sent Biffens to his town house. He will discover if she is there . . . and whether she needs our assistance."

"I can't wait!" Esther exclaimed. After a full day of calm, her reserve had quite obviously cracked. "Moments matter! While we dally, she could be in dire circumstances. She never thinks anyone will hurt her. She went directly up to a wild dog when we were children and talked him into taking some meat from her hand, when the rest of the people would have killed him." Esther was sobbing now. "Don't you understand? She trusts people to be loving . . . as she is!"

The earl was quiet, and George took her into his arms to soothe her. Both were one moment from doing as Esther had requested when Biffens returned.

The earl had a word with him and then turned to the anxious faces of his brother and her sister. "She is not at Lord Rockham's house," he began. Esther had just begun thanking God when he added coldly, "However, it is known in his household that he was planning to take Miss Laurence to his Richmond estate, and the carriage that was described is undoubtedly Lord Rockham's. She went with him willingly to Richmond."

"Fiddle!" Esther said, using a favorite term of her sister's that again caused both gentlemen to feel that Merrie herself was there denying it. "I shall go myself to Richmond and hear that from her lips before I believe it."

"And I shall take you," George cried out. And both turned to rush for their cloaks.

"There is no necessity for this lady to be distressed any further," the earl said, indicating Esther's tear-stained face. "I shall find Miss Laurence. And believe me, I will bring her back whether she wishes it or not."

"We'll all go," Esther said. "She'll need me, if what I fear has occurred. I know she has already refused Lord Rockham. And had, in fact, sent a note of acceptance to the duke."

"I shall discover whatever has occurred, and I can travel at a speed that would not be comfortable for the lady. And blast it, you are delaying me with these distractions."

Esther demurred, George discussed, the countess sent her maid down to inquire for news, and Esther was torn about taking time to respond to her. When she asked for a moment to soothe his mother, the earl nodded. However, even as she and George were going up the stairs, his lordship quickly summoned his groom to bring his chaise and matched bays instantly around, while he collected his pistol and enough money in case someone had to be bribed. Then, taking advantage of their absence, the earl calmly put on his driving gloves, stepped into his chaise, and was off. Alone.

20

For the first time in her life Merrie was forced to question her philosophy that if one assumed there was some good in each person, the other would act in kind. Lord Rockham was not acting in kind, nor being kind. No sooner had she been escorted to his apartments, than without even giving her a moment to compose her thoughts, two chambermaids were there to overlook her every act. Meanwhile they occupied themselves with duties that were alarming, at least in implication, such as turning down the bed, announcing that dinner would be served *à deux* in that chamber when she was more suitably attired, and laying out a nightdress of the most indelicate brazenness.

Panic made Merrie stand like a stock as the maids moved about her, brushing her hair and removing her dress, which was generously covered with the dirt of travel. She limply allowed all these attentions, including being adorned in a daring black satin sleep gown, assuming that it was temporary until her dress was refreshed. But her travel outfit was not returned, her request for it ignored. And when she stepped before a cheval mirror, her reflection gave her a jolt, showing a woman who had clearly stepped beyond the line, an absolute Cyprian, in fact. Merrie closed her eyes to that image, only to open them and view the woman still there, who was now taking on a certain allure. The black satin turned her pale skin to a whiteness that dazzled, and the gown was cut in such a way as to taunt, if not downright tease. She was thankful for her long loosed hair falling in a red cascade that covered a good part of her bared breasts or she would have been put to the blush even before the maids. Merrie could not help but realize the influence of dress, for as she stood in it, the satin touching her skin planted languorous thoughts, such as not being wholly averse to having her skin stroked by hands as soft and respectful as the satin now touching and tingling her body. Until the thought of whose hands would be doing the stroking intruded and Merrie came to herself in a click. Indeed she was totally in charge again, even able to dismiss both maids calmly, claiming she needed at least an hour to rest. She even went so far as to lie down on the huge four-poster.

After whispering that the lady would, to be sure, soon need her rest, and after many offensive smirks and nudgings of each other, which Merrie pretended not to see, or at least did not react to, the two giggling maids at last departed. In a trice Merrie was up to check the door. That was when her faith in humankind plummeted. The door was locked. She shook the handle again and again, unable to believe herself a prisoner so quickly, so finally. Yet still she had some time ere dinner was to be served, she remembered with relief, and Merrie refused to waste any more of it bemoaning her plight. Her lifelong determination had been never to allow her spirits to sink, at least without almost immediately bobbing back up. As they did now. It was, she admitted, a challenging situation, but not insurmountable.

Helpfully her eyes focused on the various chests. In a few pushing, twisting, fingernail-tearing moments, she had them open and was rummaging through. They contained only gentlemen's attire. And being Lord Rockham's, they were of such width that it would not be of sufficient assistance to her modesty to wear either pantaloons or boots that would slip off or trip her. But a shirt covered her quite decently to her knees, leaving only a wide hem of black satin peeping to indicate her immodest inner attire. Next she found a substantial driving cloak with several capes. It not only fully covered her, but gave the illusion that she was rather a massive person. Again, clothing had an effect, and she felt imposing and purposeful. If only she could locate a brace of pistols as well, they would go a long way to solving her problem. Yet no weapons but the irons at the fireplace were found. She took one of those, and a sporting hat of his lordship's with a large enough brim to hide her entire face. Locating her hairpins left on the dressing table when the maids had brushed her hair, Merrie made a quick attempt to tuck some of her hair under the hat. She tore off a lacing from the boots and tied the rest of her hair back at the nape of her neck. And she was ready.

Even if his lordship were to enter now, with her iron in hand and her modesty cloaked, Merrie concluded cheerfully, she would make rather an impressive stand against him. But her main object was to escape before the need for confrontation. Checking the windows through the adjoining sitting room and the bedroom aborted her plan to climb down, for there was not a single conveniently placed tree or balcony to assist her descent, as her optimism had been expecting. That sheer drop would lead only to a final ending, and heavens, she was not prepared for such a melodramatic solution. Not while she still had a chance to outwit her opponent. Her second thought of hiding in a chest or under the bed was dismissed with a grin as pointless, for with his full staff on the hunt, she would eventually be spotted. Nor did she care to be stifled, nor was she small enough to climb up the chimney. For a flash, her spirits once more began sinking, but she caught herself by saying aloud, "Never despair." In truth, it was the sound of her own voice that not only gave her the confidence needed, but that seeded a wild, madbrained scheme. For it recalled Lord Rockham's shrill voice which was always rather incongruous to his bulk. As Mrs. Prissom back at dear Moorsedge had often said when they were in difficulty: "Happen when ye falls into a pickle barrel, the good Lord has ye already half preserved." And so grinning, she pressed on. Dressed as his lordship, she need only complete the imitation of his voice.

At the outside door, rather than waiting for chance, she made her own by yelling in his lordship's high, impatient voice, "Holla there!" Footsteps sounded and she continued in even more outrage. "Oddsblood, who the devil locked me in?"

A passing footman was hurriedly turning the key in the lock, only to have it flung open upon him, nearly knocking him back as a heavily cloaked and hatted lord pushed by with a "Make way for your betters!" that had the man bowing. By the time he'd stood straight, "his lordship" had strode away.

Halfway down the hall, Merrie still waited for discovery but there was no sound of alarm. "Done it, by gad," she almost cried out and rested behind a chiffonier to get her bearings. She was hesitant about testing her disguise on more observant members of the staff, such as the butler, whom she would inevitably meet once descending the stairs ahead. And so Merrie continued on this level, hoping for a room with a balcony. She found none, yet she fretted through her brief searches of the next few chambers, for time was running out. No more of it could be wasted. With that as a nagging goad, Merrie went directly to the end of the hall and the back stairs. She was halfway down them ere the thought struck that his lordship would hardly use the servants' stairs, and thus if spotted, her bluff would be immediately uncovered, as would she. But it was too late, for she was already in the kitchen quarters. Her heart jumped as directly ahead a servant appeared, but it was a scullery maid, the lowest and most browbeaten of the staff, who would probably jump to anyone's orders and not dare question his lordship. Except the next moment a footman was there, both servants entering the opening ahead. Merrie assessed her choices. She could attempt to creep by, or confront. But once reaching that open area and peeking within, she dropped both approaches. It was the servants' dining area, and an entire group was present. Softly Merrie reversed her steps. Best not to attempt gulling them en masse, for the two maids might be there and those women seemed fly to every trick. Oh, fiddle! She should have risked the main area of the estate, after all. And quickly she turned the opposite way, striding on till she reached a large door and stepping through onto polished floors and Axminster carpets. Well, she was in the main area, after all, and not much better a choice, for she came upon the first saloon where Lord Rockham had received her. Instinctively retreating from it, she took a chance on one of the other doors on either side. With heart beating loud enough to get everyone's attention, Merrie took a breath and chose the least ornate.

One glance revealed that the room was deserted, not even a fire lit. And with further relief she recognized it as the library. The sight of so many books reminded her of her father in his studies. Surely this was a parental blessing for her course. Buoyed, Merrie rushed toward the heavily draped windows, and separating the fringed centers, she uncovered not windows, but a French door, and there behind it—yes, yes, a balcony, at last. The library was the magic charm, indeed, and she stepped out.

"Elementary," she praised herself, trying to stifle her laugh of relief, as the next minute she was running down the balcony steps and into the dark garden, shouting a silent hurrah. Now all she needed was to steal a horse, and she'd be home free.

At that very moment the earl of Warwick was at the front knocker of Lord Rockham's estate, hammering away. No sooner was the door opening than he kicked it wide and entered.

Everything he did was done without a wasted step or word, and not the slightest bit of emotion, except for a strain in his cold voice as he ordered the astonished butler, who had never had a pistol placed in his snout before, to direct him to Miss Laurence—any hesitation would be the last act in his life. With unusual alacrity for a gentleman of his years and position, the butler led the way, sputtering that she was in his lordship's rooms.

"The devil you say," Lord Warwick said, and his breath caught.

On the second-floor landing, the butler quickly indicated the correct door and stepped aside, running down the hall while the earl burst into the chamber. It was empty. A few moments were wasted rushing through the adjoining sitting rooms, and more, bending down to check under the huge bed. There was no response from Merrie to his urgent calls, but there was a shrill shout from a flushed Lord Rockham coming through the door. He had his sword out, calling, *"En garde!"* to a view of the earl's backside.

With some dignity the earl rose from his investigations and calmly responded to that challenge by cocking his pistol. Lord Rockham, realizing the inequity of a sword against pistol, especially at this distance, put down his sword and put on an affronted demeanor. "What is the meaning, my lord, of invading my property and making yourself free of my chambers?" he asked with enough outrage to have won several curtain calls on stage.

"Where the devil is she?" Brett asked, his tone low but with an unmistakable menace. And as Lord Rockham advanced into the room with sword raised again, Brett added tolerantly, "Ere you prick me with your sword, my lord, I shall have blown a hole in your vacuous brain which can ill afford any more emptiness. Although I expect an airing would do it some good."

During the earl's threat, Lord Rockham was surreptitiously looking around the room, unable to disguise his surprise, as he exclaimed, "Oddsblood, have your cohorts abducted Miss Laurence?" He was monstrously offended that anyone would dare do to him what he had already so successfully done to them. "The lady is my promised bride," he continued with his view of the predicament. "What right have you to come here and interfere?"

"Have her tell me that, and I shall not interfere," Brett said, though his eyes were promising that he might not depart without leaving as a memento some blazing mark on the lord's person.

Lord Rockham was annoyed. "How can I have her say aught to you if you have taken her out?"

"Enough of this jesting! Where is Miss Laurence?"

"I would ask the same of you. She was in this room preparing herself for our intimate supper. We were planning our happy lives together. There could be no reason for her disappearing unless she was forced to do so—at pistol point. Which is what I have no doubt has happened. And you are standing here, having abducted my true love, pretending to be her rescuer, just to confuse me. But I say, stop your performance. Miss Laurence has no need of a rescuer. She came and remained with me willingly. Most willingly."

That last had the earl twitching his finger. He thought he might well rid the world of a scoundrel, except that this thatchgallows was a gentleman, and the earl was a gentleman. A duel would be in order, and the earl was anxious to arrange one, but that was a pleasure he would delay until he'd found Merrie.

Lord Rockham used that opportunity to lunge with his sword. The earl sidestepped it without a blink and shot the lord through his dueling arm, which caused the sword to drop with a clang while Lord Rockham grabbed his injury and let out a mighty cry of pain and outrage.

"Ye gods! You've done for me!"

"Not quite," Brett said with a smile. "Merely disarmed you." And standing above Lord Rockham, Brett continued unemotionally, "I suggest you give me a thorough tour of your establishment, ere you bleed to death. I feel obligated to suggest that it would be most efficacious for your health if we found Miss Laurence posthaste."

The sound of a shot had brought Lord Rockham's servants crowding at the door, and they made a move toward the earl.

"I wouldn't advise it. I shall not waste my shot on your flunkies, but shall continue to ventilate you in every extremity, and eventually reach something you have more need of. So I suggest you walk carefully before me, dismiss your crew, and direct me to the lady. Immediately."

"I don't know where she is, blast you!" Lord Rockham exclaimed, dismissing his staff. "That's my blood flowing like a river, do you think I would not give her up to you in a hurry so I might not seek remedy?"

"Would you? Not much of an undying love, then? Might very well be a dying love, though, what say?"

Groaning and staggering, and making much ado over what was, after all, a mere flesh wound, in this complaining manner Lord Rockham led him through his manor. At last seeking the relief of his couch, Lord Rockham called for his valet to cup him, and in a peevish tone ordered the earl from his premises. "And you are welcome to her—she is not worth my heart's blood."

They had looked in every nook and cranny. So thorough had the earl been, he'd even had the bleeding lord take him through the attics. There was no possibility that Merrie was there. Nor would the groaning lord admit to having taken her anywhere else. Judicious use of his pistol as well as the funds spread amongst the staff still could not reveal a clue as to her whereabouts. For a guinea a maid admitted she had left the lady resting in his lordship's chambers, waiting for my lord and their supper.

"The devil she was!" the earl said with distaste, and exited.

He was just driving his chaise out of the gates when he spotted a gentleman, cloaked and hatted, standing directly in his path. Another of my lord's servants. Had they not had enough of his lead? Wearily the earl reached for his pistol again as the cloaked figure neared, causing his tired team to rear. Controlling them with an expert's skill, Brett was just able to prevent the chaise's overturning, during which the gentleman was halfway mounted onto the earl's chaise.

Astonished, the earl immediately pointed his pistol, only to have it blithely disregarded as the figure threw itself jubilantly into his arms.

"In the name of God!" the earl exclaimed, pulling away in shock.

Upon which a familiar voice said, "Oh Brett, Brett darling, you rescued me! You do love me! And just like a hero in a gothic romance! Pistol drawn as well!"

"Merrie! Blast you," the earl said thickly as her hat went flying and the gentleman in his arms turned out to be the lady he had been seeking. He allowed his nature to take charge, and he hugged the laughing lady to him, and even stopped to kiss her several times on the mouth. All of which she returned with total fervor and laughter.

His lordship had a clear moment of déjà vu. This was how he had first met his merry girl. And he'd taken her up and taken her to heart, he admitted to himself as he felt her in his arms.

"My hero!" she said when both could speak.

There was the sound of a vehicle coming from Lord Rockham's manor, and the earl announced that they had best defer their conversation until safely away. The chase was not long, for the grooms did not have the smallest interest in being shot by the gentleman who had already shot their lord. They followed just long enough to be able to report to their master that they had done their utmost, until the earl's carriage had disappeared past the village onto the post road.

Still the earl continued at a fast clip. And even as he slowed to a normal pace, he realized that their emotions were at too high a level to have a cogent conversation over the sound of the horses. And so Brett merely covered Miss Laurence with a rug. Concurring with the plan, Merrie allowed her relief and exhaustion to take over and in a moment had closed her eyes. His lordship looking at her was wondering what the devil she'd done and what the devil he was feeling about her. And whether he should have put a shot in her as well.

But at that point she opened her eyes and anxiously whispered, "Brett, are you there?" which shook him out of all doubting thoughts. He whispered back, "I'm here. You're safe, dear heart, and I'll keep you so."

Although still in a drowsy state, she could not but reply to that, so awash was she in satisfaction. "You came for me, proving your love, and faith. But I loved you first, from our first meeting, even though . . ."—here her voice dropped off into a small giggle—". . . you burned my hat!"

He laughed at that, and rocked her with one arm while keeping his horses at a steady pace with the other. "When I thought he had you, I knew what it felt like to have my heart torn out of me. A few hours ago I would have given the world and all for this one moment of having you safely in my arms." He pulled up the horses ostensibly for them to rest, but really to hold her in both arms and thus sense completely that she was there and breathing and laughing. He kissed her with a series of deep, connected kisses that soothed both their frightened hearts, and still they must continue holding each other as the earl whispered, "How the devil was I foolish enough to think I could live without you?"

"A complete moonling," Merrie agreed with her tinkling laugh, but soon she was drowsily sighing again and softly said, "Kiss me again so that I can sleep with that memory and wake with it, and know we shall never again be apart."

"Never again, on my oath! Merrie, my darling, my darling wild girl."

And she slept in his arms until she woke as she wished with him kissing her while carrying her up the steps of the Warwick town house.

George was the first to call out that Brett had returned. The roused household was all assembled: maids, footmen, cook, and at the entrance Esther and George. Even the countess had risen from her bed and come to see the results of the earl's quest. And there she was being carried in by the earl—Merrie herself, and all smiles, jumping out of the earl's grasp and falling into her sobbing sister's outstretched arms. The two were crying and exclaiming together, until George had both sisters in his arms, and was hurrahing, and then at the sound of the countess's anguished voice, Merrie broke away from that embrace and rushed up the remaining stairs into the countess's arms as well. "Oh, my little girl, my darling child! You're safe! You're safe," the countess was crying, and Esther was up the stairs as well, and all three ladies were sitting down on the carpeted landing and crying together in joy and relief.

George punched the earl on the arm affectionately. "Blast you, Brett, you did it! By Jove, you did it!"

Even the earl could not suppress his grin.

But he did not join George in having tears in his eyes. Rather he said calmly, "Did you not request that I bring her back? I always aim to give satisfaction." But he felt a good deal of satisfaction himself.

George hooted at the earl's mock sangfroid and called him a devil of a bloke, and then bethought himself to inquire how he had left Lord Rockham. By then Merrie and Esther and even the countess had begun coming down the stairs toward them, and all three were able to hear the earl's one-word reply, and universally gasp.

"Bleeding," was all the earl said.

"You killed him!" Merrie exclaimed in alarm.

"Merely wounded him in the arm," the earl.

George wanted to hear the particulars of the duel. The countess had to be assured that her son was unhurt. But Esther called a halt to any more conversation, feeling it was hardly the time to relive the escape, that everyone needed to rest and recuperate before reminiscing. Tea was called for, servants dismissed. The earl removed his driving cloak. Esther helped Merrie remove hers as well.

Not till Merrie observed the astonished stares of her sister and the countess, as well as George's pained one, and lastly, the furious glare of the earl, did the adventuring young lady recollect her attire. There she stood in her black satin gown with Lord Rockham's shirt above, large enough to be falling half off one shoulder and revealing some of the plunging satin bodice.

"Well," Merrie began with a giggle, "there is a very good explanation for all this. . . . Indeed, for the entire escapade."

"We are all waiting with some marked degree of interest to hear it," the earl said coldly.

"There is no necessity for her to tell us tonight," Esther said, staring at the earl with equal coldness. "I need not be told that Merrie has acted unexceptionably, if not heroically, for that is the only way she ever behaves."

"Righto," George agreed. "She doesn't have to say a word to us," he said with affection in his glance, which won him a quick running embrace from Esther, though the countess had the final word.

"Vinny has missed you, and wishes to see you," she said. And so it was decided that Merrie would tell her tale in the morning. "As long as my dear child is home in my arms," the countess said, and taking the exhausted girl once more literally in her arms, with Esther on the other side, the ladies half carried her up the stairs to her room, which they had been all this time fearing would never house her again. Vinny, at the sound of her voice, was mewing his welcome, calling for her to come. At the landing, Merrie paused and turned to wave at the two gentlemen below. And to one she could not resist throwing a kiss.

The one it was aimed at did not toss it back, but his brother did.

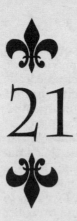

21

It was after breakfast that the earl, rather than leaving for a day on the town, as was his wont, adjourned with the rest of the family, and Merrie, who had already told the full story to Esther in her bedroom, now repeated it to the rest of her family.

At the perfidy of Lady Jane, George was enraged, the countess declaring herself justified in her belief, and taking that occasion to repeat some stories about Lady Dansville that were not at all apropos, something about wearing a similar dress. George urged Merrie to continue, and when she came to the moment when she ran up to her room and wrote a note to the earl and handed it to Simpson, the earl, who had begun to feel a certain coldness rushing through his veins at her blaming Lady Jane, was now staring at the young lady with erupting suspicion.

"But it was Lord Rockham's carriage, didn't you know?" George interrupted.

"No, for it bore no coat of arms and Lady Jane claimed it as her own, and even said she was going to accompany me to where Esther was being held."

"It did not occur to you to take our own groom along or to inform the countess?"

Those were the earl's unloving tones and Merrie was alarmed to hear them again, especially after his promise last night in the carriage to protect her always.

"Since it occurred," she admitted ruefully, "I have thought of many things I could have done, but I did what I did. I did not awaken the countess for fear she would be too overcome, and I should not have time to rescue Esther in the interim. And I hoped, I was *led to believe*, we would overtake the carriage and bring her back before anyone heard of her plight."

"But why didn't you come to me?" George exclaimed, resentful of not having part of the rescue of his love, except that his love had at that moment been with him. And so he cut off his protests.

"Your man told me you had an early engagement and were not expected back, and Esther was gone, and Lady Jane insisted we must hurry, that her standing would protect Esther from her act more than anyone I could turn to, for she by her very presence would give any act propriety. And so I ran out."

"Without hat or parasol," the countess said. "Of course, why did we not understand? Only in a true emergency would a lady depart without those."

"And so you went running out to join Lady Jane in her carriage. This tale becomes more and more fascinating," Brett continued with a tone of reserve that was veering toward suspicion as he took two steps toward the young lady dressed in one of his own chosen green morning dresses and eyeing him with complete confidence that she could say anything to him and he would believe the worst flummery. "Such an amazing transference of character this tale demonstrates. Lady Jane, who is known to all society as being rather a poor traveler, and who you recall upon her arrival at Moorsedge having to take several days to recover, and who would not commit the impropriety of even having her horse canter; this lady who was never a dear friend to you—was prepared to go against her very nature and race after a lord abducting a lady." Suddenly the earl's bitter laugh made the family turn toward Merrie with uncertainty.

"I . . . I thought it was the good in her coming out—that she would risk her comfort for the welfare of another. And I thanked her profusely. Indeed, her generosity profoundly moved me. And even when she left me alone, taking her abigail, I still believed she had wanted to help me, but just had not been physically capable, for she claimed she was overcome, and that's when I remembered about her being a poor traveler . . . but"—Merrie shook her head at herself —"it was too late. I had to carry on. . . . Ah, you had to be there, and worry about someone you loved, and know that only speed could save her."

Esther took Merrie's hand at that, and the countess the other, believing her totally—a phalanx of three against any questioning.

Still that deadly calm voice pierced through them all as the earl struck again. "You felt you were of sufficient assistance for your sister, I gather. For while you say you left a note, there was none for George when he returned, who might have been trusted to come after. Nor was there one for me, who, as you have seen, could be counted on to be of some small aid. Indeed, without my assistance you would not have been returned to the bosom of your adopted family. . . ."

"Gammon," Merrie exclaimed, insulted, but then added more diplomatically, "I was grateful to see you, but you must admit I escaped on my own!"

"Is that what you were doing in that outfit?" he demanded, revealing through his voice and stare some

of the fury he'd felt all night at the sight of Merrie
with her hair loose and wearing the type of gown only
the most wanton ladybird would have willingly
donned. Indeed, the black satin gown had given rise
to tortured imaginings of what had occurred before
he arrived. "We should dearly like to hear how he
coerced you into donning that . . . nightgown."

"He did not coerce me," Merrie admitted, facing
the earl's dark eyes without flinching. "When I arrived he told me his entire plan, devised with the aid
of Lady Jane, who apparently wished to remove me
so that her hopes of you could be fulfilled. He concluded with the pronouncement that I was compromised by just being there and assured me that no one
would believe that I had not gone willingly, for Lady
Jane was above suspicion, while I was a nobody. And
I said, those I love and who love me, will believe it."

A chorus of belief rose from all but the earl. He
continued to sight her as if over a pistol. "And so you
donned the gown and adjourned to his chambers?"

"He attempted to make free with my person in the
saloon. I hoped to divert or distract his emotions. I
am rather deft at doing that with gentlemen who allow their feelings to run away with them."

That reminder shook the earl's cold glare. He even
smiled a moment. "Yes, you are adept at causing
some diversion to distract. And so you fainted?" he
said hopefully.

Merrie smiled at his warmer tone. "Nothing so
commonplace. Besides, it was very likely that while I
was pretending to be out of my senses, he would use
that as an opportunity. He was beyond the point
where one could rely on his acting as a gentleman.
No, I merely bought time by agreeing to retire for a
while. But I was surrounded by his maids. They took
my gown under the pretense of brushing it, but then
removed it altogether and the satin gown was given

me, instead. It was that or appearing in my chemise. But I did not despair," she continued, and told her tale of dressing as the lord, and crying out to the footman to unlock the door, and how she had simply walked out. "I was hiding in the bushes when I saw Lord Warwick leaving the manor, and I ran through the lawns past the gates and confronted him on the road. Oh, it was capital! Almost a repeat of our first meeting. For we nearly had a collision, but he controlled his horses in a trice, and like the first time, took me up, and wrapped me in a rug. And told me I was safe. And I was."

The cheers were universal, and even the earl was prepared to believe that part of her story. Especially when he recollected the astonished glance of Lord Rockham when he could not find her. And later when he kept crying, "Where the devil did she go?"

Then the earl was called upon to tell his story, and Merrie was applauding with the rest of his family, and somehow all was resolved. And since the earl had already wounded Lord Rockham there was no need even to call him out. And all they could do was celebrate.

Just as they were calling for another round of tea, the earl thought to say in regret, "But if only you'd come to me, I would not have had you undergo any of that . . . disgrace. He did not attempt any liberties?" he asked, his voice husky at that.

And always invariably honest, Merrie admitted that he had kissed her in the saloon, and that was the reason she had sought to distract him.

"One kiss or several?"

"Good God, Brett," George exclaimed, "it is enough that she was not subjected to the ultimate indignity . . . I mean, to further indignities."

"There were several kisses," Merrie said, eyeing the earl steadily. "None of which I returned."

The earl nodded, and attempted to wipe that from his mind's eye. "And he never saw you in that black satin gown?"

"I have already said that. Only the maids. But they made several lewd remarks about my appearance in it, and I was put to a blush. Would you care to call them out for me?"

The earl grinned. "I do not believe I could accept their choice of weapons—dust pans and brooms."

"That might aid in cleaning out some of your thoughts," Merrie interrupted, and he bowed at her repartee. But his thoughts remained begrimed. And when Simpson entered with a note for the earl from a friend about a commitment to a race, his lordship took the opportunity to request his butler to verify having seen Lady Jane there on that morning. Everyone had been laughing and finishing their tea, and the affair pretty much put behind them, when that question called them all to attention, and reminded them that the earl still had some suspicions.

"Her ladyship was not here," Simpson replied.

There was a stunned silence.

Merrie stared at the butler. He had been with the Warwick family for many a year and his word would not lightly be dismissed. "But," she pleaded, "you must recollect—you let her in!"

"I regret not to please the young lady, but I certainly would recall if I had admitted her ladyship into the house." And that was said without a single ripple in Simpson's unshakable demeanor.

"Perhaps one of the footmen let her in," the countess said with anxiety.

"I shall of course inquire, your ladyship, but I scarce would allow any of them to take over my responsibility. And I saw the young lady Miss Laurence depart, and she was unaccompanied."

"You're lying," Esther cried out.

The family retainer gave her a look of such contempt that she was not able to continue to accuse him.

Everyone turned to face Merrie, and she shook her head. "Ah, I underestimated Lord Rockham. I should have realized that he would have another cohort. And I expect you did not deliver the note I left to the earl either, did you, Simpson?"

The unfazed retainer took a deep sigh. "You left no such note with me, miss. If you wish me to say that you did, I shall of course do so." With a bow he turned and left.

The earl was pacing in fury. "You had us almost believing that cock-and-bull story. Why don't you finally tell us the truth? You agreed to meet Lord Rockham, hoping that I should be forced to rescue you and come face-to-face with my feelings for you. And I fell precisely into your trap. And I confessed my feelings for you, so grateful was I that you were safe. But it was all done at your orchestration, as you orchestrated the Christmas affairs. . . . You treat us all as your puppets, and believe we will all jump at your signals."

He waited for her to deny but she just stared at him in astonishment, so that he took her silence as an admission. "I see you realize now, Miss Laurence, that you went too far by including Lady Jane and Simpson, both of whom I have known for a great deal longer than you and have unshakable faith in their veracity and dignity, the latter of which you have not a jot. If you had kept it simpler, your little game would not have come a cropper."

Merrie jumped up then like an exclamation mark. "Good heavens! You'd believe a servant rather than the lady you professed last night to love with all your heart? I tell you, and remember this well, for someday the truth will out—Simpson and Lady Jane are part of Lord Rockham's conspiracy. I was their victim."

"I am *your* victim, and have been since the first moment you came into my life," the earl said coldly, and walked out.

Taking a deep breath in dread, Merrie looked at the countess and George. Of her sister she had not the slightest doubt. The countess spoke first. "I expect it will take Brett some time to realize that servants are not their roles. They are people. And though it is not the thing for a butler to be corrupted, people often are."

Merrie grabbed hold of the lady's hand, and held on in gratitude. And the lady asked in surprise, "Did you really believe I should accept Simpson's word over yours? Gracious, he was my husband's butler, which should be sufficient against him. And further, he never even properly holds out my chair for me to be seated."

Merrie was uncertain how that followed, though it seemed to be the most damning thing that her ladyship could say about the man, until she recollected, "And he kicked Vinny!"

After that, there could be nothing good said about him. George and Esther had good cause to believe that Rockham, having been thorough enough to send them notes each purportedly from the other, would not scruple to corrupt a mere servant. And further, Simpson's role was obvious to them, for the conspiracy needed someone who was a member of the household, and thus aware of their feelings and schedules, to place the notes at the correct times and steal them afterward. They talked of explaining all that to the earl, and questioned Merrie if she wished them to do so, but Merrie refused. "I'd as lief he were not further cajoled or coerced into having faith in me. Indeed, I am tired of asking for what should be freely given. Trust is the key to love, and apparently his lordship has neither. And as I cannot do without those, I must do without him."

22

The last ball of the season would be given by the prince regent himself to celebrate his triumph. What his triumph was everyone knew but none mentioned other than in whispers. In effect, it was ridding himself of the two ladies in his life. After having previously all but exiled his wife the Princess Caroline, who had won the public's and her daughter's support in that royal couple's many feuds over his mistresses, this year their daughter the Princess Charlotte was also, at long last, off his hands. Just this season she had made a happy marriage to a minor princeling of Saxe-Coburg. Safely wed and on her honeymoon, there was no one his populace or even the nobles at long last could cheer but His Highness. And so, in effect, the ball was to celebrate himself. Following the royal fashion, the earl similarly was gradually emptying London and Warwick House of all its ladies.

George and Esther, chaperoned by an abigail and groom, had left for Oxford where George was to request Esther's hand in marriage from his prospective in-laws. Lady Warwick and Merrie were making arrangements for a return to Yorkshire to begin wedding preparations for the marriage to take place there. Since the earl had turned on her, Merrie had gone back to the cool formality that had characterized their first fortnight in London. And the countess, as a staunch defender of the young lady, was equally cool to her son. With George's departure, that left the earl no one to speak to at home but Simpson. And so he practically moved into his club.

He had some awareness that prior to their departure, Merrie and his mother were to attend the prince regent's ball escorted by the duke of Chumley. And somewhat in anger at the way the entire family had sided against him, and to taunt Miss Laurence, he'd arranged to escort Lady Jane. That to Merrie was the final insult, leading her to conclude that the earl was clearly unworthy of her least regard.

The site of His Highness's summer ball was to be his own palace, Carlton House, and its bird-filled gardens under the willow trees. Each lady was to be dressed as her favorite flower or symbol of summer, and the dressmakers, particularly Madame Bliss, were so occupied, there was scarcely time to fit in their favorite customers.

But Madame Bliss waited in vain for Miss Laurence, who had been a style setter this year with her throat-covering lace or gauze inserts on all her gowns, which had several other ladies anxious to copy, and coming to Madame Bliss. For without the earl's interest in Merrie's appearance, the lady herself was content with the many gowns already in her possession. True to the ball's theme, Lady Warwick was one of the many ladies who was dressing as a rose, in layers of rose-petalled flounces and of course roses in her satin cap. A yellow rose was Lady Jane's selection, and she had a petaled gown. Many dresses to begin with had floral designs or appliqués, so often there was no necessity of purchasing special costumes. But the more daring ladies went all out, and some, it was being said, were even planning to dress as birds or butterflies, and had wings fitted for their backs. Most of the gentlemen felt it sufficient to wear their formal dress and simply have a flower boutonnière, except for the younger dandies, who added flowers twined in the buttonholes of their waistcoats.

Merrie wished not to be commonplace, but as well would never again request the earl's assistance or even give him the satisfaction of resorting to his designer. So she looked long and hard at her wardrobe. There was one smashing gown in shades of orange and apricot net over a golden-yellow satin slip, not yet worn, and which gave her a sunlit image. One needed, she hoped, merely a headdress of a sort to complete it. Her first alteration was to remove the gown's apricot gauze inserts on the décolletage and sleeves. Ripping them out, stitch by stitch, was doubly satisfying since that look had been the earl's trademark for her. She would no longer reflect any of his whims.

The material then was ample to cover her large leghorn hat, alternating the strips on the upturned brim for a raylike exuberance. Naturally the green ribbon was removed, and that too with satisfaction. Nor would she wear the emerald earrings, ever again. She was in effect obliterating all his touches and asserting herself. To that purpose Miss Laurence derived a new hairstyle, simply allowing her hair to hang loose, which thus further suggested the glow of the sun at its zenith. A few crystal droplets from one of the earl's fans were added to the front locks of her hair to continue the sunlit effect. Fortunately, for modesty's sake, her hair was so long it covered her sleeveless arms and some of the bodice, now shockingly low without the inserts. Lady Warwick gave her one of her golden chains, which Merrie wore around her forehead in the current ferronnière style, with a crystal in the center.

Yet, after all this, when the duke observed her in his carriage, he said, "Orange blossom?" hoping she had marriage in mind, and made many pretty allusions to that possibility. She did not dissuade him either of his hopes or her representation.

At the ball the duke was proud to have her first dance. People parted as Merrie walked by. At first, the duke and even she thought this attention was a result of her rather spectacular appearance, but before long, as the stares continued, it became evident that something was amiss.

After meeting in the garden, the prince himself led a procession of his guests through his Gothic conservatory into the ballroom, which had more flowers than the garden. The prince regent was dressed formally with roses in his buttonholes and an embroidered rose pattern on his vest. He carried a large bouquet of roses of the most exquisite shape and fragrance. After all the bowing and curtseying he received after his parade, the prince still wished for further attention. So he walked through the guests, picking out the ladies catching his philanderer's eye, gifting each with a rose and claiming a kiss in return. Mostly His Highness chose married ladies for this privilege, basically because he had a preference for older, somewhat corpulent matrons such as his current mistress Lady Hartford. But in one or two cases he chose young ladies and gave them a kiss on the cheek. He passed by Lady Jane, and went directly to Lady Warwick standing in the background. "A perfect English rose," the prince said, "in full and exquisite bloom, egad!" and claimed a full kiss on the countess's astonished mouth.

Merrie had been dancing with the duke at the time,

and they were some distance from the event, but close enough to see the countess blush, and the duke instantly took offense. "Blast the man. Lechery is not a royal prerogative, egad! By Jove, why ain't he content with his own crowd? Has to debase a decent woman!"

The countess did not seem debased, but rather pleased. She was of mixed feelings however when the earl, with whom she had not had much converse of late, stepped up to claim a waltz. "As the prince regent's choice, I am honored, Mama, that you condescended to give me a nod," he said with some of his old warmth for the lady.

She begrudgingly smiled in return, and allowed that it was she who was much honored. And thus they continued in civility until Brett asked if Merrie was there. The countess was delighted to report that the duke had brought them both. "He has not forgot us," she could not resist adding, and the earl stiffened, and was further petrified when she pointed out Merrie.

He cried out, "Confound her, what the devil is she wearing?"

"A costume of summer. She made it herself, you know, from gowns she had. Rearranged herself from another's limited view. So original, the result, what say? But Merrie is always out of the common."

An accomplished dancer, he was tripping on his mother's feet, and she suggested they pause so that he might gaze unimpeded by the whirling crowd. Not caring how it appeared, he did cease dancing and just gazed. "She's the sun, isn't she?"

"Yes," his mother said proudly. "She is the sun and the stars and all of the best of summer warmth and joy in one. She is Merrie, my darling girl. Look how everybody is admiring her. Ah, there goes the prince regent, I knew he could not miss her. Heavens, if I got a rose, she should have the entire bouquet."

Indeed the prince had spotted her, and not only offered the rest of his roses, but was quite eager for a waltz. She danced as lightly as a ray of the sun, touching everyone with a glow as she glided by. Her hair flew out at each turn and with the shower of crystals seemed to radiate about her beautiful face.

"There is no one to equal her for beauty," the earl admitted, "and for daring, and for gall."

Lady Dansville and Lady Jane approached the earl and his mother. Lady Dansville saw the direction of the earl's gaze, and said with a laugh, "From Lord Rockham to the prince—she is mistress to them all."

"What did you say?" the countess demanded, and her face was in a flame that almost equaled Merrie's hair.

"Come now, countess, your protégée's shocking escapade with Lord Rockham is known throughout the ball tonight."

"And is your daughter's part in it equally known? I have been considerate enough not to mention it, but if you and your harpy spawn are spreading such falsehoods, I shall not hesitate to let everyone know who led my dear Merrie into the trap. Your daughter may be a lady, but she has not the slightest awareness of what that means. She is all pride, as are you. And dastardly deeds."

At that Lady Dansville, taking her daughter by the arm, simply walked away, a set smile on her lips. But Lady Dansville apparently had the last word. For gradually, as shocking as it was to accept, Merrie was clearly being cut. And not just by a few sticklers or old matrons with high notions, but by all, as dance after dance went unclaimed. For the first time since coming into society, aside from the duke and prince, she did not have a single partner. At last, Sir Mal-

colm, remembering her kindness to him, risked social
disapproval and bowed before her. But after him,
Merrie found herself standing alone with the countess, as a great many of the gentlemen who a fortnight
past had been writing odes to her eyebrows were now
actually pretending not to see any part of her. And
certain ladies even insulted her to the extent of giving
her the cut direct. Feeling a blushing flooding her
body, Merrie hoped it would be seen as part of the
sun's shadings. No need to question the cause. It was
clear that either Lord Rockham or Lady Jane had
spread the story in the manner most detracting to
Miss Laurence.

The only hope as the countess and Merrie stood
alone, and yet feeling themselves so much on display
for that loneness, was His Grace. He had brought
them; he must shield them. He had the power to do
so. And instantly countess Warwick, her lips trembling, looked for the duke. What she saw rather was
that confused gentleman being taken aside by Lord
Dansville. A few moments' conversation, and His
Grace was soon hurriedly departing from the ballroom. It could not be. They were abandoned, and
publicly so. At which Merrie and the countess exchanged glances at last of pure dismay.

"I expect her sun has set," Lady Jane whispered to
the earl, and she giggled.

He turned pale at that and was ready to reprimand
her for the unkindness of the remark, although before
Merrie's influence, he himself would have made some
such sarcastic aside. His revulsion indicated that he
had not completely reverted to type. Indeed, for every
moment Merrie was suffering, he suffered as well. He
could not bear to see that glowing creature shunned.
Yet he was proud of her pose under it all, as she continued to keep her sunlit head high, occupying herself
with chatting to old Lady Beaumaris—she of the

waspish tongue. At previous occasions Merrie had gone out of her way to listen to her comments and on the principle of bread upon the waters, she now found someone who would not join the rest in ostracizing her. As the evening continued and Miss Laurence's face showed not a trace of alarm, the earl felt she was incomparably above and beyond them all. Yet just as he was thinking that and marveling, at the very next moment her face went ghostly white. Immediately the earl turned in the direction of her astonished gaze.

It was Lord Rockham striding in, with a silk bandage around his injured arm. What story he was spreading concerning his injury, the earl could not imagine. Earlier Brett had seen the departure of the duke, and realizing his mother and Merrie were cast adrift, had planned to come to their rescue in escorting them home. But he had not acted in time, for apparently Lord Rockham had his own agenda. Carrying a large bouquet of roses, he walked directly toward Miss Laurence and bowed before her, obviously asking for a dance.

There was a buzz of delicious scandal, and everyone was gasping, and even stopped dancing themselves to observe Merrie's reaction.

She was majestic in her nonreaction. Indeed she simply walked by him as if not seeing either him or the bouquet he placed at her feet. Actually she stepped right over it and her skirt brushed against his bent head as she walked by. But Lord Rockham was not one to accept reprimands. He was determined to make a scene and had the audacity to follow her, for he was enjoying not only being the cynosure, but as well the rumors and even the lady's discomfort.

It was too much for the earl. In one gesture, he walked up to Merrie and without even asking her, swept her away from the gentleman and into the middle of the ballroom. Head high, he waltzed her all around the ballroom, and then right into its middle, determined to make as wide a swath as possible. But soon Merrie was asking him to waltz her toward the countess, for she did not wish to continue this dance with him.

"You came to this dance, did you not?" Brett demanded. "Well, blast you, best see it through. I'll be damned if I let you destroy my family's name because of your cowardice."

"If you feel I represent your family, then of course I shall stay. But surely you did not think so when you joined Lord Rockham's camp in his attempt to destroy me and openly brought Lady Jane to the ball. That showed clearly to all whom you believe. Therefore your name is cleared. You need only ask for Lady Jane's hand, and all remembrance of me will disappear from amongst this exalted group of petty minds and cruel hearts."

The dance was over and without responding to her remark, the earl returned her to the countess. But in a moment, he'd gone up to Sir Oswald, who had well earned his reputation as a rattle, and whispered a word in his ear that soon spread like wildfire.

A remarkable transformation was effected. One moment the two ladies were being ostracized, and the next, courted. Indeed, it was like a stampede, for several of the lords who had been despising themselves for holding back, and wishing with all their hearts to dance with the sun goddess, were now at her side. But most astonishing was the attentions of the ladies: They, as well, were bowing in her direction and even smiling. Pointedly the countess was once again in high favor, surrounded by matrons wishing to chat. A total flip-flop! Merrie was in a state of wonder, and the countess tearful in her relief.

After dinner, at which Merrie was attended throughout by her old crowd, the earl claimed the final dance. Once more Merrie was surprised by the lords and ladies of the ton, for actually, as the couple danced by crowd after crowd, each group applauded and applauded.

"What the devil did you say to them all?" Merrie incredulously asked.

The earl shook his head and merely answered, "Smile, my merry lady, this is your moment of triumph. Look there, Lord Rockham is shot through the heart." And she turned and saw his lordship following them with despair and sadness in his eyes.

"You told them you'd shot him?" Merrie said.

"Certainly not, that would only have added to his prestige and lessened yours. I told them he shot himself because you had chosen another."

And then Merrie genuinely began to laugh. "And whom did you choose as the figure of romance? His Grace who has run aground?"

"Good God, no. I chose that epitome of society's gallantry and that nonpareil paragon of romance."

"Dear heavens!"

"Yes, my dear heart, I chose myself."

Merrie missed her step. "Oh, fiddle!" she exclaimed, and before she could say more, he'd bowed to her and to all around, and escorted her and his mother out of the ballroom.

23

The day after the prince regent's ball, the duke of Chumley called on Miss Laurence, but she would not receive him.

After his dastardly behavior of abandoning her and the countess, when it was his clear duty as their escort at least to return them to their home, she felt no conversation due him. The countess, however, received him, for she wished to hear his excuses, and further as he was a duke, she felt she owed him that much courtesy.

A full hour's conversation had Lady Warwick flushed and determined to bring Merrie to understand the duke's position.

"I am only concerned with the position he left us in last night," Merrie said sadly. "Besides, his reason for wishing to see us today is because of Lord Warwick's announcement of our engagement, which persuaded society to readmit me—under the earl's auspices. Else His Grace would not have come."

But the countess felt rather that they were dealing with a gentleman who was suffering from a clear case of having lost his heart to a lady. For the truth of the matter was that he had heard all the rumors about Lord Rockham and had given them the back of his hand, but when Lord Dansville took him aside and told him that Lord Rockham had arrived and was going to claim the woman of his heart, and that Miss Laurence was going to accept him before all, he could not bear that sight, and left, totally overcome.

For a moment Merrie could only gasp. Was it possible for Lord Dansville to spread such a tale? Yes, knowing him, it was; and actually Lord Rockham did approach her directly afterward. "But why would not His Grace question us, or at least you, the two of you having such rapport?"

"That is true, we have. I find myself drawn to his gentle heart, and his heart explains why he could not question us. He was, I collect, too torn into tatters by the loss of you. After all, Merrie, you are not someone one can lose without monstrous effect. And to see you giving yourself to that bounder and before all his friends—how could a man of sensibility accept that without, quite frankly, going into a severe decline?"

"Well, far be it from me to aid in his decline. If he wishes my forgiveness, naturally he has it. In any case, I should always act as you advise. I have implicit faith in your instincts."

The countess was all smiles at that. And her suggestion was that Merrie promptly permit the duke to call on them. Still Merrie was wondering at his objective. Had he not heard that she was engaged to Lord Warwick?

"I hope you'll forgive me, Merrie, dear heart, but I felt it best to tell the complete unvarnished story to His Grace. He was horrified. Never have I seen him so beside himself. I had to hold his hands to stop them from trembling at the dastardly acts of Lord Rockham and Lady Jane. And he bemoaned indeed that we had not taken him into full confidence, so that he could have known how to act last night. With your permission, he would have been the one announcing an engagement, rather than leaving it to Brett."

"Then he takes my side of the case completely, unlike the rest of the ton and a certain distantly related, titled gentleman," she said, clearly showing that her hackles were still up.

The countess assured her that was the case, and that she had further hinted to His Grace that Brett had merely acted to rescue the family's name, and therefore Merrie might not be averse to a continuation of the duke's suit.

Merrie nodded at that possibility without much enthusiasm, but the countess was all aflutter at having brought about a reconciliation. Merrie's life would be so protected living with His Grace, the countess continued, and further, one could only think of all the good she could do as a duchess. Naturally, as a mother, she had throughout had the secret hope that Merrie would wed Brett. But after he had turned on them, she could no longer assume that would come to pass. Clearly he had acted as a gentleman should by rescuing them last night, but she knew, and Merrie knew, that he did not expect to be held to that proposal. And so the countess was pleased to have the duke back in consideration.

She said as much to Brett when he came for dinner and began questioning what their plans were for the summer.

"We are returning to Yorkshire."

"I cannot but endorse that course," the earl said, much relieved. "I am joining Lord Pavraam on a jaunt through Europe, but shall return to visit you and Miss Laurence sometime in the fall."

"His Grace will be visiting us somewhat earlier,"

his mother added with a small smile at her personal triumph.

That stopped the earl as he was ready to depart for his club. "Here or at Moorsedge?"

"Oh, he has already visited us here. We have had a cozy chat, and he is most anxious to renew his attentions to Merrie, and so I have invited him for a fortnight or so to Moorsedge."

"The devil you say!" the earl exclaimed. "And may I ask why His Grace should be visiting my fiancée?"

"I was not aware that Merrie and you had reached an agreement," Lady Warwick countered sweetly. "I understood your gesture, and applauded you for it, but that did not actually alter the relationship between you and my dear girl. It was all done for show, and Merrie understood that. And of course you are not to be held to your word. If, in the interim, His Grace and Merrie come to an understanding, then I expect you and Lady Jane would be free to come to yours."

"Why are you doing this, Mother? Are you so desperate for Merrie to become a duchess that you would toss her into this man's arms, despite the fact that he left both you and the supposed woman of his heart unprotected before all of society and to suffer the further affront of Lord Rockham?"

Here the countess was quick to defend His Grace, and to explain the part of Lord Dansville, and to indicate how curious it was that so many of the most dastardly acts seemed to stem from that family.

The earl did not defend them. He was sunken in his own thoughts. Then he looked up at his mother, and said in a curiously saddened voice, "When are you leaving for Yorkshire?" Told that it would be in less than two days' time, he answered, "Then I wish you would request Miss Laurence to give me the courtesy of a few moments' conversation before she has made her final plans."

The countess agreed to do so, whereupon on the following morning, Merrie awaited Lord Warwick in his own library. She was reading one of her favorite poets and looking quite unlike the last image he'd had of the spectacular sun goddess. Her hair was neatly arranged in a new style, center parted into two bunches, and she was dressed in a simple white muslin, appearing younger than her sister Esther. Yet her attitude was one of complete composure as he sat next to her.

"I understand from Mama that I have been remiss in not making my position clear to you. My remark to the ton was not meant just as a gesture. I intend to marry you. So there is no need for the duke to continue his courting."

Merrie surprised him, as she usually did—this time it was by laughing at his noble statement, concluding, "In other words, this is a genuine proposal?"

"Yes," he said stiffly, annoyed at her amusement when he'd been expecting obligation.

"No," she said clearly.

"No, what?"

"No, to your proposal."

His degree of astonishment was amazing to behold. He had to stand up and walk about the room. Then facing her, he repeated, "You are saying no to me?"

"How quick you are, my lord. That is precisely what I am doing."

"Because you have the duke at hand?"

"No, again. I had decided to reject your proposal the moment I was informed you'd made a general announcement of it, before being gracious enough to ask me. Ah, but then you never did. Ask me, that is.

You merely informed me. So therefore you cannot really complain of my response."

"Blast you! Are you implying that you wish a formal declaration?"

"That would be civil. Not that I expect civility from you."

"Is it not enough that I wish to make you my countess? What greater compliment?"

"Ah, forgive me, I am such a peagoose, but I was under the impression that when a gentleman requested a lady to marry him, she was doing him the honor and giving him the ultimate compliment by even listening to his proposal. And if she were to accept, his heart should be overcome. That is what the duke said to me just this morning in a most affecting missive. Naturally, I know you have not the duke's turn of phrase, but we are standing in a library. There are hundreds of tomes here from which you could find some gracious language, if you have it not by nature, nor feel it at heart."

The earl eyed her with his black eyes drowning in fury. He swallowed his ire, however, realizing the justice of her request. A gentleman should be somewhat more effusive in his proposals, and apparently she was going to make him go to the full extent. In a moment as he watched her eyes twinkling at his discomfort, he grinned, and refused to allow her to continue to hold the upper hand. He would play her game. After all, he was the expert at this kind of conversation with ladies.

Coming directly toward her, he surprised Merrie by kneeling down and grandiloquently making his plea. "It cannot have escaped your notice, my dear Miss Laurence, but of late I have felt a certain quickening of the heart when you are about. And so I request that you grant me the privilege, no, honor, of accepting my proposal for your hand in marriage."

He attempted to rise, when she pushed him back down. "I have not responded," she whispered.

Tolerantly, he remained on his knee.

"I am very disappointed in that proposal. No poetry?"

"You would prefer *Romeo and Juliet?* Very well, 'Your eyes in heaven would stream so bright, that birds would sing and think it were not night.' "

"That is merely a compliment on my physical self," Merrie said, and then seriously, of a sudden, "You do not really ever speak of love from your heart, do you, my lord? And that actually is the reason I am refusing your proposal. You may rise. As a gentleman, you have done everything required to save my reputation. But there is no need for either of us to continue this . . . farce."

He rose and stared at her with some coldness, feeling himself toyed with, dismissed, devalued. She had not actually wished for a marriage proposal, rather had wished him in the position of making one. "You are always playing games," he said with distaste.

"Yes, I am. That is my nature. And you always were against my joy in life, and yet it is that in me refusing you. I could never accept you, actually, because it is not what *you* wish, and therefore, I would be unable to make you happy. There is no more important a reason for refusing a union."

"You shall make me happy, blast you!"

"You don't want me for wife. Even the proposal was wrung out of you."

"Nonsense, I am delighted to offer for you. And I would be happy with you. . . . I know dashed well I have not been happy without you."

And to prove his statement, Brett took her into his arms and the two kissed. It was an angry kiss to begin with on his part, but the feel of her in his arms made him forget his anger, his distrust, all but the joy of having her there. And she, as always, was not shy in her response, but kissed him completely, without the slightest bit of ladylike restraint. As he held her close to his heart, he could hear hers beating forcibly against him. She even allowed him liberties with her body, to kiss down her neck and unto her bodice, and back up, without pause, until both were drowning in the heat and passion, and he angrily pulled away.

She was alarmed at the sudden violence in his face as he shook her. "And is this the way you incited Lord Rockham's actions till he reached the madness of his deed? And is this why His Grace is following you about like a wounded puppy, despite your reputation? Confound you, there is not the slightest degree of ladylike restraint in your kisses!"

Merrie attempted to call her heart to a sensible stillness as she pulled away and just stared. Then in pity and regret she said softly, "Ah, why do I keep assuming that you love me? If you did you ne'er would have said what you just did, because I showed you my heart is completely engaged. But then, you are always more concerned with the games society plays than the truth of anyone's feelings. You would prefer Lady Jane's restraint in such a situation, allowing you one chaste kiss, and living a cold life with her. Then, blast you, take them. And come not to me again with your pretense of love and honor."

The earl was confused again, and more confused by his own emotions. But the truth was that he did not have faith in her decency, because she did not act the lady's role.

"You never listen to your heart," Merrie continued in pity. "I expect it has long since atrophied. Isn't there even something within that tells you to forget all social conventions, throw them to the winds, and just love? To act on your love, without second thoughts and suspicions and reservations?" And her voice softened as she continued. "Nay, I'll not hold back my love for you because you are afraid to love . . . and trust. If you were capable of that, you would have long since believed me and your mother and George and Esther rather than your own enemy, Lord Rockham. And Lady Jane. Or at the very least have investigated the issue to find the truth for yourself."

The earl spoke then. "I have investigated it, thoroughly. Do you not think that with my feelings for you, I would not have attempted to prove you honest? I have questioned Simpson repeatedly, and have had the man tell me, much against his will, that not only did you not give him a note for me on that morning, but that you subsequently attempted to bribe him to say that you had. Simpson has been with my family since my father's time. To doubt him would be almost as if I doubted my father. Nay, I have implicit faith in his word. And Lady Jane's actions, I told you, are not consistent with her character. But your acts are consistent with yours. Not that I believe you realize what you are doing, but you so much believe in living for the pleasure of each moment that you would risk propriety to achieve your purpose, and think it a lark. As you thought it a lark to dress in a gentleman's cloak and run down the stairs, rather than waiting for me to rescue you. As you traveled on your own to Moorsedge, and when you had an accident simply commandeered a passing chaise regardless of who was in it, and ordered him to take you to his home. You are unguarded. And I have loved you for it, and I despise you for it. Because there are some things that, as a gentleman, I have come to respect—decency and control of behavior. I could not accept my wife constantly tying her garter in public, and expecting me to laugh with her at the joy of such uninhibited behavior. And though I love you, God help me, I would not be joyful married to a lady who plays so fast and loose with the truth and with propriety."

"Then of course you must not do it. I could assure you that I never did anything to hurt anyone, or that was really offensive except to those of the starchiest principles, but you would not believe me, and I no longer have the desire to convince you. And I do not even regret having loved you. One never loses for having given, one only loses for having held back . . . and winding up with naught."

She walked to the door, but stopped herself to give him a soft smile. "I say good-bye to you in love, for after this moment, I shall reserve my heart and love for my husband. But you will always be a dear memory for me, of what might have been if you had not been so fearful. I love, which is a way of saying, I am. Someday I hope you'll find a lady for whom you care so much that you shall say, to the devil with conventions. Until then you are . . . a naught indeed."

A fortnight later the earl, alone in his town house, received a letter from his mother. He was surprised to find that it did not come from Moorsedge.

In fact the letter itself had been franked by Chumley and he read with disapproval that they not only had taken a detour to visit the duke's estate and were still there, but further that they were being so royally entertained, it was not yet determined when they would proceed to Yorkshire. And then came her ladyship's exuberant description of the amusements being provided for them. Every day they went boating on the duke's own lake that boasted a view of such matchless beauty as to leave one breathless. She continued for a full page of crossed and recrossed descriptions of the various hills and trees, which could not have interested the earl less. He thought she'd reached her limit, only to discover subsequent pages of descriptions of the estate and the state of his plate and hangings, until the earl was muttering. And then after having endured all that, it abruptly ended, as she had to rush out to join the festivities, without really having told him anything to the purpose or whether Merrie had accepted His Grace's proposal.

The earl crushed the letter and tossed it on his desk. Since Merrie and his mother's departure, Warwick House had seemed tomblike in its emptiness. Egad, he never recalled feeling so alone. The only relief ahead was his trip abroad with Lord Pavraam, which should at least alter the boring sameness of view. His constant thoughts were on Merrie's last words, and he had been furious with himself for not crying out, "I can love and do love, but you are not worthy of it." Except that he could not think of any other lady who had ever so totally overcome him. He often wished he had insisted that she marry him. Better to have a slightly dishonest Merrie than not to have her in his life at all.

Reverting to his past devices, he attempted to forget one lady by finding another, needing continual fresh female distractions. He chose a married lady with a reputation for giving a gentleman pleasure and favored her with an evening or so, but abruptly broke off, unable to continue in his old freewheeling style. Incredibly, his most pleasurable moments were reading his brother's letters from Oxford. So warm and jolly did George's days sound, the earl had a passing thought of going there himself to make the acquaintance of her family. Pointless, actually, he concluded on second thought, needing nothing more to remind him of Miss Laurence. The sun reminded him of her in her sun outfit. And the green of the trees and plants were her eyes. And the sound of the birds in the deserted parks her laughter.

"The devil take her," he said, and remembered it was the duke that was taking her instead, and to wife.

Going into her room, he discovered with chagrin that it had been properly cleaned and straightened out by his very efficient staff, headed by her head accuser, Simpson, thwarting his hope of finding something as a memento.

Ye gods, he exclaimed, and promptly went to his standish, taking up pen. His disgust at his juvenile mooning spurred him to prevail upon Lord Pavraam that they put forward the date of their grand tour departure. Being an agreeable sort, Lord Pavraam was nothing loath, especially since the earl was so insistent. And as Brett departed, he felt some hope that an entire continent of new sights and people would at last blot out her beautiful face. He'd forgotten however that the place in which she'd apparently taken root must, of necessity, be taken with him wherever he went, even across the entire world, for she was safely and permanently implanted in his own heart.

24

It was the second Christmas that Merrie was to spend in Yorkshire. What made this one rather special was that her full family had arrived with George and Esther for the holiday season. Moorsedge easily accommodated them, for it had several wings of rooms, yet somehow the moment Eric and Winston invaded, it seemed amazingly smaller. Eight-year-old Eric was determined to play hide-the-bean in every room with Bruiser. He was the sort of lad, with his bright red hair, that elders often called a scamp, and yet he had a way of staring at one with his large, round blue eyes that inevitably had one relenting. "It was a very old vase," the countess exclaimed when he'd ridden down the banister and smashed into it. "However," she added kindly, "I must own, never my favorite. Given me by my husband's aunt, who never had anything good to say about anyone, and her vase reflected that disapprobation. Actually, I always felt it was disapproving of me in the same way."

Merrie attempted to apologize for Eric, and Esther did so again and again, but the countess would not be apologized to. She had, after all, brought up two boys of her own, and was quite accustomed to accidents. This was a far cry from the countess Merrie first remembered, who thought her greatest catastrophe was having George come home with his dogs at his heels.

Winston, now past twelve, was rather like his father, concerned with studies. He was a tall, pale blond lad, who always groaned at Eric's actions, and took on the responsibility for his siblings' coarse remarks and mad starts. Indeed, Winston went to George upon Eric's breaking the vase to consult him on what must be done in recompense. But George, who had become part of the Laurence family, merely gave him a pat and blithely claimed that he was not to fret.

And when Eric began to sense that he was not forgiven by his brother for his act, he hung his head and gave them all his pathetic blue-eyed, little-boy-lost look, until Merrie said laughingly, "There is no need to enact us a Cheltenham tragedy, young scamp. The countess has forgiven you, George has forgiven you, Esther has forgiven you, father would not wish to be disturbed in the grand library he has found here even to be told about it, and Mother you know always forgives you before you even do anything. So what's amiss?"

"Yes, but Merrie, Winston is angry. And also, you didn't say *you* understood."

Merrie hugged him tightly, and whispered, "Next time break the matching one on the other side, and the place won't look so lopsided."

He laughed at that, but still looked sadly at Winston.

"No point, old chap. I'm onto your routines. I shan't forgive you, because you'll just use it as carte blanche to break something else. And we've never had such a dandy house to live in. And Mother doesn't have to wear herself out taking care of such a thatch-

gallows like you, all the time. So I should think you'd
have a care."

Eric earnestly swore he'd have a care henceforth,
and Winston forgave him to the extent of letting him
walk with him to the edge of the moors and watch for
the earl's chaise.

The earl was due any hour, and George had very
magnanimously appointed Winston lookout, and
now Eric was junior lookout.

As they waited, using George's very own spyglass,
Eric forgot their duty, and began scouting for moor
birds. He liked best of all spooking them, so they'd fly
up wildly in a rush, like a living exclamation, into the
sky. He did it again, while Winston dutifully stared
toward the gate.

It was astonishing how well the two families
blended. The countess, who never had any interest in
housekeeping, and usually left all to Mrs. Prissom,
now could turn over to Mrs. Laurence all the responsibility of the household, as she'd once done to Merrie. And Mrs. Laurence was in heaven, once more
having maids to do her bidding—to actually clean for
her, and to be able to order fires laid in every fireplace, certainly in her husband's study, and in their
bedroom, and even in rooms that they just intended
to pass through. Not since she was a young lady
could she remember such luxury. And her girls had
never known it, until the countess had been so kind as
to take them up. She often would spend time chatting
with the countess about their early days, but mostly
she was concerned with earning her keep, till eventually she realized that the countess preferred her chatting. And Mrs. Prissom generally managed rather
well, allowing Mrs. Laurence much leisure, which she
should have been enjoying. Except that she was fretting instead. Then a joyous discovery occurred: she
spotted all the curtain hems were in shocking disre-

pair, and taking up her needle, the lady, once prized for her fancy needlepoint, could now devote herself to hemming the curtains while she chatted with the countess. Ergo, she was useful and talkative at once. A perfect solution.

Everyone was happy at Moorsedge: the young lads, Mr. Laurence in the grand study, Mrs. Laurence, and of course Esther and George, who had each other and were planning their joyous future. Even the duke was happy, for he was often invited to sit in on the conversations with the countess and Mrs. Laurence. It was Merrie, who, for the first time in her life, did not live up to her name.

And then she fell even more into the dismals at a letter from the earl. And then he sent her another, directly after.

Returning from his grand tour of the Continent in late October, the earl discovered some significant changes. The first in his very own household. Simpson had given notice directly upon the earl's departure. Roberts, the footman, had been elevated to his position. With a sense of unease, the earl sent his valet to discover the reason for Simpson's departure, and heard, in affirmation of his worst dread, of the butler's having joined Lord Rockham's household.

One did not need pictures drawn to make clear what a jingle-brained, clodpoll gudgeon he had been. After an entire tour, Brett concluded that Merrie could not be forgotten, so he'd best adjust to her failings. Indeed, he was set to challenge the duke for her hand in earnest. He was confident in his heart that he would prevail—no other outcome could be borne. Further, he had some cause for hope since after all these months of Merrie's close proximity to His Grace, a wedding date had not yet been selected. And then, this Simpson incident shattered him out of all assumptions. Doubly shaken was he after his attending Lady Jersey's soiree. For she took him aside and attempted to quiz him as to the state of his engagement.

"Are you and Miss Laurence going to marry at long last? One wonders, since one hears that our dear duke has been most consistent in his devotion as well as his presence at your home. In which case, I have a rather personable young niece who will be having her first season this coming year, and with Lady Jane now having accepted Lord Rockham, one hopes that you will be available?"

His lordship had merely bowed and returned some pleasantry about any relation of hers being undoubtedly worth meeting, and so forth, which left the lady with a smile. His lordship was left with a grim, set face. This association of Lord Rockham and Lady Jane was further proof of Miss Laurence's complete veracity. He felt himself breathing lead and left as soon as would not occasion a remark.

That very evening he wrote his letter of apology. It was short and to the point. He'd been a total gudgeon. The next day, he felt a longer letter of explanation was required, except that he had no explanation, so he merely wrote a longer apology. All plans to return to Yorkshire and challenge for the woman he loved had come to a stand, for he no longer had a stand from which to charge. Not now that it was clear he was at fault. With such a revelation he dared not even come near the lady. Every word she had said to him now echoed with truth. Except that about his lack of heart, which could not be true or he would not be feeling so much pain in that area. Dear God, he could not understand why he had not immediately believed her, when George so instantly did, and of course her sister and his mother did. They would have done so, however, if she had claimed William the Conqueror had abducted her, so strong was their faith. And the countess would have said she always believed old William was not quite the thing.

And worse, that moonling and jinglebrain of a duke stood by her and remained constant and true. What then was his excuse for his actions, when he had loved her from almost the first weeks at Moorsedge?

The answer could only be that his believing her would have meant disbelieving everything he stood for all his life—the rules of behavior and of exclusivity which underlined aristocracy. He'd been brought up to have implicit faith in his own superiority. His father by both word and example had encouraged this, as did his early attaining of his dignity, which had cut off any individual growth, forcing him quickly to conform to an earl's position. And then everywhere he turned he received naught but reinforcement of his worth, from servants, especially butlers like Simpson, to ladies of society, like all the Lady Janes.

Further, Merrie not only brought into question society but his own style. For it was inbred in him to be well bred, never to show his emotions before the public. Which gradually made him proud of not succumbing to passion at all. He was, in effect, *above* it. One did not allow one's heart to rule one's actions. Keeping to *Hamlet,* he would quote, as that prince did, "Give me that man that is not passion's slave, and I will wear him in my heart's core, ay, in my heart of heart."

And then Merrie had come along and done just that, shaken him up until his heart forgot its proper place and jumped onto his sleeve. And he'd resented that, as he did her attitude that he was just a man, like any other—a tremendous affront he could hardly swallow without choking. Small wonder he'd attempted to alter her instead, relishing controlling and remaking her in his image, until she was no longer a challenge.

But she was too wild a heart, too merry to be contained.

All in all, both were too different to come together without one changing, and he saw no reason for that to be he. He was social rules; she was heart rules. He was distance; she was closeness. He was lofty amusement; she, laughter. He, poise; she, passion—but through the latter she'd made inroads in him. "Be a man, not a lord," she had said during Christmas at Moorsedge, and had almost succeeded, aided by the first earl, in proving that love was all. "Love your family above your friends," she'd said. And there she had had some effect, bringing him to a new appreciation of his mother and brother. But when the final moment came and the contest was between his world and her love, he'd shamed his heart and chosen society.

Then how could he expect her to understand such a surface style of living, when she gave her all, even in their kisses? She never held back, while he denied all, denied her, denied love, and the ultimate in denial, even himself, fighting every changing feeling. And now when he wished to turn to affirmation and seek his joy, it was too late.

Confound it, every feeling revolted at his failure. And if he could not countenance himself, how could she? "I love," she had said, "which is a way of saying, I am." And she had gone on to love another. Well, the duke deserved her. That was the worst humiliation, having to accept that he did not measure up to His Grace, and therefore ought not even attempt to compete with him. And further galling was having to accept his defeat with good grace—an unfortunate choice of words, but apropos of the conclusion. The good grace in His Grace had won.

And then Brett was made aware that even though he'd made claim of giving up all hope of Miss Laurence, actually, secretly, he'd been waiting for a forgiving reply to his letters. Instead she had returned no reply, rather had the countess acknowledge receipt of his messages, answering by not answering. And that clearly showed that all connection between them was a thing of the past.

But his mother, writing on her own, was generous enough to urge him to attend the two weddings being planned directly after Christmas festivities; and further, she wished him also to come beforehand for another happy family Christmas at Moorsedge. All the Laurences were there and he would not believe the jollity they brought with them. The duke loved them all and was anxious to find them a house on his properties. She herself would like to give them the dower house, but of course, it all depended on his wishes. The joy of seeing Esther and George as the first couple to be wed, and then immediately following, the soon-to-be duke and duchess of Chumley, would make even Christmas pale by comparison. He must come, for he was the heart of the family, and would be prodigiously missed by all, especially by his devoted mother.

To such a letter the earl had decorum and obligation and loneliness enough to write that he would definitely be returning for the weddings, and possibly would come to Moorsedge for a last Christmas with them all.

After all, Moorsedge was his, and he did wish to see Merrie again before he lost her forever. Not that he intended to do anything to disturb her happiness with the duke, not if she truly wished that union. But if there was a chance she did not . . . And then too, he remembered the past Christmas there with so much fondness, he could not bear to exclude himself from the festivities and his own family.

So the earl was to come.

Eric was the first to spot his chaise making a capital turn into the entrance. "I say, but did you see his style with the whip, tossing it up and catching it on the thong? Ho, ho! Do you think he'd teach me that? And Winnie, spy the speed he's coming up the drive. If only he'd take *us* up—wouldn't that be first oars all the way!"

Winston, as usual, cuffed his brother and made him promise not to make a ruddy nuisance of himself, but there was no stopping Eric, he was off at a dash, almost running into the elegant earl descending from his carriage. To his lordship's astonishment he was immediately surrounded by two small boys talking at once. The younger one was demanding to know how he managed the whip, and would he show him, and the older was apologizing for his brother while agreeing it had been a smashing performance. They both had the same enthusiasm and charm of a certain lady. He gave them each a warm smile and promised without fail to teach them and to take them up on his chaise and swing them around the bend. And before Walters had opened the door, all three were getting along famously. Winston and Eric were running to report to George and Esther waiting in the hall that the earl was a top-ho gentleman, and they were very pleased he had come for Christmas, after all.

Esther greeted him with a smile and a curtsey and George had apparently picked up the Laurence ways enough to hug his brother. The earl suffered it for a moment, and then stepped back and scrutinized George's happy face. "All, I gather, goes well for you?"

George was off on a streak of assurances only cut off by the countess, having rushed down at the calls from Winston and Eric, and now claiming her hug. And the earl was willing to be hugged by his mother, although it was not usually done, but in the privacy of his home, he allowed it. The duke approached him next, and the earl stepped back in alarm, feeling that the Laurence influence might have worked on His Grace as well, and Lord Warwick had to draw the line in embracing at some point. But the duke merely bowed, saying cheerily, "What ho! Home for the holidays, eh what?"

"Eh, precisely," the earl said with some tolerance.

"Going to have a jolly good time, George tells me. I've sent to my castle for some of my people to make it easier all round for the ladies. Can't have them fatiguing themselves to lift their fingers—we must prize our ladies, what say?"

Lord Warwick agreed, but was becoming stiffer, more offended.

And still the duke was talking, and all were listening to him as if he weren't a complete gudgeon. "Jolly good season ahead. Jolly good times. Shan't we have a jolly good time . . . reminds me of Christmas at Chumley, when I was a boy. Egad, didn't we thrash about and frolic through the woods. And me gamekeeper followed us about, don't you know? So we wouldn't disturb the game, and by Jove, didn't we give him a run. Had the poor chap racing through the woods, don't you know, after us. It was a jolly good Christmas."

The earl gave him a look of disdain, but the countess was laughing at his description. "Ah, that reminds me of my two sons, they raced through the moors often enough, just like these two little angels who've taken to scaring our game," she added, stroking Eric and Winston. Eric just laughed, while Winston looked apologetically at the earl, who smiled kindly at him and assured him gallantly that his moors were their moors. And then Winston and Eric went running up to a lady entering, and shouted almost in unison that the earl was a regular trump, to which Merrie responded by nodding and giving one of her heart-breaking smiles that lit up her green eyes. And he felt his heart lurch indeed, and he thought glumly, I won't let her go. Not to that knock-in-the-cradle!

He bowed elegantly, almost as a courtier would to his queen, and came up and kissed her hand.

"I say," the duke exclaimed. "There ain't no mistletoe there, old boy. Have to restrain yourself till we put it up. Ha! Ha! What say? What ho?"

Merrie walked by the earl directly toward the duke and said to him, "*We* do not need mistletoe, Your Grace," and she gave the duke a gentle kiss on the cheek, which had him laughing, and then she turned and gave one to the countess, and then stepped away as the countess and the duke each gave each other a hearty kiss on the mouth.

"I say!" the earl said in total surprise.

"Oh, didn't you know?" Merrie asked jubilantly. "Your mother cut me out."

"Naughty puss," the duke said with a roaring laugh. "That's it, me boy. This lady and I—we hit it off, don't you know. Miss Laurence says we were meant for each other. And I won't say no to that, what? I'm to be your papa, me boy, if you wouldn't dislike it. But your mama gave me a dashed flush hit right to the heart, don't you know. That is, she planted me a leveler, and I couldn't let her get away from me, could I? Know a good thing when I see it, what? Meet me duchess or soon-to-be duchess, rather. We'll be living in Chumley for most of the year —both of us ain't much for gadding about."

The duke's face was redder than usual from his excitement at his announcement, and he leaned over suddenly and did what the earl had been dreading, he embraced his prospective son with a jolly good hug.

Over the duke's shoulder the astonished earl could see Merrie's laughing face, and he finally allowed himself to smile. There was something jolly about this after all. Merrie was free . . . free to be his.

But subsequently although Brett's hopes had risen to a high pitch at that announcement, he soon discovered that Merrie might be free but she was definitely not his. She was even subsequently rather chary with her smiles. In truth, Miss Laurence was rarely even present. She either remained in her rooms or engaged in her new favorite pastime of walking on the moors, increasing the length of her walks since the earl's return.

Merrie always felt better, freer, when she lost sight of Moorsedge, although the moors were not entirely unrestricted, being bordered by long stone walls that marked the paths and led, like arrows, directly to the flat horizon.

A sennight after the earl's return, during one of her moor walks, Merrie was given pause by a mist overtaking her. It hung low and hid the paths, making it prudent to return, lest one not only lose one's way but overstep. For there were quarries and stone cliffs that could lead to one's fall. Yet, despite the mist, Merrie could not resist taking step after step, relishing the solace of being cut off from the world as the mist swirled around, rather like a cocoon of protection. She felt loved by it and willing to trust herself to it completely in blindman's-buff motions, hands out, till she felt her hand taken and she was abruptly pulled back, a foot before a ledge. She had no time to be alarmed before she was safely walking on another flat road. And even under the cloak of the mists, Merrie knew it was Brett walking mutely beside her.

Silently they trod on, side by side, until the mists

lifted and revealed them to each other, and the moors as well were restored to the very horizon as the sun shone down, making all bright and beauteous and filled with seamless peace. Brett and Merrie gazed contentedly about. Then they looked up together reflexively at a lapwing, red and wheeling over their heads. A bonny bird it was careening above, and they both caught their breath with its swooping. They shared a smile, and allowed their eyes to meet, flooding Merrie with a warm sweet wildness she sought to suppress, while he held her hand so tightly she felt his fingers pressing through her skin, almost touching the bones.

And then his dark eyes, so fierce and searching into her soul a moment before, turned respectful as he stepped back and bowed, allowing her to walk the rest of the short distance to Moorsedge alone.

What an alteration in the man! Merrie felt it then, and subsequently, as did all the rest of the lord's family. Indeed, it was with constant surprise that one became acquainted with this decidedly different earl. A mellow, easily assessible gentleman, this Brett, who had time to notice and commiserate with Walters on all the extra work necessary for him with all these added guests. The astonished butler could only bow and wonder. Added work for servants was not generally the concern of the gentry.

Next Brett surprised the cook by coming into her kitchen, never having been there since he was a halfling, and bringing with him the two Laurence scamps, already well acquainted with Mrs. Dalton.

"We've come, ma'am," his lordship pronounced with great formality but laughing eyes, "to request a treat. It appears you are renowned for your hot cross buns."

Mrs. Dalton, who had never communicated with the earl, having come to Moorsedge during his years of London residence, and last Christmas had only peeped at him as he passed through the halls, was open-mouthed. But Eric, who had long ago made a friend of her, went running up, asking what the matter was, why was she looking so green?

She blinked and looked down at the little boy, and regained some of her sense, enough to curtsey almost to the floor at his lordship, and Eric turned and looked in surprise at the earl.

"Why is she curtseying? Are you the prince?"

His brother was mortified and gave him a shove. "You grubby little scrub, that's a mark of respect for his title. He's an earl."

"Oh," Eric said in some awe, and quickly made his bow, which rather amused Lord Warwick.

"Very nicely done," he said to Eric, and extended his smile to the cook as well.

They got their hot cross buns, of course, and brought some for their father, who was terribly keen on them as well, and thus the earl was introduced to Mr. Laurence. He had taken over his lordship's library, but with a true scholar's indifference to everything but his studies, he did not think either to apologize or concern himself over his lordship's inconvenience.

He was delighted with the hot cross buns, and stopped to give half back to Eric, and while questioning their being served at Christmas rather than Good Friday, told them all the story of the cross on the bun, treating the earl as if he were one of his young students, although he was not old enough to have been Brett's father. Indeed, he was surprisingly youthful in appearance, with the same blazing hair as Merrie's, though his eyes were blue. Totally unintimidated by the earl's position or being his host, rather he quizzed him along with his sons, and nodded approvingly when he gave a correct answer, and then dismissed all three of them.

The earl was laughing. No wonder Merrie had so little regard for his consequence, having been brought up in that gentleman's family. At the first dinner, he had met Mrs. Laurence, who was only a slightly older version of Esther in appearance. The same blond hair, but her eyes were blue. Of all the family, it appeared Merrie was the only one to have those green eyes— her own distinction. Yet Mrs. Laurence's smile was a bit like Merrie's and she continually bestowed it fully on him.

Whether it was Christmas or the coming marriages or the mingling of the clans, everyone was, almost immediately, behaving as if they had known each other all their lives. Indeed, Mrs. Laurence, having clearly taken George under her wing as one of her own brood, merely extended the sweep of that wingspan and included him as well. The countess had long been taken to her bosom. Lady Warwick, soon to be duchess of Chumley, had never enjoyed caring for others, rather felt that everyone should be caring for her, and so she was more than pleased to have Mrs. Laurence step into the mother's role.

But Mrs. Laurence in that motherly position as regard to himself was clearly overstepping, the earl felt, having a momentary relapse into pride when she, without blushing, questioned him as to his digestion.

"I beg your pardon?" the earl asked, astounded. He could scarce recollect a question that was such a blatant invasion of his person, and yet so sweetly addressed to him.

For a moment he was near responding with one of his caustic remarks, but it had been asked of him at table and Merrie was there and looking directly at him, gazing so steadily, as if his very next word had momentous consequence. Indeed, he could almost feel the green ray of her gaze melting into his bones. Therefore, recollecting his transformation, he sighed and graciously admitted that while his digestion was generally in prime twig, it had been tried sadly through all his foreign travels. And thus the conversation was smoothly deflected to the topic of travel.

Merrie sat back with relief, and the earl looked at her hopefully, as if expecting some reward for his common civility to the commoner, but he did not get it. She did not speak to him the rest of the evening. Instead, he found himself saddled with her mother. For Mrs. Laurence, having been given carte blanche to play that role in regard to his august person, did not do it by half measures. She was often in his chamber henceforth, insulting his valet by checking if the bed had been warmed to his lordship's satisfaction. It was perfectly satisfactory, Brett assured her, and wondered what she would think if told how he wished his bed to be warmed . . . and by whom. But he continued his graciousness.

Eventually the pretty little mother-lady wore him down, and Brett accepted her solicitousness and even began to enjoy it rather. In fact, he did not even noticeably wince when she stopped him from going for his morning ride on the moors on a particularly chilly day, insisting first that he must take a scarf along.

"Are you prone to the chill?" she asked with prodigious seriousness.

"I am not," he said, as if the chill would not dare to invade him, and then at her relieved smile, had to smile and laugh himself. It was impossible to be high in the instep with the Laurences apparently. And he gave way and allowed her to wrap him up with a scarf she had already sent for. Patting him on the cheek, she told him to run along and have a jolly time.

It was amazing how young he felt afterward, like a veritable halfling himself. Fortunately the stable

hands knew him as the earl and were properly defer-
ential, or he would have forgotten who he was completely.

He rode over the cold moors and saw the mist in
the distance, and attempted to clear his head of the
situation he was in. For while Merrie was not engaged
to the duke, she definitely seemed to have altered toward him. Whatever situation they'd found themselves in previously—anger, separation, challenge—
there had been in him the conviction that she cared.
But now, he was no longer certain of that, as if a
lovely tune one always heard accompanying her had
been abruptly turned off, and the silence was stabbing
him. He attempted to reinstate a connection between
them again and again, but she always turned away.
Even during dinner where everybody was asking him
about his travels, and Mr. Laurence and he had quite
long conversations on those, he found Merrie unchar-
acteristically mute. Why had his lovely lark gone silent?

Could it be possible that the duke had really given
her the slip and she was pining? They had all jested
about it, but had his mother actually cut out that
beauty? He looked at his mother and did not see her
altered in appearance in the slightest, except for a
constant smile about her lips. The duke had a similar
smile about his.

That same happy glow was about George and Esther, and naturally, Eric was like a cherub. It was
Winston who attempted to be the serious adult member at table, and he was inevitably shouted down by
Eric or George, and told to not be such a bore.

The earl wondered if there had not been such a
difference in age between George and himself,
whether he might not have been shaken out of his
own stiffness long since.

But Merrie, his happy, laughing, irrepressible Merrie, was not her usual self. Perhaps her family quieted her down, or perhaps, he hoped with all his heart, she as well as he was suffering from not being a couple, at a place that despite the season continually smelled of orange blossoms.

The earl's strategy was to give Merrie time to adjust to his being in their midst, and to demonstrate his new consideration to her and to all about. But he was tiring of scarcely hearing her voice, and of his having to take long rides on the moors to ease his feelings for the lady. For while he'd suffered a great deal with longing for the sight of her on his European travels, having her in continual sight was even more tantalizing . . . and chastening.

As for Merrie, while pleased with the alteration in the earl, she had too long loved him and been given contempt in return to feel other than wariness. Where previously she had been open to him, now she was cautiously closed. All summer the lady had told herself bluntly that she must forget there'd ever been such a gentleman in her life as the earl. With all her energy, she had kept attempting to accept the duke, but her heart had recoiled. At Chumley, though awed by the wealth, she, who had never sought position, could not be won over by ostentatious display. The countess, however, was pleased by all the staff, fresh draperies, and just the sheer indulgence of His Grace. Whether to estate or friends, the duke was lavish in his gifts and time and praises, qualities which were appealing, no doubt. But as kindly as the duke was, he had one insurmountable fault—he was not Brett. And he was too much himself.

For every evening at Chumley, they must play at cards and hear the duke's same old jokes, the conclusions of which both the countess and she could invariably contribute when he, as he usually did, forgot. And yet the countess laughed each time, whether it was she who finished the story or the duke. And she also enjoyed a game of cards every evening, and the warmth of the fire. And during the day, rather than a ride on a fast mount, as Merrie wished, the countess and the duke took out a carriage and went for a steady, quiet ride on the roads of his many villages.

Upon arriving home one day, the duke had been struck by the color in the countess's cheeks, and went so far as to kiss her hand. The countess had blushed. And both were staring at each other as forbidden feelings were stealing over them. But then both, of course, remembered themselves and continued as if naught had occurred.

But the difference was that Merrie, who had been waiting for them on the stairs, had seen the moment and sensed what was happening, and, for the first time in months, was filled with joy. At last she had a proper purpose, and she need not accept the burden of the duke, after all.

In truth, Merrie's intention had always been to spread happiness about her. So far she had a nonpareil record. Through the annuity, she had assured the happiness and security of her father and mother. Next, she had arranged and encouraged George and Esther's bliss. Now she had only the countess to provide for, and a way had been shown her—indeed, they'd started on that way themselves, so she could not take credit. Fate or God was the happy determiner, and she merely the instrument. And so henceforth, she was never accessible for walks with the duke, but always went riding alone. She ceased playing cards and took to solitary reading. She even stopped laughing at his old jokes, and he found himself turning increasingly to the countess for appreciation.

Still they would not make an open declaration to each other. All this dallying had forced Merrie to bring things to a head herself by going ahead and arranging a special celebration, she informed them, which occasion would be revealed after dinner, when the duke joined them. At this point she summoned the butler to bring forth the prearranged cake and presented it. Across the top was a paper heart that had the names of the two lovers, Charlotte and Algernon.

Why, who could these two people be, Merrie inquired, and the duke was clumsy enough to fall into that trap and reveal that it was himself and his dear Lady Warwick.

"But what can it mean . . . your names entwined in a heart? Can it mean . . . I dare not say it . . . are the two of you *pledged?*"

"By Jove, we ain't!" the duke cried out.

"Certainly not!" the countess exclaimed.

Merrie sadly shook her head. "Are you telling me the torte is mere flummery, and that despite all the time I took decorating, you are spurning its message?"

The countess, all ablush, began to laugh, and Merrie joined her. It took them a few tries to explain to the duke that it was Merrie's prank and her way of having them admit and celebrate their feelings for each other. And then when he understood it, he laughed over it half the night. A great deal of the jollity was in relief that the jilted girl had arranged to jilt herself, so to speak, and even was patently in a transport over that development.

There was a moment when the duke wondered if her joy was not an insult to him and his position, but she assured him that her greatest happiness was that two people who obviously belonged together had found each other in time, and that all must be joyous at that good fortune. And so seeing themselves as "true lovers," they could not but accept the wonder of it and make arrangements for their wedding.

The duke had often told Merrie's mother and father the story of the cake.

Mrs. Laurence's smile was halfhearted, for she could not view her daughter's being left alone as such a joyous solution, but after becoming better acquainted with the duke, she admitted that he was not the man for her daughter. Hence, best the countess should have him. Mr. Laurence smiled at Merrie's ploy and merely said, "Merrie always knows what's best for us all," and gave his eldest daughter a wink. She, since a little girl, had always been the one to encourage him in his work and extricate them from several sudsy situations, such as one Christmas when she was no older than Winston was now, and yet had taken it upon herself to secretly sit with an invalid for a fortnight for the few shillings needed to provide at least a limited celebration. She was his Christmas angel indeed, born a few days after, and always bringing a brightness into their lives. He would have been pleased to have had Merrie happily settled, but he did not question her judgment. She was too wild a spirit for the duke to handle—she, a roaring Yule log fire and he, a small albeit ornate candle. They would not suit. Later, he took her into the library and relayed a Greek myth with a moral, which was the way he always made his point. It was about a lady who loved the sun god Apollo and hid in his chariot of a morning while he was putting the sun in place in the heavens. But as Apollo made a quick turn, she fell out directly into the sun, becoming a constant flame no mortal man could ever touch, lest he be reduced to cinders. Only Apollo on his travels could love her, and he did, dubbing her the Lady in the Sun and pledging his love to her each morning at dawn and each night at twilight. And so it must be for Merrie; she could not accept the duke, for she would burn him into cinders. She must either live alone and be content simply to shine for others, or wait for one with fire enough to love her for the fire within her soul.

Merrie had been soothed by that tale, as she always was by her father's little myths. And she wondered if somewhere out there she'd find her Apollo? Yet with her brothers around her and George as a third one, and dear Esther and her parents and the countess all anxious to share their love with her, Merrie assured herself she did not need an Apollo after all. Esther, of course, claimed she knew all along that it had been Merrie's plan for the countess and duke to fall in love, and Merrie could not deny her pleasure and relief at the outcome. As well it was with Esther that she discussed the contents of the earl's letters. "He has found out that I am not a liar as he assumed, and wants my forgiveness."

With all seriousness Esther read the epistles, at one point exclaiming in glee, "Heavens, Lord Rockham and Lady Jane!"

After the sisters had discussed the appropriateness of that match, Esther could not resist sharing the news and the earl's apology with George. He immediately joined in Esther's amusement, and they had one of their little chats about Brett and Merrie. Eventually, they both agreed that Merrie ought forgive him, but then George added, "It will be dashed difficult to do, by Jove, for one always looked up to him, rather, and he has sadly disappointed."

Yet when the earl arrived, George was so delighted to see him and to see him as he always imagined his brother should be, kind, and a great gun and friend to him, that George promptly forgot all about whatever had happened in London. It was the earl himself who brought it up when the two brothers joined the staff in going on a sojourn to the woods to bring in sufficient greenery for the holiday decorations.

George assured him that he had long since forgotten that the earl had made such a cake of himself by believing such obvious shams as Lady Jane and Lord Rockham.

"I did not believe Lord Rockham," the earl inserted, willing to go only so far in his self-immolation. "I did accept Simpson's word. But ye gods, if a gentleman cannot accept the word of his own butler, whom he has known since a youngster, what is the world coming to?"

"If that gentleman takes the word of a mere butler over that of the lady he loves, the answer is obviously that he cares for his own consequence rather than what his heart is telling him."

Brett was quiet at that. "Yes, I always had a difficult time listening to my heart. The very fact that my heart was speaking one way assured that I should go another. I never could accept being passion's child."

"Love's child," George said with a grin. "There is a difference."

But when the earl admitted as much, and unlike his usual self fell into something resembling the blue dismals as they walked, George decided to encourage him, and told him that Merrie had been the one who arranged for the duke to switch his affections to the countess.

"If she told you once that she loved you, she does not alter. You have merely not to make another cake of yourself and botch up your second chance here, and all will go well."

"Then you advise me not to despair?" the earl asked hopefully.

Feeling suddenly like the elder brother, from his position as the engaged gentleman, and one engaged to a Laurence lady, he dared to pat his brother on the arm and assure him there was hope.

So altered was Brett that he did not resent that

gesture, and rather smiled in gratitude for his assurances. Therefore George risked his dear Esther's reputation and explained why he had immediately believed Merrie—or the story of the notes sent to them, which subsequently disappeared from their rooms. And also that it was his opinion that only someone from within the staff could have known enough to arrange all.

"Devil take you for not revealing this to me earlier! Why didn't you? That would have been your word against that blasted man."

"Then you would have believed my word? Or Esther's? Without the notes? Or would you rather have seen us all as part of Merrie's group, and would have assumed that she had orchestrated our stories as well? And further, I could not disgrace my darling Esther. For we had both taken advantage of that situation to spend an unaccompanied morning together declaring ourselves. In short, I had compromised the lady. Yet we told Merric and asked if she wished us to confess to you. But she would not hear of it. I expect she wanted you to believe her for herself."

And the earl cursed himself roundly after that and rode off alone.

She was perfectly justified never to accept him, he felt, all his newfound hopes crashing down. He was clearly at point non plus.

And yet, and yet, upon returning to Moorsedge and seeing Merrie being kissed by the duke, he went forth with a growl, like a beast breaking out of his cage to protect his own.

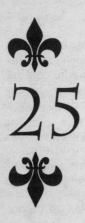

25

The duke stepped back as the tall young lord came at him. His Grace was filled with part confusion, part amazement, and then finally, alarm. Lady Warwick, who was beside, stepped forward and said laughingly, "Why Brett, dear, are you that anxious to join in the mistletoe kissing?"

Lord Warwick skiddled to a halt, and looked above Merrie's head. There the mistletoe hung, and he laughed at his foolishness, and tried to make the best of his actions. "Yes, indeed, Mama, I did not come all the way from London not to join in the best part of this celebration." With a pleased grin at his quick recovery, he stepped up and gently touched his lips to Merrie's. There was a shock that had both of them riveted. When he lifted his lips, he kept them close enough to touch hers again with the merest inclination of his head, and was set to do so, when Mr. Laurence pushed him aside.

"Play fair, young fellow. You must gather your berry and see if there are any left, or the procedure will not be precise."

The earl stepped away and plucked one of the two remaining berries, while Mr. Laurence gave his daughter a hearty smack, and one to his wife coming close, then denuded the mistletoe. "All gone," he exclaimed, and everybody was pleased at that, as if a great feat had been accomplished.

"By Jove," the duke said, almost taking personal credit, "didn't we empty that one in record time."

Everyone agreed, they certainly had. For there had apparently been much kissing before George and he had returned. George spoke for his brother too, in crying foul that they had strung the plant up before all the gentlemen had been present.

"Not such a fool," the duke said. "Not dashed likely I'd wait to be cut out by you younger lads."

There was much applause at that statement, and so His Grace was pleased to repeat it to the countess, and with a wink to Esther, who had gotten some of his kisses, and finally to Merrie, who gave him a tolerant smile.

A great many servants the earl did not recognize, some wearing livery, were occupied in transforming the rooms. Where last year it had been Merrie in charge and running around like a child putting holly and ivy and fir branches on everything in sight with an excessive delight, this year she stayed back. Rather the duke's staff, under the guidance of his own butler, joined by Walters, were doing the honors, which resulted in a very creditable but controlled greening of the house.

However, Merrie and Esther were following the servants about and applauding the effects, when George and Brett approached them, and George giving his brother a helpful grin, drew his lady away, leaving Merrie to the earl.

"I apologize for pulling you away from His Grace. I feared he was regretting his choice."

"You always seem to be apologizing to me of late —with letters, with your glances—and what are you apologizing for? That you were proven wrong, or that you did not have faith in your own feelings?"

"The latter," the earl admitted. "One must believe in one's loved one, yet I feared that if you were correct, it would prove that a good part of my life was a farce, a dashed bloody social farce. Which it was. *Is*. I realized that the moment I left England, my petrified setting. Everything opened up for me. And being in other countries, it gnawed at me that you were not there to see all the wonders with me. Each day I felt it like a fresh cut—that loss. Feverish and restless, I sought constantly to exorcise you. But a merry flame of a lady danced beside me. At the Alps, she clapped her hands at the view, and in a gondola, she kept me warm at my side. And in my mind I lived them all with you, realizing I was doomed to go through life imagining you at my side. I came back earlier to take you away from the duke, realizing I did not give a confounded damn if you had manipulated or lied, that I would be magnanimous and forgive you, just because I could not live without you. And when I returned and found that it was I who had to be forgiven, naturally that brought my plans to a halt. Although I hoped for your forgiveness, I didn't have the brazenness to imagine you would ignore my bird-witted, buffle-headed acts. Only a complete gudgeon would have misjudged you so, when you are obviously a lady of such unassailable truth. You were correct. I am a naught. A total moonling!"

There was a pile of holly branches left on the table and Merrie took one up and said, "Father says this is symbolic of the drops of blood on Christ's crown when he was being crucified. Will you feel better if you wore it?"

Her eyes were laughing as she handed it to him.

But the earl did not disdain it; rather he immediately put a branch on his head, and she called him Father Christmas. Gradually a bit of light in her green eyes that had been dimmer of late began to spark, for Merrie was never able to be quite subdued during that time of joy. Now she walked about with lighter step, adding her own touches of an abundance of greenery branches on the paintings ignored by the servants. She particularly stopped before the portrait of the first earl and ordered Brett, who had been silently following her about, "You put yours on him." And he removed his holly crown and did as she requested.

They shared a smile at how much less imposing and somehow jollier his lordship appeared with a holly crown half obscuring his face. "The spirit of the season appears to have gotten into our spirit-spook," Brett said with satisfaction, and Merrie gave him a friendlier glance, filled with deep yearning to laugh all this summer away—nay, this entire last year—and be back to last year, with love beginning in both their hearts. But there had been too many lapses of faith and trust.

"Merrie, darling," he said softly, but she turned away from him.

"Nay, I cannot dismiss it all. I do love you, and shall perhaps always love you, for I am ridiculously faithful, but there is no sweetness between us. There is distrust in my heart. I fear your fidelity, and that is not true love. True love is complete faith and joy . . . true love is Christmas. For it is a season of loving that spreads to all. And I can, in the interest of the season, accept you as a dear friend, and an old love, but"— and here she choked on her words as they seemed to be wrung out of her—"but I can go no further. I would I had been with you all summer delighting in those views, sharing the joy of seeing them, but I was here attempting to forget you, where every sight reminded. And at last I was able to let you go. And concentrate on other people's happiness."

"Do not do this to us. Let me prove to you that we are meant to be together. That I understand what you mean. That I, not the blasted duke, shall take charge of Christmas in my home . . . by gad, I shall give you a Christmas and show you that I mean always to keep Christmas in my heart."

Merrie felt a rush of joy at that proposal. The old Merrie could not resist it; she forced the cautious Merrie aside and almost jumped in happy acceptance. But Merrie was just able instead to say, "Very well, let us see what kind of Christmas you can give us all. . . ."

And she ran quickly into the saloon where her family awaited her for the Christmas caroling. But she stopped and looked back at Brett, and he kissed his hand to her as a seal of his promise.

From that moment on, the earl took on Christmas as if it were his greatest challenge. He it was who supervised all the decorations, he who planned all the festivities. And his jaunts to town were times of joy for all, even those who met him in the shops and on the road, for he always bought extra gifts and passed them around, just to see the wondrous surprise on the faces of the passersby who were stopped to be gifted and wished the joy of the season.

And Merrie heard about that, and smiled in her heart.

And he it was who planned the reveling. By the actions and whisperings of the staff, all were aware that something lively was afoot. Thus with great anticipation they congregated at the earl's request in Moorsedge's largest saloon. Brett was waiting to seat them all, which he did with great formality, even Eric and Winston, who were wiggling about in expectation.

"I have arranged for some holiday entertainment,"
Brett grandly announced, and was applauded beforehand in pure faith.

At his signal several singers from the village church
entered. They were accompanied by the old harper
who had played for them last year and several
younger gentlemen with various instruments. The
songs were much applauded and joined in by the Laurences, and soon the duke and countess unbent
enough to accompany them. "Here We Come a-Car-
oling" was very jovially performed, and even the duke
could remember the refrain, as everyone sang, "And
God bless you and send you a happy New Year!"

The earl had selected the most imposing carved
chair, and taking Merrie from the settee where she sat
with her sister and brothers, led her to it. He very
precisely draped greenery on the back of it, and
placed some under her feet, and then stepped back
and viewed her critically. She lacked something, he
felt, and then, inspired, added a sprig of holly in her
hair. Once more he stepped back in full delight to
gaze at her, as if she were perfection. Merrie could
not resist laughing at that and because of her sense of
happy anticipation.

At Brett's further signal, the harper began "The
Twelve Days of Christmas" and the carolers gave
their lusty rendition. But there was a substantial difference. For as each item was sung out, the great oak
doors were solemnly opened by the liveried servants
and the gift described was actually brought in. A partridge in a pear tree was the first of the gifts, and was
reverently placed at Merrie's feet by the earl himself.
Following in correct order and rapid succession were
two turtle doves, three French hens, four calling birds.
And then for the fifth day, when the chorus sang out
"five golden rings," Lord Warwick reached for a
gilded chest and opened it, removing five golden rings

and solemnly bringing them to Merrie. His stare held hers as he lifted her left hand and ceremoniously, reverently, silently placed one golden ring on each finger. But there was more to come.

For as the song continued, the doors opened to bring in the new gift of six geese, plus another batch of turtle doves, French hens, and calling birds, until the room was awash in poultry running here and there. And yet the earl was grinning and signaling the next round with singular aplomb, and more and more of these fowls came in to run afoul of the others. The six geese a-laying were not necessarily laying, and the seven swans were definitely not swimming, but they were there. And on the eighth-day cue, certainly eight maids came in, though in the interest of space, they were not leading cows to milk, but carrying milk cans in their hands and singing along with the entire group. For the nine ladies dancing, the earl improvised by signaling George to lead his lady to trip along, and he took Merrie from her throne, and they too attempted to skip and hop through the running hens and calling birds. The tenth day needed lords a-leaping, and the earl was quite willing to perform that, and to force the duke to jump along with him. And the eleven pipers piping were easily added to the already crowded room, followed in glorious climax by the twelve drummers drumming, until the entire room was filled with laughter and singing and dancing and screaming. And Eric was wildly running after the birds and shouting, and even Winston was on the floor making joyous cries, and George and Esther were holding hands and singing in full voice, and Mr. Laurence was observing everything with a pleased look of witnessing a very interesting ceremony of old come to life, and his wife was bemoaning the fowls running amuck through the orderly room. And the duke and countess, who at first had been too astounded to do anything but stare, had finally succumbed to living in a barnyard, and the duke did not even jump when a partridge landed smack in his lap.

But of all, it was Merrie who was laughing the most, and looking at the earl, who had indeed gone all out to entertain her in proper Christmas fashion. Even after some of the footmen were brought in to collect the poultry and allow some space, the earl had not concluded. Rather he claimed that it was an ancient tradition in Yorkshire that they were all to sing the song, and if any error was caught in the order of the gifts given to the true love, a penance would be called for. As Master of Misrule, Brett claimed he would be generous, making the penance a miming of the forgotten gift, such as a piper piping. He ordered all to stand for the game and song. By now most of the room was near to being cleared, with servants rushing to capture the errant poultry and carry off the last.

"Where do you wish all your gifts from your true love to be placed, Miss Laurence?" the earl inquired of the still laughing lady.

"I certainly shan't have them put into my room," she said, and he ordered them distributed to the carolers as they departed, or to the staff, whoever wished for calling birds and such. All were given away but for the forty-five golden rings. Already Merrie had every digit of both hands fitted to the tip with gilded circles, and those that couldn't fit on remained in the jewel box at her feet.

Accompanied only by the lone harper, the family began the song themselves. Eric and Winston knew it quite well, never making a mistake and helpfully joining in the demonstration-penances for whoever mixed up the sequence. The countess was often victim, as was the duke, but they enacted very creditable turtle doves. Even Mr. Laurence got confused and had the maids milking before the swans swimming and heartily guffawed and did a rather amusing depiction of a maid milking a reluctant cow that had all a-laughing and a-laughing.

When it came time to retire, everyone picking up a candle and going toward the stairs, Mr. Laurence was explaining the meaning of the carol: that in church symbolism, a partridge represented abandonment of faith, since a partridge is a bird that abandons its young, and bringing the partridge back to its pear tree would indicate a return of faith . . . or devotion. And further that a young girl was known to back into a prickly pear tree and cry out when pricked by it at the sight of her true love.

"Then it is a restoration of lost faith between loved ones," the earl said deliberately to Merrie, and she, all afire with the joy of the night, merely smiled. But she was humming as she went up the stairs, followed by a servant carrying the chest filled with a great many rounds of golden rings.

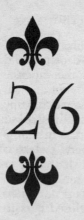

26

Unable to sleep promptly that night, Merrie spent a good hour staring at the golden satin canopy above her bed, feeling for the first time in a while a quiet joy rushing over her.

Of course, it was within a day of being Christmas, and she was always at her merriest around then. Also it was a season when the good in people was permitted to make a showing without unduly embarrassing either the benefactor or the recipients. It was a season when giving was accepted without questioning motives. It was Christmastime throughout the land and in the hearts of all, a time when one ought to forgive and risk loving again.

And then Merrie realized that that was the cause of her sleeplessness, having to decide whether she ought to love again. She rose to stand before her fireplace, looking down for answers in the bright, sparkling fire, which called to mind another fire, the one here on her very first day at Moorsedge that had burned up her bonnet. And that reminded her of the earl's admission, with one of his slow, mocking smiles, that it was he indeed who had purposely burned it, as if attempting to burn what she was, although subsequently he'd bought her a whole wardrobe of hats in recompense. Amazing how one could overcome the loss of an item but never forget the deed. Just as she was certain she had long since forgiven the earl for his distrust, but yet had caught it from him. For it was the first time she'd found herself distrusting another, and that other, the gentleman she loved. It was shattering to realize she was emulating the very fault found so heartbreaking in him. She'd blamed him for not opening his heart to others, and yet she'd closed hers to him.

Oh, fiddle, how could she continue to do so when he was so exhaustingly attempting to show her his transformation? Indeed, she noted that his heart this Christmas was opening up to all. To the neighbors that he was gracious enough to invite for a Christmas Day dance. To the staff, who'd been allowed Christmas parties throughout the whole season belowstairs, and to whom he'd sent presents and decorations from the main rooms. To her brothers, taking Eric and Winston out on a shoot, and having them come back such fast supporters. He had told them tales of himself as a nipperkin, of sleeping out all night in the stables because his good friend Pinkton, who ruled the stables, had whispered that on Christmas Eve all the animals bowed down at midnight to honor the birth of the Christ child. And they were anxious to spend Christmas Eve out there as well, until Mr. Laurence debunked that. But the earl had promised to bring his horse Caliban to the front door on Christmas morn and make him bow before them in honor of the day, and that had satisfied them.

His treatment of her mother had been the most clear evidence of his change. Or rather that her mother could reduce anyone, even one as high-flown as the earl, to being an affectionate, obedient son. And, of course, he had always been polite to Esther. Now he was as companionable to her as he'd always been to George. Brett had taken Esther and George into his confidence in regard to the "Twelve Days of Christmas" pageant, and beforehand she'd oft caught the three whispering and breaking off when she came by, and then laughing together. And frankly, she'd resented it. Last year, *she* had been in charge, at least of the festive arrangements. And while it was lovely, his doing all this as surprise for her, and singling her out as the recipient of all the gifts, actually she would rather have joined in the preparations and surprise. And yet, would she have missed that moment of sitting there and having her true love, with the utmost dignity, parading an entire barnyard before her, as if he were presenting her with rare diamonds? She would never forget that picture of him holding a partridge, and its laying an egg on him, which he accepted with unruffled ease, casually handing it to her and whispering, "A bonus."

She had dissolved in tears of laughter. As she had at the moment when he'd very soberly begun leaping across the hall, to be the lord a-leaping, and then roused the duke to follow him, all done so matter-of-factly, as if it were the most august and respected ceremony. And his pleased bows after each entrance of the day's gift, hopefully watching her face for her approval. Ah, she could not help but give it to him in full measure.

This was not the repressed, indignant lord to whom his position and dignity was everything. She'd certainly shaken him out of that.

And when she thought of the hours he had spent talking to her father about the celebrations done at Oxford. And then George and even the duke joining in to recall the stately procession of bringing in the

boar's head into the old college hall, with all the students in their black gowns singing the old carol in
Latin to accompany it.

And before Merrie could blink they'd all stood up.
With Brett taking the lead—an arm around his
brother and her father, while the duke was crowding
in to make a unity of chorus—they'd sung out:

> *Caput apri defero*
> *Reddens laudes Domino.*
> The boar's head in hand bring I,
> With garlands gay and rosemary.
> I pray you all synge merrily
> *Qui estis in convivio.*

Lord Warwick had insisted on all the verses, and
Mr. Laurence had remembered every one, and they
sang it several times for Mrs. Laurence, and then for
the countess, who came in, and again for Esther and
herself, and when Eric and Winston entered, they too
were instructed in the Latin and quickly learned it.
But they were not so keen on the song as on the
promise by the earl that he would have an entire
boar's head brought to Christmas table, with an apple
in its mouth.

Merrie was smiling as she recollected all that while
standing barefooted before her fireplace. She told herself, and her heart agreed, that Brett was the loving
man she'd always sensed there under all the layers of
prideful nobility. Whenever she was able to reach
Brett and push aside the earl, they had sensed their
connection. Such as last Christmas in the tower room
when he had declared his love, and then on the road
escaping from Lord Rockham. The thought of Rockham sent the usual shudders, but now relief and
laughter, as well, recollecting Brett's declaring the

union of Lord Rockham and Lady Jane as the perfect punishment for both.

"Yes," Merrie had agreed, "they are meant for each other. She will swoon whenever he wants to come on a villain, and he will be delighted to revive her."

For a moment the earl's old cold eyes were back as he said gruffly, "He wished to play the villain with you?"

And she said, "Of course. Not capable of giving or receiving love, he played his little game of power, requiring a woman on her knees—either swooning or sobbing. I expect my being amused disconcerted him. I do not believe he'd ever been laughed at, and I daresay he's quite experienced in having ladies at his mercy, for he was saying his lines with a degree of facility that doubtless came from much repetition."

Brett had painfully smiled, and held her hand.

"Is that for comfort, at this late date?" she teased.

"Yes, for comfort," he said softly, "but to give *me* comfort, not I to give you. For obviously my merry girl knows how to handle villains, and to spot them of both genders. But the comfort I need is for the dread that I nearly lost you and might never have heard your laughing voice again."

Merrie enjoyed the belated comfort—then and now—as she remembered the pleasure of having her hand held in sympathy, while wondering at all the people fearful of love, such as Lord Rockham and Lady Jane, protecting themselves through poses and power, when it was all so simple—one just opened one's heart. Yet she herself, she admitted, was now joining the group of people fearing love, and she had less excuse, for she knew it was wrong not to trust one's heart, which meant that it was wrong not to trust Brett, and she jumped back into bed and lastly remembered Brett's good-night words: "May your sleep be soft and your dreams of me."

And it was . . . and they were.

The next morning, she woke early, filled with euphoria at its being Christmas Eve day. Jumping up, she reached out for one of the lace wraps, part of Madame Bliss's extras, and donned that, inspired by last night's dream. Brett had been knocking on her door and then come in, lifting her in his arms, and the two had gone directly into the fireplace and there, in there, blazed away.

While brushing her hair she remembered the blazing, which comically reminded her of her mother's flaming Christmas pudding, and how last night Mrs. Laurence had checked the copper holding it, confiding her anxiety of the moment when her very own pudding would be brought flaming to table to be eaten by an earl, a duke, and a countess, as well as her own dear family.

Smiling at that and other Christmas thoughts ahead, Merrie was jolted by a strong knock, very unlike the timid notice of her maid. Going to the door, she opened it to the earl standing there, as in her dream. And he was all afire.

27

Merrie jumped back from her doorway, overcome by the surprise of the sight. The exalted earl
himself was dressed all in white, with a red sash
around the middle, and on his head he had a green
wreath that held seventeen lit candles. He bowed low,
causing all the flames to flicker wildly with his rising.

Merrie went off into a peal of laughter, stepping
back as he walked solemnly in. It was not the thing
for a lady to receive a gentleman in her chambers
unless they were wed, and even then probably there
were certain rules and times. Merrie was not a lady of
rules but of emotions, therefore she welcomed him in,
forgetting her muslin and lace gown with the barest of
lace sleeves; yet her bare arms were fully covered as
well with the cloak of her just-brushed hair that spar-
kled about her. It was his lordship, however, who was
all lit up.

"You cannot be Saint Lucia," Merrie said when
she could speak.

"No, I am not," he said with mock solemnity. "I
am her brother, Saint Lucas. And it is the tradition, I

have thoroughly researched it with your father, that on days when the gentleman of the household desires to ask the lady of his heart for her hand in marriage, he is to appear with this crown of candles on his head, and she signifies her acceptance of him by blowing them out, one by one."

"Flummery!" Merrie laughed. "There is no such custom. This is tit for tat for my invading your chambers last year, admit it. As usual, you have outshone me, for my crown did not have half the candles. Good heavens, you're a fiery gentleman."

He bowed again with pride at that remark, and returned the compliment. "But you have no need of candles on your head to blaze—you are lit from within and the flame is in your glowing hair," he whispered as he neared her.

"My lord, you are too close, and we shall both be aflame in the next moment."

"What of it? Dash it, I have been aflame since the moment I first saw you."

Merrie smiled in pleasure at that, her heart beating in happiness. It boded well that the earl was not concerned with decorum or wondering that she did not rush to cover herself with the false modesty that any lady would be exhibiting now. The soft smile on his mouth and candlelit dark eyes were comforting, reassuring. Then he recollected and revealed what the hand behind his back was holding—a small gilt chest.

"You have something good in there?" she inquired with childish delight.

"I do. But in keeping with the tradition of Saint Lucas, I do not bring things to eat, but gifts of homage for my lady."

Merrie could not resist taking the chest; it had a sprig of holly atop, which she immediately placed in her hair to complete the holiday picture. And then she solemnly and with wide eyes opened the chest.

Within was an absolute treasure of emeralds, from a necklace of five flawless emeralds in an exquisite diamond setting, to three matching bracelets, and lastly, a ring with another emerald, appearing so heavy that one might very well require a footman's aid to lift one's hand.

The riches ignited the old Merrie—gone was the serenity and quiet joy; she was now all exploding with sparks.

"Is this an attempt to buy me? You know I don't care for such . . . trinkets."

"Trinkets? Egad, this is a fortune in jewels. And further, it is the famed Warwick emerald collection. There is even a matching tiara, but I felt that would be pushing it rather."

"Rather," she choked.

"But as my countess you would be forced to wear them. I thought it best that I show you all the disadvantages of wedding me before you accepted and thought better of it."

Merrie looked at his mocking eyes, and wondered how he could be making a jest of such a moment.

"A simpler gift would have been all that was necessary," she said stiffly.

"Ha! I already gave you a barnyard of simple, common gifts, and you merely laughed at me. Twelve beastly days of them."

Merrie had to smile at that, and put in, "You also included at least forty or so golden rings!"

"And now I shall risk giving you my dearest possession, the one thing that I simply could not live without."

And Merrie watched him as he slowly took her hand and brought it closer to his chest, where his heart was beating.

"I would tear it out and give it you, but you already did that when you left me. But what there is left of it, I give to you for Christmas."

Merrie was all ablush at the feelings she felt in touching his heart. Indeed, her own was fluttering as she looked back, waiting for the one word more.

"And do you not have a Christmas gift for me in return?" he asked softly, coaxingly, almost holding his breath.

"I have knit you a very comfortable pair of socks," she countered decisively.

He laughed so strongly at that, the candles nearly went out as he threw back his head. When he could speak, he said as solemnly as he could, "As much as I anticipate the great pleasure of receiving them, I own I'd rather receive your heart. And your hand in marriage. Having achieved such a notable success with my brother and mother, you cannot stop arranging engagements for my family. Certainly I shall not countenance being left out. Do you not feel I too should be wished happy? And did you not tell me the true joy in life is to make other people happy? Therefore, since that is your aim in life, it behooves you, for consistency sake if naught else, to accept me."

But although he had proposed, he had done it in humor, and Merrie would not accept it on that level. For she felt that demonstrated he was still holding back, and so, in a similar light tone, she said, "You are needlessly confusing my belief, which is simply that one should aim to make it Christmas all year round for everyone. Have you done so?"

"Ye gods, there is no one who has so devoted himself to spreading Christmas joy."

Merrie allowed that she had heard of his happy actions in the neighborhood and was most pleased at his concern for others. He replied that she had not heard all of his Christmas sharing, for he'd already arranged to give her father and mother the permanent tenancy of the dower house as a Christmas gift.

Moved by that, nevertheless Merrie, with an incorrigible twinkle in her beautiful, glowing green eyes, concluded that all that was very well, but what had he done for her two brothers?

Not daunted, Brett immediately whisked out of his pocket two full lists from her brothers of their Christmas requests, which he intended faithfully to fulfill down to the last cricket bat. She chuckled over that, informing him that he was obviously dripping with sincerity.

"I am certainly dripping with something," he exclaimed, wiping away the wax on his forehead from his flickering candles.

"You make an unexceptionable candelabrum," Merrie could not resist exclaiming, "one that should undoubtedly be of much use during Christmastime."

He bowed in mock shyness at that and now was so fully splattered over by waxy spots that Merrie had to lean over, set to wipe them away, when she noted the fire in his eyes and stepped back, continuing their game, claiming there were other people who needed to be made happy. Instantly he parried with the confession that he had already reduced the rent of his tenant farmers. While approving of that, Merrie exclaimed that she was referring to George and Esther. Was their future secure?

The earl was beforehand with them as well. For he'd truly come to realize that the only way one could assure true happiness was to cease seeking it and be content with giving it around instead. As witness, he had already purchased for their sibling couple an estate close by, filled with books and horses. "Indeed, that deed is to be given them, as well, on Christmas morn. And now, my merry lady, do you have any other conditions before granting me your hand? If not, I request an immediate extinguishing of these blasted candles, as I have become so covered with wax, I shall soon be fit only for Madame Tussaud's."

At which Merrie lovingly leaned over and extinguished them, pursing her lips and blowing across his forehead, one after another, and then gently, with a loving hand, wiped away the candle drippings from his brow, leading Brett to toss down the entire crown and take her into his arms and kiss into flame the fire that had been between them from the first.

The kiss was fully satisfying to both, as if they had been perilously hanging from a cliff and had been at last taken up into safety, and Merrie held tightly as he clasped her in his arms. In a few moments their relief gave way to a wild rush, ignited by their kisses until quite a respectable blaze had caught in both their breasts. But Merrie pulled away . . . and held him away.

"I am persuaded I ought not so brazenly to demonstrate my 'unladylike lack of restraint' " she said, unable to resist reminding him of his previous criticism of her abandoning herself to him in love.

Shamefacedly Brett insisted he had long learned from her that a true lady and gentleman were fully giving—in *every* respect.

"Then you love me completely and without any more reservations?" Merrie asked, needing to hear him say it in so many words.

"I do," Brett confessed gruffly. "You are my heart, my soul's darling. There is no existence for me without you, for you are my life. If all the lords of society together, and all the gentlemen of England as well, declared their love for you, they could not equal what I feel in one second of my adoration."

Naturally they had to kiss to that, whereupon his lordship pronounced officially, "Actually, since you have blown out my candles, according to custom, you have already willy-nilly agreed to be my wife."

And satisfied, Merrie gave him her most dazzling smile that outdid all the candle flames he'd had on his crown, concluding that considering the season, she would follow the custom. "However, I shall accept the title of being your countess only if you do not count on that entitling you to forget to keep Christmas all year round in our home. You have made an auspicious beginning, truly proving that making others happy results in one's receiving that happiness back twofold. As witness my joy now in presenting you with my love."

"And mine in returning it tenfold," the earl enthusiastically assured her, and demonstrated that with ten more fully given and accepted kisses that were climaxed by Brett exhilaratedly stating, "I vow to keep Christmas in my heart for now and forever more —for you are Christmas."

At which Merrie gave him her hand in love and festive happiness. And the newly pledged couple quickly went off to inform their families of the joyous holiday news.

And a happy Christmas was had not only by both families and all about them that year, but all the Christmases to come. For they always spent them together, and as the family grew in size, so did their love that was ultimately shared through generations more.

COMING NEXT MONTH

THE MIST AND THE MAGIC by Susan Wiggs
A spellbinding romance set in 17th century Ireland. On a cliff high above the sea, John Wesley Hawkins meets Caitlin MacBride. With true Irish whimsey, Caitlin has just grasped a white and blush-colored rose and wished for her true love. Hawkins walks into her life, but danger and adventure lie ahead before these magnificent lovers can find a happy ending.

SILENA by Terri Herrington
A powerful romance set in Nebraska in the late 1800s. Silena Rivers is on a quest to discover her true identity, with the help of handsome Wild West showman Sam Hawkins. But along the way, they find that love is the only thing that really matters.

THE ANXIOUS HEART by Denise Robertson
An enchanting contemporary novel set in London about a courageous and feisty young woman who pulls herself out of a low-income tenement building to discover the amazing world outside.

THE MAGIC TOUCH by Christina Hamlett
Beth Hudson's husband, Edward, was a magician obsessed with the occult. He had always promised her that he would be able to communicate with her from beyond the grave; and two years after his death, his prophecy seems to be coming true. With the help of Lt. Jack Brassfield, Beth reopens the investigation of her husband's death and gets more than she bargains for.

AMAZING GRACE by Janet Quin-Harkin
An engaging romance set in Australia just after World War I. Grace Pritchard, a beautiful young Englishwoman, is forced to choose between two men . . . or face a difficult future alone in the male-dominated and untamed Australian outback.

EMBRACE THE DAY by Susan Wiggs
A Susan Wiggs classic. An enthralling and romantic family saga of spirited Genevieve Elliot and handsome Roarke Adair, who set out for the blue-green blaze of Kentucky to stake their claim on love.

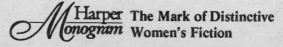 **Harper Monogram** **The Mark of Distinctive Women's Fiction**

ANALISE

Analise Caldwell was the reigning belle of New Orleans. Disguised as a Confederate soldier, Union major Mark Schaeffer captured the Rebel beauty's heart as part of his mission. Stunned by his deception, Analise swore never to yield to the caresses of this Yankee spy...until he delivered an ultimatum.

ROSEWOOD

Millicent Hayes had lived all her life amid the lush woodland of Emmetsville, Texas. Bound by her duty to her crippled brother, the dark-haired innocent had never known desire...until a handsome stranger moved in next door.

BONDS OF LOVE

Katherine Devereaux was a willful, defiant beauty who had yet to meet her match in any man—until the winds of war swept the Union innocent into the arms of Confederate Captain Matthew Hampton.

LIGHT AND SHADOW

The day nobleman Jason Somerville broke into her rooms and swept her away to his ancestral estate, Carolyn Mabry began living a dangerous charade. Posing as her twin sister, Jason's wife, Carolyn thought she was helping her gentle twin. Instead she found herself drawn to the man she had so seductively deceived.

CRYSTAL HEART

A seductive beauty, Lady Lettice Kenton swore never to give her heart to any man—until she met the rugged American rebel Charles Murdock. Together on a ship bound for America, they shared a perfect passion, but danger awaited them on the shores of Boston Harbor.